Cover Design – Thomas F. Rukas

SURVIVAL
OF
THE
VIRTUOUS

A Novel by THOMAS F. RUKAS

Dedicated to the Memory of Marylou

Survival of The Virtuous

By: Thomas F. Rukas (c. 2018)

INTRODUCTION

Let it be known that I am certainly not an authority on the concept of reincarnation, but I am decidedly a free thinker and have an unusual attraction and fascination for writing fiction.

So, that being said, have you ever driven down a country road, a road that you have used hundreds of times and all of a sudden, for 'maybe just a split second' of time, thought you were traveling another road in a completely different county, and for that fraction of a second wondered where you were? Or 'maybe at one time in your life' you've walked into someone's living room, of a house you know you've never been in before and identified the room as familiar as your own, and brushed it off as a form of Deja vu?

How about something a little different, like have you ever hung out with a friend for years, getting to know their patterns and innocent quirks, and one day you notice that they've suddenly changed, or 'maybe gradually', but the change was noticeable and out of character?

'Maybe' they were drinkers, not necessarily alcoholics, and all of a sudden, they've quit going to bars with you and in less than a year, took on a different job and lived a completely peculiar life, contradistinctive to what you've ever known them to do.

Or have you ever experienced someone who could have never been considered adequate at carrying a tune, but one day out of the blue you become aware they're suddenly a natural vocalist, an exceptional singer?

Do you believe in soulmates? For instance, have you ever spent time with an older married couple who have been high school lovers, or even childhood sweethearts who can anticipate what the other is thinking or finish each other's sentences, and always seem comfortable with each other within a healing aura, causing everyone around them to be happy by simply being in their presence?

Unanswered common mysteries and attempts to solve them have encircled our globe for centuries where sometimes we've come to the unreliable conclusion that one explanation for uncommon or mystifying occurrences is as good or as satisfying as another. The truth is, we don't seem to want the observation vindicated, for it takes away the conundrum and motivation for searching for a more interesting, or better yet, mystically creative resolution to the enigma in question. Our earthly minds sometime want the intrigue of not presenting ourselves so linear or symmetrically earthbound in our beliefs, but rather, anticipate a more boundless and interminable rebuttal to what some would argue as logic and common sense.

The story, "Survival of The Virtuous" is just that, a story positioned within certain beliefs based on an assemblage of notions and fictional superstitions taken from unaccountable stories and lore from centuries of people handing down tales through the generations of man and womankind. It also reflects the idea that the human spirit in its essence is not confined within any race, color or creed when reincarnated, as the Universe sustains it as virtuous.

Reincarnation could be taken as realistic or as legend, depending on who the reader or listener is, or depending on what is believed or inspirationally invented.

Along with the belief of reincarnation came the legend of "Walk-In" spirits, who were believed to have entered a body in order to guide the occupying soul to another place or destination while it takes over, possessing that particular body. This "Walk-In" spirit was 'supposedly' a good soul whose purpose was to mend and rectify where the previous soul has faltered, sending that quondam spirit in question to paradise, or on to a better life, reincarnated, while remaining as his or her replacement soul.

While limited on the complete knowledge of these theories of reincarnation and 'Walk-In' spirits, and since no human being has ever been 100% proven to come back from the dead to inform us of exactly what happens, one could be left open to the Universe of imagination, pondering such a tempting and inexplicable concept of life and death.

After all is said, I find it very hard to believe that there is simply total blackness and a void of absolutely nothing when we pass on from this earth.

Nor do I believe that everything in the Universe just happens, or "is" without some divine plan beyond our realm of knowledge or thinking. For I believe the Universe is a wonder of imagination and an endless generation of dimensions that our puny little human minds could not 'possibly' fathom without the gift of inventiveness, fantasy and vision.

The two ancient souls, or lovers within this story trace back to more than thousands of years of reincarnation where they, as soulmates, fortified the strength of each other, together starting each lifetime searching for truth and durability of existence by coexisting together, time and time again, modifying, balancing and forming them into ageless old souls.

They're born, then live full and happy lives and die together, only to return subsequently to another lifetime to exist in the physical realm once again with different circumstances, carrying out the quest for an eternity. Unfortunately, when there's an anomaly within the Universe and a pattern swings out of its proverbial harmonic convergence, due to an untimely removal of life, such as a murder, the Universe will successfully find a way to balance itself, which is what happened to the lives of our story's soulmates.

Three of their previous lifetimes, before the real story begins, will be portrayed concisely within this introduction to best summarize to the reader this author's own concept of life and reincarnation and what lead to the upcoming chapters in this book.

In one lifetime, our soulmates were born in the mid 1700's in the cold winter of the mid-west in two separate teepees, in the same tribe and same camp of Sioux. The camp, or group they were in numbered over two-hundred Native Americans near where today's North and South Dakota border would be. Sun Rock was the male, and Moon Angel was the female.

They were both raised by their biological parents and family and both children virtually always knew each other growing up. They courted according to the tribal traditions and always knew they were in love.

They were married in a tribal ceremony in the spring of their 20th year and remained in the group for the rest of their lives, happy and content with Sun Rock going with the buffalo hunting parties while Moon Angel was taking care of the home-front and the children.

Sun Rock was a healthy specimen of a man, tall, and naturally dark complexioned with hazel-gray eyes and his hair long, black and straight. With three eagle feathers usually cropped on the back of his head with a headband, he would be near naked in hunting parties in the summer showing off his masculine toned muscles and in the winter months, he'd dress warm with buffalo and deer skins.

Moon Angel was pretty, standing at about 5'4" with long black hair, usually in a single braid riding down her back. She was thin, strong and very well-built with a perfectly feminine contoured face with those brown eyes that would penetrate the soul of anyone looking deep into them, but she only had eyes for Sun Rock.

In their lifetime they raised two girls and three boys, whom Sun Rock eventually taught to hunt and fish, and in his old age, at least until he was seventy-five, he hunted buffalo. They seldom went on war parties against the Crow, but fortunately deaths from wars did not touch their family.

Both Sun Rock and Moon Angel lived to be near a hundred years old, both dying only hours apart, and neither of them had ever seen, in the whole entirety of their lives, a single white man.

In their next lives the man once known as Sun Rock was reborn in the late 1800's in a small rural white West Virginian town located on a railroad line as Ely Cass, the infant son of a coalminer and his wife.

He was raised as a typical Caucasian lad in the wooded hollers, attending a single room school house in the winter and fishing till his heart's content in the summers.

When he was old enough in his early teens he worked part-time at the sawmill and eventually full-time in the coalmines.

The one who was once known as Moon Angel was reborn the same year and across town as Mary Kelly, the infant daughter of the owner of the sawmill where Ely worked part-time.

That's exactly how the two met, with her working with her dad at the mill on occasion, stacking the cut wood and loading the train flat-beds.

Ely was a strong, slim figure of a man in his teens, who stood about 5'11" and already had a natural five o' clock shadow, even after he shaved. He wore flannel shirts and dungarees most of the time, but he never appeared disheveled or unkempt, as some of the local teenage boys were, giving the impression of being a natural leader.

His brown hair and deep blue eyes attracted the young ladies constantly, but those eyes were always focused on the job or responsibility at hand, that is until he met Mary Kelly.

Mary stood at about 5' and slender in her jeans and blue flannel shirt as she helped with the loading, guiding the long, cut pieces of oak onto the flat-bed car. She had flowing red hair while her skin was creamy white, with the exception of a few orange freckles across her cute nose, coloring her smiling face when her blue eyes first met Ely's blue eyes.

They had felt they knew each other from the beginning, love at first sight, sensing that they've known each other for an eternity. They attended dances together, courted, became engaged and married by the time they were sixteen, with their parents' permission.

Mary and Ely bought a house on the side of the mountain with the help of parents from both sides and made it into a little home, snug and away in the pines of the Appalachian foothills. Mary kept the home fires burning while Ely worked many hours in the mines but made sure his time at home was quality time with his family.

He did not drink moonshine like some of the others but did have a nip or two at Christmas to bring in the holiday season with good tidings and cheer.

Eventually the children were born, one after the other after the other, proving that his quality time was spent well and they both knew they were irrepressibly and relentlessly in love with each other. Mary spent most of her time in their world being a devoted mother to the kids and a loving wife to Ely, who even in his sixties, couldn't take his admiring eyes off of his soul mate, Mary.

Because of the coal dust in his lungs, Ely was only sixty-four when he died, although living much longer than any other coalminer in that particular town. Before he passed, he had helped Mary raise eight children and seventeen grandchildren. Mary had encountered a heart condition before Ely passed and she died quietly in her sleep a week or so after Ely's body was laid to rest.

In their following lives they were reincarnated again in the same sequence of time, the early 1950's as two Afro-Americans, Skip Mooney and Miranda Goddard. They were both born in two different households, and of course two different families.

Skip and Miranda were both born in West Philadelphia and in different neighborhoods, but Skip's mom and dad were killed in a house fire off of Woodland Avenue and Skip ended up being raised by a drunken uncle who taught him how to play the tenor saxophone.

Miranda was an only child whose mom had died giving birth to her and was raised by her loving, hard-working father who did odd jobs in construction, mostly hot-tar roofing.

Miranda's dad was killed in a suspicious accident, falling off of a three-story roof in center city, suspicious because there was talk about local union involvement and Mr. Goddard was not registered in any locals. None the less, nothing had been proven regarding foul play and Miranda was on her own at age eighteen by around 1970.

Miranda was a beautiful woman at the age of 18, slim, tall, about 5' 10" and busty, with long, slender legs that she was proud of showing with her stylish skirts and shoes. Her light-green eyes and naturally curly, jet-black hair complimented her full dark-brown face, and her round forehead accentuated her features brilliantly, turning the heads of men of all colors and drawing compliments and suggestions from friends that she should be a model or an actress.

Although hearing and appreciating the compliments, she never let the praises go to her head, for her personal vanity was limited to her realization of life itself, and she knew that if she was to subsist within her own independence, she would have to stay focused on the truth and sensibility of the real world.

Miranda worked as a waitress at a Club on Walnut Street to make ends meet, and that's where she met Skip, who played the tenor saxophone, accompanying a piano playing singer doing standard jazz numbers and some duet versions of top forties hits.

Skip, by this time, was about 19 years of age, saying he was 21, lying about his age so he could play in the bars, and could get away with it because he looked mature with his broad shoulders and standing at about 6'2". His hair was in a short afro and as black as his full and neatly trimmed beard, with his clothes stylish, wearing a black, silk body dress-shirt which formed perfectly around the muscles in his toned biceps and his V-shaped back.

His eyes were big and brown, and when those eyes saw Miranda, they lit up his entire face, causing him to play a very high C note, which he incorporated into "Take Five," a jazz standard the duet was playing at that particular time. It was love at first sight when they met, as if they always knew each other, and after the gig Miranda brought Skip back to her apartment where they spent their first night together in romantic bliss and were never apart for the next 11 years.

They were married within a year of their first meeting and carried on with their daily routine of Skip playing out 3 to 4 nights a week, making a salary and tips while Miranda worked as a waitress in bars and clubs while going to school at Temple, pursuing a career in law.

In that whole time of their 11 years together they never really fought, but understood each other like soul mates, living in complete harmony. They never had children, nor did they want any since their lives were busy with each other, living their existence to the fullest in bliss and pure elation within each other's company.

By about 1980 Miranda was assisting at a law office in Bucks County where she commuted by train from Center City to New Britain, PA., where she was to meet a client about a public drunkenness and drunk-driving case. At the small and secluded New Britain train platform while Miranda was talking with this client of hers; who was a white, blond-haired young man, he had defiantly opened up a bottle of bourbon and started chugging it in front of her.

The both of them had just spent hours with a Judge and because of Miranda's shrewd and judicious idiom, was able to get her client off easy with only a small fine and 7 hours of public service, charging him 'virtually' nothing for her services since she was appointed by her firm and her client was on public assistance.

Needless to say, Miranda was furious and had a few choice words, but her client wouldn't hear it. He finished the bottle then tried to accost her, making aggressive unwanted sexual advances at her, and when she refused him, smashed her over the head with the bottle, killing her instantly.

Her client was as surprised as Miranda must have been, surprised at her dying right there in front of him and since they were both alone, and it was getting dark, the man took Miranda's body while the lonely sound of the train whistle was blowing in the distance and Miranda was never heard from again.

That same night, at about the same time, Miranda's husband Skip was going over a few songs with a drummer, a woman named Libby, who was from Bucks County and could play the drums like nobody he's ever seen.

Libby was young, white, and in her early twenties and a beautiful brunette who was buxom and thin, vivacious and very talented as a drummer. The man Libby seemed to be hooked up with, Robert, who was about 30 years her senior, had a club called Bender's in Philadelphia and many more like it across the U.S., and Skip's been sitting in with Libby's band at this club for extra money. Libby liked his playing and wanted to take him on fulltime, so she invited him over to the club when it was closed, after hours, so they could talk business.

Skip watched her shoot-up a syringe full of heroin right in front of him, which in itself, shocked the hell out him and he watched her keel over while she turned purple and began foaming at the mouth. She stopped breathing and Skip put his ear to her chest, but heard no heartbeat, so he began pressing down on her rib-cage in a steady beat until he felt a pulse in her wrist, and when he was certain her throat was clear of phlegm, he performed mouth to mouth resuscitation until he heard her breathing on her own.

Skip sat with her all night, just the two of them in the club room all by themselves next to her drums as she seemed to sleep soundly. He stroked her head and hair and as he looked into her relaxed face in total peace he never once thought about Miranda while he was engrossed in reviving his musician friend Libby.

Until that night, Skip had never so much as looked at another woman in the way he looked at Miranda, even Libby, who was a natural head-turner, but Skip had never noticed her sensuous stride and her low-cut suggestive tops the whole time he's known her, until that night.

What happened was Libby had died, and unknown to Skip, Miranda's soul had passed into the body before him, becoming the "Walk-In" replacement at the moment of Libby's death, while Libby's original soul moved on into the cosmos.

Miranda had become Libby, in Libby's body, with Libby's memory, with no memory of herself as Miranda, and Skip was now naturally, *spiritually speaking*, drawn to Miranda's spirit through the physical form of Libby.

There was a fixation that a part of him, somewhere in the early morning hours started feeling an anxiety about how he felt, and that's when he thought about his wife Miranda and began to unconsciously worry about her, like he sensed that something was wrong with her physical being. That's when Libby opened up her eyes and smiled at him, and her grin penetrated his soul as she said:

"Wow, what a rush, Huh?"

He was trans-fixed, as if he was seeing and hearing someone he already knew and loved inside of her, but wasn't ready to accept any of it, at least not yet.

"If you're okay, I've got to go now. I'll call you later," he told her as he bolted out of the room.

After about six months and sporting considerable and immense sadness and heartbreak, depressed over the sudden mysterious disappearance of his wife Miranda and the thought of possibly; never seeing her again, Skip, continued to play, as he had, in Libby's band and sometimes did a lonely, haunting sax solo that lasted about ten to fifteen minutes of the show.

The police had no leads regarding Miranda's disappearance and the case soon grew cold, even trying to convince Skip that she most probably changed her identity.

Skip, although sad, felt a very strong and unusual attraction to Libby ever since the night she overdosed on the heroin and the night that Miranda was last seen, and after a while, the two of them started an affair, falling in love instantly.

Libby and her, 'supposed' husband Robert seemed to have a mutual understanding regarding seeing and romancing other people so there was no problem in that respect. The problem was with one of the partners, a bigoted manager of that particular Bender's Club called Bill Bailey, who being somewhat of a racist had a problem with people of color and merely tolerated Skip's superb saxophone playing, that is until Libby and Skip's obvious affair started. Unfortunately, Skip and his tenor sax ended up subsequently disappearing from the sight of the Bender's club, and Libby never saw Skip alive again, but she had an idea that Skip's disappearance was perhaps; due to an occurrence of foul play.

Since this drummer Libby was surrounded by a mixture of good people who she trusted dearly and also sleazy, sordid personalities who collimate the present businesslike universe of the Bender Club Inc., there was an atmosphere of bliss mixed with the shadow of distrust and bigotry which needed to be properly balanced in order for her to endure the aggravating aggregation of her present life's controversies.

But as this beautiful woman wondered in emptiness where Skip was, and what he might be thinking at that precise moment, the one thing she took from the ordeal of his vanishing was something he used to tell her in the past year regarding the surrounding hate, bigotry, and even the sadness of his wife's disappearance:

"It's not necessarily the strong who survive, but the virtuous."

So, as I said before, the human spirit in its essence does not subsist within any boundaries of race, color or creed when reincarnated, as the Universe sustains it as virtuous.

And what ever happened or became of Skip you might ask? Well, the same spirit of Skip Mooney, Ely Cass, and Sun Rock, all one in the same, will be telling the story from his own point of view and doing it from here on in within Part I, upon the opening of Chapter One of 'Survival of the Virtuous'. Enjoy. – *Thomas F. Rukas*

Survival of The Virtuous

By: Thomas F. Rukas

CHAPTER - ONE

PART I

THE SPIRIT TALKS

Where the hell am I? I have no memory of anything, but I seem to be existing on a whim, on a thread of hope. I feel as though I've been standing here for an eternity, but as I get restless I move forward, ever so cautious and as I do, I'm aware of many people around me, unfamiliar, but equally as confused as I.

"What place is this, and how did I get here?" . . .

Questions I keep asking myself with no remote expectations of answers as I maneuver through the 'seemingly' vast and endless mist. That's what this is; a sort of mist of entities, which I identify as people, all in the same God forsaken place with nothing but a glimmer of hope to determine what will coalesce from this formidable alcove of confusion.

I realize that I am a male species, but not from any physical aspects, though because the sense of sight is hard to explain or put into words, my perception and innervation are all within an unexplainable dimension of consciousness. There was another entity present, enticing me to feel as though I was sensing an uncontrollable yearning, as I found myself reaching with my entire being and drawn with an incredible infatuation, or rather passion, being gravitated toward her.

Yes, a female whose beauty was indescribable loomed in front of me and I was aching from not being with her; a warm feeling of love, almost as if she was once a part of me; but now drifting and floating just out of reach, increasing my need and want to survive before she vanished into a multitude of, what appeared to be a form of people.

The herd seemed to be moving slowly and I recognized a face, a disturbing cognizance of a profile from the past. My first thought was fear, then a disturbing anxiety that I've actually known this particular being, a fellow from a past stream of consciousness, but the fear is reflected within him thus dissolving my own distress. No memory, other than a pinpoint of association, but a force to be reckoned with as he backed away into oblivion while I presently moved forward toward his direction with a focus on the division of my recollection of him.

A gradual essence of light, growing ever brighter drew me in like a vacuum towards its warm glow before I was ordered to stop. Not by a voice, but by an infinite command, as I found myself right beside the being with the familiar face I encountered only seconds ago. There was a communication that began from, not the entity next to me but something immense, boundless, and the warmth of the light turned into a comfortable heat.

"Are you aware that you are dead?" the Voice asked.

"No, I wasn't, but I guess that answers a few of my questions," I said respectfully, and still confused.

"What's the last thing that you remember?" the Voice continued.

"I, I don't remember a damn thing."

"That's good," was the utterance.

The other being standing next to me stared directly into my eyes when I happened to glance at him, proclaiming to me he was sorry while falling to the ground and crying before other beings in bright white and red told me to follow, leaving the poor man pitifully crumpled on the ground.

"Where are we going?" I asked.

There was no response while we continued, so I asked again:

"Where are we going and who was that man? And why was he apologizing to me?"

"That is not important for you to know right now, and in time, it will be known to you. You see, here in this quadrant, time is relative and virtually uncharacteristic of your present state of reality."

"Is this heaven?" I asked auspiciously.

"No, it is not," the Voice said calmly.

Just then, I walked past a kneeling form on the ground, with a familiar figuration of what I knew in my soul to be Adolf Hitler, and he was trembling and silhouetted in a cold darkness. Then we passed another known serial killer on his knees with the same fearful expression and demeanor.

"You don't mean I'm in . . . Hell?" I stated hesitantly.

"Not Hell," the Voice said, and continued, "There was never a 'Hell' as you were taught in the reality of your life. Humans and all of creation are a part of all of the Universe, or God, and God doesn't condemn himself to Hell.

The visions you'll see here you'll find are contrary to the popular judgmental belief from your pre-death reality."

As we ambled through and past the depressing faces of gloom and doom, who were trembling and shivering in fear I grew even more bemused, since I've yet to see a happy face in this new Universe of the afterlife.

I was surrounded in a world of woe and downheartedness and feeling the urge to inquire further.

"What is this place?" I asked blatantly.

"Do you sense any evil here?" the Voice asked calmly.

"Actually, none whatsoever," I stated truthfully. The fact of the matter is that it was a different sensitivity toward these individuals now than what I felt before. There was no evil, other than their own fear itself and I felt an endless pity for everyone I saw on this walk through the kneeling and disconsolate gathering.

"There is no evil here," the Voice said. "Satan, or the idea, is obsolete, destroyed after death."

"Is this Heaven?" I asked once again, a bit addled.

"No."

"Purgatory?" I asked, as if I was on a game show and desperate without any help from an audience."

"No Purgatory either," was the response, "but a journey without the element of time as you know it toward the goal of Paradise."

Still befuddled, I was curious to know what the hell this voice was talking about, and I had no clue as to what it meant about a journey to Paradise.

"I thought that life was the journey," I said.

"For most, it is," the Voice responded, "but for some, in life, the 'free-will' is misused and replaced with evil. When death occurs, evil is destroyed and all that's left in that vacuum is the magnified fear filling its place."

Then there was a pause and the voice addressed me directly and firmly:

"Your fear fizzled to a cinder, which will eventually be totally eliminated once you've performed a task of your own."

I observed the sea of faces within this realm, all kneeling on the ground and asked why I was chosen over the thousands around me.

"You were fearless in your approach," was the reply. "You were not aware how long you were kneeling in your fractional instant of distress before you were able to overcome and address it. The ones you see still kneeling will need to face their fears and approach, the same way you did before completing their journey to Paradise."

"Even the one I identified as Hitler? In Paradise?" I inquired.

"See, you're still judgmental and you need to cleanse," the Voice said. "You have a task to fulfill before you're worthy. Everyone gets into heaven eventually and the dimension of time is relative per person, yet irrelevant to eternity. When you yourself arrive into Paradise it will seem as if it's instantaneous, with no negative memory of your life on earth, but an embellished and magnified account of reflected consciousness. You will have balanced the spiritual scale of the Universe with your task, as will the one you call Hitler, and all of the others." Then the Voice continued:

"His task however is much different, nothing to do with yourself as he will have to live and die through each and every individual life he has had the responsibility of torturing and destroying; Individuals who will have no account or memories of their own experience of these torments. His task will seem as an eternity for him; hundreds, 'maybe, even thousands of years, in his personal perception of time if he falters.

But he will make it to the other side eventually, arriving precisely when you do in your different sequence of time, and unrecognizable as he's known now.

Until then, he will back off on occasion, tormented by the pain he must bear, giving up on the suffering and torment of his task over and over, each time kneeling on the ground before continuing, going through and living the torture and death each of his victims bore; until those lives are accounted for, finally giving him the peace and strength in spirit to see the face of his Maker. You see, the Universe is Eternal and maintains an Infinite Balance, as part of the soul. Even when tarnished, the soul will always survive, remaining Virtuous in its pure state when cleansed; in the name of survival, and supreme order and balance within the Universe."

I began to understand, and I was beginning to wonder what my task was to be, and even more so, I was wondering now how I died.

"Tell me," I said, speaking to the Voice, "How did I die? And why was that man apologizing to me?"

"You were murdered, rather brutally," the Voice stated, and continued, "The man apologizing was your murderer, a serial killer with an addiction to violence, and is now going through what he did to you and the others, living it all through you so you wouldn't have to. He becomes your 'savior,' A divine intervention, if you will, so he too can be cleansed. The deaths and suffering he caused you and many others were so horrible that you or them really wouldn't want to know any of the details and the memory of them was removed and experienced first-hand by the perpetrator.

He will be experiencing it again and again in place of the others he's slaughtered until his soul is cleansed. His fear, which you recently observed within his timid face, was the guilt he felt for what he did to you and the others, and his own self-pity was knowing he will have to survive the unbearable pain and unspeakable experience that each of his victims encountered at his own hands.

That's the way death works to find the universal balance."

After a moment's thought, I asked: "Will I have to go through pain and torments to get to heaven?"

"You've already witnessed part of your heaven." The Voice replied.

"Where?" I asked.

"The entity that you were longing for, the indescribable beauty of light just out of your reach when you first became aware of your existence within this realm," the Voice said.

I immediately recalled the serene and compelling allure of what appeared a female, who was extremely warm and too beautiful to detail or convey an image that could remotely justify her existence.

"You were a man called 'Skip Mooney' in your last life," the Voice said, "and your life was taken untimely and unjustly by that spirit of man you saw groveling in the room. Your life was cut short after you had met her; and spent time with her."

"Met who?"

"The female entity, your universal other half," the Voice said.

"What do you mean?" I asked, totally confused.

"Your Soulmate!" the Voice indubitably replied. "A mate whom you have shared countless lifetimes with as you perfected your existence together.

In a more recent life, before Skip Mooney, you were a coalminer in West Virginia, happily married to her, with a family of eight children. You and her, were also in another life years before as Native Americans, living in the Sioux Nation, living a full and happy existence raising two girls and three strong boys. But from you, who once was this man known as 'Skip,' she was taken away, murdered, and her soul became a 'Walk-In' spirit to save another, with the plan of meeting up with you, but because your 'Skip Mooney' life was stolen, you shall now be a 'Walk-In' spirit for a man who needs spiritual help, and to execute a task on earth, to be set at a predetermined time before your murderer's death to aid the Universal Balance. You will once again be with this female entity, your Soulmate."

"I don't understand." I retorted, now totally confused, "am I going back as this man 'Skip Mooney'?"

"No," it said. "Skip's body is dead, and you will have no memory of him. There is a task you will need to perform, as I had stated before, but yours is one of guidance. You will have to go back the world of the living and be a personal guide to someone who needs spiritual help."

"You mean, be like an Angel?" I asked.

"The living might call it that, but I call it being a guide, and eventually a 'Walk-In'."

"Oh. . . I'm not understanding you . . ."

"You're confused now, but don't think about it anymore for you will eventually come to understand," the Voice said, and continued: "The year will be 1984, and the man's name is Horace Clowney.

He's a drywall contractor doing small jobs, and also a musician looking for a break. We need him to follow a righteous path and you're going to have the job of guiding him into it."

"I think I can handle that," I said confidently.

"You have no choice," the Voice said, and I was immediately swept away, to a small town called Doylestown, Pennsylvania.

CHAPTER - TWO

Note: For clarification, when the spirit guide speaks to Horace, his words will be identified in "*italicized text.*"

I found myself in the year 1984, in the village of Doylestown, Pa., a little community in Bucks County, north of the vast outer suburbia of Philadelphia. A quaint little burg, this semi-metropolis, located at the top of a hill has its own police station, and its own Courthouse; labeled as the Bucks County Courthouse. The pubs in town are rats-kellers and walk-in-off-the-street joints with pool tables and greasy Stewart sandwiches, however, there are a few clubs where live music can be heard from Wednesday until Saturday nights. The ostentatious shops are ritzy in the center of town, with the proprietors on occasion standing outside on the sidewalks with a classy sample of embroidered clothing or a representative piece of antique furniture, or oil painting. The town spreads out to its own suburbs where housing developments are popping up faster than the pizza joints on the outskirts of this glorified hamlet. In town the old row houses and twins are on backstreets, divided by back lots and concrete access driveways. Wood Street is one of these passages within the borough and this is the place I'm told I will find my protégé, Horace, however he's presently not at home.

Horace Clowney is a man in his early 30's, with brown hair touched with strands of sun-bleached wavy locks, compliments of the 'Month of May' sun. He just finished another bicycle ride, shirtless, and in his sweatpants cruising three times his 6.5 miles around Lake Galena, which is just north of his home town of Doylestown. Horace stood at near six feet, with a normal build for a man of his age and height, and in fairly good physical shape. He loaded the bicycle into his Ford 150 pick-up and headed homeward, by way Cheese Factory Road past the Shrine of Czestochowa, and out Ferry Road, Chapman Avenue, and homeward.

Horace has no pot belly or flab, since he rides his bike every day that he can after his drywall and masonry repair appointments, which as a steady job also keeps him physically active and 'relatively' toned; going up and down ladders and lifting a sheet or two of drywall gypsum board here and there, or cement and cinder blocks as the job calls for it.

He's in great physical shape for a man his age, especially considering he has had a past of irresponsible drug and narcotic use, or so I was told by the Voice. He's also a good-looking man, according to some of the ladies in town, including his girlfriend of 4 years, Lucy Snyder.

The looks have never gone to his head, notably because he's not aware that he's blessed with them, nor is he receptive of his passable talent for singing and extreme talent for playing his acoustic guitar. Considering himself mediocre as a musician he's happy jamming and playing music with the local yokels on Wood Street.

This is where his rented house sits back about twenty feet off of the gray and gridded sidewalk, but Horace doesn't see himself any more talented than the sanctimonious beer drinking buddies with whom he thrashes out these inebriated, whiskey-washed melodious mantras they call 'songs'.

He pulled the truck up in front of the house and Lucy was standing at the front door, and I merely observed as his spiritual bystander.

"You're taking my spot again," she said, shaking her head from side to side as if she was reprimanding a naughty child. In her hand was a pot of marigolds she was about to plant.

Now, Lucy was a fine-looking young lady about 25 or so, with short, straight brown hair and built like one of those models in a magazine, with brown eyes and very white teeth. Her sleeveless tight top and skin-tight yellow dungarees made her slinky form pop with the vivaciousness of a young and energetic woman. She waitresses part-time and is dependent on Horace for, 'pretty much' everything regarding room and board. Her only savings is a few $1 and $5 Silver Certificates, and a $100 bill worth about $2000 that she's been saving for a rainy day, and besides her, only Horace knows about, since he's the one who gave it to her a few years ago for a birthday present.

Unfortunately, her attitude towards Horace left a great deal to be desired, since she could be considered a virago; you know, a woman who tends to be controlling or domineering.

Horace is easygoing and an easy prey to this type of personality, although he does his best to just flow with the stream of the unknown, no matter how choppy the waters may appear.

"Well, why aren't you parked here?" he retorted, shrugging his shoulders as he unloads his bicycle from the back.

"Don't talk to me like that," she snapped, and continued, "I let Johnny take the car, he couldn't find a job again today so he's at the bar."

Horace in the meantime was wheeling his bike down the walk through the door, slipping past her while she blocked his way.

"Move."

"Say, what?" Lucy answered.

"Doesn't he even try to get a job?" Horace asked almost moaning, and continued, "He's always at the damn bar it seems."

"Watch what you say about him," Lucy said firmly, and following him through the house, "He's at least trying. I don't see why you can't pay him to work with you."

"Because he drinks too much," Horace said raising his voice, "Besides, what is he to you, anyway? Why is he here? I'm already paying his room and board."

"You don't have to get so nasty, Horace, he's an old friend. Friends help friends. You should show some compassion."

"He's YOUR friend," Horace bellowed, rolling his bicycle onto the back porch, and walked back through the house and out to the truck to get his cooler.

Just then, Johnny walked up, or rather, staggered like a wounded rat in a gutter and asked Horace to move his truck, while he had left Lucy's car he borrowed sitting with the engine running and idling in the street.

"Say, what?" Horace stated firmly.

Johnny stood there, at about 5'8" with his scraggly long bleach blond hair, like Peter Frampton, flowing down the sides of his clean-shaven face past his shoulders over his white muscle shirt which was tucked neatly inside his blue jeans.

The shirt was showing off his thin, soft-tanned arms with wiry muscle tone as he was pointing his half-filled beer can at Horace's truck, as if showing off the tattoo of the black rose of death on the back of his hand.

"I told you to move the truck," Johnny repeated, and added, "I'm not going to spend time looking for a parking spot when I can just park here."

"Well, I'm already parked here," Horace said, "so, find your own parking place."

"But this is Lucy's spot," he said, getting indignant.

"Look, I'm paying the rent here!" Horace replied adamantly.

"STOP IT, BOTH OF YOU!" Lucy said at the top of her lungs, as she came stomping down the walk giving Horace a shove, surprising him.

"Horace, move the truck so he can park here."

"No, I won't."

"Excuse me?" Lucy said looking him directly in the eye, and added, "My spot, right?"

Horace, taking a few deep breaths stood still for a moment, then twirling the keys around and around in his fingers and feeling defeated, he finally moved, getting into his truck, slamming the door in anger before pulling out; burning rubber as he exited his brief domain by the curb, surrendering it to Lucy's Ford Maverick and her friend, Johnny.

Horace drove for a few minutes, not looking for a spot to park his pick-up, but just thinking, reminiscing of all the times she's embarrassed him with her domineering rhetoric.

The abuse was almost unbearable anymore, but he falsely convinced himself as always, that he's used to it, rationalizing once again that he still loves her and it's all part of a relationship.

Satisfied with his chronicle of justifiable self-deprecation he continued driving out of town, northward on route 611 for the fresh air of the wide-open spaces of Plumsteadville, PA. Taking a few back roads he reflected on his life and what he really wanted to do with it, besides living with a young woman who bitches at him constantly and her idiotic scraggly blond friend who won't work but sucks up all of his income until he's at his wits end. The guy appeared there a few years back without a job, like an unwanted relative, or rather, like that relentless wart on the side of his own foot. Only, the wart, Horace was able to vanquish with a solvent, while Johnny remains in the spare room, or in the kitchen, or in the living room as an eternal irritating lump of useless flesh.

Horace one night even saved her life by stopping Johnny from attacking her with a butcher knife in one of his drunken tirades when she refused to give him money for a night out, and even then, she wouldn't let Horace call the police.

If there was just something, anything, an excuse to propel him from the clutches of this wicked wench he would welcome the opportunity, but alas, there was none.

Horace was so used to being with her and realized there will never be a change unless he decides on his own to move forward with it, leaving him once again depressed in his rationalization that it is what it is, that he must be in love, or something, which once again bypasses his thoughts of suicide.

He stopped the truck in the parking lot of a bar, Sportsman's Palace, and looked through his phone numbers for a potential customer in the area who had left a message earlier and used the phone booth to call.

A man answered, and they chatted briefly about what needed to be done and Horace told him he was in the area, letting him know he's available to stop in if it's convenient.

"Where are you?" The man named Robert asked.

"I'm at the tavern on 611 near Oak Grove," Horace stated.

"Sportsman's?"

"Yes."

"We're on 29 Bender Road off of Deep Run Road," Robert said.

"I'll be there in less than ten minutes," Horace responded.

"Do me a favor," Robert continued, "Pick me up two six-packs of Old Milwaukee, cans, and I'll cover you."
"You got it sir."
"Not sir, please, the name's Robert, okay?"
"Okay, Robert."

Horace bought the beers requested by his potential customer and pulled out of the lot and out onto Route 611 north to Deep Run Road and made the left, almost ramming a southbound diesel rig head on. That is when I decided to speak my first words to Horace, yelling:
"Go, go, go . . ." as he hesitated in his left turn, then he gunned it upon obviously hearing me.

This whole time I was watching, observing, and waiting until I saw fit to acknowledge our camaraderie of existence with something as substantial as communication.
"That was close," was, or were my next words to this poor soul, and I still wasn't sure he heard me.
"It sure was," he responded, "that woman's going to kill me yet, thanks for yelling for me to step on it."
"Hesitation is never a good thing," I said, *"especially after you've made a decision to turn at the moment you did."*
"Like I said," Horace repeated, "That woman's going to kill me yet."

I was aware he meant Lucy, and her tormenting talons were digging into his tender heart and brain, motivating his mind to function improperly, causing a near disaster. I'm certainly glad for his sake that it was only a near miss.
"Get her out of your mind, for the time being," I answered, looking at him from my hazy limbo.

"I'm working on it," he said, "the thought of that near miss with that semi cleared my head, and almost my bowels."
"Keep that sense of humor, and you'll be alright." I told him, and I realize I'm nothing more than a random thought to him.
"You've got it, Horace," Horace said to himself, as he cleared his throat and continued to drive calmly.

After about two miles or so he saw a large white complex, the size of a small town off to the right, with a white wall, appearing to be made of concrete surrounding it. Then he saw Bender Road and made the right. Bender Road dead-ended at the complex gate, where he pulled his truck up in front of the double gates and stopped. He soon heard the moan of movement, a hum, as the gates slowly opened, revealing the macadam driveway ahead to the house, a white mansion.

Along the driveway there were trenches where a backhoe was parked, 'presumably' for burying electrical wires from what it seemed, since large empty spools were visible in the area.

Pulling the pick-up around to the side, he parked and took his clip-board and measuring tape and proceeded to what appeared to be the front door. It was about 8-feet high and double doors 6-feet wide surrounded by two pillars on either side that extended up about 12-feet completing the rather, stylish white portico. There was an arch window above the door and actually above most of the windows in the mansion.

The set of four steps were marble and lead to the door from the flagstone path that Horace walked to get to the door.

Ringing the doorbell, which sounded like a distant lower-register bell chime, he waited for what seemed to be a minute or so before the door opened.

In the doorway greeting him stood one of the most beautiful women he and I had ever seen. She was in her mid-twenties, had green eyes and straight brown hair down to her shoulders, which were bare due to her floral printed casual halter off-shoulder backless crop top, with the same design in her matching flared shorts. Her smile was as priceless as it was inviting, addressing Horace with a welcoming reception:

"Why, hello. You must be Horace."

"I am," he responded, carefully speaking over his suppressed nervousness, "Here's the beers Robert requested."

"Thanks," she said, taking them from his hands, "You'll find him in the den, Horace, just walk to the end of the hall and make a right. He's watching the Phillies getting their asses beat by the Cardinals."

That's too bad," he said, "and thanks, Miss . . .?"

"Just call me Libby."

"Thanks, Libby."

Horace walked down the hall, which was more than just a 'hall,' for it was ten feet wide and had a twelve-foot ceiling. He walked about sixty feet, passing framed oil paintings, appearing to be early renaissance, and a few doors before reaching the entrance to the right, and the

'den.' He heard Robert shouting at the TV set at the top of his lungs, "Bums, you, fucking imbeciles!"
"Losing?" Horace asked.
"Lost, God dammit," he said turning the screen off with the remote before turning to greet Horace.

Robert was a middle-aged man, in his late fifties, with greying hair, but was 'apparently' in great physical shape. He was wearing a pink dress-shirt with a black tie and a black vest, and black dress-pants, looking like a lawyer in semi-comfortable mode.
"I'm Horace," Horace said reaching out his hand.
"There goes 'two Grand'," he said, smiling and holding out his hand to Horace.
"Robert Bender, at your service, you met the lady of the house, Libby?" he asked.
"Yes, I have," Horace spoke, rather meekly, "I'm here to see the work needing to be done."

The den was a large room with a cathedral ceiling of tongue and groove oak slats vaulting from ten feet to about eighteen feet high, with about six skylights and a hanging crystal chandelier, not unlike the one in the hall. The walls were painted off-white with painting portraits of Matisse, Renoir, and other Impressionists. They looked like the originals with frames of meticulously finished oak and each had their own show lights. The furniture was leather, a couch in a large semi-circle and chairs surround a glass coffee table mounted on an exquisitely finished piece of driftwood.
"Where's the beers?" Robert asked, pointing for Horace to sit in the chair and before he could say anything, Robert's

question was answered by a soothing voice coming from directly behind Horace.

"They're right here, dear," Libby said with a tray containing two frosted mugs of freshly poured Old Milwaukee beer.

She leaned over, exposing her soft cleavage for the world to see, then handing Horace the frosted mug, winked and smiled almost, as if it was a personal show for him.

"That's what I wanted to hear. Drink-up there, Horace," Robert said.

"Robert," Libby said softly, "are you going to show Horace the basement, or would you rather I do it?"

"I'll show him in a minute, dear, after a beer," he said out of the side of his face and rolling his eyes.

Libby walked away and as she did, Robert caught Horace staring at her floral bottom.

"Sweet little lady, huh?" Robert stated with a smile, "And she plays drums, and a good drummer at that . . . if you know any musicians in need of a good drummer.

"Um," Horace stuttered, "Sorry, I was lost in thought."

"Yeah," Robert said, "Lots of guys get lost in thought looking at Libby."

"I wasn't . . ." Horace began, but was interrupted.

"Don't worry about it," Robert said assuring Horace, and continued, "Our basement needs drywall installed, just on the walls, no ceiling, and spackled."

Horace, taking a swig off of the head of the brew, rejuvenated his focus onto the issue at hand and answered him.

"About how many sheets are you talking about?" Horace asked.

"Well, the ceilings are a little over ten feet high, and the section of room down there I need done is about 40' x 40', So, 40 ten-foot sheets? Standing them upright?"

"That sounds about right," Horace said, "and an extra two sheets in case of mistakes. You want them standing up, right?"

"You're the contractor, you tell me."

"The thing is, Robert, I'm working by myself these days, and I've been limiting myself to just spackling, and finishing for jobs that size. Hanging the drywall is too much for one guy on a job like that."

"If you had help, you could do it?"

"Why, yes, I . . ."

"Libby!" Robert called aloud, interrupting Horace's train of thought.

"Wait a minute, I know you have friends that can help, but I don't need you to get me anyone, like I said, I usually work alone."

"What is it, dear?" Libby asks as she walks into our area.

"Could you help Horace hang the drywall he needs for the walls in the basement?"

"WHAT?" Horace asked, out loud.

"Sure," she said, smiling, then looked at Horace tilting her head sideways, "Are you going to need me to help?"

"What, is this a joke?" he asked again, taken aback.

"Why do you think we're joking?" Robert asked, "Libby has installed drywall before, with me. She can handle it. Hell, she's been digging up the yard out there with the back-hoe and putting in the new underground line from the street. She can handle herself pretty well."

"But," Horace said, "I didn't look at it yet, and you have no idea what I charge. And I have to pay Libby, and that's not my normal way of working. . . and . . ."

"I'll pay you a flat rate," Robert said, "I'll pay you a round figure of, say, $2500, just your labor, and I'll buy the materials, and have it all delivered."

"That's . . . a lot," Horace said in disbelief.

"Look," Robert continued, "I like you, and you came out to my place the same day I called. The other guys were not trustworthy to me, nor did they appear, to be credible. You, however have an honest face and I want you to do the job. Besides, I looked up your references and you're a good contractor, and a good guy."

Just then, the phone rang, and Robert answered it in a preoccupied demeanor and began talking as if Horace and Libby didn't exist.

"Come on," Libby said to Horace, "I'll show you the basement," and she signaled to Robert, who waved his hand, flagging her in a wave to go ahead as he continued his involved phone conversation. Horace and Libby walked through the house as she continued to talk.

"He's a very busy man," she said, "He's like that all the time, and he never lets up. That's how he ended up with this mansion and the cars, and everything else we have."

"What does he do for a living? That is if you don't mind me asking."

"You mean you don't know?" she asked.

Then Libby began laughing and shaking her head as they descended the stairs into the basement with its ten-foot high wood beam ceilings and studded out walls.

"What's so funny?" he asked her with his eyebrows up in question.

"Robert Bender," she said, "You ever hear of 'Bender's'? Bender's Clubs?"

"You mean, he's Bender? The guy who owns Bender's?"

"He's the one. I figured you knew!" she said, continuing to laugh.

"Why, they have clubs all over the United states," Horace said with an amazed look on his face.

"I know that," she said, "I'm his partner. We have 155 of them to be exact."

"Unbelievable," he said, just staring at the concrete floor, and a set of metallic blue, very nice-looking Ludwig drums in the far corner of the other room.

"So, here it is," she said, smiling, and interrupting his distant gaze, "here are the walls that need the gypsum board installed,"

Horace started walking and measuring, jotting things down on his clipboard while Libby walked into the next room behind the studded wall and pulled two ice cold bottles of Michelob from a refrigerator and opening one, handed it to him.

"So," she said with a comforting smile in his direction, looking right through him with a gaze, "How long have you lived in Doylestown?"

"Well," he said, putting his clipboard down and taking a sip of the brew, "I kind of grew up there, in the area."

"What color are your eyes?" she asked moving her face very close to his and staring deep into his baby blues.

"Um, blue, I guess."

"Blue," she said, and asked, as he felt her soft hand on his chest, "what color are mine?"

Horace dropped his bottle of beer on the floor and it shattered, giving them both a jolt backward, causing Libby to begin her laughing once again.

"My," he said, "you laugh a lot don't you. 'Really sorry about the mess."

Libby was way ahead of him and grabbed a broom and dustpan, but Horace snatched them from her as he got down on one knee and swept the broken shards and suds from the concrete floor.

"Don't worry about it," she said. "I'm deducting the beer from your pay anyway," and started laughing again.

In a few minutes the mess was cleaned up and Libby had brought him another bottle, but he said he'd better not, and started gathering his clipboard and tape measure, rather clumsily, dropping the tape measure on the floor in the process.

"You alright?" Libby asked rather, sheepishly.

"Yeah," he said, "I just think I'd better be going."

"You know what you need?" she asked, grinning.

"No, what?"

"I mean, do you have the measurements and know what you need to do this job? Silly?"

He started up the stairs and was greeted by Robert, "What do you think? Easy enough, right?"

"Right," Horace replied and then said, "I could get to it in a few weeks."

"It needs to be done after the weekend," Libby said, "On Monday you can start."

"What?" Horace retorted, with a surprised look.

"She's right," Robert said, finishing off a can of his beer, "We need this done ASAP. Libby has furniture coming the week after next and she'll be painting it next weekend, which gives you a week to hang and finish it."

"But, I have jobs booked next . . ."

"Push them back," Libby stated.

"Yeah," agreed Robert, "Three thousand dollars is a lot of money for a single week's work."

Horace stared, in disbelief before saying, "But I thought you originally said $2500."

"Look, Horace, $3500 is my final offer, but you have to start Monday and finish it so it's ready for paint Saturday; Take it or leave it."

"Forty sheets?"

"I'll help you," Libby said, pulling her loose top up from slipping, after showing her generous cleavage again while bending seductively to pick up a beer tab from Robert's beer can.

"Okay," Horace said, after a moment of hesitation, but realized that Robert Bender could afford the money, and that he himself could sure as hell use it. He followed Robert to the door and on his way out, Horace stopped to pick up a pen that dropped from his clipboard. As he did he felt a soft tap from Libby's hand through his tight jeans right on his rump, and a squeeze. He ignored it as if it never happened and continued to the door.

"Everything will be ready for you here on Monday, bright and early," Robert said.

"I'll be waiting," Libby added, with a wink.

"I'll see you both at 9:00am," Horace said, and got into his truck, but before driving away through the gate and homeward, he heard drumming coming from the basement and decided to check it out. Walking a few feet to the basement window, he peered in to see Libby behind the drum set, playing a steady, rock-solid beat before rolling it into a solo that could have given Baker or Krupa a run for their money. Shaking his head, he got back into his pick-up and drove through the gate, and homeward.

CHAPTER - THREE

The sun was going down as Horace drove his way home, and I felt it was my duty as an Angel, or at least his spiritual guide to talk with him again, this time about his visit to the Benders' house, and how the whole ordeal went down.

"Libby is a pretty sweet and flirtatious little number, isn't she?" I asked.

"Oh, man," he said, "she knocks me out, and what a drummer? Hearing her play makes me feel like I want to play more, and I want someone like that in my life, but she's married and he's such a great guy, it seems."

"Well, a little flirting won't hurt anything, besides, you got a good paying job out of it."

"I know, flirting with danger," Horace said, steering his way onto the bypass, "and I have to move my other two jobs back a few weeks, but fortunately, those jobs aren't rush jobs and those customers basically said 'whenever'. Maybe she and I could jam sometime."

As he passed an underpass, sitting on a ramp was a hitchhiker who was an Afro-American, in his mid-30's, with what looked like a bass fiddle in a soft-case next to him. He was wearing a brown turtle-neck sweater under a blue-jean jacket, and black slacks. Along with the bass fiddle he also had a small black suitcase with what looked like pennants and decals.

"That guy was standing there 'thumbing it' when I passed him on my way north, a few hours ago," Horace said to himself and continued, "I'm going to see where he's going."

Horace pulled over and asked him how far he was going, but when he said Philadelphia, Horace offered to take him to the other side of town at least.

"Thanks, man," he said, loading his stuff into the back of the pick-up.

"No problem at all, I'm Horace."

"Thanks, Horace, I'm Jordan."

Jordan, it turns out, is a bassist, hailing originally out of Philly then moved to Chicago and then Memphis, and on the road, looking for a gig in a jazz trio in Philly, but he just found out the union hired another bassist because the club they were hired at wouldn't let him play due to discrimination.

"I didn't think people discriminated against black musicians or mixed color bands since 1964, or so," Horace said steering into the passing lane.

"No," Jordan said, "Not because I'm black, but because I'm gay,"

Horace looked over at him, and then looked at the road and said, "Oh, you let them know, Huh?"

"I don't hide that shit anymore," he said, "hell, I don't I hide that I'm black."

"You sure don't," Horace said, laughing.

"Does it bother you, knowing that I'm gay?" Jordan asked, staring at Horace out of the side of his face.

"Does it bother you, knowing that I'm straight?" Horace retorted.

They both laughed, and a quiet ambience fell over them as the humming of the wheels on the road spread an uncomfortable drone of continued awkward silence that was almost unbearable until Horace broke through the medium with one question:

"How long have you been playing bass?"

"Probably close to twenty years," Jordan said, and continuing, "My father was a musician, and so was my mom. They both played with Ellington and The Count, off and on, but Mom got strung out and Dad, well, I don't talk about that much anymore. I've been in foster homes for years and the music's what's kept me sane. That bass of mine, it's a Kay, given to me by my dad, and it's my heart and soul."

"He was a bassist, I take it?"

"He was a trombone player, who filled in as a bassist for some of the big bands, and he gave me the bass about a year before I went into the home. I've been playing it every day since. How about you, Horace? Are you a player?"

"I fool around on the guitar. I've got a Martin acoustic that I've been playing for, I don't know, close to fifteen years or so."

"No shit? What kind of music you like, brother?"

"'Pretty much' all kinds. I like country, rock, country rock, Blues, Jazz . . ."

"Jazz?" Jordan said, as he lit up to the word 'jazz'.

"Well," Horace said meekly, "I'm not a connoisseur, but I can play a few extended chords, and some pieces from Charlie Parker, Coltrane, and some Benny Goodman."

"No shit?"

"Now, like I said," Horace continued, "I'm not that good at it, I'm more into the bluesy side of that genre rather than being any expert in bee-bop or true jazz, but I've fooled with it."

"Can you play by ear?" Jordan responded, "Can you read sheet music?"

"I can understand charts, but I play mostly by ear," Horace said, smiling and making another turn off of the road into a convenience store in Edison.

"So," Horace said, ""You got someplace in the city to go to? I mean, if you don't have a band now, where are you going to go?"

"I have some folks there, on Erie Avenue in North Philly," he said with a smile, "Thanks for asking."

"This is as far as I can take you," Horace said, sadly, "I'm sure you can get a ride from here."

"No problem, Horace. I really appreciate the ride. It's Friday night and I'm sure I can . . ."

"Wait a minute," Horace said, "Here's a five. Catch the 55 bus, into Broad and Olney. There's one that runs through here every hour. I see you just missed one but catch the next one. Here's another couple of bucks, get a sandwich or something."

"No, don't, I've got it here," he said smiling and showing his big grin, "Thanks for everything, brother, I hope to run into you again, 'Home'."
"Home?" Horace repeated, questioning.
"Home," Jordan answered, "It means 'friend', or 'brother'."

Horace pulled away with a grin, leaving Jordan with his bass and his suitcase to the Seven Eleven lights as it started getting dark on his homeward trek, back up route 611 and into Doylestown.
"Home?" I asked.
"I know," Horace replied, "I never heard that expression. Must be a 'black' thing."
"He's a hell of a nice guy," I told Horace as we climbed the old Main Street hill up into town, driving towards the center.

We maneuvered our way down the backstreets to Wood Street and eventually slowly past the house, to see there were no parking spaces again. He found one at the end of the block, right at the end of the curb and was barely able to squeeze the Ford into the vacancy.

When he got to the steps the stereo was blaring a Robert Hazzard song, so he turned down the sound, and yelled upstairs.
"LUCY?"

The silence continued, other than a thump and a bump sound.
"Yeah? Horace? Is that you?" Lucy's voice responded.

Then he became aware shower was running and yelled up, "You're in the shower?"

Lucy came down the stairs fully clothed, breathing heavy with her jeans on and her hair wet as she combed the tangles out of it.

"You left the shower running?"

"No, stupid, Johnny's in there. Where were you?" she asked, calmly, breathing a little softer now, "I was worried about you."

She gave him a kiss on the lips and asked, "Did you eat? There's soup on the stove." Then she went and leaned over the stereo to turn up Cyndi Lauper singing, "Girls Just Wanna' Have Fun," and walked into the kitchen. Horace followed her in and looked around to see that it was a mess, with the dishes piled in the sink and food on the floor, and an odor of garbage.

"Why the hell is there a mess like this in here?" he asked.

"Well," Lucy responded, "clean it up. You got two hands. I've been busy all day."

"Doing what?" he asked her, obviously annoyed.

"Look," she answered, "What's with the third degree?"

"How the hell did this food get on the floor, it looks like eggs and cheese, with . . . shrimp?"

"Johnny made lunch and it got messy, so, what?" she snapped.

"It smells like a garbage truck backed his load into this room," he said firmly.

"So, clean it up of you don't like it, for Christ sake," she said angrily.

"Why the fuck didn't HE clean it up?" Horace demanded, "He's living here for nothing, eating my food, drinking my beer, and I'll bet fucking my . . ."

"Don't . . . you. . . dare . . ." Lucy interrupted.

Just then, Johnny entered the room, with his shirt off and wearing a pair of Horace's pants, with his hair soaking wet, dripping it onto the floor as he combed the tangles out.

"What's up?" he asked, with a big smile showing white perfect teeth, "we got anything to eat?"

Horace shoved Johnny aside and stormed out of the room and out of the house, into his pick-up and just drove into the night. Behind him the whole way was Lucy's constant yelling, "You, fucking asshole!" But he was not deterred as he floored the vehicle's accelerator and gunned the Ford down the street and onto Main Street south to Route 611.

"That was pretty weird," I said calmly.

"What else was I supposed to do? That asshole just got out of the shower, I know he was fucking her."

"Why do you put up with it?" I asked.

"I don't even know, but it's going to stop."

He headed to Edison where Jordan was dropped off and just caught him getting onto the number 55 bus.

"Jordan," he shouted and flagged his hands.

After Jordan flagged the bus onward without him, he and Horace had a brief discussion outside of the pick-up about where he can stay temporarily, instead of heading into the city.

"Why don't you hang out with me, for tonight anyway?" Horace told him, "We can play some music."

"Say what?" Jordan replied, leaning on his bass.

"Look, brother," Horace said, "I'm straight. This is NOT a pick-up line and I'm not making a pass at you. 'You want to play music? I am in the mood for jamming tonight with some good music if you have nowhere to go, that is if you're not bullshitting me and can *really play* that bass of yours. I have nowhere to go but home, tonight; In turn I'll give you a place to sleep."

"Sounds good to me, Home." Jordan spoke, loading his gear into the back and then climbing in.

"Another thing," Horace said, "use that five I gave you to help me chip in for some beers up here. We'll pick up a case of something that I developed a taste for just today, "Old Milwaukee."

"You're on, my good brother."

Horace and Jordan drove the pick-up through Sunny's Drive-Thru and with the beer in the back, headed to Wood Street and home. Horace noticed the parking space open in the front, Lucy's spot, and fit the truck in its void like a glove.

""This your crib?" Jordan asked.

"This is my pad," Horace said with a big and victorious smile, "and it looks like we're the only one's home."

The guys carried their gear, Jordan with the bass and Horace with the suitcase in one hand and the case of beer under his other arm. The beer was loaded into the fridge and freezer while the mess in the kitchen was simply ignored. A few chairs and the coffee table were moved aside while Jordan slipped the soft cover off of his Kaye upright bass. The four strings were steel and strung across a near-black fingerboard attached to the large, chestnut brown colored violin shaped body. The strings looked larger than life attached from the tuning pegs and stretched across the body on a bridge to the tailpiece. Horace, with his own acoustic guitar out and now on his lap, had never seen one of these uprights up close and admired it with a gaze as Jordan started tuning it.

"Give me a 'G'," he said to Horace while reaching up a twisting the tuning peg to the resonance as Horace complied with his guitar pick picking a higher octave 'G'.

After a few moments of tuning, Jordan pulled out a joint from his top pocket and held it up to Horace with his eyebrows raised as if to ask "Okay?" Horace responded by tossing him a book of matches and then poured two frosty mugs of brew from an ice-cold quart of malt liquor that he had hidden in the back of the fridge while they waited for their newly purchased case to get cold.

"This promises to be one of those good Friday nights," Horace stated, taking the lit joint from Jordan.

""Damn right. What do you want to play?" Jordan asked, "What are you in the mood for?"

After blowing out a stream of smoke, and then taking a long sip of his beer, Horace started a blues riff in the key of A flat, which Jordan picked up on right away. They did the 1-4-5 pattern, Ab, Db, and Eb, with sevenths and suspended fourths, and then augmented chords, which Jordan was able to fit a slow walking and sliding, hypnotic sound of slurs between the notes, giving the number a sexy tone with acoustic guitar syncopating the rhythm and melody. Soon, the chord pattern embellished and modulated to another slightly different chord pattern of distant familiarity as it went into the key of A and Horace started playing the mellow guitar lead melody to "Summertime." After a few bars Jordan started with the lyrics, "Summertime, when the living is easy . . ."

Jordan didn't remember all of the words and was not a bad singer, but Horace continued with the rest of it. It could be said that they were adequate vocalists but neither of them, were much to talk about with their singing voices, but the playing of their instruments was superb. They blended well and conversed together like they knew each other for years and years, even though they've only just met. It's nothing more than the miraculous power of music, cutting into their souls through their present situation of the blues; Jordan with his situation with the band and lack of place to go, and Horace with his situation with his woman and the derelict she forces as a wedge between them. In issues such as these, you can't help but turn to the blues, and music for comfort.

After a few jamming numbers, Jordan sat back and opened a pint of Windsor Canadian bourbon he had stashed inside of one of the pockets of his soft-cover case and after a swig, offered it to Horace, who passed. Then screwing the lid back on, sat on the couch and lit a joint before he leaned back comfortably and took a look around the room they were in, glancing with a perpetual smile at the pictures of Horace and Lucy decorating every wall. There were portraits of them together in paintings, and black and white shore pictures of their summers at the Jersey beach. There was also a picture of an infant between them in one and it caught Jordan's interest to ask.

"Horace," he questioned, blowing smoke into the air from his joint, "you got a kid?"

"Had a little boy," Horace replied, with a sad face.

Jordan's curiosity peaked as he just nodded his head, taking another long toke and waiting for Horace to respond further, but there was nothing but the still of the room as is normally heard in the empty void when the music stops. Horace was simply sitting back in his easy chair recliner across the cozy fifteen-foot room, with a full, cold, quart bottle of malt liquor. He asked Jordan for his pint of bourbon and Jordan obliged by tossing it to him, and Horace opened and drank two strong gulps of it before tossing it back to him, then guzzled his entire quart down. After a moment of him staring at the picture off to his side, the one that encouraged Jordan's question, Horace finally broke the silence with a response.

"My little boy was killed in a car accident," Horace said in a deep tone.

"Oh my God, I'm sorry to hear that, brother," Jordan replied, blowing out a stream of smoke and putting out the joint in the small saucer they were using as an ashtray.

"It was two years ago," Horace continued, "Lucy my girlfriend, and Gabriel, my little two-year-old boy, were on their way home from visiting a friend of hers when they ran off of the road to avoid a pick-up coming directly at them in the wrong lane and crashed into a tree. Lucy was thrown from the car and had a few lacerations but survived. Gabriel on the other hand was crushed, killed instantly."

"Man," Jordan whispered aloud, shaking his head from side to side.

"I'm sorry," Horace said, now shaking his own head, "we're here to have a good time, and I'm bringing you down. Just tell me to shut-up, Jordan."

"Never," Jordan said, opening his pint and taking another swig.

"Was it a drunk driver?" Jordan asked.

"Oh, the driver was drunk alright, but we're not supposed to know that," Horace answered, sarcastically.

"Say what?"

"Both drivers were drunk, Lucy, and the jerk-off driving the other vehicle, the pick-up," Horace said, slightly slurring his words now.

"I . . . don't follow," Jordan replied, "You're saying the drivers of both vehicles were, intoxicated?"

"Yes, drunk!" Horace said, and went to the freezer to put the icy beers into the fridge and brought in another two cans of brew, offering Jordan one, who happily accepted.

"Were they . . .?"

"Arrested? No," Horace continued, interrupting Jordan, "No one ever knew they were drunk. They both drove away from the scene in his pick-up to his house, so they could sober up, leaving my dead son in the car. When they were recuperated enough, early the next morning they returned to the accident scene and of course, no one noticed the car down the embankment so that's when they called the cops. There was no alcohol and no evidence of drinking or drugs at the scene and she was taken to the hospital, where she was treated for lacerations and bruises. Gabriel, however was not so fortunate and, well, he was buried at the Shrine, where my parents are buried."

There was another vast silence that fell over the room until Horace spoke up, with his eyebrows pointed down in anger and a frown darkened his otherwise serene facial features.

"She had him living here ever since," Horace said.

"Who?"

"That fucking drunken loser, Johnny," Horace said, biting his lip.

"Who's Johnny?" Jordan asked, lighting his joint back up again.

"Johnny was the guy who almost hit her head-on and killed my son," Horace said in a strong tone of anger, and continued:

"The loser's been living here ever since because Lucy felt sorry for him, and I'm mad at myself because I know I'm a fool for letting this nonsense continue."

"He's . . . living here? Really? Where's he at now?" Jordan asked, handing him the joint.

"Let's play some more music," Horace said, ignoring the question, but just then the telephone rang.

On the phone was Lucy saying that she won't be coming home tonight because she's tied up with a few friends drinking and she doesn't want to drive."

"You need a ride, Lucy? I'll come and get you."

"No, that's alright. I'm staying here. Thanks anyway, Love you."

"Love you too," Horace said hanging up the phone, but he didn't feel as sincere saying it as he used to.

He finished his beer and said, "What's next there, captain?"

Jordan started walking a bass line to a pattern of notes that matched a Gm7 to A7 set of chords and Horace played these and played the melody line to "Scrapple from the Apple." They jammed the rest of the night and into the morning on jazz and blues standards, mixing and matching melody lines and scales and not another word was spoken about Johnny or Lucy.

CHAPTER - FOUR

The following morning Horace awoke with a slight headache, remnants of the marijuana smoke and sugars from the evil powers of bourbon and beer. He was at least in his own bed, although alone, peaceful in the accomplishment of good music echoing a memorable resonance throughout his entire sense of being. I, as his guide did my usual entrance in speaking to him because I've grown to like the guy, and because it's my job, my assignment, as a spirit guide, if you will.

"How are you feeling buddy," I spoke to him calmly, reminding him that I'm still here as his guardian.

"I'm feeling; which means I'm still living, right?"

"Right as rain," I said, and once again, I'm nothing more than another thought to him 'apparently', but he senses a revived confidence as I am with him.

He immediately thought of Jordan and wondered about him as he put on his clothes and walked on down the upstairs hall to the spare room. Jordan had the door open and was sitting up on the edge of the bed, fully clothed and reading a guitar player magazine.

"This Jaco guy is something else, ain't he?" Jordan asked with his never-ending smile.

"He most certainly is, brother," Horace said, returning the grin. "You ready to go out for some breakfast?"

"Hell yeah," he said gathering his things.

They sat at a booth in the Keystone diner and ate their eggs and bacon while they shared stories about music and bands of the past. Jordan talked about a club on the corner of Broad Street and Erie Avenue where he played bass with a sax player and a jazz drummer. They gigged there and in clubs down Broad Street to Center City, "Old City" he said was what they called that section of Philadelphia, doing the trio and pulling in some serious dough. Jordan was sitting opposite Horace in the booth where he could watch people walking in and out of the diner as they talked and told Horace that seeing different people remind him of his past. For instance, he saw a guy who reminded him of his old saxophone player, and even though the person was white, he had those same mannerisms as his black friend, Skip, the way he walked, and the way he'd turn his head and grin when looking around the diner. Another time a woman walked into the diner that reminded him of a girl he knew a few years ago. He said there was a girl drummer, who used to sit in with them playing incredibly hot, showing up, once a month maybe and they'd let her rhythms roll like clockwork, catching the ears, then the eyes of the patrons as she showed off her prowess on the skins and symbols as they jammed. Then they'd let her cut loose with a solo and the place would go wild until they broke back into the song and it was always capped-off with a standing ovation, but unfortunately, she disappeared off of the scene.

"Who was she? Horace asked.

"I have no idea," Jordan said, sipping his coffee, "I never got her name either. We just called her "Sticks."

"Sticks, huh?"

"Yeah, a white chick with a nice body, my man, some really good form."

"It sounds funny," Horace said, "YOU, noticing her nice body," Horace replied, referring to Jordan's sexual preference.

"What?" he asked, "Can't I notice a nice body? I may be gay, but I'm not dead . . . yet."

They both laughed as Horace sopped up his egg yellow with the buttered rye toast and Jordan munched on a blueberry muffin before taking another sip of his coffee. Just then, there was a familiar female voice calling out to Horace from another booth on the other side of the room.

"Horace!"

Horace turned to look, and was surprised to see Libby, sitting in a booth with a dark-haired, middle-aged male companion, but it wasn't Robert.

"Libby?" Horace responded, and waved as Libby waved back.

"You know her?" Jordan asked.

"She's a customer," Horace said smiling, "I'm starting a drywall job at her place this Monday."

Libby stood up and walked over to the booth Horace and Jordan were sitting from across the room, bending sideways in order to not knock a waitress's tray over. She was wearing a revealing silk blouse and skin-tight jeans letting everyone in the diner know her ass was perfect.

"Scoot in," she said to Horace, sliding right next to him into the booth.

"Libby, this is my friend Jordan," Horace said, introducing him.

"Oh my God," she said, astonished, "The bass fiddle!"

"It 'is' you! Sticks!" Jordan replied, "I was just talking about you to Horace here. I saw you walk in and you reminded me of you."

"I what? Who's Sticks?" Libby stated, grinning from ear to ear, "What the hell are YOU on?"

"Never mind," Horace retorted, "He told me about a story of a girl drummer and it turns out, you're her."

"OH," Libby said, shaking her head while looking down and laughing, then rolled her eyes and added facetiously, "THAT - - - sure clears it up."

"Anyway, how the hell have you been?" Jordan asked, "I just found out your name's – 'Libby'?"

"Yes, and you must be Jordan," she said sarcastically, noting that she was just introduced.

"You guys know each other in past lives?" Horace asked.

"Not really know," Jordan said, "We've jammed a few songs."

"You're a good player," Libby said abruptly, almost cutting him off.

"Well, you're phenomenal," Jordan followed, "and still playing I hope."

"Where are you living now? Philly?" she asked, taking a sip of Horace's coffee.

"Maybe," he said, "I'll have to see what the man with the cards deals next."

"It's a shame," she said, "I could use a nice jam with a good bassist. I've been just playing with myself off and on for the past year."

Both men picked up on Libby's 'tongue in cheek' humor as she took another sip of Horace's coffee and looked at him closely, eyeing him almost-lustfully, up and down.

"Say, Horace, you look nice today," she said, while twisting a curl in his hair.

I was listening with my spiritual ears and hearing nothing from Horace this entire time, and decided to give him a prod. He's supposed to swing this conversational flow into a rerouted destiny, and I don't know how or why, but I know it's supposed to happen right here.

"Horace," I asked, *"Why can't Jordan work with you for a week, and you put him up in the spare room?"*

"Why?" Horace asked.

"So, you can jam this week with him and Libby."

"Libby, can we do something this week?" Horace asked, with a serious look.

"What did you have in mind?" she asked, responding in her typical flirtatious manner, placing her hand gently onto his thigh while tilting her head and resting it on her other hand eloquently propped by her elbow on the table, gazing into his eyes invitingly.

"I thought that . . . maybe we could all jam this week, at your house?"

"Doing drywall?" she asked.

"No, no, no, I mean, do you want to jam? Play music with Jordan and me?"

"Are you a sax player too?" Libby asked, with smiling anticipation.

"He's and excellent guitar player," Jordan answered, butting in.

"I thought, he could help me . . ." Horace started, but Libby interrupted.

"Help us, you mean?"

"Okay, help 'us' with the work," Horace said, "and you and he and I could jam afterwards."

"Wait one minute," Jordan said, "How the hell am I going to do that? I have nowhere to stay."

"You can stay with . . ." Horace started, but was once again interrupted by Libby.

"You can stay with us at the house," Libby said, "That's what I wanted to ask you anyway."

"He can?" Horace asked.

"We've got plenty of room," she said, "Besides, I was looking into getting some instruments and people together for a combo."

"Horace and I were jamming last night, and it was pretty damn 'rad'," Jordan said with his big grin.
"Yeah?" she asked, returning the smile.
"We had a blast," Horace said and continued, "Libby, I'd love to try a three-piece, with you as the drummer."
"What are we waiting for, then?" Libby said, as her male companion walked over to their booth, looking sullen.
"Libby," he said, being sarcastic, "I ordered, and I ate. I'm leaving now, so, thanks for your company. Let's do it again sometime."
"I'm sorry, Bill, I got caught up talking with friends. Have a nice weekend," she said to him as he stormed out.
"Was that your boyfriend?" Jordan asked.
"No way, Jordan," she snapped, then just as quickly mellowed, "He's a colleague of my old man, Robert, and he didn't care for me standing him up, especially sitting in a booth with a black guy."
"Sorry, I didn't know you were married," Jordan said.
"Bigoted?" Horace asked.
"Very," she said, "I can't see how people can be that way. Anyway, 'want to jam today?"
"Jordan? Are you in?" Horace asked.
"Daaamn straight!" he replied.
"Straight?" Horace retorted, laughing.
"Forward," Jordan rescinded, "Never straight."

They paid the lady at the cash register and as they watched Libby pull away in her red 1984 Ford Mustang GT, Horace and Jordan headed back to Wood Street to get Horace's guitar and a Fender amp. As they arrived Horace saw that Lucy's spot was still open right in front of the house and he took advantage of it. His landlord was also sitting on the steps as if waiting for him, with a briefcase parked next to him.

"Good morning Mr. Clowney," he said, addressing Horace as Horace approached him.

"Good morning to you, Mr. Detweiler, what's up?" he replied, returning the greeting and continued, "I have your rent money, and I was going to mail it to you Monday, but I'll give it to you now."

"That's fine," he said, "I wanted to have you sign a new lease today if you would, for another six months."

"Not a problem, come on inside and I'll get a pen," he said.

"I have one right here," Mr. Detweiler said.

"Well," Horace replied, "I got to run in anyway and pee, like immediately, and I'll be right out . . . or you can come in if you'd like."

Horace ran into the house and upstairs, barely making it to the bathroom, and pushing the door open, heard the shower water running and said, "Lucy?"

"Who's there?" a male voice shouted from behind the steamy, frosted shower door.

After a short pause that seemed like forever, Horace looked at the shadow behind the door and was able to make out two bodies before he heard another voice, a female voice, say: "What are you doing home?"

"I live here," Horace replied, "and what are you doing, Lucy?"

The water in the shower was turned off to a trickle before the door slid open letting a billow of steam flow outward as Horace stood his ground, not moving an inch within the small bathroom to see who was stepping out of his shower.

"Get out of here!" Lucy said to Horace, standing in complete view, naked as she was reaching for a towel off of the rack beside the stall.

Horace, acting unmoved, pulled down his zipper and began to calmly pee into the toilet while looking at her. As he looked behind her and saw Johnny standing tall with his long and soaking wet curly hair draped over his smiling face while he pushed it back over his bare shoulders, Horace said, "Hello Johnny," and just smiled.

"Hey Butthead!" Johnny said, addressing Horace, "You heard Lucy, get out!"

Horace turned, and me myself being his spiritual guide, I could feel his emotion as he walked down the stairs, but he remained calm and collected.

"What are you going to do now?" I finally asked him.

"I'm leaving, but not before I gather a few of my things, she can have the rest."

Horace was crying but only I could see it as he grabbed a few pictures, like the one of he and his son with Lucy, and a few other things before he walked outside. He told the landlord that Lucy would be right down to sign the lease.

"Jordan, can you give me a hand?" he yelled.

"Coming boss," he said running up to the porch.

They both took a reclining chair, the case of leftover beer and his guitars, an amp, and some odds and ends. Lucy never came downstairs, but Johnny did, and was insistent on wanting to know what was going on, but Horace and Jordan just kept moving stuff until the pickup couldn't hold anything else.

"What the hell are you doing with our furniture, Horace?" Johnny said, wearing only his jeans with his wet hair still dripping, "and what's that coon doing in my house?"

Horace just glared at him before walking up to him and pushed him against the wall using his two palms, bouncing them off of his chest and said, "Manners, you, fucking jerk-off!"

The landlord walked in just then and asked Horace what was going on, but Horace yelled upstairs to Lucy that the landlord was here and wanted her to sign something. Johnny grabbed Horace by the neck and tried to get him in some kind of wrestling hold, but Horace picked him up like he was nothing and walked him outside, ripped him from his hold and threw him off of the porch right into the trash bin.

"Lucy," he yelled upstairs once again, "I just put the trash out, and Mr. Detweiler wants to talk to you."

Horace shook the landlord's hand and told him that he's moving out, adding that he's not worried about the rent escrow and thanking him for being a good landlord, then he and Jordan pulled away in the loaded pick-up, and never looked back.

I was proud of Horace, being his guide, but I wasn't sure where he was going and had to ask him.

"What's the plan?" I asked.

"I don't know," he said, "other than I have to get this stuff into storage. I can't keep it in this pick-up."
"What's the plan, Horace?" Jordan asked, "You left in a hurry. You want to talk about it?"
"Yes, I do," Horace replied with a tremble of emotion.

Horace opened up to Jordan, telling him all that was going down between he and Lucy and Johnny, and he wondered if there were any places for rent in town on such short notice. Jordan 'seemed to think' that in a pinch, Libby might temporarily help out, but Horace did not want to be, or seem the least bit presumptuous about anything like that. I decided to put my two cents in again.

"Horace," I said softly, *"you will be working there this week putting in the walls, right."*
"Yeah, that's a fact, and I can use the money," he said, driving up the Route 611 bypass.
"I was wondering if there's a way to negotiate a plan of staying there at the Benders' while you're working," I told him.
"Yeah, that's a thought, at least for a week anyway," he replied.
"Yeah," I agreed, *"I mean Libby has no problem putting Jordan up, and she has the room, it should work."*
"I don't want to assume, but I can't see why it wouldn't work out," he thought, then he smiled and started singing, with Jordan joining in, "We're off to see the wizard, the wonderful wizard of oz . . ."

CHAPTER - FIVE

Saturday night was one hell of a great sounding jam with Horace, Jordan, and Libby as they played every genre from blues, to rock, to jazz, formulating their own renditions of the standards, making the music their own. Robert, who's 'apparently' Libby's husband, was away for the weekend, and all week for that matter in Georgia at one of the Bender's clubs on a business deal and the three musicians played all night long, with the help of some cocaine that Libby just happened to have. She also had some quantities of Vicodin, an opioid pain-killer that her husband was prescribed for his back.

Although I was his guide, I decided to leave the scene for now because an emptiness was surrounding my very being and my purpose became vague, as a deterrent fog entered my Universe. I was not with Horace anymore, and I found myself once again in this misty fog, like a thick cloud of sweet, odoriferous vapor engulfing my very existence. As I moved forward I found myself in a strange room, slowly moving; and passing a gentleman sitting in a wooden rocking chair, staring at the door in front of us with a terror, an unadulterated look of fear within his widened eyes. As I leaned over to look at him I recognized him, but I'll be damned if I know from where, as he looked at me and shivered and trembled before he finally spoke.

"What are you doing? You're not going through that door, are you?" he asked, with a vibrato in his vocal cords.

"I hadn't planned on it," I said, "but now that you mention it, what's behind there?"

"No," he responded, "You don't want to know."

Then he started humming "Amazing Grace" in a slightly off-tune drone that was rather, eerie sounding, tapping his fingers out of time on the wooden chair-arms and rocking very slowly. I was feeling a chill from this whole scenario, being that I wasn't sure where I was, or rather, I had veritably no idea. I realized right there and then that I was going to open that door and walk through to the other side because there was no way in hell I was going to hang out in this white, misty room of vapors with this apparent paranoid man.

I approached the door and his singing got louder with each step I made towards my freedom from him. He screamed a shrill shriek as I turned the knob, but he wouldn't leave the rocker as I slowly opened it.

"No! Nnnnnoooo!" he yelled, and the warm air blew the vapors of cloud back into the room as I walked through, like a vacuum, and I closed the door behind me.

"Sad, isn't it?" a voice asked. The voice was the same vibration I heard before I met my buddy Horace. It appeared to be coming from that same, spiritual vastness, and was inundating me with the same self-assuredness and confidence I felt before.

"What's sad?" I asked.

"The poor soul you just left behind."

"You mean Horace?" I responded with a jolt, finally remembering that I left him as he was leaving his home.
"No, I mean the soul within the room of white vapors," the voice said, with a slow enunciated cadence of parlance, like speaking with a very clear, loud quadrophonic whisper.
"Oh, yeah," I said, "he was certainly a piece of work. Is he alright?"
"It's sad," the voice said, "this existence here is actually the end of all time, and the poor soul's earthly form died years ago, and he has no idea how to move on. He was a pastor, a religious figure who does not know how to walk through the same door as you. His fears are so overwhelming that he cannot move from his rocking chair."
"Should I return to him and help guide him through the door?" I asked.
"He considered himself a Christian in his time on earth and will see you as a Muslim, and will not trust you," the voice whispered, "like the female in the room next to his who was a Muslim in her time and who's in the same dilemma. She will see you as a Christian, or a Jew, and will likewise not trust you. Both believe in their same one true God but will not yet truly accept the only true God of the Universe due to concealing their own pride, rather than eliminating it, lacking forgiveness and love."

The rooms we were talking about appeared to be in a very large complex of compartments, hard to describe to a person that is earthbound in a three-dimensional Universe with the movement of time as the fourth element. However, it was understood that this complex of apartments was a place of incubation for these beings who are wallowing, 'seemingly' hopeless within their catacombs of anxiety and discomposure.

I saw another man that was very familiar and would not let the white light of the Voice that was speaking to me near him, fearing this Voice every time it approached. The man laid on the floor as if in a tantrum whenever the Voice and I neared him, meaning, the man was frightened to death of the both of us. He was calling the Voice a 'she' and yelling for me to "get 'her' away", but the Voice was not deterred and never changed the peaceful aura surrounding us.

"The simple truth is," the Voice said, "that all these beings need to do is to rise and walk, walk forward and through the door to their own freedom from their fear. They will sit there for as long as it takes to burn off the pride, hate, guilt and other fears induced by their life of bullying, prejudice, false teachings and beliefs. You yourself experienced a similar room before we first talked, but you do not remember, because there is no need to. Time itself is relative here as it is irrelevant, and different for each individual soul, as I'm sure you've concluded by now."

"What was my fear in the room?" I asked.

"You were a somewhat homophobic among other things in your time, and you were raised in a bigoted atmosphere," the Voice said, and continued, "but you overcame most of your fears in your worldly form, along with your addictions to the false courage of stimulants and depressants."

"I was a drug addict?" I asked.

"Let's just say," the voice replied, "that you were consumed with trying to find the right path through unwarranted detours."

"So, now I'm helping Horace find the right road?" I said in a half-question, wondering if I'd get a response, but I didn't get the response I anticipated.

"You were brought back here because you were merely observing Horace, and living, rather than your task of guiding. You will return to him and guide him accordingly, as your task calls. In doing this you will also be aiding him, yourself, and the entity you had seen, your female counterpart, your soulmate."

"Where is she?" I asked.

"You will be with her in due time." The Voice said, "and your success with Horace will complete you and her also, saving her and yourself. You will understand when it happens."

Before I knew it, some time had passed in my absence from Horace and I was in the basement, the newly constructed recreation room at the Bender's mansion with new drywall already on the walls and with Horace and Libby putting the finishing touches onto the taping and finishing. I was wondering how much I missed and would need to get caught up on the scenario of life with Horace.

Horace and Libby started as planned on Monday morning with the proposed construction work and he stayed there Saturday and Sunday night in one of their guest rooms after moving out of his rented house while Jordan stayed in another one of their spare rooms. They had installed, under Horace's skilled management forty-two sheets of 4' by 10' by half-inch drywall gypsum board, taped and coated the seams and the exposed counter-sunk screws, and are now applying the final coats. While Horace was bending over, Libby grabbed his ass through his overalls, making him jump.

"Will you stop that?" he asked, "You've been doing that to me all week."

"Not all week," Libby said, laughing, "it's only Thursday."

"I know," he said, "by-the-way, do you have any more of that coke? I'm dragging again."

She grinned; then stared at him with those sensual green eyes before putting down her pan containing the joint compound and spackle knife while proceeding to pull the silver vile of the snow-white substance from her tight jeans. She sauntered towards his work space where he was applying the final skim coat and with the tiny spoon, shoved the cocaine up his nose with a strong sniff from his hairy nostril, then the other nostril.

"Good boy," she said, and then gave him a long, wet kiss, sticking her tongue almost, down his throat.

Horace received this caress of endearment with a tender approval, embracing the performance as if it was a common occurrence in the workplace. They kissed a few more times before she backed away and told him he had work to do.

"Back to work," she said, "We've got to finish this up by this weekend for the arrival of the furniture. Robert's coming home on Sunday from Georgia, so you can stay the weekend, and help me paint tomorrow night."

I watched Horace putting the skim coats on the seams while Libby spot coated the third coats on the screw-heads. The clopping of their spackle knives in the steel pans echoed through the room, making it sound like a typical indoor construction site. Libby put the stereo speakers back on to fill the air with Grateful Dead music off of Terrapin Station.

. . . .

At the end of the day, Horace was coming downstairs from his shower, that he actually shared with Libby, and walked into the den where he had first met Robert and Libby a week ago, and as his angel, I had a small chat with him.

"What are you doing messing with a married woman?" I asked.

"I know, she's gorgeous, isn't she?" he said nodding, then he walked into the kitchen to pour a victorious beer for himself from the fridge into a frosted mug.

The kitchen was a big room, about 40 feet by 40 feet, with oak cabinets in the main part where the fridge and the stove were, and the counter with the granite counter-top forming an "L" shape that enclosed that area. Ten tall stools surrounded the counter on the outside with the rest of the room serving as an eating area with two small stained white wooden tables and a large white ten-footer, all with white rail-back wooden chairs.

"And, aren't you partying a little too much?" I asked.

"I'm going through a break-up," Horace said, "and Libby is not only very attractive, but really likes me, and is in an open marriage, according to what I'm seeing. Robert has other women he doesn't tell her about and that's their own rule, 'Don't tell the other'."

"But," I said, feeling somewhat, at a loss, *"Vicodin? Cocaine?"*

"Things go better with coke, and you're forgetting meth-amphetamine," he said belligerently, interrupting me, in a confident tone continuing, "and you're not going to make me feel guilty, for I earned this." He took a big gulp of his beer, swallowing the contents of the whole can, crushing it within his right hand and continued talking while getting another.

"She knows she can book us this Saturday night, on Robert's okay, at Bender's in Philadelphia just as we are," Horace said, "as a trio, to play in the Lounge; And if it goes over well, we can do the circuit of Lounges at all of the Bender's down through Georgia to Florida. I won't have to do construction anymore."

After listening to him and thinking about it I thought I'd say one more thing.

"Isn't this all happening a little too fast?"

"Not fast enough," he said, and didn't answer me anymore that evening. I had come-to the conclusion that, he was hurting badly on the inside because I too could feel it, as he's thinking of his dead son still, and now his break-up with Lucy, and not having the Wood Street house anymore, although I seriously doubt that he's missing that dude Johnny. Just then, Libby appeared in a skimpy red top revealing everything and short shorts.

"You knock my socks off," she said, jumping onto Horace, causing him to back into the kitchen island granite counter-top as she wrapped her arms around him, caressing him and kissing his neck.

"Whoa," he said, but his objection was cut short, silenced with her aggressive kiss on his lips. As he gave in, he returned the embrace and they laid across the counter-top with her ripping his shirt off, that is until they both heard a loud "Ahem."

"Jordan!" Horace responded with a tint of guilt in his voice, unaware that he walked into the room.

They both slid off of the counter-top and stood as Horace buttoned his ripped shirt with what buttons that were left and Libby, grinning like an angel, fixed her hair.

"Don't mind me," Jordan said, "I'm just getting a beer to cool off. Anyone else?"

Libby laughed but Horace just sneered at Jordan and threw a rogue button at him while Libby walked away giggling. Jordan was already callous to their promiscuous behavior since it 'apparently' occurred all week, while I was away. Libby and Horace are truly lovers now and that could prove to be a problem, even though Horace claims she's in what he calls an "open marriage." Horace's four-year relationship wasn't finished but a week ago and he is now involved with Libby, this presumed married woman who also lured he and Jordan into forming a band trio with her.

"Horace," Libby said, "Lets jam and go over a few songs for only a couple hours tonight, then head over to Sportsman's Palace. It's ladies' night and we can have a 'two for the price of one' spaghetti dinner and shoot some pool."

"That sounds like a plan," Horace said.

"Not me," Jordan said, "I mean, I'll jam with you, but afterwards I'm heading into New Hope to meet someone for drinks at a place called 'The Rendezvous'."

"Suit yourself." Libby said.

"We didn't invite you anyway," Horace responded with a wink and a grin, giving Jordan a soft punch in the shoulder, causing him to fall backward mockingly.

"Let's get to it," she demanded, as the guys followed her downstairs and to the corner of the basement where their instruments were set-up.

The three of them tuned, then played through about 20 standards combining blues and jazz pieces, alternating the sounds and combining rhythms and styles from each of their own backgrounds to blend an acoustic conglomeration that in one night became their own sound. Although a little loose sounding, it lent originality to the old standards as they formulated a universal spin that was unique as it tightened up through the hours.

"That was hot," Jordan said after their last number, which was a rendition of "All of Me."

"It sure was," Horace said, "and I'm hungry."

"Starved," Libby said, slurping her lips comically, "Time for spaghetti!"

Jordan looked at his watch and put his bass fiddle against the wall while Horace placed his Martin acoustic in the case. Libby dialed Sportsman's Palace on the phone to ask how late they served, and they replied they had plenty of time since it was only 8:00. Jordan left to meet his friend in Libby's BMW while she and Horace drove in her Ford Mustang to the local bar, Sportsman's, for their dinner.

As they arrived, they walked through the doors and sat at an open spot at the bar; a bar which was about 30 feet long and half filled with folks eating and drinking shots and beers. There were two pool tables that were already taken and about 20 tables with chairs in the large bar room and only five were taken by couples and one family. There were two bartenders dressed in white, long-sleeve shirts, donned with black vests and matching black pants; 'presumably' their uniform. One bartender was a stocky, very physical six-foot male, in his 40's with jet-black hair and a goatee. At the other end of the bar, wiping it down and obviously waitressing the tables was a woman dressed in the same manner, but just short of five feet, well-built with long blond hair in two pig-tail braids who went by the name of Heidi, oddly enough. Her shirt was unbuttoned part way down from the collar and Libby noticed that Horace was looking at her.

"Stop it, Horace" she told him, "she's not on the special."

There was a chalk board in front of them with the evening's specials scribbled in pink and yellow colored chalk and it's what Libby was referring to.

"I was . . ." Horace responded to her comment, "I was going to get her attention."

Just then they were approached by the male bartender who was closer, and as he stood in front of them introduced himself in a deep baritone voice.

"Good evening, folks, I'm Lester. What can I get you? Do you need a menu?"

"Ah, no," Libby said, "I think we know what we want; The 'two-for-one' spaghetti and meatball dinner is what we want."

"And to drink?" he asked.

"We'll take a pitcher of draft, and two frosted mugs," Horace said.

"You got it."

"Wait." Horace said. "Can you also get us two double shots of bourbon also?"

"Coming right up."

Lester handed the dinner order through an opened window-slot behind the bar then took a pitcher and put it under the tap to fill while he got a couple of large shot glasses from under the counter and set them in front of Horace and Libby, filling them to the brim with the bourbon. Then he grabbed two icy beer mugs from the fridge and placing the frosty steins in front of them, filled the mugs from the full pitcher, then topped it off to the spout again from the beer tap. He leaned over to start a tab for both of them when Heidi approached them.

"The man at table two, over near the window says he knows you," she said with a bright smile, pointing in that direction.

"I don't know him," Libby said.

Horace looked across the room to see a man waving at him and he immediately recognized the long blond locks.
"Oh, shit," he replied, as he waved projecting his fake smile, "It's that asshole ex-roommate of mine, 'Johnny'."
"Johnny?" Heidi said, "So you know him?"
"Yeah," he said, "I don't want to talk to him though."
"Alright," she said, "I'm just waiting on his table and he said he knew you."

As Heidi walked back over to the table it was obvious that Johnny was eating alone, so Horace peered at him as if he was looking for something else. I decided to speak up as his spiritual advisor and say something.
"*She's not there*," I said to him in a whisper."
"I know!" he said loudly.
"You know? You know what?" Libby asked, confused at his outburst.
"What?" Horace asked, looking at her almost embarrassed.
"You said, 'I know'," she repeated, looking at him with a questioning daze.
"I know," he said again, and after a pause, with her pretty eyes looking into his added: "Never mind. Drink the beer before it gets warm."

The spaghetti and meatballs arrived and they both chowed down with their forks and spoons, twirling and slurping down the pasta and sauce, occasionally piling on the red pepper and ground garlic. Horace had the sauce running down his chin, so Libby crawled onto his lap and licked and sucked it off of his face, laughing out loud in the process.

"Hey, hey," Lester said, "enough of that. Get yourself a room next door if you're going to behave like that."

"That's right!" A voice came from directly behind Libby. It was Johnny, surprising them by dragging her off of Horace's lap, but Libby's arms were now pinned inside of Johnny's and she was virtually helpless. With his hands on her breasts, Johnny began squeezing them through her top as he pulled her back while licking her neck, calling her 'Lucy', causing Horace to stand instantly, pulling Johnny and Libby apart. Johnny then took a swing at Horace, but he blocked it, simultaneously giving Johnny an uppercut shot to the jaw, knocking him onto the floor, and onto his back.

Lester, the bartender ran to them from around the bar, while some of the patrons just stood and looked on, but the encounter was over quickly. Johnny was out cold, laying on his back on the tile floor and the bartender apologized to us.

"We get all kinds in here," he said, "but at least you know him."

"Well. I . . ." Horace started, but Heidi, who happened to walk over at that time handed Johnny's check to Horace saying:

"He said you were going to pay for this."

"What?" he asked, looking at it, "$128.69."

"He told me that's why you waved." Heidi said, and continued, "He said you were his buddy and had him covered. He was here all day eating and drinking."

"Why, that son of a . . ." Horace started, but was interrupted.

"Hey," Libby said, "let's just cover it. Since you know where he lives, we'll just take him home."
"Take him home?! That fu-. . ." Horace started, but was interrupted by Johnny's movements.

Just then, Johnny stood up, handed Heidi what looked like a $100 bill from his wallet and walked, swaying back and forth and staggered out the bar room door into the night. Everyone stood in silence and watched, even the eight to ten customers that were left, saying nothing, not even looking at each other while he left, but Heidi was the first to speak up when the door slammed.
"At least he's hitchhiking tonight," she said and continued, "He said his 'old lady' hid the keys to his Maverick."
"Hah! *His* Maverick?" Horace said sardonically, remembering that it's Lucy's automobile.
"Look at this $100 bill he handed me," Heidi said, "It doesn't quite cover his tab, but I've never seen anything like it."

Horace glanced at the note and realized it was the 1933 Silver Certificate that Lucy had been saving for a rainy day, worth at least $2000.

Once again, as his Angel, I nudged him to get it back off of her.

"I'll pay his tab with a check and a generous tip," Horace told her, "If you'll let me have the hundred."
"Why?" Heidi asked, as she kept turning the bill over and over, staring at it.

"Because, it's counterfeit," Horace said, lying, "and isn't worth the paper it's printed on. You see, Johnny ripped you off!"

"Take the check," Lester said listening and chiming in, "I don't want to be stuck with a counterfeit bill."

After the confusion of the short brawl with Johnny; and Horace conning Heidi and Lester out of the Silver Certificate with a check for $150 which covered Johnny's tab, and tip, he then turned to Libby to see if she was alright.

"I'm fine," she said, holding onto Horace's hand with his bleeding knuckles, "Your hand is hurt."

"I'll live," he said, shaking the circulation back into his fingers after his knockout punch.

"You certainly know how to clear a room," Lester said as he watched customers one by one walk out.

They both finished their dinner while Lester and Heidi continued their work quietly and the customers slowly and eventually all filed out the door, leaving only Lester, Heidi, Libby and Horace in the room.

"I'm pissed," Lester said, "but I hope he made it home okay. I was going to call him a cab, but I know he had no money."

"Fuck him," Horace said.

"Fuck him," Libby said.

"Fuck him," Heidi said, and poured herself a seltzer water, then put on her sweater.

"Okay, I'll make it unanimous," Lester responded, and they all laughed, then finishing her seltzer, Heidi the waitress exited the same door Johnny had previously stumbled through.

Libby and Horace also finished their drinks and decided to head homeward, and after leaving a nice tip and paying their bill, Libby opted to be the designated driver, despite the fact that they were both drunk. Horace took one more double shot and then they both walked out to the car.

CHAPTER-SIX

By 11:30 Friday morning Horace was rising from his deep slumber, sporting a mighty headache and blurred vision, physically and mentally, as he dressed into a pair of clean jeans and a tee-shirt before slowly staggering down the staircase to the kitchen. "Where did she go?" he wondered, regarding Libby as he worked his hurting brain to a frazzle trying to remember the details of the previous night. He had never 'blacked-out' like that before, for all he could recall was arriving at the Sportsman's Bar to have a Ladies Night special of spaghetti. Unfortunately, afterwards all he could remember was nothing; nothing about Johnny or even leaving the place, for all that was present in his memory banks was the uncomfortable empty void of a blackout.

He saw there was a fresh pot of coffee in the glass coffee maker and poured himself a fresh, hot cup, as he sat and gazed out into the yard through the big kitchen bay window, aware of the backhoe near the gate, a backhoe that Robert once mentioned Libby operated as well as she plays drums. As he sipped and stared, Horace saw the gate open and the Ford Mustang coming through it with Libby driving, and he leaned back, hoping now to find out some answers, like about how he got home and into the bed. In a few minutes she was walking into the kitchen looking like she worked hard, with dirt stains and smudges on her jeans, top, and face.

"What were you up to?" Horace asked.

"What do you think?" she returned the question, and continued, "How are you feeling this morning?"

Horace dropped his head and moaned, and holding it with his hands shook it slowly from side to side before saying, "God, what the hell happened last night? I don't remember a damn thing after we got to the bar."

Libby's eyes widened as she peered her sharp, hawk-like glance at his crouching figure in the kitchen chair and said, "What? You don't remember what happened last night?"

"Oh-oh," he said, "was it something I did? I can't for the life of me remember!"

"Seriously, you really don't remember?" she asked again, "Anything?"

Now Horace was starting to become worried in his lack of memory and Libby picked up on his look of concern, but she was also at the same time aware that he 'apparently' had no idea of their shenanigans in the previous evening.

"What the hell happened? I can't remember a thing?" he said in a now desperate tone.

"No?" she consoled him, then lied: "You didn't do anything but pass out at the bar. I told you I thought you were drinking too much. I woke you up, and you and I just got up and left."

"Wow," he said, "I'm so embarrassed. I should go back to that place and apologize."

"No, no. You were fine, and I told them you wouldn't remember, so don't go back there and make me look bad."

Then pouring herself some coffee added, "Wow. I can't see how someone can forget everything they did. I guess because I myself have never experienced that."

Horace took his coffee and walked into the den to sit on the couch beside the coffee table while Libby just watched and followed, then told him, "You and I, and Jordan, are playing at Benders tomorrow night, remember?"

"I remember," he said, "but if you don't mind, I think I'm going to go back to bed. I am so exhausted and pretty damn sore for some reason. I must have fallen, look at these knuckles."

"So," Libby said with her one eyebrow pointed downward, "who's going to help me finish sanding and painting?"

"Okay," he said lowering his head, "I'll work until I pass out."

They both worked together until Horace finished sanding and touching-up his drywall work and Libby started mixing the paint for the off-white color that she finally decided on. They both worked together on everything for about eight hours before Horace hit the shower again and then retired to the king-sized bed, dead to the world by eight o' clock, without any dinner. Jordan had also given them a hand and they managed to get two coats, with Jordan and Libby put the finishing touches on the new baseboard and wood trim.

Horace was the first to rise early Saturday morning in the darkness of 4:00 AM, tired and with a mild headache, phantom dues paid from the drinking and drugs Thursday night. He was fuzzy-headed and spaced-out climbing over Libby's naked form beside him and while dressing into his jeans, staggered down the stairs without a shirt, slapping at the wall light switches, lighting his way to the bathroom, then into the kitchen.

"What a weekend," he thought as he stumbled his weary way to the refrigerator to pour himself a large mug of iced expresso, then opened the sliding glass door overlooking the back yard and sat back in the wooden chair on the deck. The stars were out and there was no moon, and the air was crisp and cool, as it normally is on a late May night or early morning in Spring.

As his Angel, I realized once again that it was the perfect moment to have a nice talk with him.

"How are you feeling, Horace?" I asked calmly, as I usually do.

"Ah," he answered, "I don't know. I'm not sure where my life is going, and I can't seem to get Lucy out of my thoughts."

"You mean 'Libby'?"

"I mean Lucy," he said adamantly. "I keep thinking of her, and well, I know I still love her but . . ."

His thought seemed to trail off into thin air as he stared straight ahead into the darkness of the early morning, as if pausing to see the faint, dim light of the horizon in the east starting to grow brighter with each passing minute.

"But what?" I asked.

"When I feel like this I want to get a beer," he said and started to stand, heading for the refrigerator, but I somehow pushed him back down.

"Whoa, I was off balance, I guess," he said, and continued, "Maybe I need something stronger, like bourbon."

As he stood to walk towards the cupboard I pushed him again, making him fall off of the 3-foot deck onto the lawn, and after stumbling a few feet, fell onto his face and belly.

"What the fuck?" he yelled. But the sliding glass door opened, and Libby, who was standing in the doorway naked followed up with another yell, "What the fuck? Are you alright? What the hell are you doing?"

"I fucking fell off of the damn . . ." he started but Libby continued, "Why don't you come on in here and let me look at you."

He sat in the kitchen chair and Libby, bending over, looked directly into his face while he stared at her swaying breasts.

"Look up here at me," she said grabbing his chin to reposition his head, and then went to a cabinet for a bottle of mercurochrome. She then put some of it with a Q-tip on a small open cut above his eye and said she was going back to bed and reminded him that Robert would be coming in any time now. Horace returned to the wooden chair on the deck, without any of the beer or bourbon he originally set out to get before taking the fall, but he did carry his iced expresso with him while we, he and I, continued to chat.

"I think I've been drinking too much," he said.

"You have," I agreed.

"I've been drinking all week," he said, and took two big gulps of the iced coffee.

"More than just drinking," I said.

"More than just drinking," he agreed, and continued, "I've never blacked out before."

"Pretty scary, huh?" I replied.

"I don't want to do any of that shit again," he said, "all week it was narcotics, drugs, I mean cocaine, speed, what the hell is the matter with me?" he asked shaking his head from side to side.

"You'll be alright," I told him, *"Just stay away from that shit."*

"But I can't get Lucy out of my mind. Maybe I should go and see her," he said, as if wondering.

"Nah," I told him, *"Why don't you just not think about her for now, and play your gig tonight, and then see how you feel tomorrow?"*

"Sure," he said, "that's the ticket. I'll get busy practicing some of the songs, then do the gig with Libby and Jordan tonight."

"Maybe keep away from the shit, the drinking and stuff," I relayed to him, *"for a few days anyway?"*

"Yeah," he answered in a haunting drone, "that sounds like a plan. No more scary blackouts."

The blackout from the drinking and drugs scared poor Horace 'almost to death,' since he'd never experienced one where he couldn't remember anything he did this past Thursday night. The early morning darkness was now fading into the dusk of twilight and soon daylight while he was taking his guitar out of the case and tuning it before bringing it upstairs into the den. He fingerpicked a few songs, singing them in a mild baritone as he stared across the wide-open spaces of the yard. As he sat in the chair in front of the glass sliding door leading to another deck he saw Robert's car through the dimness of the waking day with its lights on, pulling in through the front gate. He realized then and there how awkward he felt, sleeping with Robert's wife, and sharing his bed with her while he was gone, and even though he knew that Libby had told Robert that Jordan and he were temporarily staying there, he still felt out of place.

He got up to take the guitar back downstairs to the finished basement but was met halfway by Libby, who was now completely dressed in a tight revealing top and a silk sarong that went from her hips to below the knees.

"Where do you think you're going?" she asked, raising one eyebrow.

"I'm going to put this away," he said, holding up the guitar.

"No, you're not," she responded, "You're going to relax, and sit and talk with Robert and I."

In a few minutes the front door opened, and Robert Bender walked through wearing his gray pin-striped suit and carrying his chestnut brown leather briefcase. His hair looked like it was a little grayer than before and he had a week-old salt and peppered beard growth covering his chiseled facial features. His eyes carried a stern look of self-assuredness as he moaned the word, "Home," and put his briefcase on the kitchen counter.

"Any coffee?" he asked as he glanced directly at Horace, who was sitting on one of the stools at the counter, holding the neck of his acoustic guitar resting on the floor beside him. He didn't notice Libby at the pot already pouring him a cup.

"Coming right up, dear," she said and added, "How was the trip?"

"Ah, you know, same old shit," he said as she set the large cup of the fresh brew in front of him, handing him a pill.

"That bad?" she asked.

"Horace," he said, "So you want to play at my club? I heard you did a fantastic job with my girl."

"Say what?" Horace asked.

"Libby said the basement looks good, that you guys did a fantastic job," Robert said with a big smile, blowing softly on his coffee before popping the pill into his mouth and then taking a mild, slurping sip.

"I think it looks good," Horace said with a grin, then winking at Libby, who threw him a subtle frown, slowly shaking her head.

"How long are you planning on staying, Horace?" Robert asked, a question that was unanticipated.

"Well," Horace started to answer, but Libby interrupted.

"We're playing tonight, and we're staying the night in Philly," she said serenely.

Robert looked at Libby as she told him this, then glanced back at Horace before looking back down at his cup.

"You've been pretty quiet, boy. 'You okay?" he asked Horace.

"I'm just tired," he said while Libby set a hot cup of coffee in front of him.

"How did you cut your eye?" Robert asked, slurping another sip from his cup of joe.

"He banged it using his drywall knife," Libby said, stirring her own cup as she stood at the end of the counter, 'seemingly' watching the both of them carefully. Then Libby wanted to know what the problem was with Bill, the man she was with at the Keystone Diner where she ran into Horace and Jordan last week. There was 'apparently' some friction between everybody concerning this guy Bill, an aura of animosity.

"Bill Bailey had to sign a contract," Robert stated with pride, "that documented that we're agreeing to unionize the musicians, which means Bill won't be turning away musicians anymore in accordance with their race, color, creed, or sexual preference."

Horace peered over at Libby and back at Robert, asking, "He was doing that?"

"He most certainly was," he responded, "and I knew nothing about it until last month."

"That's against the law," Libby replied, with her one eyebrow up, as is usual when she hears about outrageous behavior.

"Well," Robert concurred, "he won't be doing that again. I gave him a different management position and he has no responsibility with booking the bands. However," he continued, "he maintains management regarding the rest of the establishment but there's now an underling spy present, keeping an eye on what he does."

"Who?" Libby asked, with that eyebrow of concern again.

"Hah!" he said, with a soft laugh, "You don't think I'd ever let something like that slip out, do you?"
"I know who it is," she said, smiling.
"You just think you know," Robert retorted, returning the smile and sipping coffee.
"Anyway," he continued talking, "Bill Bailey is considered an important investor and owns 24% of the shares in that establishment and most of the others. Our other partner Phillip Phelps owns 24% and I'm in at 50%. Libby, you're already aware you own the other 2% but together, you and I own 52%, making us the majority owners. Bill has been trying to consolidate with Phillip to go against us, and attempt to takeover, but the original contract states that stock holders can only sell, not merge, and Phillip said he'd never sell."

Robert took another sip of coffee, and with his hands slightly shaking, took a deep breath before continuing in his mellow voice, now close to a whisper while Horace and Libby moved in closer to him at the counter, as if he was going to release a big secret. "Libby, those methadone tablets you've been giving me to help me withdraw from the heroin addiction may not be working the way they should. If anything happens to me, you need to take complete ownership of Bender's, I mean be the majority stock holder over Phillip Phelps and Bill Bailey."
"Nothing's going to happen to you, dear." Libby said moving herself over to him and wrapping her arms around him from behind, but he continued, "Libby, please let me finish."

"If something should happen to me, as I'm not the healthiest person on the planet, I want to make sure you are taken care of, Libby. You need to go to the bank with me on Monday and we'll take care of the Will and Last Testament, leaving you with my shares. Otherwise, God forbid I die in my sleep, or in the bathtub, you won't be left with a pot to piss in. When we take care of this, you will be the majority owner and you'll have the option to buy those guys out if you wish."

"How did Libby end up with only 2%?" Horace asked, "Why couldn't you both have shared the 52% in the first place?"

"Because she was given 2% when she moved in, as a gift from me." Robert said, nodding his head in a 'yes' motion, "And that was as a business bond, so in the will, when I die first, taking into account I'm much older than she, Libby would have my shares immediately put into her name."

"Well, so why do we have to get a Will if that's already the case?" Libby asked.

"Because, my dear, it's not the case anymore. Bill found a loophole and a good lawyer who just recently took it to court, and I was blindsided. That's where I was in the middle of last week, at a hearing. I'm told there was a clause in the contract stipulating that if any one of us single stock holders doesn't own the majority of the company, which is more than 50%, related or not, we will concede to the shareholder with the next largest interest, or percentage, at the time of death the remaining shares, unless it's stated within a Last Will and Testament recognizable in a court of law."

"But Bill and Phillip are even in shares, aren't they? I mean each at 24%?" Libby asked, and continued, "So, how could Bill possibly acquire control in that situation?"

"Because, in a recent undermining political business maneuver, Phillip sold 10% of his shares to Mr. Bailey on a handshake, at a bargain, with the intention of buying them back for the same price when the new construction he used the money for was completed in his buildings. Phillip had helped Bill out a few years back as a business favor the same way, and when Bill bought his shares back, they both made out on the deal. But this time, Bill Bailey did not, and will not sell the 10% back to Phillip, so, Mr. Phelps is screwed if something happens to me."

"Don't take this the wrong way," Horace said, "but it sounds like this 'Bill' dude is already trying to take over."

"Exactly," Robert said as he finished his coffee, and continued, "He's been doing this undermining for a few years now, but I thought we had it under control since this sort of thing simply goes with the territory. It always has been this way when you're dealing with big business and corporate politics, and now he and his lawyers are getting fierce."

Robert held his one hand over his chest and Libby leaned over him to see if he was alright, but just told her it was anxiety. She offered to postpone the gig with their trio playing at Bender's in Philadelphia tonight, so she could stay home and take care of Robert, but he wouldn't hear of it.

"Where's this other man, Jordan?" he asked her as she kissed the rough beard growth on the side of his face, telling him she liked his new macho scrub.

"He's still sleeping in one of the spare rooms," she said.

"Jordan who?" Jordan said, smiling as he walked into the kitchen surprising them.

"Hey, buddy, did you sleep okay?" Libby asked as she gave him a hug.

"Best sleep in a while," he said, then walked directly over to Robert.

"Mr. Bender, I'm pleased to meet you," he said greeting him, "I'm Jordan."

"I know," Robert said, returning the smile, "but you can call me Robert, please."

"It's a pleasure, and thanks for the accommodations, Robert."

"You're welcome, my friend. Are you ready to give it hell tonight?"

"Hell yeah," they all replied in unison.

Everyone sat and chatted for a while, digesting small talk about the upcoming evening's performance while Robert soon arose from his place at the counter with his briefcase, and with another fresh cup of coffee in his hand, retired to the den instead of going upstairs. On his way walking by Horace he tapped him on the shoulder with the corner of the case, directing him to follow with a subtle movement of his cup. Horace complied and followed him into the den as Robert instructed him to shut the door behind him. As he sat back in the leather reclining chair opening his briefcase on his lap he told Horace to have a seat on the couch. Holding up a plastic bag of white powder the size of his hand he asked Horace if he knew what it was.

"Do you know what this is?"

"It looks like powder," Horace said, pretending to be stupid.

"Yeah?" Robert asked, squeezing it in his big hand and tossing it up and down, "You're right. It does look like powder."

Robert, after placing his closed briefcase on the floor beside him, took out a razor blade and leaning forward, put a slit in the plastic and poured a small portion of the fluffy contents into a glass vile on the coffee table before resealing the opening with a wide piece of frosted tape. Horace looked on in silence while he continued talking.

"Horace," he said, "have you ever done any drugs?"

Horace remained quiet as he stared at him tapping the shot-glass sized glass vile, as if trying to pack the contents down, tapping it on the glass table-top, which rested on a piece of dried and finished driftwood. Looking through at the unusual shape of the wood he asked Robert if he found the piece of driftwood himself.

"This?" he said, pointing down through the glass top, "I don't remember, I think Libby picked it up somewhere. It's pretty; isn't it?"

"It sure is," Horace answered, "I wonder what kind of wood it is?"

"Deadwood." Robert answered, now pulling a tablespoon and a lighter from his jacket pocket.

"You didn't answer my question," he asked Horace, pouring a small amount in the powder into the spoon which he had placed on the table.

"What question was that?" he asked, obviously trying to avoid remembering.

"Have you ever done any drugs?"

"Robert," Horace retorted, "what does that have to do with anything?"

"Why, it's a question," Robert said, "and I believe you've answered it. What kind of drugs have you done? Opiates? Speed? Cocaine? Marijuana? All of the above?"

As he was saying this, Robert had taken off his suit jacket and rolled up his sleeve on one arm above the elbow before taking the spoon containing the fine powdery substance into his hand. With the other, he took the lighter and lighting it, held it under the spoon bowl, heating it until the substance turned brown and melted, bubbling in a frothy, steaming liquid. He then pulled a syringe out of his pocket and taking a small piece of cotton, swirled it using the pointed tip of the needle in the liquid, drawing it up into the syringe until the spoon was empty. Horace just stared silently as Robert took his own belt, wrapping it around his bare arm, tightening it with his teeth and stuck the point of the needle into the pencil-size throbbing vein in the crook of his elbow.

Robert loosened the belt, dropping it to the floor as he rubbed the area, removing the point and laid back in the chair, quietly.

"Are you alright?" Horace asked, staring at his eyes rolling backward in his head as he slowly closed them.

"Never better," he answered, 'seemingly' drifting off to sleep, but then he started talking again.

"Horace, you never did heroin, did you?"

"Nope," he answered, "Never had the desire to stab a needle into my arm."

"Speed?" Robert asked, but Horace once again tried to change the subject.

"So that table-top is on deadwood?" Horace asked, diverting.

"HAH!" Robert bellowed, laughing with his head tilted back onto the top of the chair, "You don't want to talk to me about it, do you?"

"Talk about what?" Horace asked.

"Libby told me that you liked speed and cocaine. You were doing Vicodin and valium too."

"Why would she tell you that?" he asked Robert, surprised.

"She tells me everything, and I mean EVERYTHING." He said, confidently winking his eye.

"Um," Horace said, feeling awkward and appearing a bit embarrassed, "I'd better go. I'll get my stuff and . . ."

"You're not going anywhere," Robert told Horace as he pulled out what looked like a .357 Magnum revolver, pointing it directly at his face.

Horace stood still, like a deer in the headlights of an oncoming semi-truck, wondering what his next move should be.

As his angel, I too stood still in my misty realm, wondering as Horace did, what 'my' next move would be when all at once, it looked like Horace was going to drop; or pass-out. I decided to say something to him.

"Horace, keep your cool, everything is going to be alright," I said as calmly as I could, asserting my strongest will.

Horace slowly sat on the couch and kept his eyes fixed on the weapon while Robert kept it pointed at him with an intense look in his eyes.

"What do you want from me?" Horace asked, slowly putting his hands up.

"I want you to stay here," he said, "Libby had a hell of a time finding a great guitar player and a great bassist she enjoys playing music with, and you're not about to quit on her. And God dammit, put your hands down. This ain't a Clint Eastwood movie."

Horace slowly put both of his hands down beside him on the couch and watched as Robert slowly lowered the gun and set it gently on the table.

"Please stay," he said to Horace, "we need you here."

"You didn't need to point a gun at me," he said, "I wasn't going to . . ."

"Leave?" Robert interrupted, "The hell you weren't. Just because you feel guilty about doing drugs in my house and balling my girl shouldn't be a reason for quitting on her. A man could get the impression you were just using her, and she would get that same impression, and we wouldn't want that, now, would we?"

"No, we wouldn't," Libby said, walking into the den to where they were sitting, and added, "Who's using who? What are we talking about in here?"

"I – I really don't know," Horace said, scratching his head.

"Horace was just telling me he's looking forward to playing tonight," Robert said smiling, and winking his eye at him.

"What's this doing out?" Libby said, leaning over to grab the pistol. "It's loaded!"

"Ah, just toying with it," Robert told her as she placed it point blank in his ear and squeezed the trigger.

"LIBBY!" Horace screamed.

"Damn you, Libby, you're getting me all wet," Robert said, standing up as she kept squeezing the trigger over and over again, unloading the water from what had come to surface as a realistic looking water-pistol.

Horace looked on in disbelief at the prevarication that had just taken place, with himself believing he was being held at gunpoint by Robert only moments ago and saw that this man's sense of humor was as dry and tasteless as one could get without any perception, or consideration on how it affected others. He then took a deep breath of relief, knowing everyone was playing around, and realized he had no idea of how to perceive them anymore.

"You guys are crazy!" Horace responded, gazing at the yard through the picture window, which was now bright in the sunlight.

"That, we are," responded Robert, now holding Libby on his lap laughing and kissing.

"Are you getting Horace off now?" Libby asked Robert, as he slowly leaned forward, lifting her up off of him.

"Nah," Horace said, "he's not getting me off. I don't do heroin."

"Are you going to be energetic enough to play the Philly gig tonight?" Libby asked.

"I'm run down, and exhausted," he said, "but if need be, I'll ask you for a line or two of meth if it's no trouble."

"No trouble," Robert answered, "but seriously, if you're going to do it at all, you'll be doing your nose a favor if you shoot it; and I've got a clean set of works."

"I don't like the idea of getting hooked on needles," Horace retorted with a grimace, "I've heard stories of people hitting bottom and that's not for me."

"Smart man, 'don't want to become like me," Robert replied.

"Self-control," Libby said, "It's all about controlling it. You're a strong enough person to handle it, Horace, and you're also a great guitarist for what we're doing. Shooting the meth instead of snorting it gives you the pure fire to make your performance greater than life, and more dynamic, besides taking the edge of depression and exhaustion from your system."

"Horace," Robert said, "I've been doing heroin, which is pure and physically addictive for a good part of my life, and that's my vice. But look at me, I'm successful, with a beautiful house, and I've got her," he pointed at Libby who leaned over to give him a kiss, "and other than the physical addiction, I have my health. With you, on the other hand, we're talking about injecting speed, or meth, which is a stimulant, but as long as you don't let it get out of control, you can make it work for you."

"I just need something to wake me up for tonight," Horace suggested, "a line or two . . ."

"A line or two is a waste," Libby said, "and you'll just be looking for the next line."
"I thought that was with coke," Horace said.
"It's with speed too," Robert replied, "remember, you've already got it in your system."
"Is this for free? Because there's no way I'd be able to afford this."
"We've got you covered," Libby told him, "Just do a 'teaspoon', which is less than a quarter gram and you'll have a nice rush. You'll play like a god all night and to get to sleep, we'll have valiums for you."

Being the angel and listening, I found it impossible to get a word in edgewise to Horace as he watched Robert open another vile of powder, dumping it into another teaspoon and using another fresh syringe, syphoned a measured amount of water from a fresh glass Libby brought to him. He squirted the water into the powder and it disintegrated, melted like ice into the water as he stirred the point of the needle with the cotton before syphoning it all up into the syringe, then handing it to Horace.
"WHAT THE HELL ARE YOU DOING?" I asked Horace with force from my realm, sending a noticeable chill up his spine.
"Robert, I don't know if I . . ." Horace started speaking but was interrupted by Robert.
"Don't do it now," Robert said serenely, "Libby will get you off right before the gig tonight."

"I'll show you," she said sitting onto Horace's lap provocatively, "It's not like you're going to get hooked or anything. You'll see, trust me."

Robert arose from the leather recliner and said he was going to hit the sack and asked if the big bed was made, which Libby replied "Yes, as always." she stood, using her arm as a lift, pressuring it into Horace's crotch and excusing herself. "Keep the cap on that syringe until tonight," she said, "And get a nap before the gig. We're going to knock them dead."

"Where's Jordan?" he asked, putting the loaded syringe away in his backpack.

"He's putting new strings on his bass," she said.

I realized that my appearance and existence here with Horace was as a guide, and somehow, I knew that I needed to do something to engage Horace and remembered that the Voice told me that my guidance would even engage Libby to stop this careless use of these drugs. But for now, all I could do is warn him.

"You're not really going to do that, I mean shoot that stuff up into your veins. Are you?" I asked.

"I really don't know," Horace told me, walking out onto the deck and climbing onto his bicycle.

"You know this is not a good idea, don't you?"

"Well, they seem to be okay, and they've done it." Horace said, referring to Libby and Robert's drug use and added, "Hell, he's been doing this 'hitting up' stuff since before I was born, probably, and look at him. He's holding up alright."

"How do you know? Besides, that's him! That's not you! You're doing alright without it, aren't you?"
"I know, but I'm young, and I've been dealt a lucky hand here, and I need to be sure I have the energy and confidence to follow through here," he said, pedaling his bike through the front gate, "and I'm also aware I have pretty good self-control. Besides, I feel Karma is with me."
"Isn't 'having good self-control' simply not doing this stuff in the first place?" I asked.
"What if I'm too tired to play tonight." Horace said, getting defensive, and continued, "Tonight's gig is a big chance for Jordan, Libby and I and they're counting on me, like I'm counting on them."
"But you're so good, you don't need this crap in your system."
"If I do it, I'm only going to try it once," he said, "I'm not going to let anything, or anyone own me."
"But you already tried this crap once, and twice, and three times without the needles!"
"So, maybe it's time to try it another way. Just, leave me alone," he retorted, pedaling faster.

Horace ignored me as he pedaled his bicycle, a well-constructed mountain bike, down the back roads off of Deep Run Road towards New Galena Road, and finally to Lake Galena, where he rode around the lake once, which was broken up with trails and back roads. It was, however, very close to the lake in areas where he pedaled and stared into the distance across the large body of water, rippling from the occasional breeze and was a glimmering platform for the sailboats gliding on its surface.

After circling the lake once, about a six and a half mile ride, plus the other six or so miles he rode to get here from the Bender house, he stopped by a water fountain and guzzled about a quart of water before sitting on a bench near the lake, taking in deep breaths and almost drifted off to a nap. Walking toward him was a woman dressed in a short white skirt above the knees and a white halter-top, and as he opened his eyes wider he recognized who she was.

"Lucy?" he said, with a slow rise in his tone as if questioning, but still sitting.

"Horace," she said, "What brings you by here?"

"I'm not in the mood for talking about anything, Lucy, I'm still pissed."

Horace was referring to their last encounter at the house with Johnny and the landlord, and of course, his blackout a few nights ago wouldn't let him recall punching Johnny at the Sportsman's bar. Lucy looked at him with her eyes watering and placed her hand gently onto his shoulder and softly patted it.

"It's alright," she said, "I understand perfectly. For what it's worth, I haven't seen Johnny since then."

Lucy leaned into him and gave him a tender kiss on the side of his face, then rose and slowly walked down the bicycle trail out of sight. Horace leaned back and stared out at the sailboats drifting past each other beneath a cumulous clouded sky, shadowing various areas on the lake beneath their dominance as they command their welcome shade over the park from the bright and torrid sunlight. As he did, he reflected his thoughts on Lucy's appearance and began to wonder why she was here at the lake, and why she was even talking to him after their fighting the other day. He was also aware that she was actually magnanimous, which was contrary to her natural state of being he was used to, at least for the past few years with her anyway.

Horace stood up and walked down the trail in the direction he saw her walking, then stopped, as if having second thoughts about something before turning around and heading back to the bench and his bicycle. Picking it up, he pedaled in the direction he last saw her walking and continued riding completely around the lake for the approximate six miles and a half before returning to the bench. He appeared exhausted and I felt like I wanted to talk to him again.

"What are you looking for?

"What makes you think I'm looking for anything?" he stated confidently.

"Do you think she's still here?

"Who?"

"Lucy."

"I'm real tired right now, and drained," Horace said shaking his head, "and I'm looking for a phone to call Libby or Jordan to come and get me. I wonder what time it is?"

"There's a phone booth right over there," I told him, pointing at a booth by the water fountain and washroom.

Horace had gotten hold of Libby at the Bender house who sent Jordan out in a Ford Bronco, another of the many vehicles parked in their garage, and he pulled into the large parking area by the bench where Horace was waiting. He had only waited for about 20 minutes for Jordan to arrive, but it was enough time for him to drift off to a small nap, and into a dream. In this dream, he and Lucy were walking hand in hand and chatting with each other, but when he awoke, he could not remember a thing they were discussing, or talking about, just the memory of holding her hand. He knew that the dream was due to him and her accidently running into each other on the toe-path in the past hour and brushed it off for now hearing Jordan's voice.

"What's up, Home? 'Ready to go?"

"Let's hit it," Horace replied, rolling his bicycle up to the Bronco and loading it in, "I'm fucking beat!"

CHAPTER - SEVEN

After a nap at home Horace was tuning his acoustic guitar and checking the strings, which were still relatively new before loading everything except the drums into Libby's Ford pick-up, another of her vehicles. This one, contrary to Horace's was brand new and had a crew cab and the cap over the bed for the equipment. This was to be their ride to the Bender's Club in "Old City," Philadelphia where the plan was to unload and play music in the lounge.

Feeling near dead to the world, Horace held the syringe full of the methamphetamine solution that Robert had given him earlier in the day and was tempted to use it for energy; but thought better of it. He left the cap on and put it away inside of his guitar case without anyone noticing and the three of them piled into the vehicle.

"Wait a minute," Robert said, walking down the flagstone path from the front door of the mansion to the driver's side of the window where Libby was sitting, "Here's a few items for later," he said, dumping a handful of something into her hand, giving her a kiss, "I'll see you tomorrow morning."
"See you tomorrow," Libby said as we pulled away on our route to Philly.

Using Route 611 to the P.A. Turnpike, they made it to Bender's on Market Street, chatting all the way there about stories of their past, getting to know each other better. Jordan laid across the crew-seat in the back as he peered through the back window into the bed where their instruments were, asked why they weren't taking the drums. Libby answered, saying there was already a drum-kit there, provided and set-up, as per her instructions to Robert. Jordan then took out a syringe full of fluid and rolling up his sleeve, pierced the edge of the needle into the crook of his arm and pressed the plunger. Horace had watched him with intense curiosity from the front passenger seat as Jordan emptied the entire contents into his vein, before saying anything.
"I didn't know you were a user," Horace said softly.
"I wasn't," he answered, "I just started last week, actually."
"Smack?"
"Nope," Jordan replied, "It's 'crank'."

'Crank' was the slang term for 'Speed', and 'Smack' was slang for 'Heroin', but Horace was now becoming a little concerned for where he was, with some influence from me as his spiritual guide.

"Horace, I hope you're seriously considering your thoughts on contemplating mainlining what should be considered as poison into your system," I told him adamantly.

"I know," he said, as he thought about his own loaded syringe obtained from Robert, the syringe containing a spoonful of crank which was waiting for him in his guitar case.

He watched Jordan rolling his head back on the headrest of the back seat and side window and a smile slowly appear on his face as his eyes opened wide, as the whites of them glowed against the dark tones of his face.

"DAMN!" he said, now showing his white teeth, "What a RUSH!"

"Good shit, huh?" Libby asked, tilting her head slightly to the side, towards the direction of his voice as she continued her concentration on her own driving.

"Damn straight!" he retorted, adding a "Whew!"

"Straight?" Horace asked with a smile, quipping to his homosexuality once again in good humor.

"Wouldn't YOU like to know," Jordan answered back sardonically, still bearing his wide grin.

He then stretched out his arms and shaking his head back and forth let out a loud yell, as if to show his appreciation to the Universe, letting everyone in the vehicle and the world how great he felt in the moment.

"AAAAAAAAAAAAAHHHHHHHHHHHH!!!!"

"Must be really good shit!" Libby stated as she let out an outburst of laughter while turning up the ramp toward the PA. Turnpike.

"I can't remember the last time, I felt this good, "Jordan said, and continued, "I can't remember EVER feeling this good!"

"Robert gets the best stuff," Libby said as she pulled in to get a ticket at the booth, "It's not cut with anything."

"How long will this high last me," he asked, "I mean, I feel like playing all night!"

"Is it you're first time shooting up?" Horace asked.

"Not really," Jordan answered, "I used to shoot once or twice a few years ago, but I never got a rush like this."

"Was it speed back then?" Libby asked.

"Once," he replied, "but is was mostly coke. But now this, I'm feeling like I can do no wrong!"

"I remember the first time I did coke," Libby said, "and it took me a lot to realize I was getting off on it, or to maybe at least recognize the high."

"Yeah," Horace said, "It's rather subtle, unless you know the high."

"Yep," she replied, "and I was trying to associate it with the 'speed' high."

"When did you start 'banging' speed and coke?" Jordan asked Libby.

"Never 'shot' coke, yet," Libby said, referring to his slang term "banging" of injecting it, via syringe, mainlining it into her system, "But speed, I started doing it when I moved in with Robert, two years ago. I overdosed on heroin a while back, and someone very special saved my life. That was the last time I did smack."

"I've never done that," Horace said, "Just speed or coke up the nose is good enough for me."

"You get a better rush," Libby said, "and it's better for your health to mainline it if you're going to do it."

"You know that's a lie, Horace. Don't be stupid! None of that is good for you or better for you, any way! Or Any time!" I said, interrupting Horace's train of thought. But no matter what I said or did, he was ignoring me. I could read his thoughts, as he was seriously thinking that he had never seen this depth of drug use, regarding needles and syringes and frankly, he was feeling as I do, that it seemed dirty and sleazy, no matter how Jordan or Libby glorified it. But then Jordan surprised me, for a little while anyway.

"I don't know if it's good for you at all health-wise," Jordan argued, "but it sure feels good! WHOO!"

"Well," Libby responded, "I've been doing it, not every day, and I'll sometimes go a week without it. But I eat right and take vitamins, which is essential to keeping my system going strong. Look at me! I'm in good shape, and the drugs have never taken their toll on me!"

"You're young, still." Jordan replied, "Give yourself a few years before the hair starts falling out, or you're losing your teeth, or you start forgetting where you parked. It happens to the healthiest people who sustain their lives on steady drug use. I've seen it first-hand."

"So, why are you doing it now?" she asked him.

"Feels good. Feels DAMN good." Jordan said, now laughing and stretching.

Libby started telling a story about a guy she met in the Bahamas and how they both were drugging and drinking the whole time.

"It was amazing." Libby said, "It was my first time I ever did it. We were in the bed, and we were both completely naked. I let him put it in me and it was a rush I had never felt before! Ever!"

"You mean, you were a virgin?" Horace asked.

"To needles I was. What did YOU think I was talking about?" she asked, half smiling.

They all laughed as Libby continued her attention to the road, passing a few semi-trucks as she weaved between the lines of the four-lane highway.

"When I met Skip, I stopped doing everything for a while, but when he disappeared, I started back up again.

"Skip?" Horace asked.

"Was he the sax player?" Jordan asked, "I knew Skip."

"Skip Mooney." Libby answered. "Yep, and a damn good one. He saved me when I OD'd."

"Where did he get to?" Jordan asked.

"He disappeared." she said. "Let's change the subject, alright?"

"Well," Horace said, still feeling tired, "I think we're going to have a good night."

"You going to do yours?" Libby asked, looking at him with her mouth slightly opened."

"I don't know," he said shaking his head, "Libby, are you doing any?"

She reached into her small leather purse on her lap and pulled out a few packets and a set of works and said,

"I'm prepared." And with a serious look added, "Horace, you look beat, please be up for the show tonight. Okay?"

Horace said nothing as he returned his stare out the windshield towards the highway watching the reflected glare in front of them off of the mirrors and chrome of the polished Corvette, lit up by the setting sun directly to their rear; a Corvette that Libby seemed to be pacing. She was handing Horace a tiny plastic packet containing white powder and then a syringe with a quarter gram of water and instructed him to squirt it into the packet. Afterward, he was directed to use the syringe to suck the dissolved solution back into the syringe and handed the works back to her. She capped it and placed it into her purse, along with the tiny empty plastic packet and a bag of marijuana that Jordan had just handed her after he rolled a joint and placed it in his mouth, lighting it.

The whole time Jordan was rolling the joint he was telling a story, about a time when he was a teenager, working at a high-class country club washing dishes during a banquet.

"This place I worked washing dishes," he said, "was top-of-the-line white people, first class, with every food you could imagine. The had lobsters, steak, and even stuff like herrings in cream sauce, Gefilte fish, chopped liver and onions, and I would also make these big sandwiches like corned beef on rye, and well, anyway, we used to get trays full of wine and champagne returning to the kitchen to be thrown out, so me and the other young kitchen workers would just drink them down."

Jordan handed Horace the joint, who took a big toke before handing it to Libby saying, "Sounds like you were having a good time, even as a teenager."

"Oh," he answered, "It was the best. Anyway, we had all gotten ourselves pretty wasted and we 'basically' couldn't work level-headed anymore. A white guy, one of the waiters named 'Keith' was drinking and became belligerent to a couple of his customers and was fired on the spot. That's when I tried to act as sober as I could, but the manager and the chef were starting to get suspicious of all of us young guys and wouldn't let any of us go near those trays with the wine and champagne.

"Wow," Libby said with a big smile, handing Jordan the joint, "did you get caught?"

"No," he said, "but we knew that we weren't getting any more-sober and my dishes I was throwing into the dish-washer were getting broken, so it was just a matter of time. But just then, the back door opened and who stumbled in but Keith, who 'by the way' was about twenty, and I was only seventeen, so I kind of looked up to him. He told me he had some stuff that would keep me sober and to come on out to see his new car, which I did immediately, but I wanted to leave without getting fired for being drunk, so I punched my timecard out, yelling to the chef that I'm going on break. Keith's vehicle, a 59 Chevy was already running, and we climbed in and he drove off of the lot and up the road. I thought we were just going to sit in the car, but I was so drunk I didn't ask any questions, other than how long he's had the car and what's this stuff to make me so-ber."

"Did he have speed?" Horace asked, furrowing his eyebrows at him.

"He certainly did," Jordan said. "He had set it out on lines on a compact mirror and told me how to snort it through a dollar bill."

"Probably kept you up all night," Horace said.

"It certainly did," Jordan said laughing. "I never went back to work, and he and I drove all over Memphis until about seven in the morning, when he dropped me off at my doorstep."

"That was nice of him," Libby said, "So, did you lose your job for not coming back to work?"

"Well, not exactly," Jordan said, "What happened was the cops were waiting for me at my house."

"Say what?" Horace and Libby both said in unison.

"Well, that 59 Chevy we were in? Keith stole it from the Country Club we worked at?"

WHAT??"

"Yeah," he said, snickering. "The customer who owned it," he continued, "was with his wife and two other couples inside the Club, so, while it was left running outside, and unbeknownst to me, Keith was stealing the damn thing! So, when I didn't return from my break, guess who they started looking for?"

The three of them were roaring with laughter, non-stop for quite a few miles before Jordan finished the story. He said that Keith eventually admitted that Jordan was totally innocent and had no idea the car was stolen, but according to him, being a minor and also black, he was still put in a juvenile home for two months.

"That's a pretty incredible story," Horace said.

"Well, Keith doesn't work here at Bender's" Libby said, "so, don't worry about anything like that tonight."

More laughter as they got onto the off ramp for I-95 South and into the city of Philadelphia, and within 70 minutes flat, arriving by 7:00. They're to play from 8 to 12 Midnight in the lounge, and later if they want provided the crowd is still in the room spending money. Robert had set Libby, Jordan and Horace up well, with some advertising regarding their act and they were getting paid $500 each, even Libby, but she had decided she would generously give her cut to the boys. Jordan was surprised that he and Horace were not even asked for room-and-board for their stay at the mansion, but Libby had insisted that it was already considered when they decided on the $500 a piece, so, it seemed Libby was paying their stay at the house.

The lounge, which was a room about forty by forty with ten-foot ceiling, was small enough for us to not need microphones for our equipment, being acoustic, but we had one in the center with a stand for singing. Libby also had a microphone, leaning on a boom-stand into her drum kit and strategically placed so her voice would be picked up over the sound of her drums. Both mikes were also carrying residue sound into the air making their instruments appear loud enough to carry throughout the room. The room was already crowded with people eating dinner in about twenty or so tables that could seat six people each very comfortably and then they were ready to go on, that is all but Horace.

Horace had pulled his loaded syringe from his guitar case after he had set his acoustic Martin up on the stand, tuned and ready to go, when he glared at the set of works, loaded with the spoonful of methamphetamine, the wakeup juice he started lusting for to guide him through the evening instead of my assistance.

"Horace," I said in the most commanding tone I could muster, *"Don't do it!"*

"I hear you," he said, and added, "But I don't hear you."

He took the set of works to the bathroom and I felt myself drift upward and outward through the proverbial mist to the Voice, once again with my dilemma.

"You have done well, but you must take over now," the Voice commanded me.

"I'm trying." I said, "but Horace is not listening to me."

"You don't understand," it repeated, then said again, "You must take over."

"I guess I don't understand," I replied, "I don't know what more I can do. He's going to shoot-up methamphetamine. That's speed!"

"You must understand," the Voice said, "You ARE Horace."

"I'm Horace's guide?" I asked, confused.

"YOU ARE HORACE!" The Voice said, and there were tremors throughout my very being.

"You have never known your new name until I told you now," The Voice said, and continued, "You don't remember how you got here, and you don't remember your name. You died a horrible death; you were murdered, but you do not recall what you died from."

"My name in a past life was 'Skip', I thought."

"Your past life is 'no more'. To you, 'Skip' is no more. Your memory was cleansed."

"Yeah," I answered, "and why is it that I don't remember? And if I died, and I'm now Horace, how could he be alive?"

"Too many questions. If you clear your mind, you'll see that your questions are answered." The Voice retorted, "'Time' does not exist as you know it here, therefore, time is irrelevant. We've undone your horrible death and we're going to give you your life."

"I'm confused," I said, shaking my head, "how did I die? You never told me."

"You didn't die. Your death was undone, because of your helping Horace. Now you must help him again. Be him."

"I'm still confused," I said.

"Undcrstandable, and understood," the Voice said, and continued, "You will remember everything that Horace remembered and feel everything Horace felt, because you will be Horace, and you will address your addictions and defeat them, while helping Libby at the same time. You will not see me for a while, but you will know I am with you!"

When I had returned to Horace, he was in one of the stalls of the restroom with the needle of the syringe piercing the skin and large vein in the crook of his left arm, and before I could say anything, he pressed the plunger, injecting the spoonful of meth into his system. I myself felt an immediate rush as I started to yell at him, and instantaneously became one with him. In trying to say his name, instead, I was yelling:

"HHAAAAAHHHHRRRRRAA!!!"

Then I felt a solid and sustained pulse of chills emanating from my entire being as I pulled the needle out of what was now MY ARM! And MY heart beating hard and fast.

As I sat in the stall with my pants on, I realized I was Horace, and it was the strangest realization I had ever felt, since I had never injected, or 'shot up' anything before into my arms, or anywhere. My thoughts as a guide had disappeared and I assumed that I was still normal other than having a godlike, larger-than-life speed rush that was now unleashed through my gorged veins as my heart was beating faster and faster. I had now come-to the conclusion, that, the speed-rush gave me small hallucinations causing me to have faded memories of a "Voice in the mist," and this disappearing thought of my being a guide to myself was now all but a faded memory, vanquished like a fart in the wind. I was ready now for anything, and feeling like a new man, I couldn't get to my guitar fast enough.

Jordan and Libby were on the stage where our instruments were and waiting for me through the noises of the clanging silverware and plates the waitresses were gathering from the meals of the well-dressed clientele. I gazed into Libby's eyes and she smiled, knowing I was different, with the adrenaline and speed rushing through my system. I felt the rush of methamphetamine before, but I never felt like this, like I was two people molded into one, with an illustrious energy and spontaneous creativity buzzing from head to toe, surging through me like a fast-moving river, and I loved it. Looking into Libby's eyes, I was also feeling this feeling that she too and I were now, and always have been connected in our souls and that she was my one and only reason for existing, knowing in an instant what seemed to last forever was that she felt the exact same feeling, and always had. Only now I was finally catching up to this feeling that had always existed . . . true Soulmates.

The first song was "All of Me," an old jazz standard which we embellished as our own version, using our bass and drum solos to extend the length. We got a standing ovation after the first song and continued to play the rest, which were hand-picked jazz standards dating to the 1940's and also early fifties, with a few modernized versions as Libby did most of the singing, and I'll add, a damn good singer. Our last song of the set, although most got standing ovations, really brought the house down with Libby's drum solo, a jazz version of the Beatles song, "One After 909." The main feature in this piece and all of our other songs was without a doubt Libby's drums, and her breaks. She knew precisely how to stretch a song out using her solos, which was interesting enough to keep the attention of the entire room. She would lower the energy down to its lowest limits with her snare rolls, leaning over her stick that fanned so fast it looked like she was holding feathers as she'd roll and roll. It also didn't hurt that she wore a low-cut, black, tight top which divided her full breasts right above her snare drum, forming a perfectly shaded cleavage in the off-white light shining on her, while Jordan and I were in dimmer lights. Then slowly she'd bring the scenario to a slow boil by moving the rolls back and forth to the smaller toms, then incorporating the floor tom and the snare and the small toms included, back and forth, up and down like a flowing river over the rocks of diverse rhythms, and combining the cymbals and high-hat with the mix, until the audience roared their applause in at the apex of the orgasmic climax.

Another time she did the walk-around, which was to get up, without missing any beats and walk around the drums using her sticks on all of the drums. On a whole note, she'd step one step over to Jordan's upright bass and tap her sticks on the strings and play the bass notes to "Big Noise from Winnetka" before we'd all come back into the mix and join her.

Libby was definitely the star of the show and the undisputed leader of the band. She was not only attractive, but had an ambience, a charisma that was not to be denied as she made friends in the room easily during our breaks, playing the room like a goddess, or a princess, going from table to table schmoozing the patrons, who were donning their expensive attire and gowns.

Not mentioned earlier, Jordan and I were directed to wear three-piece suits, furnished for us by Robert's people under Libby's insistence and custom fitted from sizes given to them ahead of time. The suits were the same gray color with the blue ties, argyle socks and wing-tipped shoes. Libby's black, low-cut gown was low-cut in the back also, revealing her well-formed posterior and accentuating her tight ass, even thru that skirt with those slits, which went 'almost' to the ankle straps on her expensive shoes. She wore the dark-red lipstick with the dark eyeliner and dark-shaded eyebrows, making her natural good looks irresistible to any man, or adventurous woman.

Bill Bailey was there, and was even making passes at her, right in front of Jordan and I, and Libby cordially and respectfully turned him down.

"Libby," he said, "If you don't want to stay with these bozos, I have a place we can go, and I can get you anything that you want."

"I already have everything that I need, Mr. Bailey." she told him with the biggest smile and pointing to us with her extended opened hand, as if she was holding us up on a golden platter.

Bill walked away from her passing by us and didn't forget to give a belligerent shove to Jordan, who just said, "Excuse me."

Bill turned to him, and with his face only inches away from Jordan's, and with a permanent intimidating smile asked, "Did you say something?"

"I said 'Excuse me'," Jordan repeated, while keeping his own smile, challenging Bill's evil grin in good faith.

"Time to go on!" Libby said, grabbing Jordan and me by our elbows, repeating the 'excuse me' phrase to Bill as we walked from the middle of the crowd. I was watching this 'Bill' character standing firm, staring at Jordan and his icy glare gave me somewhat of a chill, which I just brushed off as part of the speed rush.

When we had gotten up to play the second set, the people filled the dance floor as we pumped out tune after tune, still filling in with the solos and Libby and I harmonizing our vocals. The people were even on the stage dancing with us while the rest of them sometimes stood, watching us and clapping their hands to the jamming music.

Jordan was in his glory and in a world of his own as he slapped the bass strings hard in his solos, spinning the big violin-shaped body around and around like he was dancing with a beautiful woman, although knowing him, he preferred the opposite sex for his driving rhythms and bottom end.

When 12:00 Midnight came around, Jordan, Libby and I were wide awake and felt like we could go on forever, so we went on and played another set, with some improv, and played until 2:00am. The people were filtering out and I couldn't believe that I was still wide awake. Jordan came over to me as I sat in one of the booths that surrounded the room and held up his hand for a high-five and sat across from me.

"Great goddam night!" he said, with that great big grin of his.

"Damn right!" I answered, agreeing. "Now we have to load up."

"All taken care of," Libby said from behind us and sat in the booth, giving us each five one-hundred dollar bills a piece.

Then we saw these dudes picking up our equipment, Jordan's bass in the case and my guitar case, causing Jordan and I to rise, but Libby grabbed our hands.

"They're loading it up for us," she said, "We're staying the night here, upstairs in the hotel rooms and heading back tomorrow afternoon. Here, take a few shots of this."

She held out a bottle of vodka, 100 proof, and then said, "Here's some valiums for the crash, you're going to need them to sleep." She gave me three and Jordan three and popped three of them into her mouth.

"Do you think this is a good idea?" I asked.

"What's the matter with you?" she asked me, "You were always ready for these, just like last week with sheet-rocking the basement. How else are you going to get to sleep?"

I agreed and popped them, just like I did last week, and eventually went with her to my room, so she and I could share a double bed, just like we did last week.

The valiums I ingested took their effect during our making love in the big, king-sized bed, with the satin sheets, in the Bridal Suite on the tenth floor of the 10-story hotel adjoined to the Bender's Club. Libby and I shared the suite, while Jordan was given the room next door, which was 'almost as' exotic. As I wearily drifted off to sleep I had a dream of the Wood Street house, and of my son, Gabriel. I was holding him in my arms with my face touching against his while he giggled, and he asked me "Where's Mommy?" In this dream I told him Mommy and I, were no longer seeing each other, but that I'll always love her, and I'll always love him. Then I felt a hand on my shoulder and a naked body clutching my back sensuously, waking me from my chimera of holding my two-year-old son. The body of course was Libby, pressing her erotic, warm form against my back and kissing my neck and ear, enticing me to turn around and join the party again of rolling thunder beneath the cool, satin sheets.

I felt like I was totally and irresponsibly in love with her, as if we were one, connected more than physically. It was not unlike a spell had been put on me ever since I had gotten off on sticking that needle in my arm, but the feelings were absolutely real and not drug induced. It was hard to believe that this woman, married to the owner of these clubs and so irresistibly attractive to me would have any interest in me at all; And that her husband knows she and I are having this fling, although that word 'fling' doesn't match the ardor. Also, I'm blessed with having on hand, any drugs I could ever want if I want them, and this woman; with no strings attached to share everything with. To top it off, we're both in a band that's booked solid, if we wish, at an elite well-paying nightclub for as long as we wanted not to mention the luxury of laying in satin sheets while people are moving our equipment for us.

A week ago, I was in a half-a-twin house paying rent on Wood Street living with a woman that was constantly picking on me along with her loser, asshole friend being the 'thing that wouldn't leave.' Other than the potentially haunting sleaziness of the illegal drugs that seemed to weigh in on my subconscious, which is not unlike a dark cloud in an otherwise blue sky that won't evaporate, I'm feeling like a new man, and life in this newer world of the rich and elite is good. I'm starting to believe karma is finally catching up with me because I can't imagine it getting any better than this; for now, anyway.

CHAPTER - EIGHT

It was about 11:00 in the morning when I awoke and saw the rooftops of the City of Philadelphia through the big windows in the suite, since this building is one of the tallest in this part of 'Old City'. Early this morning in the darkness we were watching the city lights through these same picture windows, flickering to the metropolis nocturnal beat, and stars above this concrete jungle before we drifted off into our peaceful slumber. Once again, and in the light of today I felt like I was on top of the world and that everything seemed to be happening rather, fast, especially finding out that we were scheduled to play here again Tuesday and Thursday, and then next weekend again, Saturday and Sunday.

None of this cost Jordan or I anything and we were treated like kings, with a free place to live, no room-and-board, and the hotel suites were in the deal with Libby's husband Robert footing the bill for the band. There's that word; Band. Our band had no name and the act we did last night in the lounge was billed simply as "Libby Bender," in which we had no objection since as I had said before, she's the vocal and fire, and inarguably the true leader of the band.

Libby had a charisma that was unmatched by any woman I've ever met and could certainly challenge any form of the male species I've ever encountered. She was sure of herself, standing her ground on every decision of what songs to play, and she let Jordan and I take our solos for as long as we desired, and encouraged them without feeling threatened. But because of her extreme talent as a drummer, the combination of the skills from Jordan and I together couldn't match her finesse and knowledge of rhythm combinations and showmanship, although Jordan is a crackerjack bassist and I know I'm no slouch on the guitar.

Libby drove once again as we headed homeward through the musical serenade of Sunday traffic up I-95, but this time we took it to Route 413 and the back way through the lower Bucks County countryside. We drank cold beers from the cooler and Libby and Jordan did lines of cocaine from a compact mirror that Libby used as a cutting surface for her razor blade while she was driving, on which I passed.

"No coke today?" she asked me.

"No, thank you," I said proudly.

"Boy," she said, "You were jumping all over this last week. Something bothering you?"

"Why should anything be bothering me?" I answered with a question, and added, "Can't I just be 'not interested'?"

"Suit yourself," she said offering the last two large lines to Jordan. "Jordan?"

"Damn right," he said with his never-ending big wide grin.

Right at that moment a cop put on his lights behind us, and as they flashed Libby pulled the vehicle over onto the wide shoulder off of Route 413. Libby told us to relax as she hid the stuff and her paraphernalia while the rest of us composed ourselves.

"Driver's License and Registration please," the Officer said while Libby was rolling her window down.

The cop was a white male, in his thirties with the Smokey the Bear hat covering most of his crew-cut and was clean-shaven with sunglasses and stood about six-foot, two. After looking at the information Libby furnished he asked Jordan to step out of the truck.

"Why?" he asked, "Why do you want me to step out of the truck?"

"STEP OUT OF THE VEHICLE, SIR. NOW!" He repeated, in a loud forceful tone, inciting Jordan to promptly comply.

Jordan opened his door and the Officer immediately spun him around with force, throwing him face-first into the side of the pick-up bed before punching him, then kicking him mercilessly. Libby and I leaped from our seats and out the doors, yelling for him to stop but it was too late; Jordan fell to the ground. The Officer pulled his gun on us and directed us to get back into the truck while he rifled through the wallet he took from Jordan's back pocket. We reluctantly went along with his demand, acquiesced in silence as we slipped into the truck, staring at each other while Jordan started to rise from the dust.

"Here," the Officer said, handing Jordan the wallet back, "I thought you were someone else. Have a nice day," and he climbed into his unmarked police vehicle and made a U-Turn, heading in the opposite direction from where we were going.

"What the fuck?" Jordan said, wiping the blood from his mouth and carefully holding his ribs as Libby and I helped him into the crew-cab back seat.

"I know," Libby said, "That was fucked up! Horace, did you get a badge number? Or a license number?"

"Sorry, no." I said, disappointed.

"Do you think it was a real cop?" Jordan asked.

"Who knows?" she said, "But when we get to the house, we're going to make a few calls. I'm going to try and contact Robert now on the car-phone. He'll know what to do."

Libby called Robert, who in so many words told her to come straight home, so they could get to the bottom of it. In the meantime, he was going to call the State Police to report it and told us not to say anything to anyone else about it, but by that time, we were, almost home.

When we arrived at the Bender home there was a doctor with a nurse waiting for us, putting Jordan into a wheelchair, although he said it wasn't necessary, but they were merely taking precautions and examined him, finding he had a few cracked ribs but no signs of a concussion. Robert had made discrete calls to persons of interest when his calls to the State Police turned up no information on the confrontational episode with Jordan. His inquiries uncovered a dark, duplicitous strategy to undermine the Benders and their position on operating the club and the clientele, with Bill Bailey behind the design; constructed in order to intimidate Jordan with the idea to discourage him from playing the club.

As it turns out, it *wasn't* a real policeman, of course, but a person hired by Bill Bailey to harass and intimidate Jordan, partly for restitution of their brief encounter the previous night, and part of his plan. Robert called us all into the den to ask what exactly had happened and asked each of us what it was we saw and how this "ordeal" went down at the Bender's Club.

"It was nothing," Libby said firmly, and keeping her composure, "Jordan said 'excuse me' to him when Bill elbowed him walking by."

"He elbowed him?" Robert asked.

"Yep," I told him, "Just like the bullies in Junior High School used to do when we were walking down the halls."

"Well," Robert said, "Bill could be a real asshole sometimes, believe me I know. I'll have a talk with him as soon as I can. How did the gig go otherwise?"

"It went very well," Libby said, "We're playing there Tuesday and Thursday. Thanks for the bookings."

"Well," Robert said, "It's the least I could do, but it's apparently pissing Mr. Bailey off."

"Too bad," Jordan said faking pity with a smile, setting us into a roll of laughter.

"Bill would be happy," Robert said, "if the club patrons and workers were all white and straight, but that was never my intention with any of my establishments and I'll be damned if I'll let some prick in to encourage that prejudice atmosphere."

"Well," Libby said, "He's been doing it in Philly and a few of the others for years."

"Well," Robert responded, mimicking Libby, "He'll not be doing this anymore as of tomorrow morning. I'm letting him go."

Libby sat directly on his lap ad gave him a big hug, saying, "I love you when you're right!" Then she stood up and asked about Mr. Bailey's shares and what they were going to do about his corporate joint interest.

"Not to worry," he said, "Unbeknownst to Bill, you're already in the contract as taking immediate ownership of any partner stock options at the time of their departure, be it due to termination or death.

"'Sound's so . . . final," I said.

"It will be tomorrow," Libby said, with a devious grin, "I can't wait."

"Don't forget to notarize the new Will for us first thing tomorrow," he added, "the one that gives you and I joint interest in the 50%, and with the 2% you already own, it's at 52%.

Robert took out his set of works with a packet of heroin and a spoon right in front of us again as he had before, and had gotten himself off, with Libby helping as I left the room.

"I can't watch this anymore," I told Robert as he was looking deep into me.

"Horace," he said, "I wish I had your youth and freedom. You have your whole life ahead of you and the world by the balls. . . if you could only see it."

"I see it," I stated, "I wish you could."

"Can you spare a taste of that?" Jordan said, asking Robert and Libby to get him off.

I saw Libby look over at me with a look of concern in her eyes when Jordan asked her this and she immediately responded, as if she were reading my mind, telling him: "The doctor gave you prescription pain killers, Jordan, and by-the-way, there will be no more shooting-up dope in this band, and that includes me. There, I've finally said it."

She smiled, and her smile penetrated my heart as she winked at me while I was walking out the door with a subtle and generic wave to her.

I was glad to hear her make that statement, but I was also disgusted and happy at the same time as I left the house, loading my bicycle into my pick-up and driving over to the Lake Galena trail for a quiet bike ride a few times around the lake. I was happy that we had an energetic night of playing and improvising, with an audience that loved our music. This group of people I'm now involved with are a combination of great friendships and camaraderie that surpasses anything I've ever experienced. I was also happy with mine and Libby's relationship and her presence, and enjoyed what we shared together, even though she's married, and married to a hell of a nice guy. What disgusts me is the constant, 'seemingly' sleazy drug and narcotic use that's engulfed and surrounded this new universe, shading the world in a darkened shroud-like cloud that can't be denied, and would be lovely otherwise.

After I pulled the pick-up into the parking lot at lakeside, I use the restroom before unloading the bike and I began my trek around the large body of water. As I rode I glanced to my right at the large open space underlined by the view of Lake Galena itself, supporting nothing but an occasional sailboat, or a fisherman in a canoe, and sparsely formed groups of ripples from the wafts of breezes skimming off of the water's surface. I had a steady clip going as I peddled through the clearings and wooded areas and up the hills within this National Park while nearing the Nature Center. When I stop and look within the fenced area at a Red Bellied Turtle crawling into a safe area I heard a familiar female voice coming from behind me.

"Well, well, fancy meeting you here, again!" she said, as I turned around, still sitting on the bicycle.

"Lucy!" I said, surprised of course.

"One in the same," she responded, and she approached me with a smile, and added, "I thought I might catch you up here one of these times."

"Why is that?" I asked.
"Well, I know you ride your bike up here." she said, looking down at the cycle and rubbing her hand on the handlebars.
"Are you just visiting the Nature Center?" I asked, noticing how good she looks, wearing shorts and a tight flowered top.
"I am," she said, "and I like taking walks through the paths in those woods over there."

She looked bright and cheerful and I wondered where her other half was, not that I expected to see Johnny with her, but remembering our confrontation when I left the house on Wood Street.
"So, where's Johnny today?" I asked. The glow melted from her face, making me almost sorry I asked the question . . . *almost.*
"Johnny and I haven't seen each other for a while," she said, "I have no idea where he is, and 'don't care."
"He's not living with you at the house?" I asked.
"I'm not at Wood Street anymore, Horace, I left there a week after you moved out." she said, taking me by surprise once again.
"Wow, that was only a few days ago. Where are you living now?" I asked sheepishly.
"Oh, here and there," she said, and added, "Park your bike, and let's walk."

I did just that, happily, leaning it against a maple tree, wrapping the cable-lock around the frame and Lucy and I hiked together to the wooded area toe-paths and into the woods of oak, ash, and maple trees that grow well here, drawing moisture off of the small streams draining into the lake. We were quiet most of the time, other than a few words regarding safety, such as "Watch your step," and "Low bridge," when lifting random branches to walk under, and "Spider," for the web-warnings. We eventually reached a small grotto where we sat on a fallen willow tree, beneath another standing willow and we rested and talked.

"So, did you and Johnny have a fight?" I asked.

"Why do we have to talk about him," she answered with a smirk.

"We don't," I said, and then asked,"Is he still living at the house?" But she turned her head sideways at me, as if to say: 'are you kidding me?'

"The house is empty," she answered, "and I doubt if anyone moved in yet."

"Well," I said, "he was an asshole anyway."

"I know! And stop talking about him!" she said, and followed up immediately with: "What have you been up to, Horace? Where are YOU living now?"

I took a few seconds to contain myself before answering.

"I'm staying with friends," I said, "and I'm doing drywall work for them."

"Who?"

"You don't know them."

"But what's their names?" she asked.

"Who are you staying with?" I asked, mimicking her, and added, "What's their names?"

"OKAY!" Lucy said, and added, "We're going to remain mysterious to each other, giving vague answers like we always have."

"Mystery loves company," I said, pretending to be witty.

She laughed, and then we sat for a while in silence, until I saw her staring with a deep look in her eyes as if in a trance, at the ground near the base of the willow where it looked like an animal had dug away at the loose earth.

"How old do you think this tree is?" she asked me, still staring at the ground.

"I don't know," I told her, "A couple hundred years? Maybe?"

"Maybe," she said, then leaning her shoulder on my arm.

"This was always a wooded area," I said, "since way before the settlers had arrived."

"If something gets buried here," she said, "no one would ever find him."

"Him?"

"What?"

"Him? You said, 'if something was buried here no one would ever find '*him*'."

"You know what I meant." she said.

"I did, but it was a little odd. Is that why you don't want to talk about Johnny?" I asked jokingly, insinuating that she did him in.

"Get serious," Lucy said, laughing. "Besides," she added, "If I did, it would be the perfect murder because you wouldn't believe me anyway."

"It wouldn't be up to me." I said. "The police would find you."

"Not if they couldn't find a body," she said, with a victorious smile, like she had just won a football pool or something.

"Why the hell are we still talking about something like this?" I asked.

"Bingo!" she stated firmly, "Now let's get off of the subject."

Lucy stood, and started walking deeper into the woods, down the root infested trails with rocks and Jewelweed, and an occasional Box Turtle. Her gait was steady as I watched her legs skillfully and artfully sidestep the logs and meter-wide streams, skipping over them as if there was no gravity at all.

"Since when did you become so agile?" I asked, grinning from ear to ear.

"You don't remember hiking with me?" she asked.

"Yeah," I retorted, "but it's been a while."

"We'll stop up here," she said, "I just wanted to show you a cool place, where I'd love to camp sometime."

"Are we going to go camping sometime?" I asked, pushing back a low branch from a maple tree and trying to stay on her tail.

"Sure," she said, "when hell freezes over."

"What?" I asked, then I said, "There is no hell."

Then I wondered why I said something like that, something about hell that sounded familiar from my past, 'sort of like' déjà vu.

"Sure, there is," she said, and continued, "for as you know, this is hell, here on earth, and it freezes over when we die."

"A likely story." I replied.

We walked a little bit more, through a slight downgrade and then up what, appeared to be, a slight embankment, right into a grotto-like clearing containing wildflowers and dogwood trees. Everything was as green as it could get, with the foot-tall grass padded down like a bedding, just waiting for someone to lay down within the comfortable lush and verdant mattress.

Lucy and I wasted no time lying down, side by side on the grassy bed staring up at the clear, blue sky, resting in silence as our thoughts took over, sedating us into a mild high on the sounds of the soft, hissing wind through the grass and an occasional chirp of the birds in the nearby trees. My mind wandered back to the reality of being in the presence of a person who once shared a relationship and child with me and I wanted to relate to her once again, wondering what ever happened to us.

"Lucy?"

"Yeah?"

"Why did we get so . . ." and my thoughts simply trailed off, as if I wanted to take the question back, but it was too late. I froze and couldn't get the words out the way I wanted.

"I don't know what you mean." she replied, a bit confused.

"I mean," I tried to continue, "Why do you think we had such a hard time trying to get along with each other in these past years?"

"You mean, ever since our son Gabriel was killed?" she asked, glaring at me, not in anger, but as if she too questioned why a two-year-old boy needed to be taken from us.

"Do you think that had something to do with it?" I responded.

"Do you?" she asked, as she laid on her back, reaching her hand over to hold onto mine.

"Are we ever going to answer each other without another question?" I asked, now smiling.

"I think that it's where our fighting really started, or our bickering, and I wish I could take all of by bitchiness back," she said, "but I can't. All I can say is that I'm sorry for the way that I treated you all these years. I admit I was the one with issues, and don't tell me I wasn't."

"I think it was because of that, Johnny, and he . . ." I started, but Lucy interrupted me.

"Don't blame him!" she said, "I told you that it was me, and I don't ever want to hear about him again."

"Boy," I said, "he must have done a number on you!"

Lucy glared at me again, this time hard enough to send a chill through to the bone as she started pushing herself up from the grassy bed and brushed the loose, green blades from the skin on the backs of her legs, where she had grass impressions, little imprints in red.

"If you only knew what he was into." she said.

"You mean besides you?" I asked.

"It's no secret he liked me," she said, "and you already knew that. But it was all deeper, and a lot more involved than you might think."

"He was your lover," I retorted, "and I was pissed because I became the proverbial 'guy on the side,' with you and him living at my house. I felt stupid because I fucking trusted you."

"I know, I know, I know," she said, now crying, "and you're making me feel so bad. You don't know what he's capable of. You don't know what he would have done to you if he didn't . . . well . . . I don't want to talk about this anymore."

"He's a fucking wimp." I said. "I could have bodily thrown him out of my house, and I almost did, although, I guess I did throw him into the dumpster."

"He would have killed you, Horace."

"What? Come on, Lucy, get real."

"He would have killed you. Look, I don't want to talk about this anymore."

I let it go for now and I walked back down the path, and as she walked past that scratchy section of loose dirt under that willow tree we had passed earlier, she once again stopped and stared at it, saying, "Did you know that willow trees grow very fast, but their wood is too soft to be good burning wood for heating? That's why people wanted to be buried under them in the old days, I read."

"I read a lot of books, and I never heard of that." I said.

"Well, maybe I heard it somewhere."

"An old wives' tale?" I asked, trying to be funny, but my response furnished no laughter.

"So, you don't know where Johnny is?" I inquired one more time with no response from her as we kept our pace.

No matter, though, I didn't really care, and I most probably won't ever see, that bastard again, although I wondered what she meant when she said that he would have killed me. I never thought of Johnny as the 'killing' type, and the whole time he stayed at the house with Lucy and I, I never once felt threatened by him, other than him milking us of our finances and displaying his other freeloading qualities.

When we had both gotten to the clearing where the Nature Center was, there were groups of people walking by on the main trail dressed in their summer dresses, jeans, tee-shirts and bandanas, all looking like they were walking out.

"Wow," Lucy said, "It looks like it's getting late. The sun is low in the sky."

"It sure is," I said, "I didn't realize it either. I lost track of time."

As I said that, a man in his late forties turned to me, then in Lucy's direction, and back at me saying, "It's easy to lose track of time in a place like this. Did you just hike those wooded trails?"

"Yes, we did." I said. "We were there most of the day."

"So, there was a group of you?"

"No, Just Lucy and me."

"Lucy?" He asked, with a questioning look.

"Yes, Lucy here knows all of the trails back there, don't you Lucy?"

"Pretty much," she said, leaning on me cozily with my arm around her.

"Okay," the man said, shaking his head like I had insulted him, then turned around and just walked away when Lucy started talking.

"Wow," Lucy said, "He's a strange one."

"Don't matter, everybody's strange," I said as we walked up to my bicycle.

"Where did you park?" I asked her as I undid the cable-lock and straddled the seat.

"I'm over here. Hey Horace, I want to talk to you some more about a few things, alright?"

"Where do you want to go?" I asked.

"I don't mean tonight," she said, "because I have to be somewhere. How about here on the trail again, tomorrow?"

"Sure Lucy, tomorrow, it is. Two in the afternoon?"

"Sounds good," she said, and walked up the trail and out of sight as I peddled a steady pace the rest of the way around the lake, coming full-circle to my pick-up truck.

After loading the bike in, I climbed into the cab and started the engine, turning on the radio, and to my surprise, I heard a song by the Grateful Dead that was one of Lucy's favorites. I turned the engine off to lay back and listen, closing my eyes and reminiscing of the days when she and I met, a warm spring day at an outdoor keg party by the shrine at the top of the hill. Because of how tired I felt from the walking and the bicycle ride, and the wear and tear from the previous Saturday night in Philly at the Bender's Club, these thoughts caused me to drift into a sound and relaxing sleep. Unfortunately, I slept all night and into the next day, right there in the park inside my truck.

I was up at around 4:00 AM the following Monday morning in the early beginnings of the morning birds chirping. By the time I had gotten back to the Bender house it was still dark and all of the outside lights on posts along the lengthy driveway were on and beaming the way. I pulled in and parked the truck, but there were cop cars and an ambulance inside the wide macadam parking area at the front entrance of the house.

Confused and concerned, I jumped out of the pick-up and almost tripped over a step walking up the walkway to the door. There was a burning smell in the air, like burning wire, or rubber, similar to the smell I experienced in fire-restoration jobs I had been involved in. Inside of the house, I heard voices coming from the den and there were two officers coming down the main stairs to the lobby.

"Excuse me sir, are you a resident here?" One of them asked.

"Well, for now I am," I said, and continued with my train of thought, "What happened?"

"We don't know for sure, yet. Would you mind joining the others in the den?" he asked very politely.

"Sure, no problem," I said, and added once again, "What happened?"

"Just join the others, please." he said once again. "We will fill you in, but you must stay in here for now, please."

Libby and Jordan were sitting on the sofa, with Libby crying her eyes out, so I knew this was bad; really bad. When I looked out of the den's rear window viewing the back property of the house I saw there were fire engines

surrounding what Robert always had referred to as his workshop, and in the shining lights I saw that it was now nothing but smoldering rubble.
"Robert's dead!" Libby cried, "He was killed in that fire! I told him! I told him not to . . ." Her trembling narrative was lost in her wailing and Jordan put his arms around her, comforting her. Witnessing this I joined them on the couch, with my hand on Libby's shoulder, patting it lightly, but she grabbed my wrist and wrapped my arm around her waist while the police and a few firemen stood firm and quiet, looking on. An important looking man identifying himself as the Fire Marshal walked in with a few other police inspectors and a person who identified himself as the family doctor, Doctor Montgomery.

In the house were also a County Physician and a few other people who were professionals. The apparent cause of death was massive burns and the death was labeled as an accident, caused by carelessness on the record, but off the record was due to freebasing of cocaine. The body was only recognizable through a unique stainless-steel pin in the hand which Dr. Montgomery identified immediately, and also dental records, since he wore dentures. But there was no doubt it was Robert Bender in the tragic fire since Libby was the last one to see him, when she warned him not to freebase the drug, and left him in a huff when he refused. She's blaming herself and although he's freebased many times before, she was always concerned; but deep inside never thought that something like this would ever happen, no one ever does.

Obviously, the Benders have the money to get all of this done on the QT, because they don't want the newspaper reporters to be printing up gossiping tales that might embarrass the name 'Bender.' So, everything was being done quick and organized in a way that by the time the public would find this out, everything would appear as it is, a tragic accident, but there will be no mention of freebasing of cocaine or narcotics of any kind. The Benders were most apparently a pillar of the community and Robert Bender had friends in the high places within the same local community.

The Fire Marshal was insensitively talking through Libby's weeping to Jordan, the doctors, and anyone else listening or half listening, including myself. He said the barn, which was also the workshop went up in flames like it was made of tinder, and there was no direct escape route for Robert. When he freebased, he had been using all of the paraphernalia for igniting the cocaine, but the lighter he used, was obviously defective, causing an explosion and igniting the surrounding area. There's also a possibility he had a heart attack while inhaling the potent mixture, disorienting him and causing his physical limitations for escape.

"What do we do next?" I asked the Fire Marshal.

"You contact your insurance company immediately." He told us, and added, "We already notified the morgue and a general autopsy will be performed. We did one here with the County Physician and your doctor for identification, but you should get a more-thorough one done."

"We don't need another," Libby stated, "We know it's obviously Robert and we know exactly how he died. We were here!"

"Suit yourself," he said, then picked up a pad and was writing what seemed to be a report of some kind. Libby was sniveling and wiping her nose on my shoulder, then leaned her head into my chest. I held her closer as Jordan arose from his sitting position and said, "I have to stretch my legs, and go take a pee."

"Take one for me." Libby said.

"This is horrible, Libby, I couldn't believe it." I said as I leaned into her.

"You didn't come home last night. Where did you go?" she asked me.

"I was at the lake, and actually fell asleep listening to a song."

"Hah!"

"Honest! Why would I make that up?" I asked.

"Nobody would make that up, because it would be too hard to believe." she said, and continued, "I was in my bed thinking about you after I left Robert at the shop. I had a feeling he was up to no good, because he's been getting into that freebasing shit more and more. But a part of me thought he wasn't really going to be doing it anymore, poor bastard."

Libby once again went into a wailing that made my hair stand and it actually made me cry and shake as we hugged each other.

Daylight started creeping in as the ambulance left with the body and by the time the last police car left the property, along with the fire marshal's vehicle, the glare of the sun was in my eyes and I was still holding Libby's now-sleeping body, fully clothed on the couch against mine. I carried her up to the double bed and laid next to her as I once again drifted off, exhausted, to a well-deserved temporary sleep.

Before drifting off into a serene sound sleep, I thought about Robert, and what a beautiful guy he was, other than his narcotic demons that 'seemed to' haunt him mercilessly. I'm reminded of my own past drug use and those demons I've left behind long ago, only to revive them from their dormant chasms once I met Robert and Libby. Also, I remembered sticking that needle into my arm the other night after a solid week of a foggy, narcotic inebriated blur, and losing a day or two to alcohol and drug induced blackouts. I also thought about Jordan and felt responsible for dragging him into all of this, but I also felt that he was at the very least enjoying the ride, for now anyway.

That same morning, still Monday, I was the first to arrive into the big kitchen and started what I called my 'cowboy coffee' in the old-fashioned percolator. The digital clock on the stove read 10:10 as I heated the pan to start a few eggs when I felt what could be considered a light slap on my shoulder, and turning around only to see the brown, smiling face of my comrade Jordan.

"Only two?" he asked, referring to the frying eggs.

"And two for you," I said, cracking a couple more into the skillet.

"Where's Libby?" he asked, walking over to set plates and silverware onto two of the placemats on the table.
"I let her sleep in." I said. "No way was I going to wake her after last night."
"This is pretty rough for her," he said, and added, "Rough on me too. I mean, Robert dying like that."
"Shhh," I whispered, "Let's keep it down . . . Rough on all of us you mean, but it's her husband, and his house."
"My house now," Libby said as she entered the room wearing see-through flesh colored silk blouse and skin-tight sweatpants. She looked into my pan and asked, "Where's mine?"
"These are yours," I told her sliding two onto the plate Jordan set for me, then the other two onto Jordan's.

She sat down and began eating while I poured her and Jordan coffees and two orange juices and cracked two more eggs into the hot, sizzling pan. As I watched her eating, it was 'almost as if' nothing happened last night into this morning, and I actually didn't think she'd be up this early, considering.
"So," she said, chewing a mouthful of egg, "How's your ribs, Jordan? Are you able to do these gigs Tuesday and Thursday? Do you guys want to come back here each night or do you think we should stay there at the hotel for the week?"
"You mean, we're still playing?" I asked, totally shocked. Jordan too was looking at her with the same expression, but in silence.

"Of course, we're playing." she responded, "Why wouldn't we?"

"I thought," Jordan said, stumbling over his words . . ."

"Because of Robert?" she asked, interrupting him, then shoved a mouthful of toast past her lips.

"Well, you seem to be taking this rather well," I told her, turning my eggs before dumping them onto my own plate.

"We're born, we live, then we die" she said, in a relatively calm; and final note before adding, "I'm sad, but life moves on, and we must start thinking about these gigs."

"Brrr. It's cold in here," Jordan replied, while I sat caddy-corner from the both of them, but Libby simply responded to his candor with a subtle icy glare before returning to her slurping of her runny breakfast.

"The ribs are fine, since you asked," Jordan said to Libby, "It turns out they were just bruised."

CHAPTER - NINE

After a morning of privately reflecting on what happened last night, and how callous Libby seemed to be acting regarding Robert's horrible accident, I headed out at 1:30pm to keep my rendezvous with Lucy at Peace Valley, Lake Galena. Although I had the bike in the back of the truck, I had not planned on any riding since I knew I was meeting her with the intention of walking and talking.

When I arrived at the place where we were supposed to meet, I saw her sitting on the wooden bench with that distant stare she seemed to have developed since our chance encounter, peering across the wide stretch of water, that teemed of wind ripples as it reflected the blue from the sky.

"How's it going?" I asked, stepping out of the truck.

She looked at me and then watched a couple passing her by, but the couple looked at me and said, "It's going great. Beautiful day, huh?"

"It sure is," I answered, and giggled to myself because I was addressing Lucy and they answered in her silence. But then Lucy answered as I sat right beside her.

"I'm fine. Do you want to walk up to see Gabriel with me?" she asked, leaning onto my shoulder.

"Of course," I said.

She was talking about walking up Cheese Factory Road to the top of the hill where the Shrine is, and where our son, Gabriel is buried. It's about a half-hour walk from where we were so we were able to have a good talk, ironing out our past differences.

"So," I started, as we began our trek, "You don't see Johnny anymore?"

"I don't see Johnny. I told you that."

"I wonder where he's living now?" I asked, and continued, "You know what I mean, like if he's mooching off of someone else."

"Why are you so obsessed with him?" she asked.

"I'm not!" I answered as we entered onto Cheese Factory road. It was a macadam road with potholes on a steep hill with a grade that varied every twenty feet, leaving us almost breathless when we tried to talk. Lucy looked cool as a cucumber while I started to break a sweat on the steeper climb as we kept up our winded conversation. The area on either side of the road was wooded with ash, oak, some tulip poplar trees and plenty of maples shading us from the sun which was through the trees and to our backs.

"Yes, you are." she said. "You've been talking about him and I told you I'm not involved with him anymore."
"Okay" I said, "So where are you staying at now?"
"I told you before, not far from here, Deep Run Road."
"That's the road I'm on," I said, "Where on Deep Run?"
"Don't ask me stupid questions." she said, and continued, "Can we talk about something other than exactly where I'm living for Christ sake? Like, let's talk about where we first met."

It's funny she said that, because we were approaching that exact spot at the top of the hill at the border grounds of the Shrine. Years ago, she and I had made love in what used to be a field right where we were now standing off the road at the top of this hill. We had met right there when a group of us had an all-night keg party with a campfire and two quarter kegs of beer, and the car radios blasting. Lucy was with a group of her girlfriends she knew from working at a Hatboro restaurant and we hit it off immediately. She and I were also wasted, but it didn't matter as the fire of romance was not subdued by inebriation while we took ourselves into the high weeds and rolled our way into the morning light, back in those days of free-spirited fun
"This place looks familiar, doesn't it?" I asked her as we stood in the exact spot, looking around at what was now cut grass, and there were trees missing from where there once stood two tall oaks and a sparse grove of beeches.
"Not anymore," Lucy said, adding: "and boy, how time puts a spin on the glowing reality of the Universe."

"You ain't kidding!" I said, trying not to laugh at her deep perception of time. I reached my arms around her and gave her a big, long hug, but when I tried to kiss her she stopped me by putting her hand on my opened mouth.

"Don't," she said abruptly. Then she pointed her face toward the rows of tombstones in the distance and took my hand, walking with me in the direction of the cemetery.

I couldn't remember exactly where Gabriel's grave was, but she knew exactly where, as we walked through and around the different configurations of etched, cement and stone grave markers before arriving at Gabriel's.

"Gabriel Clowney 1980 -1982"

That's all the grave marker said, and immediately Lucy began to sob uncontrollably, falling to her knees and sobbing while I knelt in the grass beside her, clutching her in my arms. I also began to weep, losing control of my tears, but that's only because she was doing it and I was always a sucker for a girl crying.

Don't get me wrong though, when I first found out that Gabriel was dead, killed in a drunk driving accident where Lucy was driving, I was infuriated beyond belief and that was where something died between Lucy and me. Sure, I cried then, but I was filled with rage losing my own son in a careless, senseless act such as drunkenness, and I had gotten loaded for months after that. Now, Gabriel lays beneath the green grass of the shrine without knowing what he could have become, or what kind of man he could have been, or without ever having the chance of ever falling in love.

Lucy reached down through her tears and picked a four-leaf clover from a group of clovers and placed it firmly into my hand without ever looking up at me; closing my hand around it before squeezing it and then kissing my thumb. Using me as leverage she pushed herself up from her kneeling position while a robin flew past me, inches from my face.

"That's a good omen," she said, "Especially in a cemetery."

"Whatever," I said, standing up, listening to my knees cracking.

"You don't believe me?" she asked.

"Since when did you become superstitious?" I asked, smiling nervously, in the wake of her disappointment at my doubting her.

"Not superstitious," she said, "A mojo here and there never hurt anybody."

We both stood quietly together, hand in hand as we looked at the tombstone and the carefully etched dates, and as we did, I myself wondered once again how this horrible accident could have been prevented. Her hand started squeezing mine very hard, to the point that I had to tell her.

"You're hurting my hand," I said, "What are you thinking about?"

"I have to tell you something Horace," she said assertively, "and I have to tell you now, or I never will."

"So, tell me."

Her head was already low, and it dropped lower before she threw her head and hair back and blurted it out, saying:

"Our little Gabriel wasn't killed in a car crash."

"What? What do you mean?" I asked her, now completely confused.

"Gabriel is dead, and buried here beneath us," she said, "but he wasn't killed by me driving drunk."

"You're not helping me out here, Lucy. Say what you're going to say."

"What I'm trying to say, and don't get mad at me, or go flipping out on me . . ." she said, trailing off.

"Dammit! What are you saying?" I shouted.

"Johnny killed him!"

"WHAT?"

"It was an accident." she said, and continued, "Johnny shook him and shook him because he kept crying and little Gabriel went unconscious, so I rushed with him in my car and was taking him to the hospital, but Johnny thought I was going to spill the beans about him shaking him. He followed me and ran me off of the road where I totaled the car. The next thing I remembered I was back at his house, without Gabriel."

Lucy once again began to cry on my shoulder, but it was all I could do not to push her away. My self-control mode was in high gear and my anger was starting to boil to rage when I thought about her story and that fucking imbecile Johnny.

"When I saw that little Gabriel wasn't there Johnny knew what I was thinking and told me that Gabriel didn't make it!" she said.

Lucy and I held onto each other and cried for the longest time before she started telling me some of the truths from the past. It turns out that she knew Johnny before she met me, and he was her lover throughout our relationship of more than four years. Little Gabriel was definitely sired by me because 'apparently' Johnny was sterile, but obviously not impotent with the way that she admitted their relationship was purely of a sexual nature and has been ever since they were teenagers. She was satisfied by me, she said, but her ongoing fling for Johnny was more of an addiction and she was very clear that she loved me, still does, and admits she's been very confused for years.

My problem with all of this now is that I'm hurt by her; but infuriated with Johnny for what he did to Lucy and Gabriel and I wanted to get to the bottom of why she never told me. I mean, shit! She had the son-of-a-bitch living in my house, screwing her, rent free and I was played for a fool paying his way!

"I'm pissed!" I told her.

"I don't blame you," she said, as we both walked over to the maple tree still within eyeshot of Gabriel's tombstone, and sat in its shade.

"Why lie to me?" I asked, "Why didn't you tell me this shit years ago? You love this piece of shit, don't you?"

"NO!" she blurted, "I told you I was confused, 'still am, and he was like a habit. . . and I'm sorry!"

"Would you accept me doing that to you?" I asked, "Having a fling on the side and telling you that she was a 'habit'?"

"No, I would not."

"So," I asked, "How could you live with what he did to you and Gabriel, without telling me the truth? Is it because you know I would have killed him?"

"He would have killed you," she said, now looking at me slyly.

"What?"

"He told me that if I ever said anything to you or anyone, he would kill you in a horrible way," she told me.

As we both sat under the shade of the maple a squirrel ran between us and up into the tree branches above our heads, knocking down a few leaves which landed onto the grass and roots at our feet. It made me hold back on what I really wanted to say but encouraged me to ride a different train of thought. This woman sitting next to me is someone I've been living with for over four years and I have no idea who the hell she is, yet, I feel I know her better than she knows herself.

"You must not know me at all if you believe that piece of shit would kill me," I told her, and added, "I'd kill him first!"

"He threatened to kill you if I was to say anything to anybody, and my silence was protecting you," she said, and continued:

"Ever since I've known Johnny he's been into underhanded, outlaw stuff, like involving himself with seedy characters, drugs, smuggling, and worse yet, murders."

"Murders?"

"Yes. He's done hits for organizations, syndicates if you will," she said, "and for big bucks, which he gambled away. He also collected for loan sharks, who were some of the shadiest individuals I've ever met."

"I'm not afraid of him like you are," I told her, "I'll kick his ever-loving ass!"

"When he does these hits," she said, "It's in a gruesome way. He himself said he's a coward so what he does is knock them out with a dose of heroine, or some other narcotic, or just whacks them over the head, then buries the poor bastard alive."

"Really? Are you on the level?"

"As God as my judge," she said, "He's known for his heinous methods amongst his peers and I didn't want that to happen to you!"

"I'm going to turn him in," I said, glaring right into her eyes, but immediately got a strange chill in doing so.

"You can't prove anything," she said, "You don't even know where he is."

"Do you?" I asked.

"Not now, I don't. All I know is that I put him up to live with us, so you would be safe."

"What a crock!" I insisted, "That makes absolutely no sense!"

"He said he needed a place and I talked you into it, remember?"

"Yes," I answered, "You said he was down and out, and he needed a place, and that he could work for me sometimes . . . but he was a fucking freeloader!"

"I know," Lucy said shaking her head, "but if I didn't, he was going to kill you."

"Why wouldn't you go to the police?" I asked, "Like go to them on the QT? Or tell someone instead of moving him in with me, a person he wants to kill."

"He didn't *want* to kill you," she said, "He was just protecting his interests like he's always done. Besides, I thought that if you guys hit it off you might even . . ."

"BECOME FRIENDS?" I shouted, finishing her sentence with a laugh.

"Well, you know what I mean," she said, becoming passive.

"Still hard for me to believe," I replied, and added a sarcastic, "Sorry."

"He had the police convinced that Gabriel died in the crash, which wasn't true, he was already dead," she said in a sad, trembling voice."

"But," I interrupted, "were you drunk when you were taking him to the hospital?"

"No. I was knocked out and in shock from the crash," she said, "and the ambulance took Gabriel and I to the hospital, but little Gabriel was pronounced dead at the scene.

"So, you basically lied to me about the story regarding you and Johnny leaving the scene drunk and returning the next day."

"I went straight to Johnny's from the hospital that night and got drunk with him while we got our stories straight.

I'm just very sorry I put you through all of that, Horace." she said, weeping again.

"Well," I responded, "You went through a lot too. I just wish you could have been honest with me."

"Johnny's a bad, bad dude," she said very seriously, "And I was more concerned about you. You have no idea, you have to believe me! He was set to kill you at any time."

"I'm sorry if this is hard for me to take in, right now, but Lucy, I'm really trying to be forgiving here."

"I only hope you can forgive me, Horace, really I do. You've always had that quality and I'm begging you to please . . ."

"Don't worry, Lucy," Horace told her, squeezing her hand, "We'll be alright. I'm okay if you are."

She looked up at the sky and said, "We should start heading back, shouldn't we?"

"If you wish," I answered, and we both held hands as we walked out to the road.

As we paced our way down the road through the woods there was one car coming up the hill, so Lucy walked on one side and I took the other, so the car's passenger side was on my side, but the driver rolled down the passenger side window to ask me if the cemetery was up here. I told him to keep going and that it's at the top of the hill. I also wondered why he didn't just ask Lucy, who was walking on his side right at his window but then I realized that some guys think that asking a girl for directions is demeaning to their macho egos and just brushed off the thought.

I started telling her about working and staying at the Bender's home, and about our band playing at the club in Philadelphia this week and the upcoming weekend. I also made it a point to not tell her about Robert Bender dying in his freak freebasing accident last night, since all these depressing stories of death today are burdensome enough for me, and I didn't want her to be bothered with that particular report. Lucy told me again that for the last two years of having Johnny live with us she was tormented with the idea everyday of wanting to tell me, but admitted she fell into the trap of feeling more comfortable with the guilt, which eventually eroded our relationship to its conclusive and inevitable end. I'm still feeling an inner rage about my son Gabriel as we were walking down Cheese Factory Road toward Peace Valley Park, watching the sun flicker through the leafy trees in its late-day decent toward the western sky.

As I shut the door to the truck, I gave Lucy a kiss through the side window, harboring some imposing looks from some passersby, and I drove off into the sunset. The ride home was a long one, as I took the long way northward, driving up Route 611 past Ottsville, then Revere, then Kintnersville, Riegelsville, Easton, and eventually the Delaware Water Gap where I sat in the parking lot across from Indian Head Rock, contemplating on what life was about for all human beings here on earth.

The Indian Head Rock is a clearing of granite on the outer rim ascending the mountain on the Jersey side of the river, with the Delaware River separating us. When looking at it in daylight, from the right angle, one can see the Indian's forehead, the closed eyes, the nose, and the closed mouth when using a little imagination. While observing the face of the stone chief, I thought about Lucy, and my last few days with her and how she seemed to change, having more of a heart since she and Johnny and I went our separate ways and how my whole scenario of what happened to our son Gabriel was wrong for years, and my impression of Lucy has changed, where I'm not exactly sure of how I should feel about her. Do I forgive her? Yes. Do I love her? Yes, but not in the romantic fashion that I had once thought. I realized that I now had these feelings for Libby, 'maybe not' love, at least not yet, but they're there and feeling stronger every time I see her, although with Robert's recent and horrible passing, all of our feelings are obviously 'somewhat' shaken, or misconstrued. My mind wandered through the haze of days gone by, fiery gusts of anger, and the shallow and unforeseen rippling effect of post-mortem delirium from the afterthought of my son Gabriel and my friend and employer Robert, who was my new girlfriend Libby's husband.

As I did this I fell asleep momentarily and had a dream about Johnny, and I was in a bar or someplace, and he was grabbing at a woman I was with, but I found myself in a fit of anger cold-cocking him in the jaw knocking him out. My heart was beating so fast from rage that I woke up, and saw the Indian head rock towering above the Delaware, and noticed it starting to fade into the dusk of the late-day shadows until the serene view was interrupted by a semi rumbling past, heading north on Route 611 to its destination towards Scranton, PA.

Driving home down River Road I kept thinking of Libby; and wondered what present state the emotions in her house would be, knowing that the anamnesis of Robert's death was still lingering eerily in the air. I also wondered where that fucking Johnny was and if I should be worrying about him reflecting on what Lucy had revealed to me.

Arriving at home, at the Bender's, I parked the truck and walked past the footlights on the walkway to the door, and it swung open, showing Libby standing in front of me wearing a skimpy, black teddy, revealing the majority of her very soft and toned body.

"I was waiting for you," she said, "Dinner's on the table."

"I – I wasn't expecting dinner, Libby." I said, surprised and a little shocked.

She gave me a peck on the cheek and sashayed through the foyer into the kitchen while I watched her very toned butt move like sheer poetry in motion. She was all dolled up with almost black lipstick and the dark eyeshadow, and her hair was tied up above her head in neat curls exposing her perfectly rounded forehead. The table was set with two plates with the silverware on a napkin and a large plate in the center, and two candles in crystal holders on either side of the large plate.

"Have a seat," she said, as she dumped a wok of freshly steamed shrimp onto a large plate on the table, so fresh that the heads and antennae were entangled in the mess.

"Cajun style, same as on the bayou, or even in Jamaica," she said, "Hot and spicy!"

"Wow!" I said, "This sure looks good and is burning my eyes."

"The shrimp and spices I used are an aphrodisiac for Jamaicans and Cajuns," she said with a very sexy smile, and added, "I'm anxious to see how you'll perform tonight, sir."

She very seductively sat on my lap and wrapped her soft, naked arms around me, and pressing her breasts against my chest and her lips against mine, slowly and softly slipped her tongue into my mouth as we caressed. I never wanted it to end, but like a light switch, she turned it off, like a teasing temptress and stood on her bare feet, then pranced her way back to the counter-top for a couple of crystal glasses.

"I'm in!" I said, trying to cool down, digging my hand into the pile of shrimp, pulling the heads off and pealing while she set some extra spicy garlic sauce in front of me, her own special blend, and poured us both a glass of very dry white wine.

"I really am starting to really, really like you, Horace," she said, looking right into my eyes through the candle light as she sat directly across from me.

"Well," I responded, "I love you, Libby. Thanks for cooking tonight. Are you feeling okay? I mean, with everything?"

"Never better," she said winking her eye and then attacking her own prawns on her plate.

We ate in silence, 'for the most part', looking at each other through the candle light, lusting for each other through the flame off of the wick before she asked me if I wanted more wine.

"I'm good," I told her.

"Have some more," she said, rising to pour me my third glass, then sat on my lap again as before, hugging and kissing until I couldn't bear it any longer. I hung onto her, lifting her up as I stood and walked with her wrapped around me like a snuggling honey bear. I walked her anxiously and carefully to our bedroom upstairs, leaving the dishes and leftover food on the table.

The bedroom already had candles lit all over the room reflecting off of the full-sized ceiling mirror above the bed and the red sheets were pulled back on the king-sized bed waiting for action as I slipped her under the covers and got myself undressed. Libby and I made love like I've never made love before, rolling and turning insatiably in our own naked sweat under the covers until we finally peaked together on the apex within the pinnacle of inescapable climax.

Afterwards, we laid naked and satiated in the grotto of out temporary paradise, sleeping like two infants nuzzled together without a care in the world until morning.

CHAPTER - TEN

The next two days Jordan, Libby and I rehearsed in the basement recreation area that we had put together in the last few weeks and not another word was mentioned about Robert's passing, at least from Libby. But she seemed energized, motivating Jordan and I to play the standards in our own style, using the drums as the centerpiece of the songs; in other words, she's a fantastic showman and very talented.

On Tuesday, Libby cancelled the gig scheduled at Bender's in Philadelphia and in the evenings, she would disappear, and the notion was that she was probably taking care of the finances and closing books, reorganizing her priorities in order to maintain the books, getting everything organized and such, regarding the business and the household statements with Robert, the principal proprietor now out of the picture. There were some previous concerns with respect to the Will, and also the shares of the Bender's Club corporate positions, but Jordan and I hoped that all of those issues would settle appropriately for our friend Libby.

On Thursday night after the gig Libby was gone once again, and when we got back to the house, we sat on the back-porch patio reflecting on how well the night went, and how well we were received by the crowd. Libby, as usual, was at her best in playing and being the very center of attention during her crowd-sustaining and incomparable solos.

The manager and part owner, Bill Bailey, gave Jordan a shove again, as he had before, and it was all Jordan could do from taking a poke back at him. Libby stepped in and took Bill by the arm, walking him out of the area to have a chat with him, and that was the last we'd see of Bill for the rest of the night. Libby encouraged us to play on, to just keep playing our hearts out like nothing happened, and the audience of the elites loved us. However, Jordan surprised me with a curious suggestion, a perception which never would have occurred to me otherwise.

"Horace," he said, while we were sitting on the patio overlooking the immense green, well-trimmed lawn in the twilight of the early morning hours, "What if Robert's death wasn't an accident?"

"What do you mean?" I asked, easing back on the cushions of the outside reclining chair, sipping a beer.

"I mean, what if Robert was murdered?" he asked, this time looking right at me.

"What the hell makes you say that?" I asked looking right back at him, "They proved he did it himself."

"Did they? How do you know that for sure?"

"The doctor and the police detectives said so," I told him.

"No," he said, "They know he was freebasing, but how do you know the explosion wasn't pre-planned by someone?"

I sat for a few minutes reviewing the whole scenario from the other night and remembering everything I could ever possibly remember them saying; and determined that I was now second-guessing myself because of this seed Jordan had just planted.

"Now, wait!" I said, and continued, "Why in God's Name would anyone want to plan something like that on Robert?"

"I don't know," he said, "I just think that it looks suspicious to me, you know, Libby not behaving like someone who just lost her old man, all of the money she stands to make all of a sudden, things like that."

"Tell me something, Jordan," I said, "How long have you known Libby?"

"Well, I knew her as 'Sticks' a while back," he said, "and she was always a wheeler dealer, a hustler if you will, but she never had money like she does now."

"So," I told him, "If she already had money with Robert, why the hell would she kill the golden goose?"

"I don't know," he said, "to get more golden eggs?"

"Jordan," I told him, "I believe I've come to know Libby very well. She took you and I in off of the street, and I believe she's absolutely not the type of person who would do something like that, to anyone. Personally, I'm insulted that you would even suggest such a thing."

"Sorry I offended you," he said, and added, "You may be right, but how do you know for sure?"

"I know!" I said assertively.

Unfortunately for me, the proverbial seed was planted, and I actually started to wonder about precisely what Jordan was talking about. However, I knew from hearing their conversations that Libby only owns 2% of the shares in the company, but that she's also not entitled to Robert's shares at the time of his death unless that was stated specifically within the Last Will and Testament, which to my knowledge was not notarized until Monday, which was after Robert died. So, why would she be entitled to any more than her 2%, which she may lose anyway?

Also, in the case of suicide, no beneficiary would be entitled to any Life Insurance payout, according to most policies I've seen. So, the thought that Libby would ever have pulled something like a murder for her own inheritance was, in my book, 'debunked' and puts her in the clear from any wrong-doing.

I also thought that Bill Bailey was also someone who could stand to take over the Bender's Club business with his own accumulation of 34% of the shares, already counting what he bought off of Mr. Phelps, who own's 14% after selling Bill 10%. So, that would make Bill Bailey the majority holder now, and the perfect suspect if there ever was one, to have a motive for murdering Robert. Then, I laughed out loud at my creative thinking and runaway imagination in assuming there was a murder, an apocryphal growth from a singular seed planted deep in my fermenting brain by my bandmate and raconteur friend Jordan.

Libby and I 'seemed to be' tighter than ever, as we were not only practicing our music together, but also caught up in the warmth of a burgeoning relationship of making love every night and sleeping together in the same bed. Whenever I'd ask her if the finances and loose ends were getting in order, she'd either change the subject or avouch outwardly not to worry about it. When Saturday night came, we played our hearts out once again, enticing and stimulating from the crowd three standing ovations thanks to Libby's captivating solos and flamboyant personality. Her outfits changing between sets didn't hurt either as they were variant, from skimpy dominatrix leather for one set, a tight silk see-through flesh-colored low-cut gown in another, then another, then an all knit one-piece revealing every curve. In comparison, Jordan and I wore rented tuxedoes with blue shirts and red ties, the same ones all night but the only one's our own accouterment seemed to bore was us.

Also, Bill lightened up on his picking at Jordan on Saturday and although he simply ignored and wouldn't look at him, he still harnessed an attitude which kept us away from wanting to even acknowledge him and his existence. The gaggle of elites donning the tuxedoes, three-piece suits, and evening gowns heard and loved every note and beat we played, especially coming from Libby.

When the night of playing was over, we went to our hotel suites to unwind and get away from the still populous lobby and escaping the after-hours crowd. Libby told us she wasn't staying here, but going to a party on the other side of town and asked if we wanted to go, knowing very well we'd say 'no.'

"I just thought I'd ask if you wanted to go with me," she said, holding a lit joint in her hand, "I have to get tuned up here on the way."

"Not being careful with that stuff is going to get you busted someday," I told her.

"Not today," she said with a smile. Then looking at Jordan said, "Jordan?"

"I'm invited to another party," he said, "but I'll have a toke."

I watched them both leave, and I laid back on the hotel's big king-sized bed, putting on the TV to watch a late-night Clint Eastwood movie as my eyes started to shut. The plans were already made that Libby was taking the truck for the weekend and that Jordan and I were to take a limo or cab home whenever we wished since we decided not to play Sunday. We each had plenty of cash and were living like we were rich rock stars this weekend, which was something that neither Jordan nor I were used to, but contrary to him, I chose to lay back tonight, or rather, this morning.

In about an hour, I was wide awake from drinking coffee earlier and decided I didn't want to be bored by staying here in the room by myself tonight, so I called a cab from a Bucks County outfit and headed back to the Bender house, my temporary home between Pipersville and Plumsteadville, PA. The cab driver from Blue Cab Company, a small non-union Bucks County outfit that pisses off the union Philly cab companies, met me out front, introducing himself to me as Karma. Karma was an Italian or Middle-Eastern Indian looking man in his mid-forties, about 5'5" and wiry, with black greased-back long hair and a 5'o clock shadow shading his well-formed features and talked like he was from South Philly.

In the lights out in front of the club, I could see he had large, very light-blue eyes and when he smiled, he wouldn't squint them, making them seem to look very deep into me. He seemed very sure of himself and interesting in conversation, which is what we ended up doing on the entire ride home. I found out he used to work for a bigger Philadelphia cab company, but he settled for the Blue Cab Company only a few years ago.

I, of course, sat in the back and relaxed while he played the radio's classic rock station low, and of course he was making sure I was comfortable in my seat and assured I was okay with the music.

"I'm Horace, and thanks for arriving so quickly Karma." I said climbing into the back seat.

"My pleasure," he said.

"Karma," I said, "I never heard that as a name before. Is it Italian?"

"It's worldly. 'Covers all nationalities," he said, "but mostly used in the Far East. Dad was Hindu and Mom Italian, so you're close."

"I'm English and Scottish," I told him, "but I'm a Gemini birth sign so it balances everything out."

"Gemini!" he laughed, "I'm a Gemini too. We tend to have split personalities, or two souls, according to astrologers. And if we're mixed with any Leo, we tend to be the center of attention."

"Oh, I'm not aware of anything like that, I don't think. But actually, I've sure been feeling like that lately." I said laughing.

"You like rock and roll?" he asked in his South Philly accent.

"I love it," I said, "I like any kind of music."

"Did you play Bender's tonight?" he questioned, noticing my guitar case.

"Yes, I did," I answered.

"Well, then you like being the center of attention," he said, turning his head toward me as he drove us up to I-95.

"Not really," I said, "There's others in the band standing out better than me."

"You must be pretty good if you played Bender's," he said. Then added, "They only hire top-of-the-line bands so, what band are you?"

"We don't really have a name," I said, "Our drummer is married to the owner."

"Oh," he said, "Libby's band."

"You know of her?" I asked.

"Are you kidding me? Everyone in Philly's heard of her," he said, and laughed, "She goes through band members like toilet paper."

"Really?" I asked, "I never heard about that. All I know is she's the best drummer I've ever played with."

"You probably don't have any black guys in the band, right?" Karma asked, turning his head as I felt those blue eyes peering right through me.

"Why should that matter?" I asked, very curious now.

"Billy doesn't like the black guys," he said, "He calls them 'spooks', and they have a tendency of disappearing . . . without a trace."

I sat quietly for a few moments trying to digest what Karma had just said, and I wondered where he was coming from, asking me whether there were black people in the band and telling me they disappear. I'm also assuming that this 'Billy' he mentioned is none other than Bill Bailey, the partner.

"What the hell are you trying to say?" I asked him bluntly, "And who's Billy?"

"Billy Bailey. He can't stand having anyone but white people in his place, that is, white people who are straight!" he said, opening up a can of Piels Beer and offering me one.

"Say, Horace, you're not gay . . . are you?"

"Are you making a pass at me, Karma?"

"HAH! NO, BROTHER!" he said, starting to laugh, "I was just curious. Billy makes them disappear too."

"So, Karma, what are you trying to say?" I asked, realizing that ever since I told him I was in Libby's band he 'seemed to' assume that someone's going to vanish.

"Libby can't keep band members, they leave and are never heard from again," Karma said, and continued, "and I just heard that old man Bender committed suicide. She's got a bad mojo working, bad luck!"

"Well," I told him, "I think you've got your imagination working! Working overtime! He didn't commit suicide."

"I don't know," he said, "I'm from South Philly, the Italian Market area and I hear things on the streets."

"Like what?" I asked inquisitively.

"Like, there was this one guy who was a great guitar player, and when Billy found out he was a 'fruit', that's what Billy calls them, he roughed him up. Then Libby and her old man were never able to contact this dude again."

"So?" I said, "So the dude quit because Bill bullied him. So, what?"

"They found this dude in a shallow grave, up in Bucks County, right near where you're from! That's what!"

I sat quietly, listening to The Who playing on the radio while the cab cruised up I-95 and I watched the city lights get more and more sparse as we headed further north.

"Another time," Karma recounted, "There was a black saxophone player who was the sharpest dresser anyone ever saw in the club, and the customers really loved him, because he had flash and was very close to Libby. Libby loved playing with him and Billy told her to get rid of him, but she refused. Old man Bender really liked the guy too, but like the others, he vanished."

"Shallow grave?" I asked.

"Probably," he said, "But no one ever saw him again and even his family were involved in putting APB's and searches out for him. To this day, not a trace."

"How long ago was that?" I asked.

"Year, year and a half maybe. Coincidentally, he told people his wife mysteriously disappeared less than a year before that."

I wanted to say something to Karma about his version of Robert's death, committing suicide, but I decided to let it go for now since I'm figuring this guy's just a cab driver with an overactive imagination; But I resolved to ask how he heard his version of the suicide story.

"Where did you hear that Mister Bender, had taken his own life?" I asked, as he made a turn onto a back road that takes us to Route 413.

"From the streets." he said. "I heard that he did himself in because he was dying of cancer or something. That he had set it all up to look like it was an accident from freebasing. Also, he was upset at Libby for starting up a hot and heavy affair with someone close to them. Do you know anything about that? Horace? I mean, you see them, being in the band and all. Hell, there's even a rumor that she and Robert aren't married, and that the marriage is a front."

"WHAT?"

"I mean that I heard a rumor that Robert is actually Libby's biological father and the marriage is a mere business cover-up." Karma said, getting enthusiastic in his tone.

"I don't know a thing," I said, and added, "I'm just a musician and I don't like to gossip. It's all bullshit."

"I gotcha," Karma said and became silent as he turned the radio up for a Beatles song, "Nowhere Man."

After listening to what didn't seem like idle gossip, I contemplated the information received by the Philadelphian cab driver and regarded it as a sea of possibilities. With the way Libby's been acting regarding her cold or callous emotions towards Robert's passing and the way Jordan had been talking, combined with this new allegory spewed forth by my new buddy Karma, I'm finding myself conceptualizing 'possible' patterns and scenarios. One thing for sure, I really don't think that Robert was the kind to take his own life, but then again, I've only known him and Libby for a short while. Her father? Nah! Why would she . . .Nah! I tell myself to stop thinking about and nurturing these sparsely planted seeds of doubt and ridiculousness.

I'm very aware also that Libby and I are certainly in a very hot relationship with each other, but figured as always that her and Robert's bond was an open marriage for both of them, and there was really no room for me to flatter myself in thinking that I could have caused any deadly jealousy, but who knows? Bottom line too is that Karma is a cab driver and lives for these tales and spinning the yarns and has no real idea if they're true or not, only what he hears.

"So," he said, "This address we're headed to is Bender's residence, isn't it?"

"So, what if it is?"

"Just asking," he said.

"You take people there before?" I inquired.

"Nope. Never been. I heard it's a nice place though." Karma said, smiling.

"It is," I answered, trying not to incite too many more unneeded questions from him.

Driving through the dark night I watch the solid yellow line ahead of us on this two-lane highway and soon we were directly behind a slow-moving box truck, so close that it was blocking the view of the highway ahead.

"Hold on," Karma said, as he gunned the accelerator pedal to the floor and started swerving around his left side, slowly passing him as the truck also opened-up his engine, causing us to race for domination of the highway.

"What's this asshole trying to prove?" Karma said, keeping the pedal to the medal.

"You'd better stand down," I told him as the lights of an oncoming car crested the hill in front of us.

"Nothing doing," he said, "We're in this do or die now. That bastard's not giving up and he won't let us in. We're going to make it. We have to."

As he gunned our taxi I could feel a familiar chill and warmth at the same time, like my body was separating from my own spirit and a driving force from within me formed what looked like angel wings, bright and glowing within the oncoming vehicle's lights, guiding us in a peculiar vacuum forward and funneled us to the right at warp-speed, as we slipped past in what looked like a wormhole and were able to pull in front of the box truck in time to save all of our lives.

"What the fuck," Karma said as he then sped up, way ahead of the box truck until we got to a blinking red light in Buckingham, PA. Here, Karma pulled behind the building and told me to wait in the taxi as he got out and walked to the intersection, hiding behind a tree near the corner. At this hour, there were no other vehicles on the highways in this part of Bucks County.

Eventually, the box truck that was irresponsibly playing 'chicken' with us on the highway emerged from the darkness of the unlit roadway and into the streetlights of the intersection of Routes 263 and 413. As the truck stopped, Karma ran to the driver's door, opened it, and pulled the driver out by his hair onto the macadam highway, slamming him down hard and asked him what he thought he was doing back there almost killing us.

"Fuck you!" The driver told him as he started to get up, lunging at him but Karma kicked him square in the face, knocking him back down on his ass.

Two more men got out of the passenger side, who 'appeared to be' as big as the driver, at around six-foot, white, and were built like goliaths, one carrying a tire iron. As they approached Karma he was unimpressed as he jumped in the air and round-house kicked them both in the head. Then he grabbed the driver again, who was running at him and Karma head-butted him right in the nose, causing him to drop motionless. The other two came at him again slow and carefully, on either side, but Karma took the tire iron from the dude's hand in one quick move, and in one more, swift motion swung the tool, clipping them both in the face and down for the count. He then opened up the bay-door of the box-bed and about a hundred car and truck tires rolled and bounced out onto the road and rolled downhill into a field. As it turned out it looked like these dudes were stealing and transporting tires. Karma went to the corner phonebooth and called the cops anonymously to report an accident and road rage, then brought the tire iron with him, throwing it under the front seat and said, "Let's scram before these sleeping beauties wake up, and before the State Police get here."

We high-tailed it towards the next light, then straight up Route 413, Durham Road, toward Pipersville, carrying on a conversation the whole time about where he learned Karate and street fighting. He said he learned to fight and win in the streets of South Philadelphia from black and white kids alike, but then was beaten pretty bad by a big black dude. He said he swore he would never lose another fight, taking a few years of Taekwondo and indeed never lost another fight, but it also taught him some self-control. "You ever lose a fight?" he asked me.

"I never fought much," I told him, "I win, then I lose, but what few fights I had involved myself in, I guess I won."

"Well," he said, "You're a musician and a lover, you're not a fighter."

I couldn't have put it together better and answered, "I guess."

By the time we pulled in through the gate I was bushed, and I thanked him, offering him to come on inside for some coffee but he declined. I don't know what the fare was, but he was perfectly happy with receiving a one-hundred-dollar bill, so I gave him another. He gave me a big hug and I watched his tail-lights disappear into the night as I let myself into the front door, which oddly enough was left unlocked, so I locked it behind me yelling, "Anyone home?" Then in hearing nothing and setting my guitar case down, I locked the door behind me and went to the refrigerator, peeled and ate two hard boiled eggs, gulped down a quart of ginger ale, belched, then grabbed my guitar case and headed up to the bedroom where I stripped off my clothes and sliding my guitar under the bed, laid on my back, naked in the satin sheets and slowly started drifting off to a sound sleep.

I had the strangest dream about my old girlfriend Lucy, as she was in a colorful mist and we were walking down a set of railroad tracks, with her carrying a suitcase as if she was taking a trip, or a vacation somewhere. I couldn't see much around us, other than swirling colors of red and gold, and she was . . . not really naked, but wearing sheer material that was light and flowing as if it was windy, but there was no wind. She wanted me to walk with her, not saying it with words but with her eyes, as we stepped in an even stride, keeping up with her for what seemed to be near a mile if I was to guess. Lucy stopped and pointed to the ground next to the tracks, to a path that lead right to the edge of an abandoned quarry filled with water. We were then walking on the path towards the quarry, away from the tracks and the swirling colors made the whole dream sequence fade into a misty cloud that evaporated when a loud noise of a motorcycle rattled the bedroom windows, waking me with a sudden jolt.

CHAPTER - ELEVEN

It must have been a Harley, because it vibrated the entire room with a rumble loud enough to wake the dead, but fortunately, I was only sleeping. With all of the lights in the house off I was able to find my way in the blackness and look out the window without being noticed, observing only dark shadows moving in the driveway beneath my windowsill. I heard a jiggling of the front door knob and then silence as I was waiting for a knock, but there was none.

Then I was shocked to hear breaking glass in the living room and a jimmying before the sound of a window sliding open sent me into a panic, and then directly under the king-sized bed that had no room to spare, squeezing myself next to my guitar case, lying flat as a pancake with barely room enough to breathe. I felt my whole entire body trembling as I heard footsteps on the hardwood floor stop and open the front door, letting someone in with a deep voice, but I couldn't make out what he was saying. The other was a female and their voices echoed through the house like a badly mixed reverb feature in a cheap recording studio while I tried in vain to embody what they were saying to each other.

Eventually I heard them both coming up the stairs and the male voice sounded vaguely familiar now, but I still wasn't sure, until I heard him say, "Libby, why was the door locked? Are you sure that asshole guitar player isn't coming back here tonight?"

"Don't call him an asshole," the female voice said, "Horace is at the club's hotel and he won't be back here until tomorrow night. He'll never know about us. He can't. I guess I locked it by accident and those guys have my house key."

"Breaking the window to get into your own house," the male voice said, "How quaint."

I was hoping that I was dreaming, but I wasn't, because Libby had brought Bill Bailey back to the house and it's very obvious that I'm not supposed to know any of this so, I'm caught with my pants down; literally. Speaking of pants, I reached out into the darkness and grabbed my duds from view, sliding them right next to me here while I lay as still as I can with my nose and chest kissing the wooden box-spring. I then saw the bedroom lights go on, but because of my position, I really couldn't see much, so I listened quietly.

"Those cops surrounding the box-truck at that Buckingham intersection," Bill said, "You know who that was?"

"No." Libby said, "But you stopped to talk with them. 'Probably some goon friends of yours?"

"I stopped to let the cops know about our wipeout from dodging those tires," he said, "but yes, they were friends of mine. I did talk with them before the cops chased me away. It was Langdon, Fishman and Harris," Bill told her, "and they were looking pretty damn beat up."

Libby was moving around in the room shuffling papers like she was looking for something while I felt him sit on the edge of the bed.

"Were they in an accident too?" she asked, and continued, "Someone intentionally threw those tires out onto the road. We're lucky we weren't killed."

"No accident. They were almost run off of the road by a taxicab passing them," he said, "then they got the cabby's number. The number was 160."

"So?"

"Do you know who drove Blue Cab number 160, Libby?"

"What is this?" she said, "A guessing game? Get to the point." She was still looking and taking papers out of folders and I heard a lot of shuffling.

"All I know is that it's impossible," Bill said.

"I watched when the police pulled them away from you and told you to leave." she said, "They must have done something wrong, something bad. We were lucky *we* didn't get handcuffed the way you were nosing around."

"I knew the cop," Bill said, "but that didn't mean anything to them. They were arresting them for stealing those tires."

"So, those radials all over the road were from their truck?" Libby said, and added, "We're lucky we weren't killed, with all those tires, all the way down to the railroad tracks. Did they dump them or something?"

"How the hell do I know? The railroad tracks," Bill said . . . "Down those tracks is where we . . ."

"Here is some of the paperwork," Libby interrupted. "The passwords and the accounts. The Will is in order and the rest of the paperwork."

Bill and Libby were quiet, as if they were looking something over before Bill said, "Maybe there's two taxi-cabs with the number 160, or maybe those boys got it wrong."

"What's with you and your obsession with that taxi number?" Libby said. "Big fucking deal, right?"

"Do you remember a cabby named Karma? The big-mouth cab driver?" Bill asked.

"No," she said, "am I supposed to?"

"I suppose not. But like I said, it's impossible that it was him. Hetrick and I saw to it, yeah, that would be impossible."

"Another job with Hetrick?" Libby said, "You're such a coward, and you hired another deadbeat coward. You goddam bigshots, with your hit-men really crack me up."

"I'd like to see you even try to do the things I do," he said, "You wouldn't have the guts."

"I wouldn't have the *nerve*, to kill like you do," she said, "because you'd have to be inhuman, and I don't qualify. Besides, don't you ever involve me in any of that cowardly shit you do. I told you before, I don't want to know, and it has nothing to do with me!"

"I think," Bill told her softly, "that you're even more evil than I give you credit for, and I know I'm going to have to keep an eye on you; maybe grow eyes in the back of my head."

"You do whatever makes you happy." she said, then I heard her kiss him.

I was curious about him bringing up my buddy Karma, the cabby who just beat the crap out of those three dudes while bringing me here safely, and wondered what Bill could be talking about, saying it being 'impossible it was him'. 'What did he mean by that?' I thought. Also, he mentioned a last name of a hit-partner, 'Hetrick', and by coincidence, that's Johnny's last name. Then my mind was racing with revived thoughts of what Lucy was telling me recently about Johnny's evil ways.

Libby and he were sounding like they were undressing, and she asked where the set of works were, obviously getting ready to get themselves off. Then I realized they must have gotten hurt when dumping the motorcycle because they were looking at each other's bruises, and cuts, and she made a remark about his limping, which made me snicker, loving that the poor bastard was in some kind of pain. They were also putting on antiseptic and she was getting Bill off, deadening his pain with heroin and talking about the minimal damage to the Harley. Then Bill mentioned again about the train tracks, apparently where the bike went down because of those stray tires from the box-truck. Libby had also mentioned to him that she doesn't do needles and hard drugs anymore, but I could feel his relaxing vibe through the air of the room as he mellowed to the slow beat of the narcotic he ingested intravenously while they finished undressing.

"I'll take these aspirins for pain, it's not that bad." she said.

"What about the fruity spook?" Bill inquired, "Is your bass man staying in the City?"

"Jordan went to a party," Libby said, "And I won't see him until Monday; And there's no need to make your racist references. I don't like that, I don't like it one bit."

"A 'fruit' party," Bill insisted.

"What makes you such a hateful human being?" Libby asked as I saw her now beautiful naked reflection in the dresser mirror from this odd angle.

"Not hate," he said, "I just can't stomach his kind. He's an abomination to the human race, and his own."

"But you, being a murderer is not an abomination?" Libby asked, jumping onto the bed and banging my nose.

"You tell me," Bill said, "You're the one who killed Robert."

'Killed Robert?' I thought. Now, I was very intent on listening, and shocked at what I was hearing, like the absurdity, the idea of Libby killing Robert. While at the same time, I was getting rapidly angry with the hateful demeanor in this bigoted Bill Bailey character. I knew he was kind of a prick, but I am now hearing first-hand what kind of a mean insensitive prick he really is while I quietly listen from my closed and tight quarters from under this king-sized bed.

"You're the one who set it up," Libby replied, "You and your stinking threats. I didn't want to do him in, but because of your threats, I had no other choice."

"No other choice?" he said, "He was dying anyway, and all you . . ." but Libby interrupted:

"We could have waited until the cancer killed him," she said, "but you were impatient, just like you were impatient about Skip, my saxophonist. He's disappeared and I'm really hoping for your sake nothing bad happened to him, but you won't tell me, will you?"

"For my sake? Skip was an asshole, and only wanted you for a fuck!" Bill said angrily, as he too jumped onto the bed.

"He was black! That's the whole reason you were bothered about me being with him, that is, besides your jealous, racist attitude," she said as they started rolling and wrestling around above me.

"He was a no-good NI- . . ."

"DON'T you fucking DARE!" she said, interrupting his would be comment, and continued, "He was a great musician, a lovely man. And a fantastic human being, and a better lover than you could ever be!"

That set Bill off . . . and he started slapping her and punching her, but I heard her also getting fist shots in as they continued rolling their naked and sweating bodies around within their obscenities and angry sex, pummeling and punishing each other as they yelled.

I couldn't tell if they were enjoying themselves in ecstasy or brutally killing each other, or both . . . but one thing is for sure, it was hot under the bed and I was getting the living shit kicked out of me! I didn't know how much more I could take until I heard them both yell out in unison a long solid note of male-female harmony gratification . . . then silence.

I laid in the silent darkness beneath the box-spring for what 'seemed to be' an eternity, but was most probably about ten minutes, while I thought about what was said before their grueling act of abusive and heinous love making. 'Was Robert really murdered?' I asked myself, and I wondered that if he was, 'why was he murdered?' I did not know he was ill with a disease, other than what I heard from the cab driver, and this is really turning into a mystery.
"What happened to Skip?" Libby asked, now crying. "You damn well better not have hurt him in any way!"
"Aw, Boohoohoo!" Bill said as he arose from the sheets and started putting his pants on. "He was no good for you or anyone else. You keep it up and I'll do the same to your fruity pal Jordan . . . and that other creep too. You keep your horny hands off of that imbecile Horace."

I heard a slap, then hearty laughing coming from Bill as he said, "HAH! Is that all you got? Bitch?" Then they both dressed as Bill said to her, "Look, sweetheart. You and I will be married soon. You and I will be set for the rest of our lives with the deals we made. Both of us are the sole owners of Bender's after we take care of Phelps, and there's nothing that can stop us now, nothing!"
"Here," Libby said, "these are the passwords into the accounts. When you put this number in, everything will be copacetic. Trust me"
"It'd better be," he said. "Libby, we've been planning this for a while, but something has changed in you in the past few months or so. Don't go soft on me now, because we

don't want to take our focus off of what we started, you know, our plans."
"Like I said, trust me," she said, finishing changing the sheets and they both left the room.

They walked downstairs, and I heard someone, most likely Libby, sweeping up glass so I slid myself out from under the bed and walked, still naked and sweaty over to the door's edge to listen.

"So," Bill said to her, "Your two boys in the band have no idea we're getting married?"

"Of course not," she said, still sweeping, "They don't ever need to know that. I'll 'probably' disband us in a few weeks anyway, or, 'maybe not.' We'll see how it goes, because I like this band."

"Well, I don't like them," he said, "and I don't want them snooping around, messing anything up. They have to be moved out of here before we're married."

"Don't tell me what I have to do, and don't have to do." she said. "You should know that I don't care for that kind of talk coming from you or your asshole friends."

"Well, I don't want them around!" he repeated firmly.

"Lay off of them," she said as she dumped the dustpan of glass in the trash and added - "They're alright."

"I hope nothing happens to them," he said, "you know, like what happened to Skip and the others."

There was a pause; and even upstairs I could feel the tension in the air as I heard her footsteps slowly walking over to him.

"Nothing's going to happen to them," she said, and added, "Nothing better had happened to Skip, and nothing BETTER happen to my friends, my band!"

I noted his evil laugh as I heard them turning off the lights and locking the door behind them and heard the Harley crank-start and rumble as it pulled away into the dead of night. As the resonating roar disappeared into the distance I was already dressed and downstairs, checking out the storm window in the kitchen that had no more glass, and now had the screen in place of it. There was a note on the counter for me to call a glass company to replace the window when I came home, and it was signed, "'Love You, Libby." Wasting no time, and realizing I was totally physically and emotionally drained from the evening and morning's adventures, I took about four large swigs of wine from a bottle of burgundy and went directly to bed on the fresh sheets that Libby just turned.

I awoke by eleven o'clock in the morning, still tired and took a shower to refresh myself, wasting no time taking my truck containing my bicycle and heading over for a trek around Lake Galena, stopping first for an Egg McMuffin in Doylestown while washing it down with a coffee and bottled water; Breakfast of champions. While eating and keeping myself on the move I still kept reflecting and tried to digest all of what I heard last evening and this morning, trying not to vomit at the thought of the possible murders in my midst, surmising that it may all be some sort of a sick, practical joke. But the more I thought about it the more mixed up I was; and thinking that 'maybe I should just keep on driving, leaving it all behind, leaving Libby, Jordan, my guitar' . . . My guitar! I can't do that! But I have to get away and think right now; get away like I always have from Lucy when I lived on Wood Street in town; get away on my bicycle and the trek around the lake. Ironically, I've been actually seeing Lucy up at the lake recently, a place she would never go the whole time we lived in Doylestown together, but I truly haven't minded it, and amusingly, I welcomed it.

At the lake, and to no real surprise, and to my alleviation considering my evening, I saw Lucy, only today she was doing a powerwalk in a pair of shorts and a tank-top, pacing at a substantial gate when I called out to her, but she had already noticed my truck and redirected her focus and course toward me, barely breaking her stride. Getting out of the cab, I was aware that she was in tears as she neared, raising a concern as I asked her if everything was okay.

She spoke not a word, but gave me a big hug in greeting me, displaying her own concern as in focusing her attention directly into my eyes said, "Nothing's the way you thought it would be, I can tell, and I can tell you that you're in danger."

"What the hell are you talking about?" I asked her, confused.

"'What am I talking about'? Don't you know?"

"No," I said, "I don't know."

"You were going to tell me something that went on last night, right?" she said.

"As a matter of fact, it was on my mind to tell you," I told her, and added, "Are you psychic?"

"Maybe." she said. "A little. What were you going to tell me?"

When Lucy and I lived together I thought at times that we were so close that she could sometimes anticipate what I was going to say. Today I had every intention of telling her everything I heard from under the bed, but then thought that I'd better hold back on my impulses, lest I reveal too much, and in reality, I don't really know too much. . . just what I heard.

"You really like her, don't you?" she asked.

"Like who?" I asked.

"Libby? It's alright, Horace," she said, "I don't mind you talking about her."

"Well, there's nothing to say," I told her, still not wanting to say much.

"What you think you know about her is less than you think." she said, smiling.

"I think, you may be right, Lucy."

She and I walked down the same trails we had done before, stopping at the same places, and Lucy stopped and stood still, at the one Weeping Willow as she had done before, staring at the dirt around the base. She pointed her finger at it and a tear came out of her eye, running down her cheek and then she sat, peering at the spot of earth between the roots, 'almost' as if it were a grave.

"What's the matter, Lucy? You look as if you've seen a ghost." I said, sitting next to her now, rubbing my hand softly on her back.

"Maybe I have," she said.

"Is there something buried there, or something?" I inquired, very curious now, thinking she may have buried something she regretted.

"You may want to dig that up someday." she said.

"What's there?" I asked, very curious now.

"You'll have to dig it up and see." she said. "Johnny and I are the only ones who know. He showed me this. Remember that I told you he was a bad dude, and that he did hits for people in the city?"

"You're not going to tell me that there's a body there, are you?" I asked.

"Let's get out of here." she said, standing up and I followed her back out the main trail, and closer to the lake.

I walked behind her and watching her walk in that sensuous sway that she's perfected, was as attractive to me as ever, reminding me of how her feminine way had always excited me to be near her. In the last two years or so of our relationship, to right before we split up, we were not in synch with each other and, for the most-part, I was blaming that on Johnny. Johnny Hetrick, the man who was supposed to be a 'cowardly hitman' and a gopher for Bill Bailey, it seemed, then I asked Lucy if she knew anything about, or what she knew about the Bender's partner Mr. Bill Bailey.

"Johnny never mentioned any names of people," she said, "just gravesites after the murders, trying to impress me, or threaten me, I guess."

"Gravesites?" I asked. "You mean to tell me there's more than what you showed me?"

"Do you feel like taking a ride, Horace?"

"Where too?"
"I'll show you, trust me." Lucy said as she climbed into the passenger side of the pick-up.

Under her direction, we drove down Route 313 to Swamp Road, then Forest Grove Road over to Route 413, and the old train station on Forest Grove Road at the corner. The cab of the truck was as silent as a graveyard until I asked her where we were going. Looking at me with those pretty eyes, she just smiled, telling me that it's not much further. Lucy seemed, 'almost as if' she was on something, like some weird drug, reminding me of the time that she and I were drinking at a party where we were invited by biker friends of ours, and no one told us the wine was spiked with what was known as angel dust. We were both in parallel Universes trying to communicate with each other within this mass of crazy people, but I became aware that the reason we were not relating was because she was completely speechless, silent and deaf to what was going on all around her, and a way of her keeping her sanity while I was freaking out with everybody else.

We parked the truck and began walking down the railroad tracks through the woods and fields toward the railroad crossing at Route 413, right about where Karma and I had passed that box truck just east of the Buckingham intersection where he also put a hurt on the driver and his crew. I could tell by the fresh scrapes in the macadam and two rogue and newly treaded radials, this must be the place where some of the runaway tires had scattered around on the highway and where Bill Bailey and Libby must have wiped out on their motorcycle. As we crossed the road on the tracks, looking both ways of course, we entered the forest of maples, oaks, hemlock, cedar and ash trees now surrounding us with their green, leafy canapes shading us from the early afternoon sun. The birds were chirping their songs high in the treetops while our footsteps created a steady beat, adding depth and rhythm as we paced ourselves in conversation, feeling the scented cedar breeze on our faces.

"So," I asked, "where are you taking me, Lucy? I can't say I've ever been in these woods, although it reminds me of a dream I had last night."

"Oh?" she replied.

"Yes. In the dream though," I continued, "there was a quarry a little further down, containing a reservoir of water within it."

"What?" she exclaimed, stopping to look at me, and causing me to stop and look right back at her.

"Yeah," I said. "In the dream, Lucy, you and I were walking down these similar tracks in the woods, and see that little jeep trail? That was in the dream, following along the tracks, and up here there was a quarry cliff above us to the left, and acting as a wall holding a lake of water.

"I thought you said you've never been here before." she said.

"I haven't," I told her, "except in a dream."

She stared at me with those same eyes that I've looked into for years, those eyes that have given me warmth in bad times and pleasure our good times of kissing and love making. Then remaining silent, she turned, focusing on the tracks ahead and continued walking as I followed.

"Is there something wrong?" I asked.

"No," she said, "but the quarry you're talking about, the one in your dream, is right up here as you said, on the left."

"Well . . ." I said, "Maybe I was here before and I just don't remember, because I think that it's too much of a coincidence otherwise."

"Didn't you ever hear of instinct? Or premonition?" she asked. Then continued, "Maybe you're right, that you were here before and it's a lost thought or memory, but I believe in premonition, a protective instinct that could be trying to tell you something."

"What? That I'm in danger?" I told her, thinking about one of her first comments to me earlier today.

"Are you making fun of me?" she asked.

"Not at all!"

We rounded a right bend in the train tracks and about a hundred yards later, we saw the distant cliffs of the quarry on the left and leading towards it through the woods was a toe path next to a jeep trail, which we followed carefully after descending the hill from the rails. After about five minutes of walking through the thick bushes and scrub on either side of the trail we were at the lower cliffs looking down into the abandoned quarry's body of water.

It was a lake, serene and still, with the exception of a few ripples from the mild breeze of the warm Spring day. The body of water was the size of about two or three football fields, with a clean, clear color as we could see the rocks at the shallow bottoms along the edges before it made a steep drop to a cold subaqueous darkness further out from the granite and bedrock shores. As we trekked a bit further along the side we heard a voice shout from down below, a person, male, wearing jeans and a t-shirt with his both feet soaking in the clear water waving for us to come on down. On the rim of the cliffs, only about fifty feet to out left I saw the rear of a blue taxicab with the number 160, and knew right away who's voice I was hearing, but wondered how and why he was here.

"Is that Karma?" I yelled down.

"Horace!" he said, sporting a big smile, and also said, "Lucy!"

"You know him?" I asked her, as we were negotiating our way down over the solid quarry rocks.

"Sure, I do," Lucy said, smiling her big smile that I've missed.

"How the hell did he get that cab back in here, and what the hell is he doing here?" I asked as she stopped me from stumbling by grabbing my arm.

"He took the jeep path," she said, "and he likes it back here."

"Where do you know him from?" I asked her.

"Oh, be quiet. I know lots of people." Lucy told me as we arrived at Karma's little spot by the water.

"Have a seat. There's some good sitters here, and comfortably hard," Karma said, referring to the round rocks and added, "How's things, Horace?"

"I'm fine," I said, "I didn't know you knew Lucy."

"I know lots of people," he said. "I'm a taxi driver."

Lucy got up and sat next to him, taking off her shoes and putting her bare feet in the cool water while I just looked on, wondering now what we were doing here. I felt like a third wheel as they started talking and laughing, splashing their feet at each other while sitting on the same rock above the huge reservoir. Karma lit a joint and we passed it around as he told the story on how the lake came to be, how when in 1955 the workers were digging when they struck an underground spring which shut-down the progress of the quarry business by filling the man-made hole, replacing it with the lake we see today. He told us that there's still cranes and machinery underneath the surface along with dead bodies of the quarry contractors accompanied by the more recent free-lance divers that didn't make it up from their daring dives from the cliffs; Then he added, "Not to mention the unsuspecting victims of a murder here and there.

"Like who?" Lucy asked.

"Well," he said, "you know, if someone wants to dump a body, get rid of the evidence . . ."

"Did they ever find bodies in here from murders?" I asked.

"I don't know. They never found a searching diver," he said, "but one particular diver that was looking for the body of a lost swimmer last seen jumping off of that cliff over there was lost for a month before his body was found, but get this, it was found in the Atlantic Ocean."

"What?" Lucy said.

"Yep." Karma continued, "They think that there's a strong underground spring or river that washes though here to the ocean."

"Is that possible?" Lucy asked.

"Anything's possible," I said, "but it's hard to believe the story about the body ending up in the ocean, although it is a good story."

"It's a true story," he said, "and there's another true story, this quarry lake is haunted by a beautiful dark-haired woman."

"Here we go." Lucy said with a skeptic grin.

"Really," he said, and continued his tale: "About 20 years ago there was a murder over in Jamison, a young woman in her early twenties. She had gotten pregnant by some dude who only used her for sex, lying to her and promising her he'd marry her. He wanted her to have an abortion when she approached him about her pregnancy, but she refused, and he beat her, nearly causing her to have a miscarriage."

"Why that son of a bitch!" Lucy exclaimed, as she handed the smoking reefer to Karma.

"Shush!" I said interested, "Let him tell the story."

"Anyway," Karma continued, while drawing in a lung-full of smoke, "The woman hid from him long enough to deliver a baby girl, which was about nine months later and then she approached him again, but this time regarding child support. Out of an enraged anger, this dude punched her in the face, knocking her into unconsciousness, but not dead. So, the dude took her to this quarry, to the top of that crag about a hundred feet up over there, on an old jeep trail and dropped her into the lake, with a big rock tied to her feet where she drowned."

"Oh my God," Lucy said, sliding her butt onto a more comfortable rock for listening. "how horrible!"

"Yeah," Karma said, "and her spirit has been here ever since, waiting for her baby girl to return to her, and for her murderer to return to her, so she could rip him apart, getting her vengeance. There's even another rumor that besides the infant she had left behind a little two-year old girl, both would be in their early to mid-twenties by now. Sometimes, I'm told, you can hear her crying at night when the moon is full, or maybe it's when there's a new moon."

"I'm told 'New Moon' is a powerful time for ghosts." I said, laughing of course.

"Shut up." Lucy said, giving me a swat with the back of her hand. "I love that story, even though it's sad."

"Sad and scary." Karma said as he took the joint from me.

I could see that Lucy was a bit smitten by him, but it could also be that I'm feeling a little bit insecure, and out of my realm with this instantaneous hike to the quarry lake, plus the fact that I didn't expect to see my taxi buddy from the other night sharing a rock here with her.

We talked a little more and I was getting stoned, so I laid myself back onto a flat stretch of granite and closed my eyes for a while, reflecting on what I heard last night when I was under the bed. I was curious on what Bill Bailey meant when he had mentioned Karma's name, and his cab number, and wondered how the hell Johnny was involved in all of this. In the meantime, Karma and Lucy were laughing and having a good time with each other, like they were the best of friends, or something. I then told him about Bill Bailey and Libby coming home unexpectedly and them mentioning something about the box truck and police and heard them mentioning his name and taxicab number, and something about it being impossible that it was him or his cab, and that "Hetrick" and Bill seeing to it that it couldn't have been he or cab 160 that they saw.

"It was me," Karma said. "You were with me. You know it was me."

"But why would he doubt it?" I asked. "And why was he so explicit about him and Hetrick 'taking care of it'?"

"I don't know," he said.

"Hetrick?" Lucy said, "He mentioned Johnny Hetrick?"

"Yeah, he did," I said.

"I don't know," Karma said. "You'll have to ask Bill himself about that one. I know he had a hitman he was working with, or so I heard."

"Well, I'm getting confused and mixed signals here," I said, "like 'why are we here', and just 'why did you bring me here' Lucy?"

"It's pretty here," she said, and continued, "I had a feeling that this Bill Bailey was a sleaze after hearing Johnny talking about him."

"Do you think Johnny did hits for him? For Bill Bailey?" I asked.

"I know he did," she said.

"You mean, like that mound of dirt under the willow tree?" I asked, but she got quiet and was now kicking her feet nervously in the water.

"What mound of dirt?" Karma asked with a grin as he handed me the joint.
"Never mind," I answered, taking the smoky spliff and drawing a long toke.
"You worry too much, Horace." he said, then started telling a story about the quarry, and about a dream he had.
"A while back," he narrated, "I had this dream that I had died, and had gone to a place where all the souls met . . . all the souls of the Universe. They had to take account of their lives; good people, bad people, and basically; just exist as human beings in an afterlife. A voice had told me that everyone goes to heaven, and arrives precisely at the same instant, since there is no set time in the afterlife, only a special time sequence delegated to each individual for their individual tasks, according to how they lived their life. The only catch is that everyone has to take an account within their own personal Universe for things, good and bad that they had done."

As he was talking it was reminding me, like sort of a déjà vu, and my own personal account of a dreamlike state that was at this point, vaguely familiar, and I was fascinated and now intrigued with his allegorical tale as he continued.
"In the dream, a voice said the people here in this pre-heaven limbo place who have for instance murdered someone, taken another life before that person's time, will face the same exact circumstances that they inflicted upon their victims before they can enter Paradise. Another person may go through a different and less drastic task to get to the

same place, in different time sequences, entering Paradise at the same time."

"That's pretty deep," Lucy said, taking the joint.

"No winners?" I jokingly asked.

"Everyone wins," he said.

"But that means that the bad, those evil people who murder and rapists, and molesters get in too?" Lucy asked, handing the joint back to Karma.

"Yeah," he said, "but you're missing my point. The evil will have to go through the pain and suffering they had inflicted upon their victims."

"And the victims have no memory of what they had gone through?" I asked.

"WOW, Horace." Karma told me. "Were you in my dream too? That's exactly right! The voice in the dream told me that the victims never experienced the pain and suffering, because their tormentors, the rapists, the murderers, etc. are living that part of their horrible moment to balance out the Universe so everyone gets into Paradise, and the inflictors of the suffering have no choice but to physically experience it."

Handing the joint to me, he took another out of his pocket and lit his new one off of the one he gave me, and handed it to Lucy, continuing to tell his narrative of his dream.

"Anyway, in this dream I saw Bill and some dude that looked like Peter Frampton driving along the top of that ridge up there in a car, but I couldn't make out the car. I was sort of, in a misty void, but I could see them very clear. They were scared to death and were unable to get out of the car as it was being pushed by someone over the crevice and into the lake, exploding into flames as they screamed, and it eventually sank beneath the surface while they both burned, then drowned in the submerged, infernal wreckage."

"What a horrible way to go! Oh My God, Johnny looks like Peter Frampton." Lucy said, holding her hand over her mouth, as if shocked, when she handed the newly lit joint over to me.

"So?" I said. "It's a story, Lucy, a dream.

"Anyway," Karma continued, "It didn't seem like a dream and those people I saw were experiencing a murder that they themselves caused, and they'll spend the rest of their time in their limbo undoing each and every murder they caused before they get into their final paradise."

"Well," I said, "Bill Bailey's alive and well the last time I looked, so your dream was just a dream . . . and a great story for a campfire. But you know what? I was reminded that I had similar visions, or dreams, about a Voice that spoke to me about the same kind of thing, a pre-heaven limbo, and souls waiting and paying their debt with tasks. Unfortunately, it's all too, too vague right now."

"I don't know, Horace, just keep your eyes open and ears to the ground," he told me.

"I had a dream last week. He's in danger," Lucy said, regarding me.

"Danger is a broad term," Karma said, taking the joint from me and handing it to Lucy, who threw it into the lake.

"HEY!" he said.

"I think we should be heading back, Horace," she said.

"I'll give you a lift," Karma said as we all started to get up, stretch, and made our way to the crest where his cab was parked. On the way Lucy shared a dream where she said she remembered me as clear as day hugging and holding her and comforting her as she sat in a bathtub, and before that, she remembered looking for her friend Johnny while she was carrying a baseball bat because she knew that he was going to hurt me. She said she'll never forget how sweet she thought I was being to her but that was all she could remember of the dream, other than being on a lot somewhere and hitting Johnny in the head with the bat and apologized that it was not as adventurous as Karma's mystifying memoir.

"Bathtub?" I curiously asked.

"Yeah, bathtub."

We all climbed into the cab, Lucy in the front with Karma while I jumped into the back seat, and upon starting it, he was able to loop his way down through a few trees and onto the jeep trail. We were slinking in and out of the tall oak, maple and poplar trees and protruding rocks, finding our way through the late day shades in the forest to Route 413, then over to Forest Grove Road, then the train station where I left the pick-up. I climbed out of the back seat and to my surprise, Lucy stayed, saying she's getting a ride with him.

"I don't mind taking you to where you want to go." I told her.

"I got her Horace, if you don't mind," he said, "Besides, it's getting late, and she asked me to take her."

"No worries," I said. And with that, I watched him pull away, with my Lucy. 'My Lucy'? What the hell am I thinking? I have to undo this selfish juvenile attitude of mine regarding her and my past with her, because it was my past.

On my way home to the Bender's I reflected on the day, and also last night and I'm wondering where all of this is leading. All I know is that I have a different outlook towards Libby and the band now, and that in order to resolve my discrepancies I'll need to talk about it to someone I can trust. Although Jordan has been somewhat, suspicious of Libby and the 'accidental' death of Robert Bender, I'm finding it hard to feel as if I can put my complete trust in mentioning any of my findings to him, but I felt I must cross that bridge. I'm also replaying Karma's story, his dream tale in my mind and find it fascinating that in a strange way, I had similar dreams or recants about a 'misty limbo pre-paradise' type of place in the annals of my distant memories back when I first met Libby and Robert, but I thought that all of that was drug induced from a not-so-clean lifestyle; Maybe I'm hallucinating all of this.

Something tells me that something happened during that blackout at the bar, the Sportsman's Bar that night that Libby and I had the spaghetti dinner, something that might be a key to a lot of what's been going on, or 'maybe I simply think too much about nothing.'

CHAPTER - TWELVE

It was dark when I arrived at the Bender's home and the house was lit up like there's someone home, with all of the lights along the driveway. I see Jordan leaving as he had just walked out the front door and I flag him down.

"Where are you headed, brother?" I asked as I jumped out of the pick-up.

"New Hope," he said with a big smile. "'Got a date, and I see you have one too, so I'm out of here, dude."

"What?" I asked, tapping him on the shoulder, "What date?"

"It was a great gig we had last night too." Jordan said, and added, "You missed a good party afterwards, but I know that's not your scene."
"What do you mean I 'have a date'?" I asked again.
"Libby." he said. "She really looks good too. She's been cooking up something special for you and was waiting for you to get home."
"She's crazy, you know." I told him, shaking my head.
"Uh huh, crazy about you."

I gave him another punch to the shoulder and he hit me back saying, "Don't do anything I wouldn't do," and he was off, taking the BMW for the night. I was wondering what was going on with Libby and remembered the dinner the other night where she looked ravishing, fixing us a hedonistic night of pleasure and surprising me with it at the same time. And now, walking up to the front door I was expecting something of the same from what Jordan told me. However, after what I heard last night from her and Bill, I'm not sure what to expect here, or how to react, so, I'll just have to walk through the front door and play it by ear.
"Hello! Anybody home?" I yelled, letting her know I'm here.
"Hey!" she said as she greeted me, running from the kitchen. Libby was wearing her black slingshot bikini and thong, leaving nothing to the imagination, revealing everything.
"Are we swimming tonight?" I asked, jokingly.
"You and I are doing the hot tub tonight," she said as she hugged me close to her and my hands couldn't help but

squeeze her firm behind. "The pool's finally ready too. You haven't seen that yet because that part of the house was closed off for the winter. The guys came to set it all up today."

"You mean that area on the back of the house?" I asked. "I thought that was a sun room under construction."

"A sun room with a heated pool and a hot tub sauna." she said, taking my hand and walking me into the area she was talking about as she continued, "The one wall is opened to the outside now so it's like the indoor pool is an outside patio now. We do that every year before summer."

"This is unreal." I said, walking into the area with the hot tub and pool. It was an open patio with the pool next to the concrete patio leading to the back lawn and the part closest to the entrance was all under glass skylights that open like a drawbridge to the night sky with a push of a button. The back-patio wall opens and closes as a sliding wall, keeping the heat in if winter swimming is desired. Libby said that she might keep it open and operating all year round now, but in the past, they only opened it up for the summer months, and tonight is a warm night.

"Horace, you were sensational last night," she said, taking my hand and leading me back toward the kitchen.

"Last night?" I said.

"I know I didn't get the chance to tell you," Libby said, "but you had gone to bed early and must have left the hotel early this morning. I thought you were flawless in your delivery."

"Thanks," I said, smiling and giving her a peck on the cheek as we entered the kitchen, "You're sweet, and you sounded pretty damn good yourself."

The savory aroma of her cooking permeated the house and was making my belly growl with hunger, as I hadn't eaten all day and I was still a little stoned.

"Libby! Wow! What are you making? I mean, this house really smells like some serious home cooking!" I said.

"I thought you'd never ask." she said, as she sat me down on the stool at the counter while I looked at all the pots and pans on the stove steaming, giving off the coveted redolence pervading the air while she went to work, and purposely kept bending over, purposely showing off her derriere through the thong of that new skimpy slingshot bikini of hers, knowing I was watching.

"These fish are fresh, just caught from the stocked pond." she said, holding up the large pan they were in. "I was out there fishing for only an hour before I hooked a 2 lb. trout and about a 2 lb. catfish, skinned and cleaned them right there on the dock."

"You wore that suit fishing?" I asked.

"Sure, why not? I needed to get some sun." she said, spinning around, with her arms out like a model, showing her ample top and firm bottom through that tiny suit and added, "How do I look?"

"You always look great." I told her, then asked: "Shouldn't you be wearing an apron over that or something? I mean, how the hell does that thing stay on? You might get burned."

"Nonsense." she laughed, and continued, "and don't worry, I showered before I started dinner. I just love this suit."

I love her 'new suit' too, if you can call it that, there's nothing there but three stretchy strings holding it together formulating eye-candy as an appetizer for, what she's 'apparently' cooking up for this evening. Her body was perfect and as I watched her I'm suddenly reminded of last night's adventures and me hiding under the bed when I glance over to where the window was broken from her climbing in. I asked her about it and the note she left, but I wanted to hear her story on how it happened as she brought over a large tray of raw oysters on ice."

"How did the window get broken?" I asked, as she sensuously sucked down the first oyster inches away from me, staring into my eyes.

"I forgot my house key, and the door was locked." she said grinning.

"So, you came home last night?" I inquired.

"I was here early this morning," she said, holding another slimy mollusk on a half shell, squirting lemon on it, right in front of my face. "Eat it! It's an aphrodisiac."

I slurped it in and it was delicious, but I almost gagged because I thought I felt it moving in my mouth, so I swallowed it whole.

"It moved!" I said, holding my throat.

"Of course, it did," she said, laughing hysterically, "they're fresh too!" Then she slurped down another and handed me a salted rimmed glass containing a margarita after she took a large sip herself.

"Did you call the guy to fix the window?" she asked.

"No," I said, "I didn't get the chance. I went over to the lake for a ride and just . . ."

"Don't worry about it," she said, "that can be taken care of any time. Have some more oysters, and I have filet mignon cooking too, and a nice salad."

"Well," I said, "I can eat a horse."

"Better leave room in there for a wild night of Libby!" she said, rubbing her full chest in my face, then leaving me the oysters and turning her attention to the stove.

Libby looked so good that the thought of being with her tonight melted away all of the feelings I was having about last night's episode in the bedroom regarding her and Bill, but this wouldn't be for long, for there were a lot of questions I need answered if I'm to maintain my present relationship with her and the band.

Libby placed a steaming plate of catfish filet with a salad beside it in front of me and my hunger took over, as I relished every morsel and ate it like I was famished, because I was.

"You certainly like catfish," she said, smiling at me while she ate her trout. "Both these guys put up a good fight for their lives too, but as usual I always win," she added, giving me a wink.

"I didn't know you fished, nor did I know you had a stocked pond." I told her as I chewed.

"The pond's always been there," she said, and added, "and there's a lot you don't know about me."

"Well," I said, "I know you're a good cook!"

"You are so sweet." Libby said. Then she walked around the counter from her plate to give me a long, and very wet kiss, sitting on my lap, then passionately kissed my neck.

"Wow!" I said. "You're making me hungry in more ways than one!"

"I aim to tease," she said getting herself up, then laughing and finished by saying, "I mean, I aim to please!"

She was right the first time, for I was feeling that sense of my erotic blood-flow, right beside my craving for food, and the passion for both was so strong that I finished up everything on my plate right before Libby plopped down the cut of steak onto it with more salad greens.

"Eat up," she said, "but remember you're going to take care of me too."

She kept serving and I kept eating. I was like a bottomless pit, inhaling all of the food that was put in front of me like a lion with its kill as I ripped apart the steaks and gnawed at the corn on the cobb. That joint I had smoked earlier with Lucy and Karma and the fact that I had nothing to eat since this morning put me into a 'munchy mood' that it felt like I couldn't stop eating, but I did, and only because I was full.

"Wow," she said, "I'm impressed. I'm ready for dessert now. How about you?"

"I-I . . . dessert?" I asked.

"I'll tell you what," she said, "let's go for a swim first."

She pulled me up from my stool and started to undo my pants, but I stopped her, and I took over from where she left off, slipping off my pants and shirt while she tossed me a skimpy pair of black swim trunks. Then as soon as I slid them on she had me by the hand, pulling me toward the back of the house where the pool area was. She let go of my hand and ran for the diving board, where she sprung and did a double flip like one of those Olympic divers and popped flawlessly into the water.

"Damn," I said, "I didn't know you could dive like that."

"Like I said, there's a lot you don't know about me!" she told me, turning onto her back and doing the backstroke.

"Well?" she said. "The water's not coming for you, you're going to have to come in!"

I jumped in and swam to the end of the pool and back before she and I started tossing the frisbee and enjoying idle chatter in the dim pool lights beneath the open moonless night sky. Soon I was on my back in the chlorine-scented water doing a soft backstroke and bumping my bare shoulder against hers as we looked at the Universe together under the night sky talking about the energies of the cosmos and the reasons for creation, and how we may have gotten here in the first place. That's when she told me that she stopped doing the needles and hard drugs because of a total spiritual realization she came to the other day when she hit-up meth for the last time, and it reminded me of my previous experience of the exact same thing.

The water was warm, and the air was cool and clear as we played and talked about music, the band and a little about Bender's Bar before I asked her a question that had been eating away at me to inquire about all night but was subdued by my lust for her and my now satiated appetite.

"What's the deal with Bill Bailey?" I asked. "Are you two seeing each other?"

"What kind of a question is that?" she asked. "Who have you been talking too?"

"What do you mean who have I been talking too? I'm just asking. I always see you two together." I told her.

"I'm not with him now, am I?" she said, swimming the sidestroke up to me. "Besides, what business is it of yours?"

When she said that, she was close enough to reach out, surprising me and dunking my head under the surface, holding me down by my hair. With my eyes opened I could see her firm abs beneath her full breasts barely hiding behind those slingshot straps in front of me and I reached for them, but she anticipated my every move, rendering me powerless, and at her mercy, like an angled catfish. I began to panic remembering hearing Bill the other night accusing her of murder and my imagination was going wild as I desperately tried to reach the surface, but she pushed me deeper, wrapping her thighs tightly around my head. I grabbed at her legs and scratched and punched and tried to pull those strong gams apart, but my efforts were fruitless because she had dragged me to the ladder and used it as her body's leverage, and I started to black-out. Just at that moment, she pulled me by my hair to the surface, where I gulped a large breath of air and coughed incessantly. She was already on the pool's edge pulling me onto the wet concrete, pressing down on my chest which caused me to cough more.

"Are you alright?" she asked.

"What the fuck is the matter with you?" I yelled, hoarsely in a mild cough. "You almost drowned me!

"I'm sorry," she said, "I forgot what you asked me. What was the question?"

"I forget . . . and get off of me!" I said as my coughing soon subsided.

"You're not good at holding your breath under water, are you?" she asked, fixing her skimpy bikini straps with an evil grin.

"You sure like to play rough!" I said, shoving her by her firm butt from behind, back into the pool.

I watched her toned figure splash the surface and sink, slowly to the bottom of the 9 feet of water and lay flat on the pool's tiled base, motionless. As I smiled, I yelled at her that I'm not going to fall for her droll humor and her wishes to entice me to rescue her.

Her apoplectic form appeared to be paralyzed when, as air bubbles flowed freely from her faced-down, lifeless framework I realized that I may have caught her by surprise and actually hurt her. Upon surmising this, I immediately dove in and straight to her helpless figure, grabbing her under the arms and pulled her dead weight, with all my might to above the water's surface, where she was facing me, inches away from my eyes.

"Libby!" I shouted in a panic.

Her eyes opened, and she spit a mouthful of water in my face and bit me on the nose, laughing her heart out before she started breathing heavy.

"You are soooo gullible!" she said, continuing her laughing and catching her breath. "I can hold my breath for 4 minutes, sometimes longer." she said.
"You scared the hell out of me." I told her, climbing to the pool's edge once more.
"'Still hungry for dessert?" she asked.
"Dessert?" I said.
"You and me, babe, dessert! Filet of banana Libby split!" she said, as she jumped onto me while I stood; and wrapping her arms and legs around me tightly slipped her long and sensuous tongue into my mouth.

That was it! That was all I needed to completely put behind me, and out of my mind everything I heard her and Bill talking about last night, for now I'm acting on the impulse of the moment, and all I could think about is carrying her upstairs to the soft, silk sheets on the king-sized bed she and I have shared ever since I had first met her.

'This woman has an incredibly strong and forceful way about her every being', I kept thinking to myself. Not only have I seen her play the drums like no one else, but she's very pretty and sexy; and she can cook, do construction, drive and operate a backhoe, fish and clean her catch, and at the same time, carry herself as a soft and effeminate woman, caring for me and satisfying my every need, while allowing me to satisfy hers. I'm falling in love and there's nothing I can do about it, at least, at this lustful space in time anyway. We blew off using the hot tub tonight.

Libby and I made love like there were no tomorrow, and as if it was the last thing on earth we would ever do together. The earth moved for us over and over and over again as our sweat and passion ran through our skins while we slid mercilessly on each other, front and back, top to bottom, for what seemed-to-be days, but was merely hours before we both rested in the ecstasy of our erotically intimate encounter. As she lay on her back next to me breathing heavily, and in unison with me while we looked at the full mirror on the ceiling, I could see her smile. I could recognize it past her complete nakedness in our universe and sense her feeling of satiated joy percolating through her very being, and when I touched her arm with my open hand I felt in her warmth that those feelings were sincere and mutual.

"Damn." she said. "You have the knack, don't you, Horace?"

"I don't know what you mean," I said, "I love being with you, so, what's wrong with showing it?"

"No one's asking you not to." she said, rolling over to kiss me all over my face. "You're one talented guy."

"I aim to please." I said.

"Modest too." Libby said, as she cuddled up next to me while I stared at the both of us in the mirror for a while.

I'm trying not to think too much, but I can't help it as the thoughts of the strange happenings were returning. Robert's sudden 'accidental' death, Libby's cold reactions and lack of resonant mourning for her husband, Karma the taxi driver, Lucy, the experience of Bill and Libby's comments the other night, it was all swirling around in my head now, like an endless whirlpool and I was stuck in the vortex, helpless. I then decided to ask Libby what her real relationship, with Bill Bailey was all about.

"Libby." I said, but there was no answer as I observed her nude reflection in the mirror.

"Libby."

"Libby!" I repeated, but I could hear her dainty and faint snore while she lay motionless.

Exhausted from the day and weekend, I gave up my quest for waking her while I closed my eyes and drifted off to a peaceful and well-deserved slumber.

CHAPTER - THIRTEEN

When I awoke from my abeyance of a peaceful and welcomed sleep, I became aware immediately that Libby was up and making a racket downstairs as she was cleaning up the pots, pans, and dirty dishes. While dressing and looking out the bedroom window at the big front yard lawn I became aware of a figure standing in the middle, on some of the new turf sod. It was a female form and upon looking at the form more intensely and becoming better focused from a night of bliss, I realized it was none other than Lucy, waving for me to come out to meet her. I finished putting on my socks and sneakers then ran down the stairs through the kitchen with Libby yelling from behind me, asking what was going on. I ignored her and ran out to Lucy who had given me the impression that the situation with her seemed desperate, so when I got within a few feet of her she said, "Hurry! There's no time to waste!"

"Where are we going?" I asked as I tried to catch my breath.

"To Lake Galena," she said, "Hurry!"

She and I ran to my pick-up and jumped in without looking back, while Libby kept on hollering and asking me where I'm going. All the way to the lake Lucy was crying and apologizing, and telling me that she had just seen Johnny, who told her where to find it.

"Find what?" I asked.

Just then, and almost 'on cue' as a distraction to my thoughts, I turned on the radio, and on it was the news about three men found dead by hanging in the New Hope woods along the toe-path, right out back from a gay bar that Jordan used to frequent. They said the men were stripped naked and painted with Nazi signs and writing in black stating: **"Lifeless with no morals, no virtue!"**

"Oh my God!" I shouted. "What the hell is happening in this world of ours? I hope Jordan's alright."

"Just keep driving, and please hurry!" Lucy said.

"It sounds like it's a matter of life and death," I told her, "the way you're acting!"

"It is! It is!" she cried, and added, "Oh, please hurry!"

We got to Lake Galena and Lucy jumped out of the truck running, and I followed, now running as fast as I could to just keep up with her. She was wearing a thin, long summer dress, which flowed behind her in the wind she created by her running like a ghostly presence as she sprinted, with me following down the trails that she and I had previously walked. Zigging and zagging through those woods wasn't easy with the rocky trail and the untrimmed brush overgrowing onto the paths, but my inquisitive sense of soul and imagination was curious and now anxious of what this was she intended to bring to my attention so hysterically.

When we entered a grotto with a few maple trees she suddenly stopped, then started trail-blazing toward the right, through a series of rhododendron shrubs before stopping completely, looking down at the base of a maple. The look on her face was sullen and pale with tears flowing from her eyes when her arm reached out and pointed directly at the mound of fresh overturned brown earth and said, "There!"

"There?" I asked. "There, what?"

"Dig there! NOW!" she demanded.

"What's there?" I asked. "What's buried there?"

"There's no time!" she said, and repeated, "Dig! Now!"

To me . . . it reminded me of a fresh grave, but in the middle of the woods and in the middle of nowhere, but I was so curious and befuddled at Lucy's desperation that I got down on my hands and knees and started digging, using a flat rock and a pocket knife to remove the soft topsoil mixed with subsoil that was still freshly mounded. In minutes I was hitting something solid, like what 'appeared to be' a top of a hollow-sounding wooden shipping crate, causing my anxious energy to rejuvenate, inciting me to dig away harder at the remaining soil.

Lucy's tears were flowing as she wept, sobbing directly behind me and my heart was pounding while I used the screwdriver feature in the knife to pry the edges of the box, lifting the lid, still having no idea what I might find.

"Oh my God!" she shouted in an emotional yawp when the lid was removed.

"Jordan!" I screamed.

Inside the buried box was none other than my friend Jordan. He was very still and laying on his side, fully clothed in the garments I last saw him in, but his fingers and knuckles raw and injured from what appeared to be scratching and clawing at the lid. I couldn't tell if he was dead or alive since I couldn't find a pulse, but his arm was warm as I lifted him from the wooden crate and laid him on his back. I began mouth to mouth resuscitation and at first, had gotten no response. Then, in a few minutes, Jordan let in a large gulp of fresh air on his own and began to cough while I sat him up.

"Thank God!" Lucy said, over and over while she fell to her knees.

Jordan didn't say anything as he sat, staring at the tree while his breathing slowly became stabilized, along with my own with a sense of relief, which soon turned to confusion. I couldn't figure out what the hell was going on here, other than my friend was buried alive, 'apparently' by that screwball, Johnny. I then heard another female voice calling in the distance from behind me, at the same time that I became aware that Lucy had gone, leaving Jordan and I on our own.

"Lucy!" I yelled, wondering where she went, but there was a response from another female, and the other female was Libby, who had followed me from the house when I didn't answer her.

"Horace!" she called, as she walked closer to us from down the path.

"Libby! Over here!" I said, now sitting directly across from Jordan, while he sat with his arms wrapped around his knees pulled up to his chest, with his bloodshot eyes, peering from his black face looking dismal and hopeless when they glanced up at me.

"These people are animals," were his first words to me.

"What people?" I asked as I heard Libby's footsteps closing in behind me.

"Her friends!" he said, leaping up as if to lunge at her but his weak legs collapsed beneath him.

"What happened?" Libby asked, shocked and surprised, "What happened to Jordan? What's he doing here?"

"I don't know!" I told her, "Lucy came by the house and brought me here, to save Jordan."

"Lucy?" she said, still shocked and surprised.

"If it wasn't for her," I said, "Jordan would have died. She saved his life!"

Libby looked around as if looking for the lady in question and said, "Where is she?"

"I don't know," I told her, "she was pretty upset. I hope she's alright. My main concern is for my friend here and finding out just what the hell happened. We need to go to the police."

"Don't do that," Libby said, "It's not a good idea, not right now, anyway."

"Somebody tried to kill him!" I told her. "What better time to go to the police?"

"They won't do a fucking thing!" she said adamantly.

Jordan sat up and leaned forward, glaring at her and said, "Your friends are fucked up! They're murderers!"

Libby didn't say a word in response to Jordan's accusations but glanced away, and her gaze went toward another tree a little further across the grotto and closer to an extension of the trail, a Weeping Willow, the same willow that I remember Lucy and I staring at, or rather, it was Lucy who was looking at a strange mound beneath the tree.

"Horace," Libby said, "I had the strangest dream last night, and I don't usually get frightened easily, but I was terrified."

"You're going to tell me about a dream you had!?" I said, "You're going to tell me that NOW?"

"It's important and pertains to all of this." she said.

"In the dream I saw that guy Johnny Hetrick, the guy you were talking about at that bar, the night you blacked out," she said.

"Go on," I told her, now curious while Jordan just stood up, stretching his legs.

"In the dream he had brought me directly here, to this very place where we are right now, and I was going to tell you about it this morning," she continued, "The thing is, Johnny had told me to go to that willow tree over there and to dig."

"Dig for what?" I asked.

"I don't know," she said. "Did you know what you were digging for? I'm telling you, Horace, I'm getting goose bumps all over. This is very creepy!"

"Are you making this up?" I asked her.

"Are you making 'Lucy' up?" she responded.

"You had a dream to dig over there?" I asked, but she responded: "You had a dead person tell you to dig under the maple tree?" she said.

"You're confusing me," I said, and added: "What dead person?"
"Lucy is dead!" Libby said. "You don't remember?"

Libby stood there, and her glare went right through me, as if she was seeing right into my soul and I had gotten a chill staring into those beautiful green eyes of hers. I nervously looked down and away from them to see she had beads of sweat on her tanned chest, revealed by her low-cut blue top, and I instantly looked directly back into her pretty face.
"How could she be dead?" I asked. "She was just here!"

Then looking back at Jordan, I said, "Jordan, tell her that Lucy was just here." But Jordan just walked over to the tree, still trying to stretch before sitting back down, against it, totally ignoring me.
"I have to do this," she said, and continued with: "Don't you guys leave, or go anywhere."

Libby walked over to the willow and started digging, using a shovel she had carried in with her already prepared for the excavation. I sat quietly with Jordan while he kept shaking his head occasionally and mumbled something that was incoherent, but when I asked, 'what was that?' he just shook his head again, as we listened to the digging sounds of Libby's shovel. I also thought about how we had all originally gotten together, and the coincidence that he knew of Libby before me, and our 'chance' assemblage of this band. Neither he or I would have ever, even remotely, envisioned this particular scenario of our time together as a summary of our present accomplishments, sitting under this tree and wondering what the hell is going on here. We just wanted to play music, for Christ's sake!

"Hey!" Libby shouted, and out of breath. "There's a dead body here! And I'm afraid it's Skip, my missing saxophone player!"

As I slowly walked over, leaving Jordan sitting under the tree while approaching the hole in the ground under the willow, I saw it was a shallow grave, not unlike Jordan's, at about a foot and a half to where the lid could be lifted. There laid a decomposed body of a man holding a saxophone snug in his arms, as if his very life depended on it and there was a note scribbled out in pen, which Libby pulled free from within the boney and decomposed hand. She slowly stood up from her crouching position while unfolding the paper fully open, so she could read it out aloud over the remains of her friend Skip.

"BILL BAILEY - HETRICK – LANGDON - FISHMAN – HARRIS – ALL MURDERERS!"

Libby began sobbing, like I saw her sob the night that Robert was pronounced dead, and she fell to the ground, laying herself across Skip and his saxophone. Just at that moment the sky opened up and a surprising sun-shower rained down on us through the willow and the maple and the surrounding trees sounding off a mellow hissing echo all around us that came in like a ghostly sonnet serenading the dead with the accompaniment of a soft breeze on what we had figured was the first day of summer.

I stooped beside Libby, putting my opened hand onto her bare upper back as I crouched beside her, and sensed someone directly behind me. Turning around, I looked up at Jordan's face, also with a quiet, single tear creeping down his cheek as he stared directly at Skip, holding a distant stare which soon turned into an angry glare.

"AAH! FUCKING PEOPLE! THESE FUCKING PEOPLE!" he said, ripping the note from beneath Libby's hand and holding it in front of his face, he said, "YES!"

"Jordan!" I said, but he interrupted me.

"Four of these guys, I know, and I saw what they did to friends of mine! They did this to my friend Skip too!"

Jordan was becoming irate and continued, "I knew Skip! He and I jammed with Libby years ago! The other night," he was rambling, "The other night! They sodomized friends of mine, and me, they tortured them because they were gay! They lynched them right in front of me, made me watch, in the woods near Solebury . . ."

"JORDAN! Take it easy!" I said.

I was standing up by now, grabbing him because I thought he was freaking out, but he backed away, taking a boxer-style swing at me that I successfully blocked, then ducked the next one. The third punch didn't miss, catching me clean under the eye, knocking me back and causing me to lose my balance, falling directly onto Libby.

By the time I was able to get my bearings Libby had already slipped herself from under me, leaving my ass on the decomposing Skip and my hand on his sax, but Jordan had disappeared down the trail like a puff of smoke. At this time the sun-shower was petering out and Libby had simultaneously dried her tears by lifting her top over her face, wiping them clean away with her emotions as she started her demanding spiel.

"We can't go to the cops." she said. "I hope Jordan isn't going to do anything stupid."

"JORDAN!" I yelled down the trail.

"Shush!" she said, continuing, "He's gone. He's lost it too, and I hope poor Jordan pulls it together."

"What's happening?" I asked her, not expecting a straight answer from the way she's looking around, those pretty green eyes darting about the area as if searching for a solution.

"We need to cover Skip," she said, "Lay him to rest."

"Bury him again?"

"Yes," she said, "of course!"

"That note," I said.

"Bill, and his henchmen," she replied, "buried him alive. This man lying here saved my life once. They killed him, but he may have been drugged or beaten first; it's a horrible way to go, none the less."

She and I shoveled the dirt back over the closed box containing Skip and his saxophone and packed it down firm, and Libby also replanted some flowers she had uprooted from the other side of the path with the bulbs, inserting them in the fresh topsoil across the top of the mound along with fresh tuffs of grass.

"Gardening?" I said, sarcastically, wanting us to evacuate this depressing spot but she ignored my humor and comment as she finished up.

"We have a lot to talk about," she said, "but let's get back to the house."

There were only a few leisure people scattered in typical weekend fashion around the park and on the paths as it was already late afternoon while we walked back to the pick-up, and as we did I was looking for signs of Jordan. I had hoped I would at least see him waiting at the truck, but the pick-up was sitting empty in the shade right where I left it and there were no signs of my musician friend.

"We won't see him." Libby said.

"See who?" I answered, acting like I didn't know who she was talking about.

"I know you're looking for Jordan," she said, "and he's gone, I'm telling you."

"Oh." I said being a smart ass, "I guess he's dead? Like you said Lucy was?"

"You really don't remember, do you? About Lucy?" Libby said, now beginning to scare me with her insistence.

"I have no clue what the hell you're talking about!" I stated.

Libby backed me softly against the side of the pick-up and looked up into my eyes, with a deep and penetrating gaze.

"Horace," she spoke softly, "do you remember the one night we played at the club? Do you remember the connection?"

As she was telling me this I couldn't take my eyes off of hers if I tried. The same warm feelings that were always there, but dormant, were now surfacing while she was staring and pressing herself up to me and I started to tremble.

"Yes. Of course, I do." I happily responded.

"You and I are spiritual lovers," she said, "the spiritual 'walk-in's' completing Horace and Libby, and now we're completing each other."

"You're going to have to clarify yourself, Libby." I told her. "I'm not getting it."

I was beginning to think that the drugs and narcotics that she had been doing before and after I met her were finally taking their toll on her pretty brain cells, because what she's trying to relate to me came across as pure gibberish.

"That first night at Bender's, at the club." she said. "You became aware and whole, recognizing yourself and me."

As she mentioned that, a strange sensation came over me, like an aura of peace and understanding while I remembered the evening, and the first and only time I ever stuck a needle into my arm. I remembered the sensation of a feeling of separation ending and becoming one, but at the time I wasn't sure it was the drug, the methamphetamine, but more of a metaphysical nature while being drawn towards Libby at precisely the same time, a kind of an awakening. But when it all was happening and due to having never shooting-up drugs before, I resigned these sensations and emotions to the nature of the amphetamine I had injected into my blood stream.

"I remember." I said.

"Let's go home," Libby said, smiling in relief, "we have a lot to talk about, and a lot to do."

Libby had brought her Mustang following me to the lake so in the drive home I was alone and was of course quiet, and I had a lot to think about. I felt like I've known

Libby forever, like we've always been together, even though it's only been a few weeks or so, and I do remember reading about the new age beliefs of some folks; who believe in Walk-In spirits or angels who take over for a spirit who's ready to leave a body of a human being. I've also read about reincarnation and soulmates, but up until now, it was only reading, simple entertainment for my simple mind.

As I was thinking about it and trying to concentrate on my driving I became aware of a tinge of déjà vu surfacing, bringing me to a not so distant memory of separation, an angel, and a misty universal room between heaven and hell, and an entity known to me only as 'the Voice'.

Back at the house Libby and I showered together, refraining mutually from having sex but cleaning and washing each other thoroughly before dressing into matching purple silk pajamas. Neither of us were hungry as she made a tall pitcher of ice-cold tea, taking it out to the patio by the indoor pool where we sat in the comfortable black-cushioned chairs side by side overlooking the lawn. Libby was the first one to speak, reminding me about Lucy and asking me about her.

"I thought you and Lucy broke up, you know, when you moved out." she stated as she poured our glasses full.

"We did," I answered, "but I see her now and then at the lake when I'm taking my bike rides."

Libby sat up from her lounging and taking a sip of her tea, leaned back again and told me that I have to listen to her carefully, because what she's going to tell be may sound unbelievable, but she was hoping to jog my memory of the other night when I blacked out. She pushed my lounging chair back and laid herself on top of me, telling me to think really hard about that night at the Sportsman's Bar and about what had happened. I was holding her, and we were lying comfortably while she said to concentrate, and meditate with my eyes closed, but to try not to drift into sleep. As I did, the strange sensation came over me again as I felt a tumbling into an oblivion, but it was more of a peaceful floating rather than a fearful falling. I felt myself outside of myself, a familiar notion I've experienced before, but I couldn't put my finger on when or where, and had no particular memory of it, just a sensation I couldn't zero in on.

All of a sudden, I remembered that I did not fall asleep at the bar, like Libby had originally told me, and that Johnny was there, and I remember hitting him, knocking him to the floor. I also remember a $100 bill from Lucy's collection of silver certificates and him tipping the waitress with it, and then me getting it back off of her. I remember Johnny leaving and I remember Libby and I leaving. However, I cannot remember anything after that on that night, because everything fades to black in my memory of us walking out to the car.

"I can't remember any more." I said quietly.

"Shush." she said.

After that, with Libby still laying comfortably on my chest, hugging me harder with her head on my neck next to mine, I meditate further into a realm, where there was a Voice telling a story, narrating the evening when I blacked out from the moment we had left the bar, from where I couldn't remember anymore, but the Voice was actually from deep within my memory, reading a journal documented by an angel who recorded the entire night and morning as if taking notes on an episode that was blacked-out of my mind; an angel who was watching over my very being, urging me to sober up my life . . . a presumed "walk-in" spirit angel.

"Can you hear it now?" Libby asked, cuddling quietly but I went into a trance as the entire room radiated an eye-hurting bright light while I answered "Yes," and listened to my own voice as the angel, reading the passage and the words, painting a picture of the past, dimming the bright light. It was like watching a movie of what happened after Libby and I left the bar . . . as I narrated the lost journal of that night from the third person, as the spirit guide:

HORACE'S BLACKOUT MYSTERY REVEALED IN A TRANCE: A TOTAL RECALL FROM THAT ONE THURSDAY NIGHT INTO FRIDAY MORNING:

{{{{{They were both very, very inebriated and Libby started the car while Horace undid the cap from the little coke vile, dumping the fine powder onto the compact mirror and chopped at it with his credit card, scoring it into two large lines.

"You're going to save some of that for me, right?" Libby asked.

"Of course," he said, as he took the dollar bill and sucked an entire line of the white dust up one nostril.

"Give it here," Libby said, as she started pulling out onto the road heading north. There were no cars coming so before leaving the lot, onto Route 611 with the Ford Mustang still moving, she leaned her head down to snort her line of cocaine off of the mirror.

Suddenly, there was a loud thump at the front of the car, then the vehicle jolted, as if going over a speed-hump, causing Libby to jam on the breaks.

"Shit!" she said, sniffing as hard as she could not to lose any of the coke from her nose.

"What the hell was that?" Horace asked looking around into the darkness, "Are we in a ditch or something?"

"I don't know," she said, opening her door to step out.

Horace got out on his side with a flashlight from the glove box and saw they were 'almost' on the road, but still on the flat gravel parking lot belonging to Sportsman's Palace, but over the edge of a ditch. The tires and wheels looked alright as he walked around the car while Libby went to the back, but then Horace said, "Oh no."

"What?" Libby asked.

"Come over here," he said, looking down.

There was an arm, someone's arm sticking out from under the vehicle at the front of the car. As Libby walked to the front, she had her hand over her mouth as if to stop herself from talking or screaming. But she stayed silent while Horace examined the situation.

"Is it the waitress? Heidi?" Libby asked, remembering that she had just left the bar a little before they did.

"It's a guy," Horace said, feeling for a pulse, but there was none. Then he continued talking:

"And I recognize that tattoo of the black rose of death on the back of his hand. It's that asshole Johnny."

Horace leaned in and slid the body out from under the Ford carefully while Libby held the flashlight.

"Shouldn't we go inside and get help?" he asked.

"No," she said in a half whisper, "and it's a good thing there are no cars traveling down this road late at night."

"Why are you saying that?" Horace asked, as they saw headlights coming south.

"Never mind," she said, "and put out that flashlight."

"What's with all the secrecy, we've got to get help," he said almost shouting.

"Keep your voice down," she said, and added, "we've got to get out of here."

"Are you nuts? There's a dead man here, and we're the ones who ran over him. I'm not . . ."

"You're not what," she interrupted, "drunk driving? What about me? And, my good man, lets show the officers an eight-ball of cocaine while we're at it, just for shits and giggles, not to mention that our veins are engorged with coke and methamphetamine, and opioids we took yesterday. You get my drift?"

"Ah, yeah . . . so," Horace retorted, "what did you have in mind, Libby? Did you plan on simply taking off and leaving him here? Then a dead body is found on a lot and their forensics will figure out that it was your car when they conclude he was hit around 10:30 pm Thursday night. Lester will say 'Yeah, that was Libby and her friend Horace, and Horace punched him in the jaw right before Libby paid his bill because he was grabbing Libby's boobs and they were all friends'."

"You're sick," Libby said, then laughed at his reenactment of the altercation that took place an hour or so before.

"What do we do?" Horace asked, growling.

"What do we do!" Libby said, mimicking him and his growl comically, "We throw him in the trunk!" she said, with such a determination and self-assuredness that Horace had no choice other than to follow her plan.

Libby opened the trunk and with her help, Horace lifted Johnny's dead weight into the back of the vehicle but as they did, Horace farted, causing Libby to drop her end with Johnny's head as she broke into a fit of laughter.

"Wow," she said laughing, causing Horace to laugh too as she continued, "That was loud enough to wake the dead."

"Come on," Horace semi-whispered, "we haven't got all night."

"You'd better check your pants after that one," she said, laughing out of control.

"Libby!" he shouted.

She grabbed his shoulders once again and with Horace on his legs, they finally folded him into the trunk.

"That wasn't me, by-the-way," Horace said, "That was Johnny."

They both laughed at that and climbed into the car with Libby, drunk as she was, being the designated driver again.

"Counting Johnny, we're acting like the Three Stooges," Horace summarized.

"Where to?" she asked, looking at him through the shadowy glow off of the green dashboard lights.

"Something tells me we should head into Doylestown with him. I'm sensing something is wrong with Lucy."

(As his angel, I'm documenting that all night since the fight with Johnny, Horace has been sensing something was wrong with Lucy, and why was Johnny holding that $100 bill, when he shouldn't have even known about it.)

"That coke-vile better not be empty," Libby said, referring to the cocaine container.

"It's not," Horace said, turning the dome light on and dumping some more of the powdery cocaine onto the mirror. Then he asked her, "One line or two?"

"Two, of course," she said, and added, "Look at us. We're crazy. . . crazy to be doing what we're doing now."

"I am so, so, fucked up!" Horace said out loud, gulping a pint of bourbon.

"You're telling me," Libby said, "that's why I'm the one driving! You're talking to yourself over there."

"You don't miss a thing, do you?" Horace asked.

"I don't know," she said, "Tell me where we're going. We just bypassed Doylestown."

"SHIT," he said, "You gotta go back!"

"Pay attention," Libby shouted.

"No, you pay attention! It's on Wood Street."

(They eventually circled around and found themselves in the center of town and on Wood Street, in front of Horace's old house which he had moved out of less than a week before that night. Libby's spot was open and there was no sign of her Ford Maverick, so they pulled into the space.)

"She'll bitch like hell if she sees your car in her spot," Horace said, "but she's probably not home if her car's not here."

"What are you going to do now?" Libby asked.

"It's dark, and the neighbors are asleep, so we're going to carry Johnny into the house," he said, whispering.

"You're fucked up!" Libby said.

"We've already established that," Horace said, "but we're going to do it anyway since we're both fucked up; Come on."

"But, he's dead, and looks beat up." Libby said, "You're going to, um, just put him like, on the couch?"

"I haven't thought of that," he said, "but that's a great idea! What little blood there was, is dried up now."

Pulling Johnny out of the trunk, the two of them carried him through the darkness up the walk, and as Horace fumbled for the keys, the dead weight caused him to fall backward, with Johnny through the door that opened as he unlocked it and the three of them stumbled through the threshold.

"Shit!" Horace said in a loud whisper, "Get off of me!" as he rolled Johnny and Libby from on top of him.

"You're the one who dropped your end!" Libby shouted.

"Shhhh!" he retorted with a slight smack to the top of her head.

"Don't shush me!" she said, smacking him back as they lifted Johnny and carried him through the foyer and plopped him onto the couch, and with Johnny, it was like they were the three stooges.

"Let's get out of here," Libby said.

"Wait. I want to put this $100 Silver Certificate back in her 'safe-place,' where she's been hiding it," he told her, "After all, he's certainly not going to take it again."

"How do you know she didn't give it to him?" she asked.

"How do I know? Because, I know Lucy."

Horace walked up the stairs to her room and found the place behind the bed, under the baseboard heater where she's been keeping the music box that housed the bills. Then he went into the bathroom to pee but was surprised at what he saw.

"Oh My God!"

"What's the matter!" Libby shouted, running up the stairs.

"This is too much!" Horace said, falling to his knees.

Lucy was naked in a tub of red-tinted water, but she was breathing as she held a towel, soaked with blood against the center of her abdomen where blood was dribbling out like smoke under the water.

"Lucy!" he shouted, "Lucy! Can you hear me?"

He wrapped his hand around the bloody cloth she held firm against her tummy and was attempting to pull it free to look at the wound when Libby shouted.

"No! Don't!" she said, "You take that out and she'll bleed to death, I think she's still alive . . . isn't she?"

"She's breathing," he said, slowly letting go of the cloth as he placed his hands on her face.

Lucy, as if sensing he was there, opened her eyes and stared right at him and tried to talk.

"Johnny!" she said.

"I'm not Johnny," Horace said, "It's me, Horace."

"No." Lucy said, breathing heavily now, "Johnny stabbed me! I – I hit him with a baseball bat on the Sportsman's parking lot, I waited outside for him and I was trying to -"

"You rest, we're going to get you to a hospital," Horace said.

Libby went in desperation to grab the telephone, but there was no dial-tone, so, Horace ran to where he knew there was a cordless phone, but it too was dead, and he noticed the coffee table and a few lamps were broken, as if thrown. As a matter of fact, it looked as if the whole place was ransacked, with clothes, pictures, furniture and silverware scattered everywhere.

Running back into the bathroom he saw that Lucy had stopped breathing and was turning blue, so he pulled the blood-red towel free from her belly with the mindset of performing CPR, but there was no heartbeat and the blood-flow stopped, and the life of his Lucy that once was, was now gone forever.

Silence fell over the whole house, and the quiet of death chilled the air as the two of them, Libby and Horace, sat in the bathroom staring at the nude lady in the tub of

crimson water, wondering in their synthetic, melancholy high of cocaine and alcohol what their next move would be.
"I'll call the cops," Horace said.
"Are you nuts?
"What do you mean?" he said, "Now we've got 'two' dead people here."
"Yes," Libby said, "and we're breaking and entering, and our fingerprints in blood are all over the place."
"But I live here!"
"LIVED here!" Libby responded, "Your landlord saw you fighting with her when you left over a week ago, remember? This doesn't look good for you, or me for that matter!"
Horace had a deep look when he asked, "How the hell do I get myself into these God forsaken messes?"
"Beats me," Libby said sarcastically.

Horace just stared into oblivion as she continued talking. "Horace," she said, "I'll bet you that this bastard ditched the knife, and I'm also willing to bet there are no blood fingerprints of his anywhere, since she said this happened at Sportsman's."
"So?"
"So, are you willing to go to jail for murder?" she asked him, "I'm certainly not."
"They can't put us in jail, we didn't do anything." Horace said, still bewildered over Lucy's death.
"We would never be able to explain our way out of this!" she said, "Your fingerprints and hand prints are all over the tub, the walls, her body . . ."

"So, we'll wipe them clean," Horace said, shaking his head in mild frustration.

"And be here when they arrive? With everything wiped clean?" she said raising her voice to a hoarse whisper, "Haven't you ever seen those shows on TV? Circumstantial evidence dude. We're here in the midst of it all, and we're too fucked up to think straight enough to figure our way out of this."

"Yeah," Horace replied, "But we could just tell them the truth, that he killed her."

Libby laughed and then stopped abruptly like a crazy woman would, cutting her emotional outburst to a sharp halt saying: "Yeah, right. Would you believe that? We're in a pickle dude. The truth of the matter is we can't be here, and we certainly can't leave them here." Libby paused, looking around before saying, "We all have to leave, and leave this place immaculate."

"What did you have in mind?" Horace asked.

"You will go to my house," Libby said, "and get your pick-up. You will bring it back here and we will take these two tonight and lock-up this house, since you still have a key, right?"

"They have sets too," he said.

"Right! So, we'll take the two bodies, lock up and return tomorrow with a box truck, which we have at the house for moving large items, and we'll move everything out; Tonight, we'll clean the blood and fingerprints."

"Move out the furniture? Are you crazy?" Horace asked with his eyebrows raised high.

"You told me once she probably wouldn't sign the lease, right?" Libby asked.

"Not yet she didn't," he replied, "So, what does that have to do . . ."

"Everyone knows you're moving," Libby interrupted, "and no one will question her disappearance, at least right away. And that 'Johnny' character won't have any friends missing him."

"But, that seemed . . ."

"Look!" Libby interrupted again, "I don't need a doubting Thomas! I need you to work with me on this. Trust me! There's no way I want to miss playing the gig on Saturday night."

"You're still going to play? after all of this? How the hell -"

"You'll do it too, and like it," Libby retorted, "and I'll make sure you'll have the artificial and spiritual means to lift you into a playing mood."

Horace knew she meant amphetamines and coke as the artificial stimuli to successfully perform the list of songs they had planned, and he knew they'd be exhausted if they were to move all of the furniture out of the house by then.

As fantastic as the idea was, Horace had returned with the pick-up as planned, and both of the bodies, rolled up in carpets, were loaded into the bed and after locking up the house, headed to Libby's. They drove the separate vehicles down back roads to avoid cops since they were both intoxicated and upon arriving at her house, stopped at a one of the newly dug electrical trenches next to the back-hoe on the lawn along the driveway about a hundred yards from the gate. Libby instructed Horace to help her place both of the bodies into the trench in a box and lay them flat at the very bottom, right beside the cables.

"What are you going to do?" he asked her, "You going to bury them?"

"Of course," she replied, "Out of sight, out of mind."

"But, how the hell . . .?"

"Don't worry about it," she said, "You go in and take a shower and get some sleep. There's a lot we have to do tomorrow. Besides, you're so fucked up, you probably won't remember any of this anyway."

"I'm fucked up?" He bellowed, and continued, "You had as much as me . . ."

"Get in the house, I said." And Libby's tired and inebriated body, still stable although saturated with cocaine and alcohol started moving the bodies into place.

As Horace walked wearily into the house he heard the back-hoe start up and saw its lights as Libby stood next to it, yelling for Horace to go. She stood there waiting above where he knew Johnny and Lucy would be laid to rest in an unmarked grave.

Horace took off his clothes and dropped them into the washer in the laundry room and climbed directly into the shower stall and as he showered and let the hot water spray across his shoulders and hair, he started to weep. He soaped himself up and breathed in the steaming air as he tried to wash the guilt of hiding bodies from his entire being. As he washed, he thought about Lucy, and how the thought of her in the tub, with the gash, the blood and the look she gave him reminded him of the same look that made them both fall in love over four years ago. He felt responsible, and that if he hadn't left, if he had just stuck it out with her a little while longer this whole scenario would never have happened. He slid down the wall and sat himself at the base of the stall whimpering uncontrollably with his arms wrapped around his knees, and he fell asleep to the rhythm of pulsating water droplets bouncing on his neck and shoulders.

He awoke to a naked body embracing him as Libby's entire presence huddled around him, and as she hugged him, he embraced her.

"Come on, love, let's get you to bed," she said trying to lift him.

He said nothing as he carefully stood and staggered to the big king-sized bed, where Libby had the covers already pulled back for him, then pulled the cotton sheets and the silk covered comforter over top of him. She held a glass of water in one hand and a Quaalude in the other, and in her soft tone, sitting in the nude on the bed next to him insisted he take it. In a swallow and a gulp, Horace was on his way to a sound sleep while Libby crawled onto the mattress cuddling next to him and drifted into peaceful oblivion, for the night.

Horace laid in peaceful slumber early Friday morning at 6:30 when Libby arose from her sleep, and as she lovingly patted him on his butt, decided to let him rest. She got herself dressed, in jeans and a low-cut skin-tight top and organized a group of movers, friends of hers, to do the chore of removing the furniture from the Wood Street house where he, Lucy, and Johnny used to live. She went first to the house to box and pack up the smaller items, also cleaning up the blood residue from the crime scene so when the movers arrived by noon in the large box truck they could load up without any delays or suspicion from any of the neighbors, since none of the three, Horace, Lucy or Johnny communicated much with them anyway.

For myself, being Horace's spiritual guide, I had to see what was going on with him and I found Horace and I sharing a dream, a dream that took us back to the place where my story began, to the misty Universe of the Voice without a face, where we all seemed to communicate as a trio of entities.

"What is this place?" Horace asked.
"What do you think it is?" The Voice answered calmly.
"I'm – I'm dreaming, right?" Horace asked.
"Horace, do you know who I am?" I asked.
"He doesn't know," the Voice answered. "Horace is not going to remember any of this, nor is he going to remember anything after he arrived at the bar on Thursday night."
"Why?" Horace asked.
"Because," the Voice answered, "you were blameless in the events, and your judgement was blurred and altered with the use of intoxicants, leaving you without your proper rudimentary skills of rationalizing what happened. You were misled to believe you were guilty of something that was not

of your doing, and despite your irresponsible use of intoxicants, the outcome of your situation would have been unfair to you and Libby if reported to authorities. Thus, you will be protected, not only by the spiritual guide here, but by a lapse of memory of anything that had occurred on Thursday night."

"But, I killed. . ." Horace started, but was immediately interrupted by the Voice.

"You and Libby killed no one that night. The truth is; The man was already injured, wounded with a baseball bat in a confrontation with your other friend Lucy before your vehicle ran over him. He was not dead that night. You, however, are not meant to recall any of it, or any of this dream Friday morning when you awaken. The purpose of this meeting with us in this dream was 'mainly' for your spiritual guide's benefit, who will soon be your 'Walk-In' spirit and to impose an aura of peace over your present existence. You're spirit guide prevented you from suffering the horrible fate he suffered from his same murderer."

"Will I remember?" I, as his guide, asked the Voice.

"You will guide Horace," the Voice spoke assertively, "you will not remember anything after leaving the bar regarding that night, and Horace's friend Libby will remember everything. Horace will remember nothing after arriving at the bar.

Since this night, you have already become one with the physical body of Horace, and Libby will know your heart and soul, and you both will finish completing the plan."}}}}}

THIS WAS THE END OF HORACE'S TRANCE AND TOTAL RECALL REVELATION OF HIS BLACKOUT MYSTERY.

CHAPTER - FOURTEEN

When I came to, from this trance, Libby was still holding me tightly as she rested her whole body on my chest and legs. It was already evening, and I had no idea of the time while I stared with fresh insight at the clear night sky, surmising that every star must have been out, some winking more brightly than others against the prodigious, pitch-black backdrop of eternal space. The monumental light-pierced picture of the Universe from laying back in the comfort of this lounge chair on the patio with my lover had given me a refreshing look at its inordinate vastness and countless galaxies and stars, not to mention its exorbitant expansion from its eternity out there to the eternity within us all.

Both of my hands were resting flat on Libby's bare back and I realized she was completely naked, and to my surprise, so was I. Somewhere in the trance we had both lost our clothes and were lying in our own sweat and soon came to realize she was sliding off of me; but waking up at the same time.

"Wow." she said. "I wonder what time it is?"

"Are you kidding?" I asked. "After all of that? That trance? Or whatever it was?"

"So now you know about Lucy." she said, slowly climbing off of me and diving naked into the pool.

"Yes." I said, as I stood up and walked to the edge of the patio, looking into the darkness where Lucy was buried. I could barely make out in the dim glare from the night lights in the driveway Lucy's form, standing where the vision informed me she was buried, killed by Johnny.

I said nothing, but I waved to her, not knowing what to expect, but she disappeared, just like the hallucination she was; But I remember her being real. In the background I heard Libby splashing around in the pool and I turned around to face the reality of the present while watching her swim from one end to the other, then back again before I dove in to join her.

After a few minutes of swimming I was anxious to finally ask her about a few details of the visional trance I had experienced and was curious about some unanswered questions in my mind, such as, 'Did the trance mean that Johnny wasn't dead?' I also wanted to know more about these screwed up people that are in the mix, the conglomeration surrounding Libby and the Bender's Clubs, and what the hell her involvement is in all of it.

"We thought Johnny was dead, when we thought we hit him with the Mustang." I said, after we had climbed out of the pool and found ourselves in the lounge chairs, reclining in them next to each other, staring up into the heavens once again. This time, we were nursing a couple of glasses of ice-cold wine coolers.

"I know," she said, "I didn't tell you about that."

"Did you bury him alive next to Lucy?" I asked, in a sarcastic tone, causing her to spit out her wine cooler in a spray and laughing hysterically.

"Wow! What an ironic end that would have been for Johnny," she said and continued: "A paradoxical demise for an individual who drugged, sexually abused, then buried his victims alive to do away with them, because he was too cowardly to murder them outright. It's what he did to Skip and quite a few others, but to answer your question, no, he's not out there with Lucy."

"I can't believe 'she's' dead," I said, "God, she was so real to me when I was walking and talking with her these past weeks."

"You still say you were talking with her? Actually, seeing her since that night?" she asked.

"I certainly did, I told you that before," I said, "and she took me to that spot where the willow was, but I had no idea that the grave was your friend Skip."

She sat up and climbed into my chair beside me, both of us still naked to the world and said, "You may not believe this now, or ever, nor would you ever understand, but you and I were together in other lifetimes before. I was once, in a previous lifetime, Skip's actual wife until she was murdered by Johnny, then placed in an unmarked grave somewhere, and you were once my husband Skip. After death, I was a Walk-In spirit for Libby when she overdosed months before you met her, and the rest was history when you became the Walk-In spirit for Horace the night his body overdosed on the meth from that syringe at the club, remember? The one and only time that you, Horace, stuck a needle in your arm?"

"Am I supposed to take that as a compliment?" I asked, "that I'm someone who took the place of someone who accidentally killed himself? I 'am' Horace."

"The original Horace and Libby are at total peace now." she said. "The forces that are to be, don't want you to remember a previous life, they usually don't, but for some reason, I'm remembering some, a very little of mine."

This would have sounded like crazy talk from any other person, but from Libby, and right now, it relayed vibrant and warm feelings as I listened and believed, for it was too ridiculous and absurd to be untrue. Her descriptive impression or notion that we were supposed to be spirits from somewhere else was absolutely real. Her insistence was so sure that we were intended to be these supposed "Walk-Ins" that she made it sound almost romantic, or rather, romanticizing it in such a way that it brought us closer together. It was similar to the way that a man and a woman at an art museum would observe a romantic painting together, deliberating and pondering thoughts and imagination as one soul, before surrendering to the inevitable kiss. She even said that when she was revived from that overdose, it was Skip who had saved her, and she eerily felt that same connection with him that she did with me.

Almost knowing my thoughts, she then leaned in and kissed me so warmly that I didn't care about anything, nor did I want to think about anything but her and I, in our chair, as we merged as one under the same stars our Native

American ancestors viewed; and made sweet and sensuous love into the oblivion of the passing early morning hours. It was the way it always was for us for what was meant to be an eternity; and we fell asleep right there on the cushions of the lounge chair.

When I awoke the following morning, I was alone in the chair, still naked with a few large towels thrown over me. The sun was already high in the east and I guessed the time to be about ten or ten thirty in the AM. I saw a pair of clean jeans, underwear, socks, a tee-shirt, and my sneakers all laid out for me in the other chair, with a note saying, "GOOD MORNING, SUNSHINE!"

I dressed and went to the kitchen where a breakfast of three eggs over easy, bacon, and home-fries was just being set in a place for me at the kitchen table.

"Just in time." Libby said.

"I'm starved," I said, but waited for her to sit first.

Libby looked great, wearing her yellow shorts and red, low-cut tank-top showing her firm belly, the norm for her in the morning hours on these warmer days, and in her bare feet. Her hair was up, and her early summer tan had seemed noticeably darker in the dim lighting in this side of the room. Her eyes even looked greener as she sat with her plate directly across from me with her contagious smile.

"Eat it before it gets cold, dear." she said, placing another dish of toast in front of us and cutting into her eggs.

"So," I said, "What a night."

"I know." she said, smiling as she took a mouthful of yolk. "You slept okay, I trust?"

"Yes, I slept like a baby."

I was aware that this was just small talk and conscious of the fact that she was aware of it too, so I cut to the chase with the conversation.

"Why the hell didn't you tell me that people died that night, and that Lucy was buried out on the lawn?" I asked frustrated.

"You were there," Libby said calmly, "I thought you knew."

"I was asleep; Out cold the morning that you cleaned out her house," I responded, "removing all of the evidence so the law wouldn't falsely convict us, or something to that effect!"

"No one knew or knows she's dead," was her response.

"What about her family, her friends . . ."

"You told me she had no family, other than Johnny," Libby answered.

"I don't know that for sure." I told her.

"It doesn't matter, love," she said, sopping up her eggs and potatoes with toast, "we can clear that up later. Right now, there's a lot I need to fill you in on."

"I'll say!" I said almost sardonically, "There's so much here that I obviously don't know; and need to find out! If for nothing else, for my own sanity!"

"In due time, lover." Libby said while swallowing some tomato juice and handing the half-glass to me across the table with a smile.

"Here," she said, "this is low-sodium tomato juice and excellent ice cold."

She was right, it was delicious, but it didn't end my train of thought on aggressively pursuing at this moment in time, finding out as much as I could about what's been happening.

"Jordan was buried alive!" I said as calmly as I could, but it came out loudly.

"But he's not dead, thanks to you."

"You mean thanks to Lucy!" I said sternly.

"Here we go again." she said. "Lucy's dead. And Johnny killed her."

"I saw her."

"You saw her ghost." Libby stated, looking right at me in disbelief.

"Well, I guess I saw her ghost." I said, not knowing if I believed what I had just said.

"That," she said, "I believe. There's a lot in this Universe we don't fully understand, and I know you believe you saw her. 'Maybe' it was your imagination, or maybe you've really seen a ghost."

I had thought about that and remembered the times I was walking with Lucy and it looked as if no one else I had talked to at Lake Galena, while she was with me, seemed to notice her, and I thought that was odd, that is, with the exception of Karma the cabby, when we were at the quarry lake, so, at least he saw her too.

Anyway, Libby sat, looking across the table at me almost, as if she was undressing me with her eyes while I felt her stare looming deep within my soul. It was an erotic moment, to say the least, but I needed to put her sensuous glaring aside to inquire further about that night I had the blackout.

"So," I said, "I wonder what happened to Johnny Hetrick?"

"You cold-cocked him at the bar, knocking him on his ass." she said, picking up her empty plate with mine to place the dishes in the sink.

"I mean, after that, and after we ran over him." I said. "My understanding is he wasn't dead, and you didn't bury him alive."

"Correct." Libby answered.

"So, where is he?" I asked.

"Let's go in the den with a couple of coffees and I'll tell you. It's a long story." she said, fixing us a couple piping hot cups of expresso.

After making ourselves comfortable in the den, the exact room where I had first met her late husband Robert, she and I sat across from each other with the coffee table between us, containing the two very large, hot cups of fresh foaming expresso. Behind her was an original painting by Monet, one of the hundreds he had done using a bridge, and was a good backdrop framing her face while she told me an unbelievably true story about what had happened following that particular evening.

Before I had passed out that morning, Libby became aware of movement, and a pulse detected in Johnny's body while she was placing Lucy's corpse, wrapped in blankets in a steel box two feet or so beneath the electric cables, which were run about six feet under the lawn. To her surprise,

Johnny came to, grabbing Libby forcefully and she said she gave him a swift punch in the jaw, knocking him out again. "I couldn't bury him alive," she said, "but I had an idea, which I eventually ended up following through with."

Libby dragged Johnny's unconscious form out of the trench while I was in the shower and back to the workshop, where there was a spare room and a bed. She undressed him, noticing no broken bones, placing him naked on his back on the mattress and tied his hands and feet to the bed-posts for the time being, where he wouldn't cause any trouble. Then she covered Lucy's corpse with the earth, filling the trench using the backhoe then placing the turf across the mounded area.

The following day, she and some people she knew and trusted cleared out the house on Wood Street, making it look like Lucy had simply moved out, leaving no trace of anything that might look like there was any foul play. Libby said that she had previously cleaned up the blood thoroughly so there were no questions asked by her helpers, although they wouldn't have said anything anyway, and the place was as clean as a whistle when they were finished. The items were put into a personal storage area on another property owned by the Benders and Libby said I could go there anytime, to recover anything that I wanted that might have been left behind.

Lucy's Ford Maverick was also found and parked in a garage on the same property, and since Lucy had no known living family members needing to be contacted, and Johnny and I were her only kin, we decided to worry about everything at a later date, after Libby had finished her contrived scheme to counteract Bill Bailey's sleazy and murderous takeover of the Robert Bender empire.

The following part of the story was almost hard to believe, but it most certainly happened, and I found myself intrigued with the tale. Libby already knowing that Johnny was linked to suspicious disappearances of people affiliated with the Bender Clubs, 'apparently' had tortured Johnny, encouraging him to talk, trading his pain for the extraction of information from him regarding Bill Bailey and his associates. She promised she'd let him live, setting him free if all of his information proved valid, such as the corroboration of Bill's ultimate plan of taking over the Bender enterprise. What she found out was Johnny followed up on a contract to murder her musician friend Skip, and also murdered Skip's wife Miranda a year before, after she got him out of jail as his lawyer. He was also on a mission to kill me, then under contract to kill Jordan, but what was worse for her to accept was that he was contracted to murder her husband Robert.

Because of this realization, Robert and Libby had worked out a plan between them, taking into consideration that Robert actually had an illness of terminal cancer. Libby decided to fake Robert's death to put the proverbial wrench in the undermining strategy Bill Bailey had theorized and assembled. To do so, she would have to con Bill into thinking she was working with him, like a double agent, and convince Bill she was going to murder Robert, so she and Bill could take over, but in reality, setting Bill up for their own plan.

For this they also would need a body that was about the same size and build as her husband Robert, which Johnny was, as a close to a spot-on match. Libby had then drugged Johnny, using a dose of some barbiturate before untying him, befriending him and asked him if he wanted to go for a swim.

"I originally didn't want to kill him, and I was going to back out of it," Libby told me. "He was in a pair of swimming trunks because I had given him the impression I was letting him go and wasn't sure I wanted to go through with the murder, despite him being a murdering pig. You see, other than self-defense, committing murder is not my bag. I ended up giving him some cocaine to wake him up from the Quaaludes I had previously given him, and Horace, remember how he came at me in the bar? Well, he attacked me just like that! He began ripping my one-piece suit completely off, and I jumped into the pool to get away from him, but he dove in after me."

Libby then got pretty animated and excited explaining the rest, like she was reliving the ordeal between her and Johnny in the pool.

"He followed me to the deep end, swimming his heart out to catch up and cornered me against the pool's edge, at the ladder," she said, then continued: "He told me he was going to fuck me, then kill me. He was also coming at me with my big kitchen knife he had in his hand, with the intention of gutting me like he did to Lucy. I turned toward him, wrapping both arms around the ladder behind me and when he was in front of me, I lifted my entire body out of the water, and with my legs completely spread, punched my groin against his face, a move I learned in a class I took; quickly wrapping my thighs around his head, and against my groin and plunged him under the water beneath me, causing him to drop the knife. Needless to say, his struggles were hopeless against the strength of my legs and my thigh muscles."

"I'll say amen to that!" I said grinning, in spite of myself.

"While I sensed his screaming and felt him struggle, even trying to scratch at me, my leveraged position of my hands held his arms fast rendering them helpless and prevented them from reaching me. I kept my arms firmly wrapped around the ladder with my head barely above the water and my thighs around his head and my hands on his wrists. While I was holding him under I was thinking of Skip, and of others that the pig murdered, smothered, not to mention his coming after Robert and you, and me for that matter. Even after he went limp and remained motionless I kept squeezing my thighs tightly around his ears out of sheer anger and waited about twenty minutes before I pulled his body from the pool.

"You're lucky he dropped the knife." I told her.

"It's a grip promoting panic that I had learned for self-defense." she retorted. "When done right, he had no choice, especially being under water."

Libby went on to tell me about faking Robert's free-basing accident, that she and Robert staged the whole crime scene to look like an accident, resulting in the body being burned beyond recognition. Libby had pulled one of Johnny's teeth out in her attempts to draw information from him but pulled the rest out posthumously to fit Robert's dentures into his mouth before setting the fire. The explosion burned away part of his skull and hands but left enough convincing evidence with drilling the unique bone pin into the hand and placing the dentures. The investigation was also not as thorough as a suspected murder investigation, leaving a lot of room for educational guess work.

"So, where's Robert now?" I asked.

"He's upstate under a different identity in a place we have, with doctors looking after him." Libby said. "He'll be there and under care until this whole masquerade is finished with Bill Bailey. His new identity is actually a fictitious person he had created, conjured up for transferring money and profits to the accountants who work together to control all of the Bender's clubs throughout the country. Because Robert and I are the majority owners of the corporation, we're the only ones who control that main part of the business and as far as Mr. Bailey's concerned, I'm handling all of that through these accountants and he doesn't even know who they are, and never will."

I stared at her for a moment, wanting to believe her, not that I didn't, but I had my doubts, at least a couple anyway.

"I remember Karma the cab driver telling me that there was a rumor that Robert did himself in because he was dying of cancer," I told her.

"When did you hear that?" she asked.

I realized that I would now have to tell her what I've been dying to tell her since she had started opening up to me, that I was under the bed, hiding, the night she and Bill were at the house.

"I was under the bed the night you and Bill came here, the night of the gig," I told her.

"I knew that," she said, but added, "Bill didn't know though, and I didn't let him know."

"That was the night I took a cab ride with Karma." I told her. "You mean, you knew I was under the bed?"

"Yes, I was aware of it," she said, "but you couldn't have seen Karma, because Bill and his palookas had him killed."

"What the hell are you trying to say?"

"I'm telling you Karma is as dead as a door nail, at the bottom of a quarry lake with his taxicab," she said assertively, "and you couldn't have seen Karma, unless you saw another ghost."

"He brought me home the other night," I said, "and he kicked the shit out of a couple of goons in a big box truck who tried to run us off of the road when we passed them."

"That's what Bill was talking about that night after the motorcycle ride home," she said smiling and staring into the floor like she just figured something out, and at the awareness of his comments, "and he kept saying something about the taxi number, number 160. The Universe is sure filled with mysterious surprises."

Libby then looked directly into my eyes, as if she just recognized something, and her green irises were deep and true, like windows into her soul and I realized once again that I was completely and totally head-over-heals in love with her; and have been all along, despite her knowing I was under the bed when she 'did' Bill Bailey, oddly enough.

The depth of this sensation that I was finally coming to comprehend was almost mortifying since we were not even talking about anything remotely relating to a romantic scenario, but rather, an argument about death and seeing a ghost. Slowly, a smile penetrated her deep stare as I could plainly see she reflected the notion and it was like we were reading each other's minds, coming to terms with what had existed for what felt as an eternity, forever bound and free within each other.

"I don't care about anything anymore." she said, then wrapped her arms around me as we hugged and kissed like high school kids with their parents away and rolled around on the den's sofa, fully clothed, laughing and making our tongues dance together as we continued our embrace of arms and legs as she rolled me under her and onto my back. Her top came off first, exposing her full breasts above me as I reached up from my pinned position to cradle them gently, when all of a sudden there was a voice. . .

"Wow! Should I come back another time?"

Libby jumped up and her sheer top was back on in an instant, reminding me of my teenage years and being raided by my high school sweetheart's parents' coming home early.

"Bill!" Libby shouted at Mr. Bailey standing in the threshold of the den's entrance in his expensive three-piece suit. His hair seemed to be dyed a little darker than it had been, along with his thick mustache and eye brows.

"You left the front door open," he said, "Lucky for you I wasn't some sleazebag."

"You're not?" I said impulsively with a smile, still sitting up, if you know what I mean.
"Shush." Libby said, touching my mouth with her finger and sitting next to me.
"You," he said, pointing his finger at me, "you had better behave yourself!"
"Who the hell are you?" I asked heatedly, and continued, "Who are you to talk to me that way?"
"She's my fiancé," he said, "You knew that, didn't you?"
"No, he did not." she told him. "He didn't know, and I didn't tell him yet."

I grinned and winked my one eye at him while placing my hand on her right breast for him to see and he immediately came at me, but Libby stood up to block him from further advancing.
"LAY OFF!" she shouted, with her face inches from his, but he just grinned at her, turning away, and walked toward the fireplace mantle and leaning his elbow on it, began talking.
"Libby," he said, looking right at her, "does Robert have any children that you know about?"
"No, we never had any," she said, sitting back down across from me in the other leather chair.
"Not you and him," he said assertively, "but from someone previous? Another marriage?"
"Why do you ask?" Libby said, picking up an old 'Rolling Stone' magazine and randomly paging through it.
"Because," he said, "there's a clause in the Bender contract between Robert and the company that if you as a partner, due to him as a partner being deceased," he said, and con-

tinued, "if you would marry a person who was another stockholder in the corporation, all of and any other stock holders would automatically be bought out by you and your husband, and you'd automatically own 60% to your new partner's 40%."

"So?" Libby said, "That was to protect my assets if anything was to happen to him, you know, foul play or a surprise death. That shouldn't change anything between you and me. Robert established the corporation years ago and placed that item in the contract when he incorporated; at least that was his intention."

I listened and tried to follow while they were communicating, but the whole time, Libby was looking directly into my eyes. Not that she was trying to get my attention or delivering any duplicitous notions, but as she spoke, it was merely a blank expression which prodded me to step in with a comment.

"So, Bill," I said, "why would you want to know if Robert had any children?"

"Shut up you!" he bellowed, "Who the hell asked you?"

"I asked him." Libby said, in a mellow tone.

"You asked him what?" Bill stated in a more calming tone to match hers; almost, as if she was controlling him.

"I asked him what this has to do with Robert having any children," she said serenely.

Bill walked across the room past the Matisse painting and put a cigarette into his mouth from what looked like a solid gold carrying-case but before he had a chance to light it with his gold-plated lighter, Libby shouted: "HEY!! No smoking in here! EVER!"

He grinned a sly grin at her, slowly turning it into a smirk before removing the cigarette and returning it to his case and sat in the leather chair that was caddy-corner from Libby and I, continuing with his presentation about the contract.

"It's stated, that any siblings of the majority shareholder, at the time of his or her demise, would automatically be entitled to split between them 100% of his shares. In layman's terms, if Robert has any children, they're entitled to everything he owned in the corporation, and the minority shareholders must sell if the child wants to buy out Bender's."

"So? What are you worried about?" she asked.

"Children." He said, again asking Libby if there were any.

"How many times do I have to say 'no'?" Libby stated again. "We didn't have any, and there's no bun in the oven here, if that's what you're inferring."

"I'm just saying . . ." Bill started, but she didn't give him a chance, and started in on him.

"I'm tired of listening to this bullshit of yours. You and I are going to tie the knot, Bill, and that's been established. We've been seeing each other for a while now-"

Libby stopped her train of thought and looked directly over at me saying, "-and Horace, I'm sorry but Bill and I have planned this for a long time. He and I are going to own Bender's together, but I'll still have the band and take care of you." Then she winked.

Just then, Libby and Bill started to argue, but I didn't hear a thing they were saying. I was too caught up in the confusion of what she had just told me and wasn't sure I was supposed to be believing her, or was this just a razz, a spoof of gibberish that I was to understand as banter to delude Bill, who was 'apparently' believing the spew she was telling me. I was still in the dark, regarding her intentions, but portraying a pretentious humbleness that . . . even "I" believed when I finally drifted from my thoughts back into the den of lions, still arguing.

"What do you mean still have the band?" Bill asked her. "I thought you were going to end all of that."

"*'All of that'* is my life," she said, "and it's my music, and I'll give that up for no one!"

He stood there glaring at her, silently staring with those dark eyes before she stood up and padded over to him in her bare feet and slithered her bare arms around him lovingly and said:

"Look dear, we'll work it out. We're going to own everything, and the partners will sell whether they like it or not. Trust me."

CHAPTER - FIFTEEN

PART II

THE AUTHOR NARRATES

So, Horace realized now that something was very special between Libby and himself, since he's never in his life had an attraction such as this for anyone, causing him to wonder about all of this mystical "Walk-In" spirit talk that she was propagating. Her delivery of what he thought might be her own perception of acquired religious lore and speculation was so convincing, that it disseminated his own theories through his inquiring imagination and psyche and Horace found himself looking up the "Walk-In" phenomena.

Looking through Libby's and Robert's bookcase he found a few volumes pertaining to spirituality and paged through them. Horace had no personal memory of anything pertaining to Skip, nor did he remember anything other than being born as Horace Clowney. He did, however, remember a sudden change in his own personality forever at the Bender's Cub, the night he did methamphetamine by sticking the needle into his arm. He realized it wasn't just the speed that was streaming through his veins that night, but something else took over, changing his whole thought process, making him a totally different person and Horace needed to investigate more thoroughly into this anomaly that Libby was talking about.

What he realized was he felt that he himself had changed as a person, stopped doing drugs like he had been, and had now somewhat of a personal driven force and purpose compared to before, and an unusual bonded attraction toward Libby, other than the fact that she was a physical beauty. Horace also was aware of her attraction toward him and almost understood, mildly believing her, that she was somehow reincarnated from another life and person, and into the body of a person called 'Libby.'

Months had passed now, and it was mid-summer in Pennsylvania, and there was still no sign of Jordan, the incomparable bass-fiddle player for Horace and Libby since he had disappeared on that horrible day at Lake Galena, when he was discovered by them, thanks to the ghost of Lucy. The police were never told about Skip's murdered body, the cover-up, and Jordan's rescue, nor was it ever mentioned to Bill Bailey. Libby just acted like it never happened and to not raise any suspicion, she'd occasionally ask if anyone's seen Jordan, and make it a point to ask when Bill was standing nearby. His response was usually the same, saying he didn't know where the 'spook' was, nor did he care.

Bill and Libby were married in a quiet ceremony at a Justice of Peace on Route 202 near Spring Valley, PA. with only two witnesses, Horace and an old friend of Libby's named Zoey Romano. Zoey was a young lady in her early twenties with dark hair that flowed long, soft and freely down her back to her butt. She was built thin, well-toned and voluptuous, and for the small wedding service she wore white dress slacks and a thin white blouse proudly showing off the fact that she wasn't wearing a bra. Zoey was introduced as an old friend of Libby's who shared the closely-knit group of female friends that Horace and Bill and the others have seldom seen, since they had only gotten together a few times a year. Zoey, however, was in town for a visit from her hometown of Pittsburgh and was more than happy to witness the marriage for her old and dear friend Libby.

Needless to say, Bill started in with his classic demands that shouldn't have surprised anyone and soon Horace was moved out of the house, and into an expensive home in Chalfont which Robert had already owned. It was a beautiful four-bedroom stucco covered rancher with ceramic-tile roofing and with large, furnished rooms that made you think you were in a mansion, like the Bender's place when you stood in the living room. This place was conveniently located at the top of a hill, just on the edge of the wooded forest above Lake Galena, and within walking distance from the bicycle trail.

Libby was tolerant of Bill Bailey's behavior because she was up to something, and Horace knew in his heart that this whole marriage of Libby and Bill was a farce, a well-contrived scheme for her to get to the bottom of something, but what? Horace was aware that she knew that Bill was in on, and a part of what had happened to Jordan at the lake, and also Skip's body being buried there. Also, there was something about the business end of the marriage and ownership of the Bender corporation, and it certainly doesn't appear to show that everything is, how do you say, 'Happily Ever After' between the two of them.

Of course, without Jordan, there were no gigs at the club as there were before, so Libby decided to come up with the idea of a duet, featuring Horace on the guitar and herself on vocals and drumming. This idea lasted as long as the cups of coffee they had been sipping, trying to put it together, and they put the idea to rest over a customary roll in the hay between them at Libby's house while Bill was out somewhere.

Horace and Libby's love-making never stopped after her marriage/merger with Bill and they did it whenever they could, and seemingly wherever they could, under the back deck, on the lawn, in the pool, in the big bed, on the roof, and sometimes in the back seat of Bill's classic 1955 black Cadillac. But most of the time, she would drop by Horace's new place near Lake Galena where they would spend most of their time in the king-sized bed or on the patio under the stars. They were acting like two mischievous teenagers, hiding out from the mean parent who forbids them to go steady until they're in college.

Bill wasn't completely oblivious to their shenanigans either, as he had become aware that she was not spending any quality time with him, nor did he expect a marriage made in heaven when they had tied the proverbial knot. What his male super ego expected was for her to at least show him some respect, which was not going to happen, because Libby had a plan that only she knew the outcome, and Horace knew all along she was cooking something up, even though he hadn't a clue what it was.

Bill started showing up at Horace's place unexpected as always in order to surprise the two if he could, but they were always way ahead of him, camouflaging their rendezvous with immediately jumping off of each other and into their clothes and onto their instruments, instructing each other how a song they were pretentiously working on would end, or begin.

Libby's creative fibbing and prevaricating was all part of her devious plot against Bill Bailey and she noticed, through her own guileful behavior, that it was slowly taking its inevitable toll on eroding his nerves, but she wasn't going to let-up with her constant push of being a duplicitous bitch to him. Horace, although not knowing where Libby was headed with it all, just went along for the fun of it and was enjoying his blissfully euphoric moments of being with her. But when Bill and Libby were by themselves at their home she was lovingly teasing him and leading him on almost, in retroversion of how she'd been acting toward him an hour or so before. That's when there was an unexpected knock at the door, and ringing of the haunting, ethereal echoing chime of the doorbell at the Bender home on Deep Run Road. They both happened to be home when she had opened the door, and Libby, on an impulse screamed at the top of her lungs.

"AAaaaahhh!!" Libby shouted as the body of what appeared to be a man hanging by the neck in front of her, fully clothed and in a three-piece expensive suit slowly rotated limp in the Bender doorway. Hanging from over his shoulders off of twine string was a white cardboard sign that read: "This isn't Bill Bailey. Maybe-NEXT TIME. The virtuous will survive."

When Bill saw the dead man hanging by his neck with his feet about a foot off of the doorstep and the body slowly turning he just stood and stared at the near unrecognizable deformed looking face of death, then told Libby to call the police while he took switchblade from his pocket and cut the man down. Whomever placed him there had vanished.

"Fishman!" Bill said, with fear in his face, identifying the deceased while glaring at his mutilated neck.

"What's that?" Libby asked.

"Fishman worked for me." he said. "Brian Fishman was one of the vendors to the club and a personal associate."

"But what do you think happened . . ." Libby didn't finish when Bill shouted, "QUIET!" in a rather, sharp tone.

The police had arrived momentarily, taking fingerprints and asking all of the usual questions before leaving with the coroner and the body. Bill was in a daze and Libby tried to engage with him, in her humanitarian effort to at least appear to comfort him, but it didn't last very long as he stormed out of the house, taking off in his black 1955 Cadillac. Remembering that phrase "The virtuous will survive," and how he remembered it as the last words Karma, the cab driver had said to him. He made a few calls from his car-phone to two of the others, Ed Langdon and Joe Harris and he got them to get scuba gear together and a tow truck with a strong winch and cable, asking them to meet him at the abandoned quarry.

They all met on the rocky lower part of the overlooking cliffs, about fifty feet above the deep water of the quarry's lake and Langdon, with Harris, shimmied down the rope with their scuba gear and began slipping into the black dive skins, flippers, masks and tanks. Langdon and Harris were both in their mid-thirties, six-footers, built well, but not necessarily athletic, just strong. Both had dark hair and were clean-shaven except for the hairy chest. Harris had hair on his chest and back, like a grizzly, and both had mild pot-bellies.

While they were getting ready they started chatting about the ravine they were in at the water's edge and out of ear-shot of their boss.

"He's afraid to come down here," Langdon said, slipping his leg into the suit.

"You mean Bill? Yeah, I got that impression," Harris replied. "He afraid of water?"

"Kind of," Langdon said, "but he's more afraid of her."

"Her? What are you talking about?"

"The woman," Langdon retorted, "the woman who was thrown into this quarry lake about 20 years ago."

"That's an old tale," Harris said, "about the haunting lady and all . . ."

"He's the one who killed her, Joe." Langdon told Harris. "I thought you knew about that."

"Where the hell did you hear that?" Harris asked.

"Bill told me about ten years ago when he was drunk," Langdon said, strapping on his tank. "He went into all of the details on how he knocked her out, tied a rock to her feet before throwing in right here at the deep end."

"But," Harris rebutted, "he was drunk, Ed. He was just rambling, I think."

"I don't know," Langdon continued, "he really believed what he was telling me. And when he heard that Karma the cabby was spreading that story around this past winter, about this place being haunted by the ghost of a woman, he decided to have us get rid of him, and get rid of him here."

They were strapping each other's tank firm when one of them reminded the other about Jordan and the night they accosted Jordan and his friends at the gay bar in New Hope.

"You should have hung him with the other fruits from that bar." Harris said.

"No," Langdon said smiling, "I couldn't. Bill wanted him to see his queer boyfriends swinging by the neck before taking him to Lake Galena. He wanted to watch us bury him, sick prick."

"Bill's a little psychotic," Harris responded. "Don't you think, Ed?"

"You're just finding that out Joe?" Langdon said laughing, then slipping the mask over his face. "Let's get it. Grab that hook."

After Bill Bailey, who stayed at the top, lowered the end of the thick cable and hook, the both of the divers plunged themselves into the cold lake water. In about fifteen minutes, Harris returned to the top and yelled to Bill that they found it and said that Langdon was hooking it up now. In another five minutes both were at the surface and swimming to the rocky shore, where they kicked off their flippers and gave the signal for Bill to run the winch.

As the cable tightened and whipped through the surface of the cold, murky and still waters of the basin it became obvious the tow truck winch was moving something heavy from the bottom and lifting it, pulling it to the surface. Then, the blue color of an automobile came into view, and the automobile appeared as a charred taxicab with the number 160, with water gushing from a broken window.

After the water had drained enough, the vehicle was placed onto the rocky beach and inspected by all three of them, and all three concluded in total agreement that the body within was none other than Karma's.

"I told you he was dead." Langdon said. "Nobody could have lived through that."

They all observed the mutilated, charred and water-logged decomposing remains of Karma the cabby inside of cab number 160. It most certainly was him.

"Then, who was it we saw the other night?" Harris asked.

"Are you sure you saw anything at all?" Bill retorted sarcastically.

"Someone beat the crap out of us." Harris said.

"You mean, 'beat the crap' out of you!" Langdon replied angrily.

"Well, someone knocked you out cold." Harris responded, shaking his head.

Just then they heard a yell from up top, "Hey! You guys know this is private property, don't you? What do you have there?"

"We saw something in the water," Bill shouted, and then whispered to the others, "We have to get this asshole fast before he calls the cops. Go!"

"Well," the voice from the top of the cliff said, "the cops are on the way!"

"Never mind!" Bill whispered to his crew, "Now we have to get our story straight for when they get here, got it?" And he added: "Just let me do the talking!"

The cops arrived, and Bill Bailey, Langdon and Harris 'apparently' had their story straight in time to give their fake report. They stuck to the basic story of seeing something blue in the water and wondered if it might be a car that accidentally drove off of the road and off of the cliff.

The police brought their own tow truck and took the vehicle while the coroner collected Karma's body. The cops also mentioned another report regarding a body and remarked about how coincidental that the both separate bodies seemed to be associated with the same person finding them, Bill Bailey. One being a murder, they told Bill the same thing that another crew of policemen told him at the house, to not leave the state because they might need him for further questioning later.

As it turned out, Karma's death was ruled a homicide as was Fishman's, but there were no leads as yet and Bill Bailey was getting worn-out from the questioning and the police detectives constantly dropping by. Libby, however, was enjoying the excitement and seeing Bill squirm over every question, every time the doorbell would ring. He wasn't giving in to what he called harassment and would vanish to the club on occasion, but they'd find him there too.

In a few weeks the detectives virtually seemed to withdraw from sight, giving everyone a break, and that's the day Horace showed up. Bill was at the club, so Horace and Libby hung out and after their ritual of making love on the couch, they talked at length of Karma, and how he was murdered, and when.

"The cops are going to question me," he told Libby, "should I be honest?"

"You've got a point," she answered. "The only time you've seen Karma was well after February, the month of his death."

"When did you yourself last see him" Horace asked her.

"I never met the guy," she said, "I only heard you talking about him, and Bill mentioning him and his cab number . . . but I had no idea what that was about."
"I don't know," he said, "they're going to think I'm crazy."
"Let them." she said. "Just tell them what you know, then maybe they'll leave you alone."

Karma's full name was 'Karma Ansara' and he had a family in Newark, New Jersey where the body was taken and laid to rest, interred in the family plot. The police had begun investigating and Horace told them everything he knew about Karma from his cab ride with him. Since Karma had been dead ever since February, it was hard for the police to regard with any credibility the meeting Horace had with him at the quarry lake, causing the cops to begin questioning his credibility about the cab ride.
"Are you telling us it was Karma's ghost you were talking to?" one of them said, rolling his eyes and laughing at the other officer.
"I was talking to a man with your description, named Karma, driving Blue Cab 160 on the weekend night I mentioned." Horace stated firmly.
"Have you seen him at all in this past February? Or before?" The officer asked.
"No, I have not." Horace replied.

The two officers packed their pens and notepads and said, "Good day, we'll be in touch if we come up with anything else worth asking, or if we think that you have any information of value." Then they left Horace with just as much useful information as they came with while they

walked, laughing out loud once in a while, towards their vehicle.
"They're easily entertained," Horace said, staring at them leaving.
"They're assholes," she said, "but my plan is working."

Now, Jordan hasn't been seen by anyone since that day he was found and rescued by Horace, Libby, and Lucy's presumed ghost down at Lake Galena, and Horace finally mentioned him to Libby while they were cooking breakfast at his new place by Lake Galena.
"Where do you think Jordan is?" Horace asked her while he was flipping the pancakes.
"I have no clue," she said, squeezing fresh oranges.
"I'm wondering if he had anything to do with that guy 'Fishman' that's dead."
"You don't think it was Bill who set that up?" she asked.
"Why the hell would Bill kill his friend?" he asked, looking directly at her.
"He has no friends," she said, looking directly back at him, and added: "He has acquaintances who work for him, and all he does is use them like rags, at his disposal whenever he wants."
"Yeah, but it would make no sense," Horace stated as he plopped the done pancakes onto a plate on the stove's center on a low heat, then poured the batter for three more.
"What does make sense about a senseless murder?" she asked.

"What makes sense is that Jordan had a clear motive," Horace said, "He was laid in the ground facing certain death by these guys so he's out to get them now. Make sense?"

"What makes you think that Fishman was one of these people?" she asked.

"Because Jordan killed Fishman? He had the list, remember? It can't be a coincidence."

"That list was Skip's murderers. Your theory will never hold up in court!" she said to Horace, laughing and funning in jest as she put the two glasses of fresh-squeezed orange juice onto the table. "You still can't prove he killed Fishman."

"Coincidence? He looked at the list and said he knew them," Horace said laughing and putting a plate in front of her as she sat, "and here, eat your pancakes."

They both sat at the table after Horace placed the blueberries and the maple syrup in the center between them and began eating, but both of them were wondering where Jordan had gotten to. Horace looked up at the wooden oak cabinets behind Libby and asked her if the cabinets were part of the original kitchen.

"This house used to belong to Bill." she said, taking a mouthful of pancake. "This section was added-on to make the kitchen bigger."

"I thought so," he said, "and when was this kitchen added-on?"

"Oh, about a year and a half ago? Maybe?" Libby said looking around at the same cabinets. "Why?"

I don't know," he said, "just a feeling."

Horace stood and walked over to the cabinets and stood directly in front of them and stomped one foot, causing the small cabinet above the countertop to swing open. Then he looked down at the floor where it had a hollow sound where he had previously stomped his foot.

"What the hell are you doing?" Libby asked, now not eating while she turned her body around to observe Horace as if he was on a detective TV show.

"Don't you think it's peculiar that all of this floor is solid, but only right up to here where there should be some support under this counter?" he said. "There's a lot of weight over here and no support. I think that's odd in a house like this where everywhere else the structure is perfect. You're saying this is all new?"

"Only a few years old, the addition is." she said, then went back to eating.

"How old is the house?" Horace asked.

"This was built in the forties, from what I remember them saying," she said, "and Robert's family owned it since the fifties. He sold it to Bill Bailey in the seventies when he and Bill first became partners, then Robert bought it back off of him this past winter."

"How long has Robert known Bill?" he asked, stomping his foot one more time making the cabinet door open once again.

"They were in the same Fraternity in Penn State University," Libby said, "but Bill screwed Robert over, and I'm not sure of the whole story, other than he took Bill Bailey in as a favor but there's something deeper, an old debt he wanted to settle."

"Is that why you married the bastard?" Horace asked, with a sinister grin.

"My, 'can't get anything past you!" she said sarcastically as she walked over and hugged him, and they once again stripped and made passionate love on Horace's kitchen table.

The next day, Horace and Libby, curious and energetic in their jeans and t-shirts worked together disassembling the kitchen's oak cabinets and countertops, clearing the way for empty wall space and floor area, only to find that it all had covered up an old trap-door to a crawlspace below. The wooden trap-door was made of oak also, because it was the beginning of where the original house once was, before the addition was added, and the line where the original oak flooring started towards the main part of the house from the newer plywood.

Horace used a claw-hammer and a prybar to remove the mixture of cut-nails and common two-inch nails from the perimeter of the trap-door, freeing it up. With the prybar he was able to open the wooden floor-door, releasing a musty, peculiar odor that was alien to his nostrils.

"We don't know what that odor is," Libby said, handing him a damp towel to put over his mouth and nose, while she did the same, "and hopefully it's not toxic."

"It's pretty rank." he said, as he looked into the crawlspace from the kitchen.

"Here's the flashlight." Libby said, handing it to him with it already on, 'almost' as if she was purposely refraining from shining it into the pit, leaving that task up to him.

In shining the large flashlight, he saw the dust settling enough to make-out shapes within the area beneath them, and surmised it was about six feet to the bottom. In the corner, to Horace and Libby's horror, they could make-out what looked to be a skull and the skeletal remains of what used to be a human being, wrapped in what looked like a clear plastic laundry bag, the kind Horace remembered his mom would use from the laundromat.

"WOAH!" Horace shouted, just as he realized what it was he was looking at and fell back into Libby, who saw the corpse at precisely the same time from over his shoulder.

"How long was that there for, I wonder?" Libby asked.

"At least a couple of years, don't you think?" Horace said, still shaking from the initial shock.

"We had better tell someone." Libby said, still leaning on Horace from behind, peering over his shoulder as he continued shining the light on the skull of the human carcass. Suddenly an icy-cold chill pierced Horace's skin and into the marrow of his bones when Libby announced, "Oh my God, this is Miranda!"

"Miranda?" Horace said confused, like he thought he should know who Miranda was, by Libby's tone.

"Miranda," she repeated, and added, "Skip's wife. Miranda disappeared and was never found, from what I remember Skip telling me. She just vanished."

"Vanished?"

"Disappeared," she said, "but I know now she was murdered by Johnny."

"Murdered? And put here?"

"Yes, and Skip never saw her again." Libby said, now with her voice emotionally trembling. "He was so hurt and lonely soon after I met him and hurting over her disappearance, knowing as he had mentioned to me, that something horrible had to have happened, like foul play, for Miranda would never have disappeared on her own."

Horace and Libby notified the police and they promptly arrived to pick up the body and ask the routine questions and also of previous home-owners and when the addition was built and who contracted it. Of course, as it turned out, Bill Bailey was the previous owner who had added-on the newer addition and there was now an APB out for him for questioning. Also, neither Libby or Horace mentioned the possible identity of the victim since as yet there was no physical proof to determine identity or cause of death, and Libby being married to Bill, wanted to keep herself appearing as clean as she actually was of suspicion.

CHAPTER - SIXTEEN

Bill Bailey was called down to the police station and was bombarded with questions regarding the body that was found within the crawlspace of the house he once owned, and not happy at all with their attention toward him being a suspect. He was also not happy with the blossoming relationship between his new wife Libby and her guitar player Horace, a relationship that seemed, at least in his mind, almost intentional with the sole purpose of angering him.

There was some truth to what he was thinking, but it wasn't their sole purpose, since Horace and Libby were truly head over heels in love with each other, brought together as soulmates by the Universe itself. There wasn't a thing in the world that Bill could have done to destroy that bond that they shared spiritually, and 'literally' for thousands of years.

The police, with the help of forensics were able to determine the cause and approximate time of death, the sex, and eventually the identity of the victim due to the approximate time of death. The cause was a blunt force to the head, cracking the skull of what they determined was a female, Afro-American, and 'approximately' twenty-five to thirty years old. They searched for missing persons in the files from that time period back in 1980 and came to the same conclusion that Libby originally speculated; that the body was Miranda Goddard-Mooney, who was married to a saxophone player named Skip Mooney. The police said that Skip Mooney could not be found, and was an immediate suspect to the alleged murder, as was Bill Bailey, opening up a homicide investigation into the crime.

Bill was able to channel their focus toward Skip by virtually lying his ass off, making recommendations where to look and bringing up names such as Johnny Hetrick, and also Brian Fishman, the dead man found hanged at his front door threshold. This, however, brought the law's consideration to the other two Bill Bailey partners who were not exactly happy with the attention, namely Edward Langdon and Joseph Harris.

Langdon and Harris reported under protest for questioning, raising even more suspicions by the detectives but were cleared, under the condition that they didn't leave the state. Bill Bailey was not yet charged with anything but was a suspect and asked to remain available for contact while the detectives continued investigating the house and premises where Miranda was found, which caused Libby to have Horace stay at the Bender house, despite the contesting of Bill Bailey.

Libby and Horace had walked up to the house from her Ford Mustang and were standing right outside of the front door of Libby's house when the confrontation occurred, with Bill blocking the entrance.

"Not in my house!" Bill stated adamantly to Horace. "You can't stay here!"

"Not your house!" Libby replied, just as forcefully, "My house!"

Bill grabbed her and pulled his right arm back like he was going to punch her, but her relentless glare into his eyes may have been the force to suddenly change his mind as he let her go and walked out to his car. Horace watched him and told Libby that he would have clocked him if he hurt her, but Libby responded by giving him a gentle kiss on the lips, saying: "You're so sweet, thank you."

Libby and Horace went to the Dublin Diner the next morning and sat at the booth in the corner and ordered breakfast. Libby requested the three eggs over-easy with home-fries and a side of bacon while Horace ordered the cream-chipped beef on toast with potatoes and onion.

"Gassy, huh?" Libby said, smiling.

"I guess. Or rather, I will be," Horace said, winking and returning her smile.

"You guys should try the grits and onions if you want gas," a voice from the booth behind them stated.

Horace slowly turned around to see a familiar face. It was Jordan, smiling and looking down at his menu, but not turning around to look at the couple.

"Jordan!" Horace said, in a loud whisper as he threw his elbow up on the backrest.

"Shush!" Jordan said in a loud whisper, "I'm supposed to be dead, remember?"

"I think under the circumstances we should put a conservative lid on this right now," Libby said, inconspicuously peering around the restaurant.

"I agree," Jordan said, continuing in his whisper, "Just talk low and face the other way. I can hear you."

"What's going on?" Horace asked, cutting his creamy toast with a fork.

"Did Bill get the gift I sent?" Jordan asked, eating a mouthful of scrambled eggs with a piece of steak.

"Was that you?" Horace asked, as Libby kicked him under the table for talking too loudly.

"There's two more packages you can expect, if you know what I mean," Jordan added.

"Tell him to stop sending packages to my house!" Libby said in her own loud and frustrated whisper.

"I heard you, Libby, and I'm sorry. Where would you want them sent so Bill knows I'm coming for him?"

"I think you should think about what you're doing," Libby said, "and just stop. The police are going to eventually nail Bill if my plan isn't interrupted."

"I'm sorry Libby," Jordan said, faking humility, "I'll have to do this. The law would be too merciful."

"He's already trapped like a rat in a tin shithouse," Horace said, "just let the cops do the rest."

"With all due respect, Horace, have you ever seen a friend, or a lover raped and hanged by the neck? Right in front of your very eyes and made to watch? It's something I can never forget," Jordan said, with his whispering voice trembling.

"Jordan," Horace started, "You can . . ."

"When the blood is streaming," Jordan interrupted, "from their mouths and their kicking legs, struggling to live . . ."

"HEY!" Libby said out loud, shouting it twice as she stood and knocked the pitcher of ice water all over Horace, breaking Jordan's concentration and his verbal delivery of the personal onslaught he had witnessed.

The waitress had come over to help with the cleaning-up of the watery mess and in the confusion, Jordan seemed to have vanished; as mysteriously as he had appeared.

Horace and Libby finished their breakfast in silence and eventually exited the diner, and as they climbed into Libby's Ford Mustang, they both looked around the parking lot for their friend Jordan, without mentioning anything about him to each other. But as they drove off north on Elephant Road and down Deep Run Road, they replayed the event of seeing him at the diner in their conversation.

"Did he look alright?" Horace asked.

"I was facing the top of the back of his head," she said, "and didn't get a good look, but it was definitely Jordan."

"The poor guy had been through hell and back." Horace said, shaking his head.

"Yeah," Libby said, "he's reliving his hell, and I hope he doesn't do anything stupid."

"If I can only sit and talk with him," Horace lamented, "if he would only let me."

"Right now, it's good that Bill thinks he's dead. It might add to my plan," Libby articulated.

"This plan of yours . . ." Horace started talking but she cut him off, saying: "Bill Bailey is a bad dude, and prison is way too good for him."

Libby had had a plan for a long time regarding the Bender Corporation and ownership of all of the clubs, and the plan had been augmented and modified according to the immediate surrounding situations. It was time that Libby came clean to Horace on a few standing issues, such as her being married now to Bill Bailey, and if Robert's still alive, she'd be legally married to him still. Horace was never one for complications in his life and was deeply in love with Libby, and Libby with him. So, at this point Libby had decided to reluctantly bare her soul to him, because she loved him, and because she knew that for her plan to work, she must be completely honest with the one she loved.

Bill had disappeared again, taking off in his '55 Cadillac to address some issues in the Atlantic City Bender's Club while Libby and Horace hung out together, swimming in the pool. Bill was becoming very jealous of their relationship but there was nothing he could do about it. He knew that the marriage between himself and Libby was only for business reasons, for the purpose of cementing his ownership of the corporation, but his ego, as usual for Bill, was getting the best of him. Horace swam to the end of the pool and was sitting at the edge of it on the concrete steps under water, allowing his shoulders and head to be above water and leaning on the pool's edge. Libby swam up to him and placed herself between his legs, resting her elbows on his thighs, looking with her green eyes into his from her weightlessness in the pool.

"Horace," she said.

"Libby?"

"Horace, I'm not married to Robert, never was."

"Really?" Horace responded.

"Have you ever seen us romantically involved?" she asked him.

"No," he said, "I've seen you kiss and hug, but that's none of my business."

"You've seen us kiss and hug," she said, "but we've obviously never been together. Bill and others thought we were married too."

"So?"

"So? Well, don't you want to know why?" she inquired.

"Libby!" Horace exclaimed. "That's between you and him, and if he's impotent, or gay, or had his pecker shot off in a war, it's none of my business."

"He's my biological Father." Libby said.

"WHAT?!" Horace yelled, standing himself up above the water on the underwater steps.

"Robert is my dad, I'm telling you! Our marriage was faked years ago to undermine Bill Bailey's plan to corrupt and takeover Bender's, and it was all Robert's idea. Bill assumed we were married, so we went along with it.

"You'd better start from the beginning." Horace said, sitting himself back down.

"I first thought Robert didn't know I existed for over twenty years. My mom and Robert had a relationship for only a few weeks back in 1960, but despite the fact that Robert was well off, and on his way to becoming the prominent businessman he is today, my mom didn't like the fact that Robert loved drinking and drugs, so she promptly ended the relationship."

Libby continued, "Well, it turned out that Mom was pregnant, and I came into her life in '61, and she raised me as a single mom for a few years, without Robert ever knowing. She raised me on her own, working as a waitress and in a factory until she met Bill Bailey, who treated her nice at first."

"Did she meet him through Robert?" Horace asked.

"No, Bill Bailey and Robert Bender were in the same fraternity at Penn State, but they didn't hook up in business until about five years ago, and if you listen, I'll tell you how."

"Sorry," Horace said, "and please continue."

"Mom was pregnant again, this time from Bill Bailey. This was a surprise to both of them and Bill wanted Mom to abort the child, but she decided to have it, causing Bill Bailey to bail out of her life altogether, but not before beating her, almost causing her to miscarriage. After Mom had the baby she looked Bill up and told him she wanted him to at least support the child with the monthly child support payments. Bill showed up at our little apartment and I was in the back bedroom hiding when it all happened. One thing led to another and Bill punched her, knocking her lights out, causing her to tumble to the floor, but not killing her."

"Horrible." Horace said.

"Tell me about it," she said, "I was two years old and I'll never forget it. I saw it all through the crack in the door and I just stayed as quiet as a mouse while I watched him dragging the body out. My little infant sister was in the cradle next to me, sound asleep so I just sat and waited for someone to come into the room, but no one ever did. I watched him through the bedroom window putting her into the trunk of his car and pull away into the darkness. I never saw my mom again.

"I feel so bad for you." Horace said hugging her, "That had to have devastated you. I can't even imagine."

"It was rough for the next few years, not knowing where my mom was, or if I'd ever see her again. When the neighbors asked me where my mommy went I tried to tell them that she was knocked out by a man and carried out, but being two years old, all they understood me to say was that my mom went away with a man and abandoned us. I remember the cops putting an APB out but when there were no responses and no one knowing that the guy she was last seen with was Bill Bailey, the search was a dead end and they figured she simply abandoned my sister and I, but I always knew better.

"How, at two-years old did you know it was Bill Bailey?" Horace asked.

"My mom sang a song with his name in the lyrics back then," she said, "and engraved that name in my head."

"But there are a lot of Bill Baileys." Horace said.

"It was the one my dad was friends with." she said. "You see, his voice, and that face, when I saw him through the crack in the door punching my mother; it was a face and voice I never forgot. When I found out how to find my biological father, I saw that my dad was also linked with him as a fraternity member. So, when I first got together with Robert to let him know he was my father, I told him what I remembered about that night my mom disappeared, and about Bill Bailey, and Robert didn't doubt for a moment that it was him who caused her to vanish. Because a few years before I had the reunion with my dad, Bill had old a few people at a Penn State fraternity reunion that he had knocked a woman out that demanded child support from him and sort of, made it into a sick sounding joke, saying he tied a rock to her legs and threw her into that quarry lake."

"Wow," Horace said.

"The thing is," Libby continued, "when he sobered up, he didn't remember telling it the following day when everyone had asked him again about it, and Bill said he must have made it all up. Robert told me that he heard him tell that same story at two other reunions, without changing anything in it, leaving him to believe there was some truth in it.

Something else I found out was that Robert was secretly sending child support on his own to both me and my sister, and kept it secret out of respect to my mom, and he made sure we were raised in proper care. He never wanted anyone, even me to know that, and figured that I'd find him someday if I really wanted to."

"About the mysterious quarry lake murder," Horace said, "Karma told me that same story when Lucy and I were sitting with him at that quarry. He said that the quarry lake was haunted by the spirit of a woman, waiting patiently for her murderer to return, so she can drown him, and rip him apart."

"Is that particular quarry lake," she replied, "I mean, the spot where this haunting lady is supposed to be, the same place where Karma and his taxi were dumped? Where you saw his ghost?"

"Yeah," Horace replied, "I thought you knew about that."

"Not until now." Libby said, staring at the floor as if finally realizing something, then saying: "That has to be the place where my mom was dumped. It's obviously a favorite spot for Bill Bailey."

"Do you know about other murders he's committed?" Horace asked her.

"I know he's been involved in that shit, but I heard it through Robert and that's where I came in, with his own plan to eliminate Bill. When Robert found out that he was doing these things he didn't want to tarnish the Bender's

Club. You see he couldn't turn him in because it would be a black mark on his and the club's reputation. So, he had hired a group of people who immediately stopped anyone working for Bill who was doing underhanded schemes like the loan sharking and skimming off of the top. He also put a tail on those in Philly working directly for Bill, like Fishman, Langdon and Harris. To this day, Bill had no idea, and him marrying me is going to choke him out of his fortune he's expecting, because as Robert's daughter, me and my sister that survived are the sole owners of the clubs and profits if anything happens to Robert."

"Your sister?" Horace said, and continued, "That's right, you had that little baby sister in your room, but she's Bill's daughter, isn't she?"

"Robert adopted Zoey." she said.

"Zoey Romano? Was that your mom's last name?"

"Yes," Libby replied, "but Bill never recognized it and 'probably' never knew our mom's last name, the prick. However, Robert remembered."

CHAPTER - SEVENTEEN

Libby had told everything she knew about her relationship with her mother, sister, and even Robert Bender, who is and was her biological father, but there were things that she did not know. Such as, Robert thought that Libby's mom, whose name was Elizabeth Romano, was one of the most beautiful women he's ever known, and he was smitten by her. It was true that Elizabeth decided to keep her life separate from Robert's life and lifestyle, and even though Robert was out of her life, he knew about Libby and would send money anonymously knowing that she would know who was sending it and accepted it gracefully. Robert also knew that his fraternity brother, Bill Bailey, started seeing her out of sheer spite, knowing that it bothered Robert, but the way Robert saw it was that she was a grown up and capable of making her own decisions.

When Robert secretly looked into Elizabeth Romano's disappearance, trying to find her, he knew something had happened, but was not in a position to explore it further with all of the dead ends. Instead, he made sure that her children were raised in the best of foster care and observed from a distance as they grew to become healthy and happy young ladies. Libby had taken up the drums during her growing years and developed her natural talent, proving to be exceptional at her skills on rhythms.

Robert always knew that Libby was his daughter and Zoey had to be from her relationship from Bill, but that didn't stop him from sending money and proper care for both of them, and he kept himself incognito out of respect for Elizabeth's wishes. He also hoped that someday Libby would seek him out as her biological father, and he had never told Libby that he supported and watched over her that whole time, but somehow, in some strange way, she knew.

Through the years, and listening to the rumors that were circulating, either from Karma the cab driver or even Bill himself in a drunken spew of storytelling regarding the haunted quarry lake and disappearances, Robert Bender had concluded that Bill Bailey was responsible for the vanishing of Libby and Zoey's mother.

. Now, when Libby had found out that Bill was the one who had murdered her mother, she had originally devised her own scheme with reference to getting even with him by fabricating her marriage to Robert. But she was abusing drugs and living a life of promiscuity by having a habit of sleeping with different men, even Bill Bailey, the enemy, which Robert had no control over, or at least not yet. But a better strategy was devised once Libby's new 'Walk-In' spirit entered and took over her center, leading her to, over time, start to think and project more clearly. Robert's original plan was starting to fall into place, with the help of her new lover and soulmate Horace entering the picture.

Robert was correctly diagnosed with cancer and is 'literally' dying so the plan was to fake his death to clear the way of Libby being free to marry Bill Bailey, knowing he would follow through on the wedding since there was a fortune to be had by tying the knot with Libby. Little did Bill know that this fortune would be short lived, or at least that was the intention, to ruin him by taking it all away as easily as it came, sending him out in the street into the gutter, or even prison to be with people he had originally ratted on to save his own ass. He never saw that a stipulation in the business contract also stated simply that upon Robert's death, a marriage partner to a sibling (Zoey or Libby) of Robert Bender was automatically excluded from any ownership of shares in the company.

The next morning Bill Bailey had come home to the Bender's house very early and Horace arose immediately from Libby's king-sized bed and rushed through the door to the spare room unnoticed, but Bill knew immediately what was going on as he stomped up the stairs with a sawed-off shotgun and kicked the door open to the master bedroom.

"Get up!" he shouted to Libby, pointing the gun directly at her face from across the room.

"You're fucking drunk!" she said, then she rolled herself out of bed calmly in her total nakedness and strutted her slim body into the master bathroom, never taking her eyes off of him while Bill stood still, glassy-eyed, and stared as she shut the door. The gun went off, blowing the door completely apart but Libby had quickly exited through the other door to the spare room where she and Horace ran down the back stairs and out to her Ford Mustang. One more shot echoed the grounds shattering the back window of the vehicle, but both Libby and Horace escaped unharmed.

They put on their clothes in the car while they drove to the State Police barracks to file a police report and subsequently, Bill Bailey was arrested and charged with aggravated assault with a deadly weapon and held on $500,000 bail.

Libby and Horace went back to the house while the police investigated the crime scene and removed their necessary belongings, moving themselves into a five-bedroom rancher off of Powder Valley Road on the edge of Bucks County, near Lehigh County. There, near a small creek the both of them set-up house and living-space while playing music and waiting for the next phase of Libby's plan, which was to divorce Bill Bailey and leave him high and dry with nothing but the clothes on his back for murdering her mother over twenty years ago. Even though she'll never be able to legally prove he was the one who did her in, and the body had never been recovered, she knew she'd have the satisfaction of seeing him go under financially, which would be the ultimate attack on his inflated ego, the disintegration of all of his material world.

The rancher was a humble abode, with a brick-front and connected to a two-car garage, and where there wasn't brick there was aluminum siding and windows with blue shutters. Inside was a cozy area with eight-foot ceilings and large rooms, bath areas, and a modest kitchen with the cooking counter in the middle of the room, and stools where folks could sit and talk to the person or persons cooking. The five bedrooms were each 12' by 12', plenty of space in the house for at least ten people to live.

In the meantime, Libby's sister Zoey moved in to stay, along with a few of her friends about her age, Rita, Harold, Bonnie, and Zack. Back when Horace's live-in girlfriend at the time, Lucy, died in their bathroom tub, these were the folks who helped Libby clean-up the house and move Lucy's belongings into storage for Horace.

Rita and Harold were high school sweethearts and have been together ever since, and the same with Bonnie and Zack, all who went to Central Bucks West and graduated around 1980. Zack was thin with long red hair and a scruffy beard and his girlfriend Bonnie was a petite blue-eyed blonde, and smart, graduating at the top of her class. Rita and Harold both had long dark hair and creative tattoos on their arms and legs. Rita had a pretty face with very dark eyes and was full-breasted, showing off the tattoos on her pronounced cleavage whenever she could.

Harold, who was part Afro-American with a mildly dark complexion had a well-cut masculine build for his young age and showed it off with the muscle shirts and also went shirtless, showing off his hairless chest when possible. In short, the group is a party of young people looking for adventure wherever they can find it, but in the past years, since high school, they've been working in some of the out-of-state Bender's Clubs on a generous salary from Libby and Robert.

They all had an unusually strange attraction to ancient African history and learned from reading books on ancient weaponry, such as the unsophisticated blow-gun tubes from bamboo and the fabrication of ancient bows and arrows. All of them get together occasionally and plan paint-ball battles with each other, using biodegradable water-paint balls and guns they've fabricated on their own. Zack and Bonnie have both used their homemade blowguns to project dart syringes to sedate a grizzly bear on a hiking trip in Wyoming last summer, so they're not complete novices in this field.

They however were a good audience for Libby and Horace when they jammed as an unplugged duet, with Horace playing his acoustic Martin guitar and Libby on the brushes with the snare drum, the cymbals, and at times roaring on the congas, filling in the rhythmic gaps. For a whole week it was a good time of jamming and some beer drinking, but no drunken blackouts anymore since Libby and Horace had really found each other as soulmates and thoroughly enjoyed each other's company and the relationship with their friends. Libby's sister Zoey was especially tuned into watching her sister play and even joined in on the congas when Libby switched back to the drumming.

Both, Libby and Horace, missed Jordan's solid bass lines and sensed each other's thoughts on wondering where and how he was doing, and wondered if they'd ever see him again. Jordan is a distant cousin to Harold and the only one new to this group was Horace, who said he felt like he's always known everyone. Libby even stated that the reason they were all together and sharing compatible chemistry was because they were all together before in past lives sharing the same synergy and consonance.

At one point, after a sit-down meal in the dining room Zoey and Libby cleared the dishes off of the table and Horace started washing while Libby dried. During the cleaning Rita, who was somewhat of a medium, practicing her craft whenever and wherever anyone would listen, decided tonight was the perfect time for a reading. She said the grounds they were on were ancient Lenni Lenape holy grounds and that the spirits were right for the enlightenment of a group meditation on our past lives and past souls.

Horace continued with finishing up while Libby put on some coffee as Rita shuffled some strange looking tarot cards, then laying them on the table one by one face-down, slowly looked at the persons sitting around the table; first at Zack, then Bonnie, then Harold, with his shirt off, and finally at Zoey. She told Libby and Horace to stand arm in arm directly behind her, which both were more than happy to oblige as they cuddled close.

Rita drew the one card in the air and laid it face up then each one, one by one. Those who looked on observed that each tarot card was blank, without any markings or numbers, or pictures and they all remained silent since they all felt that everyone looking saw the same blank cards. The only one who didn't see blank cards, however, was Rita, who started reading what she observed.

"Zack." she said. "You were once a son of Libby and Horace, who at that time were known as Ely and Mary Kelly-Cass in a past life. Your name was Peter Cass, and you were one of eight children living in a log cabin in a holler within a coal mining region. You eventually went on to be a railroad engineer, moving freight across the United States and died an old man, surrounded by your family in West Virginia."

"I thought so." Zack said, in his comically cynical nod, making Bonnie laugh, giving him a nudge in the ribs. Then Bonnie said, "I suppose I was his girlfriend in a past life too."

"Not exactly." Rita said as she turned the next blank card over, and while peering at her continued:

"Zack, I mean Peter, was married to me, Brenda Pruitt-Cass. He and I had a roller-coaster relationship but, in the end, we held it all together well, raising five children, but he was always on the road."

"That's too bad," Bonnie said grinning and then added with a humorous tinge of arrogance, "I would have treated him better if it was me."

Everyone laughed at her quip, but Rita followed up quickly with another revelation.

"Actually," Rita replied, "You did treat him better in some respects as Alice Chandler, a prostitute he had known on the road all of his life until he finally retired at home full-time with Brenda and the kids."

There was more laughter in the room and Libby stated: "I told you we were all together before, but in another life-time."

"What about Harold?" Bonnie asked. "You forgot to mention Harold. Wasn't he somebody?"

"Sure," Zack said, "he was probably married to that whore, Bonnie."

"Alice!" Bonnie shouted, correcting him with a big grin and laughing at Zack's comment, taking a loving poke at him. "My name was Alice, and I resent that!"

"Actually," Rita continued the reading, "Harold in another life was Arthur Cass, brother to Peter Cass. 'By the way', the illegitimate son of Alice was none other than the one and only Robert Bender, who with the help of Peter Cass was raised as a fine, upstanding young man, who joined the Airforce in 1950, and piloted a P-51 Mustang but was shot down by a Korean MIG-15 over the Pacific and rescued. As he recuperated in the hospital back in Hawaii a nurse, Angela Warren fell in love with him and they were married right there in the hospital, but his wife Angela had died from tuberculosis only a year after they were married."

"I've got chills." Libby said, squeezing Horace's hand, "That was my biological father! He mentioned that once to me."

"Actually, Libby, if you remember what you and we talked about before, you are a 'Walk-In' spirit for the life of Libby you're living now. Her spirit moved on to a better life. Through you replacing her spirit, he became your father."

"Where did her spirit go, the original Libby spirit?" Horace asked.

"That answer's not in the cards that I can see." Rita said in almost monotone. "That's not for me to know. Just like your spirit Horace. You too are a 'Walk-In', replacing what was once the temple of another soul, who likewise moved on to a better life."

Rita glanced at the cards again and added: "Horace and Libby, those spirits you both replaced were twin spirits, meaning that you were always with them in other lives, but as twins. Horace, you and your twin soul you replaced were both on the Asian Continent about 1,000 or so B.C., as twin brothers, and Libby, you and your twin soul you replaced were once in what is now Peru, in the Amazon Jungles in a tribe as twin boys at the dawning of the Aztecs. You were twins on earth many other times too. What's your birth signs?"

"We're both Geminis." Horace said. "I'm a few years older but we were both born on June 13, on a Friday, at precisely 12:00 Midnight, coincidentally enough."

"I should have guessed," Rita said, "Gemini, not a coincidence."

"What did Robert Bender do after Angela passed?" Bonnie asked, pouring everyone more coffee.

"He got out of the service and went to Penn State to graduate as a business major after the war." Rita said as if she was reading dictation off of the cards.

"Don't tell me. . ." Zoey hesitated. "So, I was . . ."

"The nurse was you, Zoey," Rita said, "Your previous life was Angela Warren-Bender, soon to be reborn once again as Libby's sister through your mom's relationship with Bill Bailey."

"Yuck!" Zoey said, causing everyone to laugh.

"This all makes for some fascinating conversation and brain teasing, but I don't know if I believe it." Harold said smiling and taking a large sip of coffee, carving a bamboo into a perfect tube, and then comically peering at Rita through it.

"It's all in good fun." Zack said with some skepticism, putting the finishing touches on what 'seemed to be' an arrow without feathers.

"I believe it," Bonnie said standing and stretching.

"You would!" Zack said, causing her to punch him in the shoulder while he mockingly faked being knocked out.

"Something else," Rita started another reading, "whether you believe it or not, we were all located together, in the same tribe in Africa around 2,000 BC. We all hunted and defended ourselves from other tribes using blow-gun poison darts and bows and arrows. We were a very closely-knit tribe."

"Still are," Harold said, holding up the man-made blow-gun tube while standing and stretching his long muscular arms to get the blood flowing and asked, "It's getting late, isn't it?"

"It certainly is," Rita said, looking at her watch and gathering her cards. "I'm turning in."

"Into what?" Zack said.

"Into a love machine." Harold said, wrapping his arms around Rita and lifting her playfully while she laughed.

"Sounds like a good idea." Libby said, wrapping her own arms around Horace as they all turned in for the night.

When the week was over, and Libby and Horace felt that the smoke had cleared from the abhorrent and harrowing shotgun incident, they headed back to the house, leaving their friends on their own to the back-woods rancher and headed to the Bender home on Deep Run Road. All the way there they talked about what might be happening, since they've been out of touch and Libby was concerned that if they let Bill Bailey out of jail on bail, he might be crazy enough to come after the both of them.

Their deepest fear had come to pass when they had gotten home, and they discovered that someone posted bail and Bill had gone back to where he had been living before he married Libby, at his residence in a beautiful mansion in Huntingdon Valley. The Bailey place was surrounded by a wall and a gate, not unlike the Bender place, but the grounds were limited, containing a well-manicured lawn and shrubs and concrete statues of the ancient gods looking over the place. The police stayed parked outside of the Bailey grounds and although he was released on bail, he needed to report every day to the probation officer at least until his trial, which would be in a few months. Bill Bailey was free to come and go as he pleased, but usually had someone tailing him whenever he left the Bailey grounds.

"What's to stop that maniac from paying us a visit?" Horace asked as he walked into the room where the shotgun blast shattered the door.

"Nothing." Libby stated. "But he is under watch and certainly forbidden to step on these grounds."

"Do you really want to stay here?" Horace asked.

"No." Libby said. "Robert has another big place, the same size as this in Buckingham, Pa. You'll love it."

"Does Bill Bailey know about it?" Horace asked worried.

"Aww," Libby said, in a comforting tone. "You shouldn't be afraid of that asshole," she told him, as they took only a suitcase of clothing they'd need for a few days until they could move everything else to the Buckingham mansion Robert Bender owned on Lower Mountain Road.

With just the Ford Mustang and a few suitcases they drove to their destination, and down a long dirt driveway through a wall opening without the protective electric gates they saw the big stone two story farmhouse that was, in all respects a mansion.

"What's the matter Horace? Are you worried?" she asked, noting what she thought was a spark of fear within his eyes. "Don't you trust me that we'll be alright?"

"This place isn't as secure as the other place," he said, "and what if he just kills us off? He'll get nothing out of it, right?"

"Well," she said, "I wouldn't say that, but he won't be able to pull it off."

"No, it's not just that. I mean, like, I'm not a business genius, but doesn't he still own almost half of your Bender Corporation?" he said, while they were carrying their suitcases into the large big-roomed house, that was well kept and cleaned regularly by a rental company Robert Bender personally contracted.

"When we get to court," Libby said, putting the suitcases upstairs in the master bedroom, "Bill Bailey will end up surrendering all of his shares to me and also Zoey. Like I said before, Robert Bender's children are the sole heirs to the entire business, unless something happens to us."

"What then?" Horace asked.

"Don't worry, nothing's going to happen. 'Never will!" she said again, while making the large king-sized bed with fresh, clean sheets.

"Famous last words," Horace stated. "Never say never!"

"Alright," Libby said, "If anything happened to Zoey and me, Bill 'could' end up with everything, if he had very smart lawyers. But since Robert is technically out of the picture by proxy, Bill would have to eliminate me and Zoey, and to tell the truth, YOU!"

"ME?" Horace asked, shocked and surprised. "What do 'I' have to do with it?"

"You," Libby said, "are the designated heir by means of a few binding signatures of mine and Robert's own delegating. We trusted you from the beginning and we know you aren't the type to wipe us out to gain everything we own.

"How do you really know for sure?" Horace asked meekly, as they both undressed completely and climbed into the bed between the cool, fresh satin sheets.

Libby softly wrapped her arms around him, then looking steadily into his eyes which were equally transfixed on hers said, "Because I know your heart, and you know mine."

She kissed him, and the kiss was warm, sweet, and compelling as the softness of her moist lips and tongue penetrated his very being, causing them to roll into a world and universe of their own, inducing a moment that lasted the rest of the night and into the morning hours.

Horace and Libby both awoke at precisely the same time, but realized they were not in the same warm bed they had so romantically slumbered for what seemed to be only hours ago. They were both aware of a sharp pain of a pounding headache and had come to the frightening conclusion that they were confined between slabs of solid wood on six sides . . . like a coffin.

"Are you alright?" Libby asked in the cool darkness.

"Where the hell are we?" Horace answered with a question, and then another: "What the hell happened?"

"Maybe we should try to save our breaths for now." Libby said, as she reached around in their very tight quarters to pound her hand on the walls to see if it was solid.

Both of them were now sweating and were sliding their naked bodies on each other trying to feel the walls and surmise the predicament. One conclusion they had drawn was that Bill Bailey had found them and that he had placed them alive into a box to be buried. They figured the wood walls were too hollow-sounding for them to be surrounded by dirt, but that didn't mean that being buried alive wasn't ruled out.

"Damn," Horace said, "I wonder what he hit us with? My head is pounding."

"He didn't physically hit us," Libby replied, "I'm pretty sure he used a gas on us to put us under. He and his cohorts must have been at the house first and had set it all up for us."

"I wonder what he's going to do with us?" Horace pondered, "I don't want to die."

"Trust me," Libby answered, "neither do I. We're not going to die here, love. I can feel it."

Libby could sense the uneasiness inside of Horace and she tried to turn him on by touching him, hoping it would relax him, but all it did was create anxiety.

"What if you just tell me a story," Libby said, "you know, something about your past that's funny, or something that would relax the both of us."

"What about using up our oxygen?" Horace said.

"Horace, you'll use up more oxygen just breathing and being nervous than you would relaxing your heart and telling one of your stories."

Realizing she was right, Horace thought for a few moments within the darkness of their confined and tight quarters. As he did he rubbed Libby's back with his gentle fingers while she faced him with her warm body pressed against his chest and thighs. All of a sudden, he started laughing, remembering something from his past that caused Libby to also laugh out loud.

"I've got one." he said. "About ten years ago I was in a band that played a party for the Philadelphia Rugby Team. They were having an Autumn keg party to encourage locals for team tryouts and we had a five piece that was willing to play for $100 a piece."

"That sounds like it was fun." Libby said, hugging him tighter.

"It was." he said, smiling in the confined darkness. "My friend Skeeter, who was a bass player was looking forward to the bash and asked if there were going to be lots of women there. I didn't know, so I told him 'definitely' while we were rehearsing for it the day before. Well, it was a bit chilly that October and Skeeter went out and bought a brand-new, snazzy reversible jacket; very stylish for that year and that time of season.

When we were loading up the equipment he entered the house where we rehearsed wearing it, asking: 'What do you think?' as he spun around like one of those models on TV.

'Look's great, Skeeter' most of the guys said, but Tommy, the lead singer and harmonica player laughed and told him that the orange color looked like puke. Skeeter just shrugged his shoulders and said that he liked the color, and then turned it inside out to the yellow side and spun around again to show it off. Tommy, who had always good-naturedly busted on Skeeter said, 'Look's even more like puke, I can't look at that.'

Shrugging his comment off like it was never said, Skeeter finished helping Tommy load-out the rest of the drums and we were all off to the gig in Philly.

We were in a separate car from the van the equipment was in and stopped to pick up two girls we knew who wanted to go. Skeeter got out of the car and spun around for them with his arms straight out, showing off his brand-new reversible jacket, causing them both to smile as he let them into the back seat, sitting on either side of him.

We arrived and set-up the equipment and drank beer, played music, drank beer during the break, then played more music while drinking the icy-cold beer out of the mugs we brought with us."

"You must have gotten ripped." Libby said, cuddling tight against Horace's naked body as he told the tale.

"We all did," he said, "especially Skeeter. I watched him during the breaks with a crowd of women around him and their boyfriends, seeing him spin around again and again. Boy, he sure was very proud of that jacket.

Anyway, we had finished playing our songs and in our drunken madness signed up for rugby tryouts to the surprise of our audience and then went on to load the van. Then we had to place Skeeter in the backseat of our car, a Buick Skylark, because he was passed out drunk. Tommy was also loaded, drunk as hell, and making passes at one of the girls who came with us, so, in order to avoid him, she sat Skeeter, who was completely passed out, right in the middle between her and Tommy. The girl was also pretty drunk . . . and like I said, we all were, and it was a miracle we all made it home in one piece."

"I'd say you're right, from what you're telling me." Libby said, enjoying Horace's story.

"On the way home, as I drove, and in the rearview mirror I saw them all passed out, with Tommy leaning on Skeeter's shoulder. The girl, 'Sally' I think was her name, was resting and sleeping against the window.

Well, after about ten minutes into the drive I heard some hacking and then retching. The two people in the front seat with me were Erin, who was Sally's girlfriend, and our guitarist Gary, both who were now looking back to check where the noises were coming from.

'Oh my God,' Erin said, 'Gross! Tommy's throwing up!'

'Tommy's puking all over Skeeter.' Gary said, as he reached back to try to push Tommy off of him.

He was somewhat, successful in his efforts causing Tommy to lean the other way, but by that time Tommy was on empty. So, with the entire car smelling like fresh vomit and us being too drunk to pull over for fear of cops, we continued our trek northward on Interstate 95. But after about another ten minutes we heard Sally waking up and asking 'Eww, what's that awful smell?' 'Almost on-cue,' she leaned over to Skeeter to see if it was him who was rancid and as she did, puke projected from her mouth, 'almost' as if she was possessed, covering Tommy's vomit with her own warm blend of sardines and chips and hotdogs from the party. You see, Tommy was getting Sally to eat these oily sardines he was packing, saying that the oil in the sardines will coat the stomach, thus preventing the beer and liquor from having an effect, causing them to be able to drink more."

"That's so, gross!" Libby said, unable to control herself from laughing.

"I know," Horace stated, "Tell me about it! We had to smell that shit all the way home. Anyway, Sally immediately passed out again after dumping her guts and slept on Skeeter's shoulder the rest of the way home.

Upon arriving at the house where we were staying at the time, everyone but Skeeter who was in the backseat woke up like nothing happened. Tommy, who actually had absolutely no vomit on himself said, 'what's that smell?' as he climbed out of the car. On the other side, Sally was saying 'virtually' the same thing as she couldn't get out of the car fast enough, and she too, had no signs of the regurgitant. Gary and I started calling to Skeeter, trying to wake him up, and realized that all of the puke, every damn bit of it was on Skeeter's reversible jacket and his lap. We both carefully lifted him as to not get any of it onto the car's upholstery and carpet, sliding him out to the lawn and set him on his ass just as he started waking up.

'Are we home?' he asked.

'Yep.' Gary told him.

Skeeter looked down at his new reversible jacket and at his pants with a look of terror and asked, 'What happened here?'

'What do you think?' I asked him, trying not to laugh at it all."

"You are soooo bad!" Libby said to Horace, still squeezing him against her now more relaxed naked body.

"I know," Horace said, "but not really. You see, Skeeter figured that he had too much to drink and thought he simply threw-up on himself. About a year later we had told him what had really happened, but he never believed it. It's too incredible and could never happen, but it did."

"I can believe it," Libby said as they both shared the laugh.

"Listen," Horace said, as they were now hearing dirt being thrown over top of the box they were in.

Horace started banging on the walls but just as quick as he began his pounding, Libby grabbed his wrist to stop him.

"Save your strength," she said, "I don't believe we're meant to die this way, and I can feel it."

"How do you know?" Horace asked.

"We weren't put at random into this life for it to be thrown away like this," she said. "We're virtuous beings."

"We're no different than anyone else," he told her. "What the hell do you mean, we're virtuous?"

"You believe because I believe, and we're the believers, protected by someone or something angelic, a greater power because we believe."

"You're losing me," Horace said, and Libby could sense his skeptic grin, causing her to smile herself.

"Maybe so, at the moment anyway, but have I ever been wrong about these things so far?" she asked.

"You got me there," he said.

"That's what keeps your belief in me," she said, softly touching his shoulder and continued, "Did you ever wonder about reincarnation, Horace? You know, about what it is, or what it means?"

"I'll admit," Horace said pausing, "You're telling me about it, but I don't completely understand how it works. You say we die, then are 'supposedly' reborn into another time, another place, and another body, and not remembering our previous life. So, how are we to be this same being? I mean if everything's different? We become someone else, so we're not the same person or persons anymore."

"Horace," Libby said with utmost confidence, slowly rubbing his sweating back in the darkness of their confinement. "The best way I can put it is it's like when you're listening to a song. So, think of it this way: We're the song, you see, our spirits are nothing but a beautiful song that somebody sings; any 'body'. Did you ever listen to a song like 'Ooh Baby Baby', sung by Smokey, and then hear the same song again sung by Aretha? Reincarnated. Beautiful, but in a different way. That's what reincarnation is. And if that song has two people trading off on verses, then that would be comparable to a 'Walk-In' spirit taking over. Same song, same life, different souls. Two people put their heart and souls into that song."

"But the song itself is a past soul sung by another person? Another life?" Horace asked.

"The soul is the same song reincarnated into another vocalist singing its praise," she said.

"You make it all sound so simple," Horace said, "and beautiful."

"The concept is simple to understand," she said, "but try to match those voices in those songs, especially Aretha's. 'Can't be done, so, it's not simple at all. Right there is the purest example of heart and soul."

"I see what you mean," Horace said, hugging her close and getting an emotional shiver.

"Are you crying?" Libby asked in a whisper.

"No," Horace said, "Just emotionally drained."

Just then, there was more digging and scraping noises coming from directly outside if the wooden walls that were immediately surrounding them and a muffled, desperate panting sound that eventually said, "Hello?" Then it repeated as the digging continued, "Hello in there. Help is here! Hang in there!"

"Hello?" Horace yelled at the top of his lungs and the digging and scraping became clearer and louder. Soon, the top of the box opened, and a blinding light pierced their pupils as the both of them sat up hesitantly, covering their eyes and slowly opened them as the break of daylight was shining brightly on their nakedness.

"Here," a familiar voice said, "throw these around you if you want."

The familiar voice they heard was none other than that of Jordan, who was throwing them two large pairs of sweatpants and sweatshirts to dress themselves.

"I always carry extra sweats for my bass fiddle," Jordan said jokingly, "but I've never needed them until now."

When Libby and Horace finally adjusted their eyes to the light of day they were able to observe the area and notice that they were back at those burial places by Lake Galena where they first discovered Skip and Jordan, by and near the big willow tree. They themselves, it seemed, were temporarily buried within a shallow grave as were the others and their apparent hero was Jordan, who was now helping them up and out of their would-be coffin.

Looking past Jordan, as their eyes were still getting adjusted to the light, they saw a dead man hanging naked from a sycamore tree with his neck in what looked like a thirteen-coiled hangman's noose, the same kind that Jordan said had hanged his friends right in front of him, right before their killers buried him alive.

"Yeah," Jordan said, noticing Horace and Libby staring at the dead man, "It's something you never forget once you see it, especially when it happens to a few very close friends."

"Who is that up there?" Horace asked, displaying a shocked expression while Libby gasped.

"It's Langdon." Libby said, horrified.

"Langdon was left here to finish burying you guys," Jordan said, "I followed them here. Harris is next, and his brother Mike Harris, and finally that prick Bill Bailey.

"Mike Harris?" Libby asked. "There's two of them?"

"Mike Harris is a bigger asshole than his brother Joe. Yeah, there's two of them, but Mike is worse because he's a coward; 'beat up and abused 'just about' every woman he's been with, and he's murdered some of them. I'm glad he wasn't the one involved in getting you guys."

"How the hell did we end up there anyway?" Libby said. "I don't remember a thing."

"It was Bill Bailey and Ed Langdon," Jordan said. "They had used a gas that was supplied by Joe Harris' brother Mike, who worked in a chemical plant, and on fishing boats, but they kept Mike away from you Libby, because of his history with women and Bill felt some sort of obligation to you still, because you're married."

"Bill's such a respectable guy," Libby said sarcastically.

"Bill's setting this all up to make it look like there's a serial killer burying his victims and he's going to leave clues for the cops to find the bodies. His intention is to pin it all on Johnny Hetrick."

"He has no idea where Johnny is, does he?" Libby asked.

"Hell no," Jordan said, "but he figured that if anyone can find him, it'll be the police. He himself hasn't seen Johnny. When the cops come here they're going to discover that Langdon has been murdered and you guys won't be here. But they'll find Skip buried over there and probably tie that to Johnny too."

"It was Johnny who buried Skip," Horace said.

"I know," Jordan agreed, "and they'll be after a serial killer called Johnny Hetrick. But Bill is going to be the one in shock hearing about Langdon through the police report, and Skip, then finding out you two are gone," Jordan paused before speaking again. "Hell," he said, now laughing hysterically, "Bill will probably think you guys hanged Ed Langdon!"

Libby and Horace were both quiet about their knowledge of Johnny to Jordan, the fact that Johnny is dead and how they had substituted Johnny's body as Robert Bender's charred remains while Robert is actually alive and in upstate Pennsylvania.

"Joe and Mike Harris are going after your sister Zoey next," Jordan said, "because they now know about her, and also you and her both being Robert Bender's daughters, the child heirs of Bender's. I heard it all through them, how they're going to leave evidence that would seem to involve Johnny Hetrick. These guys are evil, and I don't know how they can even trust each other."

"How the hell did you find out all of this stuff that they now know about my sister and me?" Libby asked.

"Well," Jordan said with a sly and crazy grin, "when you're in a box and you got nothing else to think about but dying, you listen to what's going on around you and remember everything you hear, just in case you survive."

"Look, Jordan," Horace said after hearing him out, "Libby and I are appreciative of you rescuing us, saving our lives. Believe me, we're grateful! But you can't be going around hanging everyone."

Then Jordan said something peculiar. "You know, Mike Harris can't swim like his brother, and he's deathly afraid of water. That's why he couldn't do any of the scuba stuff with Joe. I think I know how I want to get that male-chauvinist perverted mother fucker. I'm going to get him over here to Lake Galena again somehow, and I promise I won't be hanging his ass!"

"Mike must have really hurt Jordan," Horace whispered to Libby, "if you know what I mean."

"I'll tell you one thing," Libby whispered back, "My sister would show no mercy to that bastard Mike if he tried anything with her and if she ever got her hands on him."

"I heard that," Jordan said overhearing and laughing, "but if she ever gets her hands on him, I want to be there to watch!"

CHAPTER - EIGHTEEN

Once again Libby and Horace were back at the ranch house off of Powder Valley Road on the edge of Bucks County with their friends Zack, Bonnie, Harold and Rita. Zoey was also with them but was spending a lot of hours in the gym and swimming at a club near Emmaus, Pa. She had arrived at around the same time as Horace and Libby and the both of them greeted her outside by the wooden split-rail fence.

"Damn you look great!" Libby said hugging her and looking her over.

"I'll say," Horace agreed while Libby gave him a smirk.

"Stop staring at her," Libby added, directing her snide comment to Horace.

Zoey had become more toned due to her workouts, and it showed in her butt through her tight, skimpy spandex bottoms and a tight, very revealing spandex tube-top showing her abundant cleavage.

"He can stare," Zoey said, "I'm not proud."

"You should be," Libby said, "I'm going to have to go to the gym with you."

"You don't need it, sister," Zoey said, squeezing Libby's tight ass, "but I'd love it if you came with me tomorrow."

"I wasn't staring," Horace said, shaking his head, knowing that they weren't listening anyway.

The three of them walked into the rancher, carrying a few suitcases of clothing from the other house and greeted the rest of the crew. Horace and Libby made themselves at home and the plan was they were going to stay until there was word from Robert's lawyers and accountants on what the next move should be.

Meanwhile, Bill Bailey and the Harris Brothers, Mike and Joe, were gathered at Bill's Huntingdon Valley place waiting for the arrival of the police, who had just gotten the report about Ed Langdon's body hanging from a tree near Lake Galena. The cops found what looked to be an empty grave, and located another shallow grave containing the remains of a dead man holding a saxophone. Bill, needless to say was furious and certain that Horace and Libby had somehow escaped and killed Langdon, just like Jordan had predicted. Bill also thought that they would have found Jordan's body in the same location but of course, and unbeknownst to him, Jordan was rescued and was alive and healthy.

He didn't want to say anything at all about Jordan in case the police had found his body and were holding out to see if someone would speak up about him. He didn't want to say anything that could incriminate him in any of the murders, so when they were asking questions he was like a clam when they inquired about the area and answered only questions pertaining to their working relationship.

The detectives also asked questions pertaining to finding Fishman hanging in the same manner in the front-door threshold of the Bender's place, but he knew nothing and could offer nothing. How the cops were alerted in the first place about those shallow gravesites was he had Mike Harris place an anonymous call to the Park Police about what looked like a fresh grave down that particular nature trail under a willow tree about a hundred yards or so from the lake, but the police saw Langdon's body hanging in the nearby sycamore tree, easily marking the crime spot. There was also another note in ink by a black magic marker written on Langdon's chest, similar to what they found with Fishman, saying: "The strong will survive with the virtuous."

As Bill Bailey had planned, and as Jordan had predicted, the police were looking for a man named Johnny Hetrick to question as their number one suspect, thanks to the answers Bill, Joe and Mike have delivered to them, guiding the trail of suspicion directly to a dead man. Only Bill and his cohorts aren't aware that he was dead, and figured that Johnny simply took off, or left the state 'maybe' since no one from their circle had heard from him for maybe a few months, making Johnny their perfect patsy.

Bill had Libby and Horace under surveillance by his own people, two goons known only as Stu and Blue. Both guys were white ex National Guard officers in their mid-thirties, both had shaved heads and clean-shaven faces and were a bit paunchy, looking like androids at about 5'11', about 250 pounds each but were able to carry themselves satisfactorily in a one-on-one fist fight, since they were originally hired as bouncers for the Philadelphia Bender's Club. These two were assigned to follow and listen in on conversations that would give Bill Bailey leads to whatever Horace and Libby were up to at any given time.

Horace and Libby, however, weren't the easiest to put a tail on so the two goons working for Bill had their work cut out for them with being as inconspicuous as possible, but it was easy for Horace and Libby to catch on, and actually use it against them to try to corner Bill using his own plan.

Stu and Blue were sitting outside of the Bender Deep Run Road home about a quarter mile away with binoculars to see that the couple had stopped in for clothing and other items, listening to a microphone-bug they had planted. Stu then radioed via car-phone, information to Bill Bailey regarding the couple's next moves, without police being aware of what Bill was up to. At this point Stu and Blue had become aware that Libby and Horace planned a full-moon midnight swim, a skinny-dip at the quarry lake that night, but that was all the info they could obtain from listening in.

Zack, Bonnie, Harold and Rita knew that Zoey had left to join Libby and Horace for a moonlight swim at the quarry and decided to do an all-nighter of paintball and prehistoric war games in the surrounding woods near where they'd be swimming but wanted to wait until after they had their private swim and fun. They wanted to surprise them by showing up at around 3:00 am and seeing if they could sneak up on them. Zack had manufactured the 'virtually harmless' toys that could be utilized as weapons if needed, but that was all part of the games. They had homemade paintball guns that shot harmless paintballs that would wash clean from clothing, and the misses would rinse easily from trees and rocks in the first rainstorm and made with products like flour and water that would not damage the environment but might cause the eyes to temporarily burn if not protected. The guns could also be altered as weapons if need be for self-defense if loaded with gravel, or Zack's favorite, loaded with marbles and set with a pump of high compression, but no one was expecting the latter.

Zoey met Horace and Libby at the Bender house and they all left together in the pick-up, all three sitting in the front with Horace driving.

"I'm glad you could come with us Zoey," Horace said as he pulled out through the main gate.

"No, he's not," Libby said half kidding, slapping Horace on the knee, sitting in the middle with Zoey by the window, "Horace wants it to be just him and me, swimming naked and fucking."

"Oh, come on now," Horace said wearing a big smile.

"No," Zoey responded, "I figured that, but I plan on leaving you guys on your own when we get there. It's a big enough lake at the old quarry."

"Aren't you afraid of the woman who haunts the lake?" Horace said.

"You mean our mom?" Zoey said laughing. "If she's there, she'll more than likely be watching over us."

"I'm not afraid. Besides, I'll bet that the clan will be here sometime tonight to try to scare us," Libby said.
"The clan?" Horace said, questioning.
"Yeah," Zoey said. "She means Zack and them might show up for their wargame fun in the moonlight. I know they were thinking about it when I told them I was coming with you guys, but I wouldn't put it past them to show up tonight, you know, make it a party."
"Well," Horace said, "so much for privacy!"
"I'm sorry, Horace," Zoey said, leaning in front of Libby, showing her pouty lips, "I'll get them to leave if they show. I want you guys to have a nice romantic moonlight swim in privacy. You deserve it."
"Don't worry about it," Libby said, putting her arm around Horace as he made the turn on to Route 313, "We'll have a good time no matter what."
"Yeah," Horace said leaning his face against hers.

After about twenty minutes they pulled into the old train station lot and parked the truck in the woods and out of sight. The moonlight through the trees cast powerful shadows around them as the moonbeams lit the way down the path to the tracks, where they followed the rusted rails on the wooden ties through the forest.

The warm air was dry, with very little humidity so the sky through the branches and leaves above them was clear and displaying a blanket of starlight that faded into the glow of the full moon. The scent in the air was a mixture of honeysuckle, some spruce and the distant fragrance of tar, pitch leftover on the old ties they were treading on, and the sounds of the wood beneath their feet creaked with each step as they hiked their way closer to the quarry's lake.

The crickets and katydids were singing a very loud serenade to the night sky as their song echoed off of the solid bark of the oaks and maples. An owl was cooing in the distant, trying to scare up a rabbit or two for a late-night dinner while the occasional loud and haunting screech of a mating fox filled the air from the north base of Buckingham Mountain. The three of them walked in silence listening to the night and worshiping the surroundings as they nurtured the works and word of God whispering to each one of them from the moon shadows.

Within twenty more minutes they were at the crest of the big open lake, looking like a flat sheet of glass shimmering in the lunar reflection. The cliffs in the distance were glowing, almost pale gray, with red and orange in the glow off of the full moon. Their reflection on the water's surface was spellbinding to the three of them, since none of them have ever witnessed this midnight garden of light until now.

"Fucking beautiful, isn't it?" Libby said, almost crying. "I wonder if my mom can see this, wherever she is here."

"They never found her body," Zoey said.

"No one knows she died here, except for us and Bill Bailey," Libby said.

"And Karma," Horace said, "at least that's where I heard the story about the woman who's haunting this place."

"That'll be my mom," Zoey said, "but what better resting place could you want than this?"

"Fucking beautiful!" Libby said again.

The three of them left the tracks and started through the thicker woods down an isolated deer-trail that lead to the water's edge, where they hiked their way on rocks and logs down an uneven path toward a spot that was a clearing of solid bedrock at the water's edge, a perfect place to rest and swim from.

From this clearing they could see everything clearly across the lake to the moonlit glowing cliffs, and to the other side, the hazy darkness with the glowing treetops of the forest. Behind them was light bluish lighting from the lunar light mixed with the darkness of tree shadows and occasionally there was the huffing of a buck clearing his nostrils, echoing from the woods followed by a trampling heard of the white-tailed deer he signaled, playing in their gloomy, tenebrous playground.

Libby was the first to take off her denim shorts, sneakers and top before wading into the lake and feeling it out.

"This feels great," she said, sliding the rest of her naked body under the shimmering surface.

Zoey asked where the deep water started, and Libby said that it drops off to 'no bottom' about five feet out. Zoey slipped off her sneakers, peeled her top and shorts off and dove her perfectly trim body head-first into the lake, returning to the moonlit surface about thirty feet out. Horace was the last one in, taking his time unloading his sneakers, shorts, and tee-shirt before wading himself in after them, then dropping like a stone below the surface at the underwater cliff, surprising him but he was soon swimming with Libby and Zoey about thirty feet from the shore line.

Libby directed Horace to follow her toward the cliffs while Zoey swam on her own out to the middle.

The lake was the size of two or three football fields and Libby warned Zoey that there may be currents or eddies within the vast body of water caused by underground streams feeding the lake. Zoey, however, didn't seem concerned as she continued to swim farther out while Horace and Libby remained so close in their strokes that their hands were sliding off of each other.

"Turn on your back," Libby said, "and do the elementary backstroke, so we can look at the stars and the moon."

"I hear you," Horace said, slightly out of breath as he flipped himself around and was in awe as he looked to his zenith. They were close enough to the cliffs that he viewed them as the 'cut-off craggy line' to the stars in the sky, and the moon was to his left far enough that it made the backdrop of sky behind the stars above him appear pitch black against the reflected light off of the cliffs.

"Magical," he whispered in his heavy breathing from the swim.

"You know it," Libby said as she placed her arms delicately around his chest and pressed her lips against his while they both kissed, dancing their tongues together inside of their warm and lusting mouths. The lukewarm water on the surface surrounded their every move around and between as they made love slowly and passionately within the trusting womb of their own place on the lake.

"I love you," Horace said in a delicate whisper within his soft but heavy breathing into her ear as they heard their own ripples slap against the nearby cliff face.

"I've always loved you, Horace," Libby answered in the same serene, whispering blend of rhythm as they continued their sub-surface dance within each other's arms, and legs, while they stared deep into each other's eyes, and aura of a seductive moonlit glow.

Meanwhile, Zoey was swimming to the far side where there were shorter, twenty-foot cliffs and where there was also a known sub-surface drop-off at those crags that, as with the rest of the cliffs, dropped to over a hundred feet or so below the surface. She dove her well-developed and toned body, like the gymnast she was as she spread her legs completely opened above the surface with her back arched, then lowering her butt and legs into the water, and positioning herself upside-down, closed her outstretched legs, propelling her downward and deep into the abyss. Opening her eyes, she could see the full moon behind her getting dimmer as she descended fearlessly deeper, pushing again with her open arms and feet, feeling the water around her getting cooler, then colder with each passing fathom. She felt her ears starting to pop while she soaked in the silence of the lake, now completely surrounding her as she held her breath for yet another minute while watching the moon slowly getting brighter as she neared the surface.

Breaking the water's crest and heaving a gulp of fresh air, Zoey was satiated with the joy of her surroundings and in a few minutes, repeated the dive, only this time she felt the warm water of her own urine while releasing the pressure from her bladder about twenty-feet down before surfacing once again.

With a smile she swam to the water's edge at the 20-foot cliff and scaled the steep bedrock to the summit, using her hands and feet to cling, and eventually up to a smooth spot where she sat on the edge, overlooking the beautiful lunar reflection off of the lake. Zoey thought about her mother, who was murdered in this beautiful quarry lake but generated positive thoughts, as a prayer, knowing she was at peace and wished she could see how her daughters have grown into strong and healthy young women, free spirits enjoying life to its fullest. She then sighed to herself thinking about her sister and the love of her life, Horace, and laid herself down onto her back, her glistening nakedness in in the moonlight and stared at the face of the goddess of the night before closing her eyes in a meditative dream state, bringing peace and tranquility to her own very being.

Suddenly, and in a mere instant her peaceful Universe came to an end as she became aware of three individuals who were strange men in tight, black jump-suits accosting her, wrestling her to the ground with force, one in particular punching her and going out of his way grabbing at her private parts, and caressing her breasts while the others were attempting to tie her down to steel stakes they were driving in between rock fissures. Two more had jumped in to help restrain her and the man that was grabbing at her breasts and crotch ended up with inciting Zoey to head-butt him, cracking him directly on the nose, then when she had an arm free she punch him with a closed fist with the power of a boxer's left jab precisely in the same spot, causing him to scream out loud like a child and fall backward.

"You keep that up, Mike, and I'll give you worse!" Joe Harris said to his brother.

"No touching the merchandise," Bill Bailey said to everyone. "We tie her down tight until we get the other two, then you can play with this little toy later. She's a real hellcat, like her mother was, and if she's anything like her, you guys are in for a real treat!"

Zoey struggled even harder and more furiously at that comment and tried to scream at them while they laughed, but her attempts were fruitless as she was being gagged while they were tying her with ropes and nylon ties to the steel stakes driven between the rock cracks.

"I can't wait," Mike Harris said in painful agony with a trembling voice, now holding a rag over the broken cartilage. "You'll pay dearly for this, bitch."

"It looks broken," Stu said while holding Zoey's legs spread as the others tied her. "You know your nose is bleeding?"

"No shit . . . A fucking genius you are!" he answered.

"Does it hurt? Mikey?" Blue said sarcastically, tying Zoey snug with a gag and laughing.

"Not nearly as much as you're going to hurt when I get through with you!" Mike snapped.

"Sounds like Mike has a hard-on for you Blue," Stu said snickering as they were finishing up with tightening her nylon restraints.

"Must be for me," Blue said. "It's certainly not for this fine piece of meat tied here."

"You're a fucking asshole!" Mike said as he stormed towards Blue, but his brother Joe stood in his way, bracing him.

"Knock it off! All of you!" Joe Harris said angrily, curtailing his brother. Then inches from his face looked at his bleeding nose and said, "Man, she did a number on you. That's going to need surgery."

"It really hurts Joe," Mike said with tears. "I'm going to get her."

"You have first dibs on her, Mike. But like I said, that nose is a mess and will need to be rebroken and reset."

"I got a knife and a hammer right here," Blue said with his surly grin reflecting the bright moonlight.

"I said knock it off!" Joe said again, this time inches away from Blue's face.

"Joe's right," Bill said while picking up the hammers and leftover stakes. "We've got our work to do and you all know what to do. You can come back for her when we're done with the others. They're the ones I'm interested in."

They collected their tools and left Zoey on her back, with her arms and legs outstretched and tied to stakes with the nylon ties and ropes firmly gripping her elbows, knees and torso. Her head had a gag wrapped around her mouth causing any attempted vocal noises to be muffled and pointless, so she just laid back and concentrated on moving her arms and legs in a circular motion in hopes to loosen something.

Blue and Stu were sent to the tops of the cliffs where the jeep trail was while the others, Bill, Mike and Joe meandered through the brush and rocks towards their next phase of the plan. The moon was a little higher in the sky and there was an occasional breeze as they stole their way through the rhododendron and marshy areas towards where Libby and Horace had undressed before their swim.

Meanwhile, Horace and Libby had begun swimming back to the spot from the cliffs where they had just touched the Universe with their heart and soul, united as one in another glorious orgasm of life itself. Satiated and fulfilled, and head-over-heels in love, and unaware of the evil surrounding them, they swam together towards the spot on the other side where they had first entered this marvelous, delightful and gratifying world of water.

"Just think," Libby said on her back looking at the moon and stars, breathing heavy due to her legs kicking and her waving arms sweeping under the water while she pushed herself artfully across the surface, "Mom is buried in the water beneath us. What more of a gorgeous place of rest could anyone ever want?"

"It is beautiful!" Horace said, duplicating her exact moves beside her as they propelled themselves closer to shore.

"How deep do you think it is here?" he asked her in his heavy breaths from swimming.

"I'll let you know," she said as she spun and dove as Horace watched, sliding her pretty ass above the water first then her legs, and she disappeared. Below the surface she continued to dive, looking back and upward with her eyes open at Horace's silhouette against the moon getting fainter and dimmer. The water was getting cooler, then colder and she realized she needed more air to go further and decided to return to the surface.

After a few long minutes Libby resurfaced with a deep breath, then catching another before saying anything. Horace held her tight and told her she shouldn't be doing that in this uncharted quarry lake, what with the stories and yarns that were spun regarding bottomless pits, currents to the ocean and sea monsters.

"Sea monsters?" she said laughing. "I never heard that one."

"Oh?" he said, "I added that one in, figuring they might come from a bottomless pit with a strong ocean current."

"You're crazy!" she said, splashing him in the face then said, "I'll beat you to the shore."

"You probably will," Horace said, swimming right behind her to their spot.

The two of them swam hard and fast with Horace soon catching up as they neared their rocky target. Just as they were within arms-length from the embankment of bedrock they were surprised by a large fishnet raining down on them, entrapping the both of them closer together the more they both struggled to free themselves. The net was originally from a shrimping boat and was thrown over them by the Harris brothers who have both worked together on fishing and shrimping boats in the gulf. They, with the help of Bill Bailey had the two caught like fighting marlins and tightly entwined, now facing each other within the snare of the nylon ropes.

"No use trying to struggle," Bill told the both of them as he raised them with a pulley on a small make-shift manual crane fabricated by Joe and Mike. "But I will say, you both look rather cozy in there."

"Poke, poke," Mike said, jabbing at Libby's boobs with a stick. "Nice ones."

"Fuck off!" Horace said, grabbing the stick from his hand and stabbing his ear.

"OOWWW!" Mike shouted and grabbing his bleeding ear while Mike's brother Joe took the stick from Horace and punched him through the net in the jaw.

"Let me look at that," Bill said holding the flashlight on his ear, and in touching it Mike let out a loud screech.

"Damn, that hurts!" Mike said, then seeing Horace in the dim camp-light flipping him the bird, started running toward the netted prisoners but once again Joe was there to cut him off.

"Grow the fuck up, will you?" he said. "Then these stupid things won't happen to you. Got it?"

"There's going to be some payback," Mike said with a smirk while working with his brother to tie the both prisoners with another piece of rope as Horace and Libby just wrapped their arms around each other with a few snaking movements while they finished.

"Okay, get these two into the boat." Bill said. "Put them in the front and tie the concrete footer securely."

"I know." Mike said to Bill. Then he looked over at his brother and said, "You'd think I'd never done this before."

"I know," Joe replied, "but although you're good at this I'm going to double check as I always do, and don't be touching her!"

With Horace and Libby wrapped tightly and hopelessly secure, and placed in the rowboat, Joe and Mike tied to their feet and net the weight of an 80-pound concrete footer that would weigh them both down.

"So, what are you planning on doing?" Horace asked, while unseen by the three captors Libby was beginning to sob quietly on Horace's neck and shoulder.

"What do you think?" Joe answered with a chuckle.

"Horace and Libby," Bill said confidently, "like Robert, you don't exist anymore. And you Libby, will soon be saying hello to your mother."

Libby hugged Horace tighter while she continued to sob silently and shake while Horace whispered to her: "Dear, this isn't over by a longshot."

"Don't cry," a voice whispered from behind them, and when they turned they knew it wasn't coming from their captors, who were busy untying the anchor line and launching the skiff.

"I'm right here with you and nothing's going to harm you. Trust me," the whispering voice said.

"That sounded exactly like Robert," Horace said.

"So, you heard that too?" Libby asked him, drying her tears. "It sure sounded like Robert's voice."

Zoey, in the meantime, laid quietly and kept to herself, and silently looking at the stars she asked the Universe for help from deep within her gut and continued to slowly move her arms and legs, in hoping for a miracle to loosen the binds that restrained her.

"That only works in the movies," a voice whispered from beside her.

"Who's that?" she asked from within her muffled gag.

"It's your lucky day," the voice said, and removing her gag added, "Be quiet."

"Who are you?" she asked as the black-faced man began untying her.

"I've been stalking these guys and followed them here," he said, "I'm Libby's and Horace's bassist."

"Jordan!" she said out loud.

"Shhh," he insisted, cupping her mouth while still untying. "Don't do this to me. We've got to get them, and he's coming up the hill now. He'll never know what hit him."

"I know," she whispered, "but can you do me a big favor?"

"What's that, love?"

"Leave me here, and can you make me look tied up?" she asked. "I have a treat for my buddy Mike, if you know what I mean. I want him, please."

"Mike Harris?" Jordan said. Well sure, only if I can watch."

"Sure thing," she said, "I'll need you here anyway just in case there's more of these assholes, but I want 'him'."

"You've got it," he said and fixed the ropes, so they looked tied in place and Jordan hid himself in the rocks and trees. Jordan then said, "But we have to make it quick if we're going to help your sister and Horace."

Jordan looked from the lake's twenty-foot overlook to see the boat containing Joe Harris, Bill Bailey and the entwined in fishnet Horace and Libby rowing out from the shore from the other banks about a hundred yards away toward the center.

"What are they doing to our friends?" Jordan asked Zoey.

"I overheard them," she said, temporarily removing her gag. "They want to drown them then put their bodies near the shore where they'll be found."

"Well," he said, "If I see those bodies going into the water, I'm diving in."

"We'll be okay," she said, "just keep an eye on them. I'll be right behind you."

"Shhh," Jordan said, "I hear him coming."

Approaching was someone humming and giggling singing, "tasty, tasty, tasty, lady," over and over and he was obviously getting closer. The singing was coming from Mike Harris, and he was obviously doing this to intentionally intimidate Zoey, believing she was tied securely and also believing there was no one around now to stop him from having his way with her, any which way he wanted.

The men in the boat were under the impression that Mike was on shore with the walkie-talkie waiting for the word to head up to start on Zoey after they drowned the two prisoners like rats, but Mike decided, after a few shots of bourbon in attempts to kill his pain, to head on up to get what he figured was coming to him.

In the boat, Joe was rowing to the point they wanted to throw the two overboard with the weight on their feet and the idea was to have them drop about twenty feet below surface, drowning them, then afterwards place the bodies near shore to ensure that authorities would be convinced they were accidentally drowned somehow, leaving the metal rowboat capsized along the shore nearby. When they had gotten to the spot, Joe tried to contact Mike on his walkie-talkie but there was no answer,

"Fuck!" he said, "Do you think he already went across the way to nail her?"

"Did you give him bourbon?" Bill asked.

"I sure did."

"Well," Bill said to Libby, "I'll bet he's riding that sister of yours right now, right as we speak."

"Should we dump them in in now?" Joe asked.

On top of the twenty-foot ridge where Zoey was, she had the back of her head on the edge of the overlook with her naked body outstretched with the impression of being tied in place, the way Mike believed he had left her. As he appeared in the clearing he gazed lustfully at her and said, "Man oh man, do you look good enough to eat!" He then took off all of his clothes, exposing his naked lean male body in the moonlight, observing her toned and curvaceous form in the heavenly moonlit glow. On his hands and knees, he crawled, barking like a dog and inched his face closer to her with an evil laugh, hanging his tongue out like a canine in heat as he made lapping noises at the air to intimidate her while his face was now at ground level right in between her fully spread gams. As she watched she could see his bleeding ear and blood-stained broken nose inching closer as he lapped the air like a madman pretending to be a dog, and his hissing evil laugh between his ridiculous panting.

"Billy boy said your mama was a hottie too," he whispered, "and you're lookin' and smellin' hot, baby. Let's just see what you've got you tasty little hellcat!"

Just as he couldn't get any closer without licking her, and at a point where she couldn't stomach the sound or view of him any longer, Zoey clamped both of her strong, and toned muscular thighs shut on his head while locking her legs, pulling him into her, hugging and crushing mercilessly against his broken nose and gashed ear, causing him to shriek and screech with muffled, painful squeals. Being previously untied by Jordan, she threw off the gag and still locking her feet together, putting the crush on his head, and using the leverage of the slanted cliff-top, she maneuvered her body into a jujitsu backflip and propelled him swiftly and head-first over herself and the ridge. They both tumbled naked through the air twenty-feet into the deep water of the lake as Jordan watched from the shadows of the rocks and brush with a smile.

Zoey hung onto his head in her thighs until they hit the surface of the lake where they temporarily separated, and as he surfaced in extreme pain and fear, trying to swim he began screaming, "Help! Joey! I need help! Help meeee pleeeze!"

Joe, who was about fifty yards away didn't see, but heard the splash, then his cries, and assumed that Mike had lost his balance somewhere due to the bourbon and had clumsily fallen into the water. In the midst of it all Bill was asking Joe to stay put and to help him lower the two prisoners into the lake.

"Ignore him," Bill stated, "and don't forget what we came here to do!"

"He can't swim," Joe refuted, "and he's my fucking brother!"

Joe then dove into the water, swimming toward Mike's begging pleas.

Zoey had resurfaced and swam toward Mike, her surprised aggressor, who in desperation was at her mercy but able to get himself to the steep cliff face extending above the water's surface and began pulling himself up and partially out of the lake. With her one hand and arm slowly wrapping around his bare belly from behind and the other grabbing him by his hair, he felt her warm body slide up on his back while she said, "Aww, don't you like me anymore?" and dragged him terrified and squealing back into the water. Now keeping her body at a distance, she positioned him firmly while punching him in his broken nose once more, causing him to let out a girly yelp.

"I'm coming!" Joe yelled out between deep breaths as he approached a few yards closer but was unaware that Zoey now had his brother in her clutches.

"What was that you said about my mother?" Zoey asked Mike, aggravated, "You're a worthless piece of shit!"

Using her training from martial arts she grabbed him in a hold that instantly dislocated both of his shoulders causing him to shriek once again in pain, then in a single move, using her limber body, spinning like a pretzel and flipping like a python clutched his head between her thighs once again, pulling his entire struggling body under the water's surface and beneath her, restraining him as she treaded the surface very quietly with her arms beneath the water, watching with just her eyes above the surface like a stalking gator as Joe swam by only about ten yards away.

"Mikey!" Joe kept calling. "I'm coming Mikey! Where are you, brother?"

Mike was too panicky under the lake's surface and was trying to punch and pull her legs apart but having no strength in his arms, now out of their shoulder sockets, he was unsuccessful. Almost losing consciousness from the pain and lack of air, she finally released him, pulling him up by his hair to the surface. As he gulped his first breath of air Mike once again yelled for help and fruitlessly tried to wipe the water from his eyes, looking directly into the fierce eyes of his adversary. Zoey, who, using his hair as her grip, kept shaking his head in anger, bitch-slapping his face while he did nothing. After a few seconds she just said, "You will never hurt another woman, but I've got friends that need me now. Say good night and goodbye to your brother."

"HALP!" Mike cried in a very high-pitched squeal one last time causing Joe to turn around again as Zoey dove head first beside Mike, sliding herself against him downward, and grabbing his kicking legs, squeezed them together firmly under her breasts and against her belly, containing them while she swam kicking her legs, using one arm and pulled Mike beneath the surface for the last time. As Zoey swam downward, dragging him behind, Mike was terror-stricken and trying to swim in shear pain toward the fading moon through the water, while watching it grow dimmer and dimmer as the water grew colder and colder and Zoey's agile and trim body swam stronger, deeper and faster.

Bill in the meantime had dumped Horace and Libby overboard and they had sunk, with the help of the concrete weight to the line's limit at about twenty feet. He had called out a few times to Joe and heard nothing but the distant yells of him calling out to his brother Mike. Within a few minutes he saw the line moving and bubbles surfacing by the boat, causing him to surmise that Horace and Libby's struggling for air were at a near end.

"Come on!" Bill yelled to Joe. "I'll need help in a few more minutes to pull this dead weight on board here."

In a few minutes he saw Joe swimming to the boat before pulling himself aboard, dripping wet, but there was no sign of Mike with him, and looking around the moonlit lake's surface he saw nothing.

"Didn't you get him?" Bill asked.

"I couldn't find him anywhere," he said. "I swam underwater in the area looking, searching, but couldn't see him anywhere. Even with the moon out it's still dark out there."

"Maybe he made it back to land," Bill said.

"I hope so," Joe said, still worried and calling Mike one more time. "Mikey!"

"Let's just pull these pieces of shit to the surface and get them on board," Bill said, "then we'll look for him."

With Joe still dripping wet from the swim, he and Bill pulled the line slowly to the surface, and in the lunar light grasped and pulled the dead cargo aboard the skiff, cutting free the concrete weight.

"What? Did we lose one of them?" Joe asked, "There's only one here."

"I see that," Bill replied, "which one did we lose?"

In cutting away the netting they saw it was a male, certainly not Libby, but in the glow of the moon and the twisting of the net it was hard to make heads or tails of anything, until . . .

"Oh my God!" Bill said. Joe's jaw dropped before yelling, "MIKEY!!"

The body inside of the netting was none other than Mike Harris. Zoey had drowned Mike and having a plan, dragged his body to the rowboat containing Bill, Horace and Libby while surfacing once or twice for air. In seeing her friends being dumped overboard Zoey immediately submerged herself with Mike and was able to cut them both free, then with Libby's help, placed Mike's body within the netting, securing it, then they all swam to shore, surfacing for air discretely and undetected by Bill or Joe who were distracted by the search for Mike.

"That bitch!" Bill said.

"I'll fucking kill her!" Joe said, furious.

Bill immediately sat at the ores and began rowing, as fast as he could toward the shoreline where they had discovered their clothing and where the makeshift crane and pulley were. When they had gotten within about six feet from the rocky edge Joe felt a looped rope lasso around his neck and tighten quickly, faster than he could grab at it and the rope immediately tightened, pulling him airborne above the water, swinging back and forth, gagging and kicking hopelessly.

"Hello Bill!" Jordan yelled from the rocks. "It's good to see you again!"
"Jordan?"
"In the flesh!" Jordan answered as they both heard Joe's neck snap.

Obviously in a panic, Bill began rowing furiously back toward the other side of the lake by himself to see if he could contact Stu and Blue, who were 'supposedly' ready with a vehicle on an old jeep trail. As he approached the opposing shoreline, at the base of the smaller cliffs where Zoey was originally wrestled down and tied-up he started calling for Stu and Blue.

Zack, Bonnie, Rita and Harold were all just arriving as originally planned to the wooded area near the quarry lake and heard Bill's voice out on the water calling for his accomplices.
"What the hell is he doing here? That's that guy Bill calling for those imbeciles who work for him." Zack said.
"It can't be good," Rita said, clutching Harold's hand, "let's see what's going on!"

Hanging on to their homemade paintball guns and homemade primitive slingshots they spread out towards the lake to investigate the situation while Bill continued calling for Stu and Blue. Finally, Stu waved his arms in the light of the full moon, directing Bill to row towards him where he was standing amongst a few young sycamores at a fairly level rocky grade to dock the boat. Just as Bill arrived and was starting to drag the boat up he was splattered in the side of the head with a paintball, then plunked in the back of the head with a jettisoned marble. When Stu turned around he was splattered with an eye-burning salted paint-ball, causing him to scream, inciting Bill to relaunch the skiff back out onto the lake under a barrage of raining rocks and stones. Stu, barely able to see, threw an axe he was carrying onto the rowboat and climbed into it himself. From the fifty-foot cliff they saw Blue dive head-first, followed by another barrage of rocks and stones into the lake and swim desperately toward them as Bill rowed. They met at a cross point and Blue told them there was another jeep trail where they could reach the property owner's house and a vehicle.

After Blue climbed successfully in, and after rowing in circles they changed direction, rowing across the base of the cliffs beneath the road where previous so-called accidents and murders originated as Libby, Horace, Zoey and Jordan watched them from the opposing shoreline.

"That moon's so bright I can see everything they're doing," Horace said.

"The reflection off of the cliffs makes it almost look like daylight in that spot," Libby replied. "Magical."

"Do you think they'll get away with all of this?" Zoey asked.

"Time will tell," Horace said, "and if they can make it out of here we'll have to somehow prove they were trying to kill us."

"They're not going to get away with this if I can help it, I have good lawyers!" Libby retorted as they finally heard Zack, Bonnie, Rita and Harold coming up from behind them.

"Wow," Bonnie said, "we tried. But it looks like they're getting away."

"I'm glad you guys are okay at least," Harold said, patting Horace on the shoulder.

"We'd better get out of here, cause how are we going to explain 'this' with all of us standing here?" Horace said, pointing at Joe Harris's body swinging from a rope hanging off the crane pulley.

Just then, there was a large burst from the calm water beside the skiff carrying the three fugitives while Bill was desperately rowing for the destined shore. Out of the burst was a beautiful naked woman, standing on the water's surface, who instantly grabbed Blue by his bald head and pulling it firmly against her flat belly ripped it at the neckline with a slit of her long fingernails, tearing apart his juggler vein, almost severing his head.

"Wow!" Zack said, "Did you see that?"

"Holy shit!" Horace said, "I see it, but I don't believe it!"

"The haunted lake is really haunted." Harold and Rita both said out of sequence.

"Mother?" Libby said, shocked as anyone else.

As the mutilated body fell back into the boat spurting blood, Bill screamed, sounding like a terrified woman and was rowing the ores like a madman without taking his eyes off of her. The nude lady, who in the full moon appeared athletic, trim and toned in shimmering beauty, with the face of a sensual goddess with long, dark hair grabbed her second victim, Stu, who was now screaming louder than Bill.

"Oh my God." Bonnie said, "She's going to cream them one by one!"

"This is awesome!" Jordan said with a sardonic grin. "That prick Bill is losing his mind!"

The mysterious goddess then, as with Blue, hugged his head tightly to her bare belly then twisted it sideways and with one pull of her sharp fingernails gashed his neckline and juggler, causing Bills screams to be higher pitched and louder while the blood and life flowed from Stu's torn body. Bill's screams were now sounding like pulsating shrieks in perfect timing with his arms, compulsively thrusting the ores strokes through the water surface as she now climbed completely on board and with her bare foot on his face, pushed him back and downward face-up onto the floor of the boat while he kicked and bucked his now pinned body, unable to pull himself free from her as she said, "I told you I'd get you, and I've got you right where I want you now!"

"He's not going anywhere now." Zoey said laughing.

"Poor bastard," Jordan said sharing the laugh. "He's just going to lay there kicking like a tool."

"FREEZE!" A male voice said behind them as the area lit up with what appeared to be dozens of bright police flashlights, rifles and handguns pointed at them.

"Out there!" One policeman yelled to the boat where the woman stood motionless in her glory pinning Bill to the floor with her foot.

"What's the matter with him? HEY, YOU OUT THERE, BRING THAT BOAT IN!" A cop yelled.

"It looks like a man on his back in that boat, having some kind of an attack," The other policeman said holding his binoculars on him.
"He's in convulsions or something, and there are two or three men next to him who look like they're dead," Another said.
"They don't see the woman," Libby whispered.
"I still see her," Rita said, with her eyes wide open and staring.
"What woman?" Jordan said. "You see a woman out there?"

A few cops popped open a couple of those yellow rubber rafts and went out to the rowboat while the officers surrounded Libby, Horace, Zoey, Jordan, Rita, Harold, Bonnie and Zack, questioning all of them briefly before letting them go. They convinced them that they had come to play a moonlight game with a moonlit swim and were accosted by this group of crazy people trying to kill them. Their only crime was they were trespassing on private property and were let go, with the promise of being further questioned later.

Bill Bailey, on the other hand, was a different story, considering that when they approached him he was laying on his back inside the boat still moaning and screaming and clawing at the air above him. The cops who surrounded the lake and the boat did not see what Bill told them he was seeing, a naked goddess, a woman standing above him holding her bare foot on his chest preventing him from moving. Inside the boat with Bill were three bodies of three men, two were almost beheaded and still bleeding while the other was soaking wet, wrapped within a wet fishing net. Beside the bodies was an axe with blood covering the head and handle, and Bill's prints in blood were all over the alleged weapon used in the murder and all over the boat.

When the cops were cutting down the man hanging in the noose over the water they discovered that the rope used had Bill Bailey's name on it and assumed they'd find his prints on it also. He was immediately arrested for suspicion of murder due to the circumstantial evidence surrounding him and eyewitness accounts, and pending further investigation there was no posting of bail. It wouldn't matter anyway, since they all figured he was insane with the way he was carrying on and talking about the beautiful naked lady, who he named as "Elizabeth," "Elizabeth Romano." Bill insisted that the naked woman in the lake was Elizabeth Romano and that she was the one who was the perpetrator of the crimes committed here, with the exception of Joe Harris, who he insisted was murdered by Jordan, however, the eyewitness accounts said Bill was crazy, clearing Jordan's name. Zack, Bonnie, Rita, Harold, Zoey, Horace and Libby all saw the naked lady of the lake on the boat standing above Bill, but never admitted it to the police; Jordan was the only one in the group who didn't.

CHAPTER - NINETEEN

The entire group of them, Zack, Bonnie, Rita, Harold, Zoey, Jordan, Horace and Libby all went back to the rancher off of Powder Valley Road early that morning while the moon was still shining brightly and while everything was still fresh in everyone's mind. They stayed up into the daylight hours talking around the kitchen table, discussing everything that had happened, trying to understand it all. Daylight was now coming in through the paned, squared sections of the kitchen windows and the sun was about to creep up from the horizon, glowing brightly through the sliding glass doors at the end of the dining room as their conversing continued over a few shared half-gallon bottles of burgundy.

"Do you really believe that woman was our mother?" Zoey asked Libby.

"I don't know," she said, "I wouldn't want to believe that Mom was or is now an evil lady of the lake."

"I wouldn't say she was evil," Harold said, "just because she gave some people exactly what they deserved."

"I don't think that makes her evil either," Zoey said.

"What the hell happened to that other one?" Libby asked, staring at Zoey. "You know, Mike Harris?"

"The evil daughter got him," Jordan said laughing.

"Damn right!" Zoey said, taking a big swig of wine. "It was all in self-defense, and I enjoyed every minute of it."

"What woman are you talking about?" Jordan asked. "I thought you were all kidding, I didn't see a woman on that skiff."

Rita was taking her cards and spreading them in the corner of the big wooden table while everyone was passing the half-gallon bottle of burgundy around and she let out a shushing sound, in an attempt to inspire everyone to mellow out for a few minutes while she concentrated. She had asked Zack to put a blanket over the window to block out the light and Bonnie and Harold drew the light-lock shades on the windows, making the area pitch-black with darkness. While they were doing this, in the center of the table Rita placed a large, white candle, wide enough to fit into the top of an empty half-gallon burgundy bottle shaped like a round globe. She had peeled the labels off of the green tinted glass and lit the candle to melt some of the wax to use it as a more stable mount for the wick before sitting back in her corner and staring at each one in the group one by one.

Everyone was quiet while Rita was doing all of this and watching her intently, but Jordan was not used to the group and was, understandably, getting a little impatient.

"What is this, a séance?" he asked with a half-way grin.

"Jordan," Rita asked, gazing directly into his pupils, "What did you see out there on the boat?"

"What is this, the third degree?" he asked frustrated. "I told you I didn't see any woman."

His brown face, now with a sparse, scruffy band of whiskers, glowed with a sheen in the candle light while Rita stared at him, unmoved by his retort then smiled.

"I'm just asking you what you saw, Jordan," she said with her hands flat on the table. "I understand that you saw something different than what we all saw."

Jordan looked around the table at everyone else, who were all sitting quietly, intently waiting for him to give his account on what he had seen. With the candle being the only means of light, their faces were carrying a dim, yet comforting aura to the serene life force surrounding the table and Jordan felt compelled to oblige, as out of the whole group, Horace and Libby, and now Zoey were people he felt very relaxed with.

"Well," he started, "I saw Bill Bailey with those two creeps he had picked up from the other side, Stu and Blue, and he was rowing toward the other side of the big cliffs when all of a sudden, out of nowhere, he stood and started chopping at those guys. Didn't you guys see him doing that?"

"No," Bonnie said, "I did see him pick up the axe and start swinging it at that woman though."

"He stood up," Zack said, "but I just watched him freeze until she went for the other guy, then he sat down and started rowing really fast."

"But he never stood up," Harold said, "I saw him just scream and yell like he was crazy while she fucked those two dudes up."

"Yeah," Horace said, "That's how I saw it."

"Me too," Libby said, "Bill never touched the axe."

"The hell he didn't!" Jordan said.

"Right," Bonnie agreed, "I saw Bill swinging it at her."

"I saw him swinging it at her too," Zoey said laughing. "How could any of you miss that?"

"There was no woman!" Jordan shouted completely frustrated. "What fucking planet were you all on?"

"STOP!" Rita said, trying to maintain control, causing everyone to slowly mellow and sit back quietly looking at the flame in the candle.

"Now, apparently we all saw something," Rita said, "and most of us are, in agreement that there was a lady in the boat."

"She wasn't acting like a lady from what I saw," Harold said snickering, inciting Rita to throw a sideways glare his way before continuing.

"But we're not in agreement of the sequence of events we each had seen," she said, "which leads me to believe that we were seeing an illusion created by Bill himself."

"What?" Jordan asked in his cynical tone.

"Yeah, 'what'?" Horace retorted.

"I'm saying," Rita answered, "that what we witnessed was a strange phenomenon that caused us to see Bill Bailey's own self-created deep fears of this woman he had murdered years ago there in that quarry lake. I believe his own fear was so real and deep enough that his visual became our visual, and that we were witnessing something really rare and special in the metaphysical realm."

"I'd say you were all nuts if I didn't know you," Jordan said, and continued, "So, why didn't I see this woman. I saw him, Bill with an axe, chopping at their heads. I swear on the powers that be that I saw no one but him butcher those guys."

"I couldn't possibly answer that," Rita confided, "All I know is that the woman was not the soul of Libby and Zoey's mom. That woman's soul left the earth twenty years ago."

Zoey and Libby went to a room in the house away from the others and talked briefly about their glorious escape and rescue from Bill and his henchmen and how Zoey had been working for years, with the help of Robert Bender to finally get these guys to justice, although it wasn't exactly how they had planned it. Libby told her that Robert originally hired Bill to ruin him for what he knew Bill had done to their mother, but had no idea that Bill was in cahoots, through the years, with the lowest and seediest people they could ever have imagined. Zoey had researched where Mike Harris had come from as well as his brother and found out they were in the Klan for years and were both involved in doing hits for them, and actually, that's where Stu and Blue came from, through Mike and Joe Harris. In hindsight, if Robert had known this shadiness was going to occur from making Bill a partner, he wouldn't have done it and in a way, never forgave himself for taking him on.

"So," Horace said, "what's going to happen now with Bender's and all that goes with it? What do you need me to do, Libby?"

"We're going to talk about that later," Libby said, leaning the jug of wine to her lips. "Robert has had all of it under control this whole time and I don't think we'll be getting any more problems from Bill Bailey."

"I sure hope not," Jordan said, taking the jug from Libby and helping himself to a swig.

"I'll have some of that too," Zoey said, but Bonnie slid her jug across the table to her, inviting her to share from hers. The rest of the morning the group got themselves a little drunk and they all ended up sleeping through the afternoon and into the evening in their own self-assigned rooms, except for Jordan, who slept uncomfortably on the couch.

The following week Libby and Horace had returned to the Bender house on Deep Run Road and were greeted by the police and detectives who said the whole place was ransacked, with all of the valuable paintings gone from the den and a few of the other rooms. However, they were all recovered and will be returned after the investigation is completed into the murders on the quarry lake and at Lake Galena since the murders and the theft were all tied in with the same person, Bill Bailey.

The detectives told Horace and Libby that Mr. Bailey had staged the theft in the house and the thieves were all part of the gang of thugs that were murdered on the lake. He had planned on taking the paintings and selling them to a black market overseas that he had been using for years to launder cash profits he had skimmed off of the top from the Bender's Clubs he had been overseeing. 'Apparently', Robert Bender was aware for years of the embezzling of funds and had put a private investigator onto his transactions, on the sly, of course.

The people who Mr. Bailey were using were corrupt individuals who, as the detective put it, must have crawled out of the gutter because they had a slimy trail of dirt behind them that was easy to follow. Michael Harris and his brother Joseph Harris were two accomplices who were notorious for their beatings in a loan-sharking racket they were running years before, with Langdon and Fishman, all coming from the same gutter. The bodies that were found dead, beaten mercilessly, in their neighborhoods where these rackets were run could never be linked to Joe or Mike, due to the lack of solid evidence and witnesses; Same with the bodies of the dead prostitutes that would occasionally surface.

Stu and Blue, alias Stuart Smith and Lester Bloom, were merely thugs who were hired hands for the ride. They had worked on fishing boats for years in the past whose main catch was pulling up nets of cocaine from off the shores of Panama and Mexico. They had gotten a better paying job from Mr. Bailey a few years back through his contacts Joe and Mike Harris and worked as extra muscle, hired hands.

Johnny Hetrick was the only one who is still on the loose, according to Bill, and Bill is blaming him for the murders of Karma the cabby, Miranda Mooney, and her husband Skip Mooney, Ed Langdon and Fishman. Police are puzzled regarding Johnny and other than these bodies, there were no signs of him anywhere, 'almost' as if he had vanished from existence. The police also questioned Libby again regarding her father Robert's death and asked her again why she was sometimes telling people that he was her husband, but she told the truth, that anyone who thought that assumed it and she just never corrected them. "It was none of their business anyway," she'd say. But what Libby didn't tell the detective was that Bill assumed they were married, and that Robert used it to his advantage to corner the scoundrel, but Bill gave them the gift of cornering himself.

At this point Bill Bailey's credibility was all but completely destroyed, especially since he was still talking to the fictitious lake lady and occasionally screaming in fear, sometimes impulsively, swearing she was right in front of him telling him she's going to rip him apart when everyone's gone. He was so adamant about this that the guards were given an order that he was to never be left alone, for fear he might do himself in.

Despite all of Bill's talk about the murderous lady on the lake, all of the evidence pointed to Bill being the murderer of Joe and Mike Harris, Stu, and Blue and weeks later he was convicted. At his trial his lawyers pled insanity and he was locked away in a place where they keep criminally insane convicts for life, without any hope of parole. It's said that he screams himself to sleep every night because this lady he sees in the cell with him every day said she's going to cut him to pieces.

Although there was an All-Points Bulletin put out to locate the notorious Johnny Hetrick, they were, of course, unsuccessful in their endeavors to find him. They also included 'Lucy Snyder' in the search as a person of interest, but the FBI and local police forces in the entire country couldn't locate either of them and assumed they were either out of the country or has taken up some alias identities. Also, they were able to come to terms eventually that Lucy was totally clear of any crimes or wrong-doing, as was the deceased Skip Mooney.

Libby and Horace were now driving north on the Pennsylvania northeast extension of the turnpike heading to the place where Robert Bender had been in hospice care, surrounded by his most trusted business staff and friends.

They had just found out that Robert Bender had passed away peacefully in the morning hours when they were on the quarry lake, and the precise time was about the time they were on the skiff, about the time they had thought they heard Robert's voice whispering from behind them. It sent a chill through Horace's bones when he heard the news but by the same token, not so surprised when he had considered all that had happened ever since he had met Robert and Libby. Libby wasn't surprised in the least, but very disappointed that she wasn't with her dad at the time of his passing.

"Well," Horace told her, "he was certainly with you."

"And you," she responded, shedding a few tears. "He really liked you, Horace. I just wish that I could have been there, but at least he wasn't alone. I heard that the whole staff of people he had trusted for years were all around him. That's good."

"That is good," Horace said, "and he at least knew and lived to see that his Bender empire was in good hands now."

"He still felt guilty, to his dying day," Libby said, "about taking on Bill as a partner just to get him back for what he did to Mom."

"*No,*" said a separate voice coming from behind the two of them. "*Not a speck of guilt anymore. The lake water washed it all away.*"

Horace was driving and pulled the pick-up to the shoulder immediately, but in turning around neither of them saw anyone behind them.

"Now, that sounded like Robert," Horace said, visibly shaken.

"It was Robert," Libby said. "He was talking to us as clear as day."

"*It is me,*" he responded in the same whispering tone, "*but you won't be able to see me.*"

"Where are you?" Libby asked in a more desperate tone.

"*I'm here. That's all you need to know.*"

"What's going on?" Horace asked Libby who answered, "I don't know."

"*Libby and Horace,*" Robert spoke, "*there's a reason that you cannot see me, which is the same reason we cannot remember our past lives. Don't worry about what you can't see, but be tuned into what you know, and you know I'm here.*"

The two of them, Horace and Libby remained reticent in the front seat and simply waited for the other shoe to drop, another voice from within their heads sounding like it was coming from directly behind them. It was a strange sensation for the both of them, but they went with it for now, somehow knowing that this voice, this sensation of communication from the beyond was coming from none other than Robert Bender.

"*I was directed to come to the both of you to relay to you that you've both completed your tasks here, whatever that means, but my tasks are just beginning.*" Robert said, then continued: "*I was concocting a shady plan here on earth to bring an enemy, closer with the sole purpose of destroying him because of what he had done to your mother, Libby, and in the process, I managed to grow the Bender Corporation beyond my wildest dreams. Unfortunately, bringing him on didn't make me a better person and I grew addicted to the personal revenge and eventually heroin took it over. Evil gravitates to evil, and when Mr. Bailey began bringing in all these derelicts to mastermind his scheme to take over the success of the club, that's when angels from beyond thought it was time for them to step in, with the help of your mom, Libby.*"

Horace began scratching his head and looking around inside the cab of the pick-up truck uncomfortably while Libby glanced over at him, sensing his stress and tapped his thigh with her hand, rubbing it softly before he heard a familiar voice besides Robert's, a voice he had remembered hearing ages ago. It was the Voice from a misty limbo, the place between life and death he had experienced before he had become Horace Clowney's 'Walk-In' spirit. He now realized the voice he had heard back then was actually a female voice, indistinguishable to him before, and the voice was that of none-other than Elizabeth Romano, the mother of Libby and Zoey.

"Horace," the Voice said, "My task was directing you to your task, and in turn, your task saved a multitude of lives, including the lives of my daughters, and I'll be the first one to tell you that your task was a job well done! Bravo!"

"Are you Elizabeth?" Horace asked.

"Who are you talking to?" Libby asked.

"Libby won't be able to hear me right now, Horace, but I personally wanted to thank you," The Voice responded again.

"*He's talking to your mom.*" Robert said. "*You'll be talking to her later.*"

"Yes, Horace," the Voice said, "I was Elizabeth in my previous life, the mother of Libby and Zoey. My life was cut short by a brutal man just about, twenty years ago from your time perspective, but it seemed like just yesterday from mine. I was granted the task of redirecting fate, with the help of angelic forces, to derive an alternate and fair destiny for everybody involved, but without controlling the outcome as it was left within the hands of the individuals involved.

In order for the strategy to be a success and come to fruition, I would have needed the persons I trusted, like you and Libby as the spiritual 'Walk-Ins,' to come through in good faith as righteous human beings, and at the same time, save the original souls of the new bodies that you possess as 'Walk-In' spirits. The twin souls which you replaced were working on the same task with me as one, in order to finalize our mutual goal.

You see, after passing through the shroud of death, we are all eventually cleansed and become one with the 'one' who knows all at the center. Between the shroud of death and the final gate of Paradise, Horace, there is a place of cleansing, the same place where you started your new journey as a 'Walk-In.' This life in which you took over as Horace Clowney was a result of entering and fulfilling a task delegated from beyond the shroud of death, compromising what would have been an alternative outcome, and generating and achieving an equitably fair and just conclusion for everyone involved. When justice is served, we all pass through the final gate cleansed, and it is the task of Angels and the spiritual guides to guide everyone as they see fit within the balance of the spiritual center, the 'One.'"

"That's all pretty deep, and a lot to think about," Horace said, appearing to be in deep thought, "but I get it."

"Think about it, and know that you did good, and thank you," the Voice said before vanishing.

A State Police vehicle had pulled up on the shoulder behind the pick-up truck and asked if they needed any help, and after the response of 'No. we're alright' they asked Horace and Libby to please move along. Libby decided to take the wheel and continued the driving to where Robert was staying when he had passed away.

"You know," Horace said, "we're really lucky."

"I'd say," Libby answered, "those cops didn't harass us at all."

"I'm not talking about that," he said as they were heading north on the long and straight four-lane highway called the Pennsylvania Turnpike; "I mean we were lucky to not have been killed by those freaks, and also lucky to have ended up with each other, the way that we did."

"It's not luck, it's fate," she said smiling at him while keeping her eyes on the road, "fate with the help of angels."

"Yeah, I guess," he said and then stared into the passing forest of trees and hills while Libby laughed in spite of herself.

Robert Bender was right, for when they had arrived in the small town everything was taken care of regarding the services and privacy that Robert wanted. He was cremated, and his ashes were given to Libby to have them spread over the quarry lake where her mom was. Libby, Horace and Zoey were the only ones who knew, along with seven trusted lawyer/accountants he had worked with, that Robert Bender was still alive until the early morning hours when Bill and his cohorts were apprehended dead and alive on the quarry lake. These people were the continued handlers of the Bender corporation, free to appoint those who would take on the managing responsibilities and 'cleaning house' as it were. Helping with the management was the notorious 'Fearless five', as they named themselves, Rita, Harold, Zack, Bonnie and Zoey, who made sure that everything was being run on the up-and-up.

Libby and Horace were married at a private ceremony at the quarry lake by one of Robert Bender's most trusted lawyers, who was a local Justice of the Peace, with only Jordan and Zoey as witnesses. After the ceremony Robert Bender's ashes were scattered from the cliffs into the deep waters of the lake as in accordance with his final request.

Libby took a long walk afterwards by herself and beneath the ash, oaks and maple trees of the deep forest surrounding the lake she began to cry for her father and mother and fell to her knees.

"What's the matter dear?" A voice whispered softly from behind her, and although there was no one there, she knew who it was.

"I don't know, Mom. I'm missing you and Dad." Libby said, weeping quietly.

"I know," the Voice said, "I'm here, and I'll always be here, as long as you are."

"But," Libby said, emotionally, "I feel like I shouldn't be, I mean, I was a 'Walk-In' spirit, and I didn't originally come from . . ."

"Now, now." The Voice interrupted. "You don't understand the workings of the Universe, Libby. Your twin soul and you are one with the Universe, and although you have a faint memory of me, I am and always will be your mother. There is a universal reason why we're not to remember our past lives for the same reason we never remember most of our dreams. If you remember a dream, it signifies that you never finished a thought, and dreams are nothing but the brain itself solving and concluding issues. In reincarnation, we solve our tasks from life to life and when the final task is met, we don't return, but move on, Virtuous, onto a more-worthy cause in a pure state of Paradise."

"I kind of understand," Libby said.

"Libby, remember when you were talking to Horace, trying to describe to him what you thought reincarnation was like?"

"Yes." Libby said. "You mean you were there?"

"Of course." The Voice said. "You told him how a soul in reincarnation was like a song that takes up a new life each time a person sings it. The song possesses that person giving it life, and if that song has two people trading off on verses, then that would be comparable to a 'Walk-In' spirit taking over. Same song, same life, different souls. Two people put their heart and souls into that song, mixing with it, however, your explanation to him regarding reincarnation and 'Walk-In' spirits is a raw analogy of the more and deeper realization of the actual existence of what can only be considered as a mere concept in your life form, and you should at least know that the 'Walk-In' can only work with the mirrored image of twin spirits."

"Sounds confusing, but I think I understand." Libby said, now standing and walking toward the lake. "But Robert, my dad, he seemed so troubled and . . ."

"Don't worry about Robert, dear," The Voice interrupted. "He's with me and his tasks were finished. His pain is long gone and his time passed in your instant, for our realm here is in what would be your future."

"I guess this is too much for me to understand," Libby responded, wiping away a tear.

"You'll understand better if you live your life to the fullest with your husband and enjoy the great gift of life that's around you, and know, Libby, that you are not alone, and never will be." The Voice said this, then vanished into the air surrounding the ash, oaks and maples while Libby walked closer to the lake and the others.

When she reached water's edge and looked facing the cliffs, she saw a young man and a young woman, naked to the world, walking hand in hand on the water's surface toward a distant shore that had not existed until now. The area was a natural paradise with a very tall waterfall and a garden of flowers, plants and shrubs that she had never seen before inside a green hillside that in her mind resembled Hawaii. She knew that this was her mom and dad and it made her happy that they were entering Paradise together.

Libby and Horace went on to live a full life, raising four children, two boys and two girls in the Bender home on Deep Run Road, playing music with Jordan, and even incorporated Zoey on vocals. The yard area where Horace's friend Lucy was laid to rest became a garden of marigolds and roses, which were flowers that Lucy had loved, cherishing the roses in the early days when Horace first started courting her, and it became the garden that she had always wanted. Lucy Snyder, being raised as a foster child by people who died when she was a teenager had no family or anyone who would have missed her, so a plaque was placed for the garden to be in her memory and they actually named their oldest girl Lucille.

Horace and Libby played and sang their songs like the virtuous spirits they were with soul, spirit, and each other's inspiration and loved each song as if it was life itself. This life on earth was and is a mere stepping stone and they both knew it. For it was a path in the direction of eternity and they recognized that in the endless realm of the Universe they would be together as one, for always, in an unfathomable and incessant harmonious symphony of their own as virtuous beings surviving simultaneously with an infinite number of others within the cosmos.

THE END.

ABOUT THE AUTHOR

Tom Rukas is a musician and a songwriter residing in Bucks County Pennsylvania. Along with some poetry, he has produced and recorded three albums containing some of his original music: "Forgotten Words and Rumblin' Wheels," "The Possession of Abraham Cactus," and "Watching the Wagons Roll."

He has also written two previous novels, "THE LOST MARBLES STORY" and "THE POSSESSION OF ABRAHAM CACTUS."

In his leisure time, Tom plays bass guitar in a local classic rock band.

Made in the USA
Middletown, DE
07 October 2018